Tales From The Loon Town Cafe

A Novel

Dennis Frahmann

Tales from the Loon Town Cafe is a work of fiction. Names, characters and incidents are products of the author's imagination and are not to be construed as real. Any resememblance to actual persons, living or dead, is entirely coincidental.

TO ROBERT

CONTENTS

Prologue   1

Spring Into Summer   5

Fall Into Winter   107

Spring Forward Again   315

PROLOGUE

Years later, I was jolted into reflecting on that curious time in my life, a fateful year in the '80s when I owned a cafe, when I mingled with scoundrels and saints, when I learned that even the smallest of towns has its secrets, its plots and its dreams.

It took an earthquake, the Northridge quake of 1994, to jostle free those memories. The shaking woke me from a dream and the digital clock read: 4:31 am. A huge boom echoed throughout the house. Everything was in motion. Each nail in the old wooden frame building screeched as it was pushed and pulled by the rolling of the earth.

I jumped to the floor, just as our big color television flew from the falling bookcase to land on the bedspread. Outside our bedroom windows, the Los Angeles basin spread before my little house perched in the Silver Lake hills. And the lightness of the city fell out. The glittering bowl of streetlights and neon signs rolled into darkness, with only the emergency lights from the Kaiser Permanente Hospital now glowing as a beacon.

"Move away from the windows," Stephen shouted to me. "It's an earthquake." And he pulled me to the side, as another shelf of books collapsed on top of me. And I fell into unconsciousness.

I came to, slowly, groggily, with the worried face of Stephen bending over me. "Are you alright?" he asked. "I think this might have been the big one. Everything is a mess." There was a yeasty, herbaceous smell of cabernet floating through the air. Stephen noticed my wrinkled nose. "The wine rack collapsed," he said in explanation.

I just wanted to escape outside before there was another tremor.

We stood in the darkness of the cold January morning, as our neighbors began to emerge with flashlights, walking the perimeters of their houses, checking the exteriors for damage. Above us, the electric transformers still popped and crackled with a weird glow.

Another aftershock hit, and the light poles swayed in front of me. I began to walk the neighborhood to calm myself and see what damage might exist. Up ahead a cheap apartment building from the '50s listed dangerously above its car ports. Walking toward me was the neighborhood hermit and packrat. He never spoke to me. As was our custom when we passed, he nodded solemnly. But today I wanted to reach out to this old man who always seemed so alone.

"How are you doing?" I asked. "Are you okay?"

"Yes indeed, young man. Thank you for asking."

I reached Sunset Boulevard, a tawdry, tired section near downtown Los Angeles, totally unlike the tony reaches that curved through West Hollywood and Beverly Hills. In an alcove of a thrift store huddled a neighborhood bag lady I saw every week. She wasn't hard to miss, since she always wore antennae made of aluminum wrap.

"Are they invading?" she shouted out to me in a surprisingly strong and clear voice. "Have they come at last?"

"It was just an earthquake," I said, but she didn't seem to hear me. She only rocked back and forth in the narrow entry way. The shopping cart filled with her life sat next to her.

"Come with me," I said. "You need something to eat." She seemed surprised and wary. "I won't hurt you. Please come. We just had an earthquake."

She stood, wrapped her tattered blanket around her shoulders, and together we began to walk back up the hill toward our little house. Because she would not leave it behind, together we pushed her overflowing shopping cart over the cracked sidewalks.

As we made our way, I waved and shouted greetings to all those who were in their front yards, all unwilling to go back inside while the earth still shook. We came up to the hermit, who had continued making his own slow inspection of the neighborhood.

"Where you heading young man?" he asked.

"I'm going to get this woman some breakfast," I replied.

"Mind if I walk with you?" and he did.

The old woman tugged at my sleeve. "I was wondering if you would have any wild strawberry jam. Just hoping."

In our front yard, amidst the birds of paradise in full bloom and the beds of calla lilies not yet in flower, I saw Stephen standing over our gas-fired grill, a turner in his hand. I could smell the cured smoke of bacon and the crispy odor of frying eggs. The aroma of coffee, made cowboy style in a pot on the grill, intermingled with it all. In the yard with Stephen were our neighbors Josh and Daniel. A young woman from across the street had also joined them, as had the fat and ponderous Neighborhood Watch captain, who was always prone to stick his nose into every bit of business.

"I have two more for breakfast," I shouted out, feeling so overjoyed to see Stephen there in the new daylight, surrounded by friends and neighbors, undamaged by the quake.

"No problem," he replied. "There's plenty."

And in the cold morning air, we sat together over coffee, with eggs and bacon, united as much by the joy of being alive as the fear of going inside. I looked around the small group and it suddenly seemed so familiar. "I was dreaming when the quake hit," I said. "It was about my hometown in Wisconsin, a wondrous place where everybody cared, and everybody knew everything, about everyone, all the time. And it was like all of you were there."

Stephen laughed, "I know you got knocked out, but I didn't know you'd wake up thinking you were in a Judy Garland movie."

"The dream was just so real," I started to say, then I stopped. I looked at everyone around me, their faces turned to me expectantly, even the wearied faces of the bag lady and the hermit. There was something in each of their eyes and smiles, a sense of life worth living, that I had never seemed to notice before. I felt suddenly giddy with a new-found joy. I reached for the coffee pot.

In the lifegiving breeze of the morning wind, I extended my hand. "More coffee anyone? This loon town cafe is open for business." And for a moment, it was as though my original Loon Town Cafe was back in business, but without its scoundrels. For a moment, I was reliving a year and a dream that truly mattered.

SPRING INTO SUMMER

CHAPTER ONE

"Welcome to the Loon Town Cafe."

"Get me a beer," snapped back the old woman, all decked out in a big black-and-white bird costume.

What better way to start a chapter of my new life story than to serve an ice-cold Leinie's to the town loon? I dug out a bottle of the local brew from the cooler. "So what's with the garb, Claire?"

The woman dolled up in a north woods loon outfit was accompanied by Bromley Bastique, the rotund, full-of-himself, self-proclaimed mayor of Thread, Wisconsin. As usual, he was quick to dismiss any question of mine as nonsense. "Wally, you should know the answer to that god darn question. Claire's the town mascot for the Loon Fest. Always has been. Always will."

Bromley had quite the knack to exasperate me by lecturing on things I already knew. "Of course. It's Loon Fest. I was just wondering why Claire is already in costume." Did the town mayor really want his town mascot wandering the streets lugging an opened beer bottle? "Loon Fest is why I've been working like a dog to get this place ready for its grand opening. Everyone tells me it's the best weekend for tourists. Miss this weekend and you miss the summer. That's what you tell me." And yet here I was, sitting in my otherwise empty cafe with the mayor and a woman dressed as a giant loon who had wandered in before I had a chance to turn the sign on the door from "closed" to "open."

"Quit your bellyaching," said Claire. "It's not like you get snapped at every morning before the sun comes up by those spindly little men."

Bromley took advantage of my confusion with Claire's statement to go behind the bar and open his own bottle of Leinenkugel's.

"Hey, where's my beer?" asked Claire. I slid the opened bottle down the bar. She picked it up, took a swig, then stopped and looked around. "You know, I like this place. I remember when Al Capone stopped here, back in '33, or was it '34. Over fifty years ago, but I can still remember the meanness on that man's face. You remember, Bromley?"

"You weren't even a teenager then. Why would you remember?" Bromley asked with a dismissing tone. "Just a little kid, and Capone was here for ten minutes. It's not like your supposed spacemen who stop by every morning to chew the fat."

"They have never chewed my fat, just collected it. And there's nothing supposed about them." Claire turned her attention back to me peering through her thick glasses. "Wally, I've been thinking ever since I heard that you were coming back, and I just can't figure it out. I remember when you were just a kid. Kinda pudgy and short, as I recall. Never liked Thread either, if I remember right. Seems to me you wrote some kind of article in that school paper about how every single kid should leave this town and run off."

"And where would one run off to?" A newcomer had just walked through my restaurant door. Did no one pay attention to the "closed" sign? The town eccentric Mr. Packer was tall, over six feet, missing an arm, nearing eighty at least, and with a yellowish-white beard that reached to his waist. He wore a heavy knitted red stocking cap, even though the heat of this late June morning was already well into the eighties. "Is there possibly more to the universe than Thread?"

"If anyone knew, it would be you, Mr. Packer. How are your collections?" I asked.

"Passable. Passable. What fool thing have you gotten yourself into, Claire. You look like a giant loon."

"My God, Mr. Packer, that's what she is. She's our Claire de Loon. You know she walks in the Loon Fest parade every year." Bromley stomped around the bar, his rather ample stomach proceeding him as he turned the polished mahogany corner, and pulled out a second Leinie's. Our Mayor was a quick drinker. I was just hoping he was planning to pay for them. He wasn't only the town mayor, he had also been my realtor for this place, and maybe he thought his commission included a lifetime pass to my bar.

"Is it the Loon Fest again? I had hoped to have gotten out of this danged town this year before it came up. All those summer people showing up. Bunch of fools."

"Well, Mr. Packer, it takes one to know one. What we would be without our fools? Take our young Wally Pearson here. Abandoning the bright lights of Manhattan to come back to our little Thread. Opening up a fine cafe . . . "

"Say, Wally, did you know that Al Capone once drank a beer here?" interrupted Mr. Packer.

"Of course, he knows that," said Claire. "We were just talking about it. I remember how mean he was. My first gangster."

"I bet he was," muttered Bromley.

"Such a nasty looking man. They were on their way to Timberton. He had some actress with him. Beautiful woman."

"Frances Farmer," said Mr. Packer.

"She was going to be in that movie they made about Timberton. What was it called again?"

"*Come and Get It*," said Mr. Packer.

"Get what?" asked Bromley.

"The movie. That was the name of the movie," he replied.

"I remember Frances Farmer. She was quite the looker," Bromley said. "Do you remember her in *King Kong*? What a movie."

"You got it wrong. That was Jessica Lange in *King Kong*." For some reason, I felt compelled to interject and correct Bromley.

"Bromley's right. It was Jessica Lange before she went crazy and had all that electroshock therapy. Just like they did to me," said Claire. "I remember her in that movie. They made a movie of her life, too, you know. And someday they're going to do the same for me. Jessica and I are so much alike. Beautiful women. Misunderstood." She glared at Bromley.

"You're confusing Frances Farmer, an actress from the '30s, with Jessica Lange who played her in a movie," said Mr. Packer, providing a perfectly reasonable fact that was completely ignored by both Claire and Bromley.

I polished the bar counter as this conversation flowed, and questioned my sanity in coming back to Thread. I had known Bromley, Claire, and Mr. Packer when growing up. Bromley had acted as mayor for years. Claire Moon, once the beloved town tramp, now just beloved, had slept with so many men for so few dollars that many wondered if she had lost a little bit of her mind each time she claimed to have lost her virginity. But that was so many years ago. And Mr. Packer had his own story, although who knew what that story was. Even the Mayor didn't seem to know Mr. Packer's first name, and Bromley never referred to anyone without using their first name.

My little cafe was filled with warmth and I liked it. The late June sun streamed in through large plate glass windows facing onto the Square. White painted letters, Loon Town Cafe, cast short morning shadows across my square tables with their varnished birch tops. I had kept much of what had been the Thread Tavern. The great Art Deco mahogany bar was still in place. It looked a bit rough when I arrived, having been kicked by many a lumberjack over the years, but now stripped, restained and properly polyurethaned, it was ready for the eighties. The old vertical board wainscoting along the walls had also been stripped. Much to the horror of the local workman, I bleached the boards until they were nearly white. Manhattan had been dark enough. Coming home was meant to lighten my mood.

"So what you going to serve here?" asked Claire. "Fish fries and beer. You gotta do that or nobody's going to come. But what else?"

I handed her a copy of my menu. "Take a look and try something. I'm not officially open yet, but my new cook's already in back."

"Maybe later. I'm too excited. You don't know what I have to go through to get this costume. Everyone knows that it's always my job to be the town loon for the parade, but that school principal won't let me borrow the team mascot costume. Like that mascot does the basketball team much good."

"Lost forty-five games in a row," said Bromley.

"But the game against Grosselier in February was lost on a technicality," said Mr. Packer. "Only four players showed up for the Thread team."

"Anyway, you see," continued Claire, "each year, I get this idea in my head that it would be great fun to walk in the parade as Claire de Loon. You know, my last name Moon really is Lune in French and that's just the same as loon."

"A homophone," said Mr. Packer.

10

"Now don't go calling Claire names," titched Bromley.

I went back to looking at my menu for the Loon Fest grand opening lunch. I needed to get my head around officially opening, and this disjointed conversation with three of the town's oddballs wasn't helping. "I think Miss Moon was talking about her plan," I pointed out.

"Exactly," she said with a sharp look at Bromley and at Mr. Packer. "As I was saying, it seems a shame not to have a town mascot in our Loon Fest parade. And no one seems to care. But I do. I have to be Claire de Loon. It's a cosmic thing."

"Like your visitors," muttered Bromley.

"And so, just like I've done for the past five years, I break into the Thread gymnasium, and go rummaging through that's coach's storage room. He saves everything."

"Coach Shapely is anal-retentive," said Mr. Packer.

"Listen to that man," Bromley said in a near shout. "He can't talk about anyone without calling them a dirty name."

"You're the mayor," I joked. "Banish him."

"So I rummage through this stuff. Basketball uniforms from forty, fifty years ago. Who's going to use them again? He has all this stuff, all disorganized, all the better to hide the costume for Nanoonkoo so I won't find it."

"Nanoonkoo?" I asked.

"The mascot for the Screaming Loons. Don't you remember your childhood, boy?" replied Mr. Packer.

"And don't loons call, not scream." Bromley cupped his hands around his mouth and let out a deep, unearthly shriek that rose from low tones to high only to drop back down into muffled tones.

"That's not how a loon sounds. After all, I should know. I'm the town loon. Listen to me." And with that Claire cupped her hands and began a more melodious and lonely sound. Bromley just continued even louder. Mr. Packer sighed as though he heard this once before and he too put his hands up to his mouth and emitted a sound so plaintive and echoing, wild and laughing, that both Claire and Bromley stopped their cries and just looked at him.

"Knock, knock" a teenaged girl poked her head just partway through the door. I really needed to go turn the sign over to read "open" and make things official.

Bromley turned toward me and whispered as though telling me a secret I didn't already know. "Cynthia Trueheart. Red's her father. A stingy son-of-a bitch, that Red. Don't tell him I said so. He always gives me a lot of support at election time. But why shouldn't he? He owns half the god darn town."

I nodded to Cynthia to come on in and join the story. She walked in, a big smile on her face, as though she were eager to join up with this crazy bunch of town folk. Claire paid no attention and continued with her tale.

"So I'm in the gym storage room, rummaging around until I find my bird costume, and what happens, but the door slams shut on me. And it's locked! I'm locked in the school gymnasium. It's early summer and school just got out. I figure I'm done for. So I put on my Claire de Loon costume, because if I'm going to meet my maker, I want it to be on my best terms. And I stand in that hot little room thinking of all the years I have spent in Thread, good years they've been. Lots of fine people have come through here. I liked them all. They've all been very good to me. Treated me like a lady. I had no complaints. So in my costume, I laid my head down on the basketball uniforms and said my prayers."

"And that's when I opened the door," squealed Cynthia.

"She squealed just like that," said Claire.

"What do you think? It's a storage room, and I thought someone had left a corpse there. Wrapped it up in Nanoonkoo to rot away. What would we have done next year for our cheerleading routines if we didn't have Nanoonkoo."

"Won a game?" snipped Bromley.

"Mr. Bromley! My dad wouldn't like it if he heard you talk like that? You know he thinks you should be more positive about this town and everyone in it. We will win a game. Maybe next year. The boys can't help it. They're just outnumbered and outsized. They've got the heart." By now, Cynthia was completely inside the circle and sizing up the look of my cafe.

"This is really neat," she said. "I like it a lot more than when Daddy owned the place." Yes, Red was the former owner of this building, just as he owned so much of the town. As I recall, he had also been my parent's landlord when I was growing up. "Daddy kept this tavern so dreary, don't you think? These are nice flowers. Did you grow them out back?"

"Oh dear," Claire said, "I think I hear the band tuning up. It must be time to get in place for the parade. I'm the grand marshal this year."

"You most certainly are not," replied Bromley. "You know perfectly well that I lead the parade this year, as I have for the past thirty years. It's the responsibility of the mayor. You're not even supposed to be in the parade. In fact, you're not even supposed to use that costume. The school superintendant forbid you to ever wear it again after last year's event."

"If you're the grand marshal, you better follow me or you're going to be late." Claire trundled out on her webbed feet. Bromley waddled after.

"Some say they're brother and sister," Mr. Packer observed. "But who knows for sure. Not many left in town who remember those lumbering days. Twins is what they say. They certainly have turned out different, if that's the case. I think I'll just follow along and see that they get to the schoolyard in time. Last year, they got into quite a squabble and missed the parade." He left the cafe, a slight odor of unwashed clothes lingering behind.

"Aren't they just wonderful," Cynthia swooned. "I could spend all day with them."

It's a peculiar thing that I ended up back in Thread after plotting my escape for all my high school years. During my adult time in Manhattan, Thread was a place in my past, an interesting set of anecdotes and stories. It held no future for me. The locals were too isolated, too strange. I was meant for better places.

But last winter in Times Square, a mugger's knock on my head forced me to rethink my convictions. All I could think of was how much safer and quieter life would be if I went home. The big city held too many problems for me. The old home town offered something simpler. True, Mom and Dad had already moved away. Neither my brother nor my sister lived within a hundred miles of the town. And I hadn't kept up with any of my old classmates. Yet as I rose back to consciousness from that mugging and horrible day, I could smell the Friday night fish fries of my youth in Thread. A nostalgia welled up for the sense of belonging I once had, and I knew I needed those old feelings back.

I never saw a bar in any New York establishment as beautiful as the one I recalled in the old Thread Tavern. I never had as much fun writing for the fancy East Coast magazines as I did during those summer waiting jobs in local restaurants working my way through college. Cooking old favorite recipes for my famed dinner parties was one of the few bright spots in my Manhattan life.

I mused on setting up a beer with a brandy chaser for the old men in Thread, of dogs waiting outside an ice cream parlor for their young masters to attack their sundaes, of women lingering over lunch to finish a cup of coffee and a homemade piece of apple pie with a flaky crust that could only come from a good lard pastry. I was bringing Norman Rockwell back to life, and it was beguiling.

Thread is an odd kind of town. Its last big transformation had been the arrival of electricity in the days of Roosevelt's REA act, or maybe the closing of the last lumber mill just before World War II. Or, if one were really honest, it was probably the dismissal in 1969 of Wanda, the local phone operator, when direct dialing reached the citizens of Thread. Until that year, Wanda kept tabs on the comings and goings of every man, woman and child as they made and received their calls. Red Trueheart had always paid close attention to Wanda. He trafficked in information – along with his groceries, the tavern, a hearty portfolio of mortgages and women's hearts.

The summer of 1969 also ushered in the final run of the Great Lakes Rail Road Northern Highlands Express. The Express was an old steam-engine, three-car passenger train that worked its way north from Chicago and Milwaukee. Each evening at nine, it would squeal to a stop at the Thread station and a handful of summer people disembarked. The summer resorts' drivers stood patiently by station wagons with wooden sides, ready to whisk the arrivals to their week on the lake. Saturday evenings were the busiest times for newcomers, always keeping pace with the Saturday 10 am departure of the previous week's leisure crowd.

By the time Amtrak evolved into the national service provider, it was clear the vacation tour to northern Wisconsin was no winning route for Federal policy makers. To most Theadites, it hadn't seemed that that many summer people rode on the Highlands Express. Everyone thought that those who did would start to drive instead. But they didn't – even though the car trip would have been hours shorter. Most folks felt it was just too far to drive after working all week. And there were so many other more enticing, livelier towns that had to be driven through before arriving in Thread. Who could blame them if the tired workers of Chicago and Milwaukee stopped short of their original destination? And so Thread became a little lonelier

But the lakes still glistened with clear, clean water. The towering pines still cast shadows over the lapping shores, and the loons still called in the evening light. That was the town to which I would escape back in time. When I returned to Thread in 1986, little had changed in the 14 years since I had graduated and left. The same stores encircled the town square. The same World War I cannon sat in the middle of an unkempt square.

Founded in 1887 by James Thread, a renegade son of a Vermont dry goods family, Thread followed the layout of its founder's childhood New England villages. He placed the town's center around a square that nearly ran edge to edge of the isthmus separating Big Sapphire and Little Sapphire lakes. This town square connected two broadening triangles of developed land between the lakes, laid out in a series of neat streets in geometric trapezoids, leaving space for parks on the north side fronting Big Sapphire Lake and on the south side fronting Little Sapphire Lake. The old pike road that wandered up from central Wisconsin moseyed along South, turned into the south side of the town square and then marched steadily north through the woods toward Timberton, the next town up the road.

The Great Lakes Railroad tracks, the rationale for the town, skirted the other side of the town square. It didn't leave much room for growth from the town square, but then it never mattered much. It took thirty years from the town's founding just to build up the stores and offices surrounding the square. And in the fifty years that followed, it was a struggle to keep those storefronts filled.

The lumber barons barrelled through and stripped the hillsides of their virgin timber, leaving only junk wood in the many marshes and swamps. The copper and iron titans emptied the hills of the Penokee and Gogebic ranges of their ore to ship it on giant freighters across the Great Lakes to foundries in Michigan, Ohio, and New York. Workers came and went, as one natural resource boom followed another.

A few foolhardy farmers found their way to the far north of Wisconsin, mostly new immigrants from Finland, who didn't have enough relatives with good sense to warn them away from the weak soil. They struggled at being dairy farmers, but over time they fled to others

15

endeavors, and their barns eventually caved in after one too many winters of heavy snow.

The hardwood forests all felled for their lumber and then cleared of stumps for short-lived farm fields were slowly abandoned. Eventually, the fields grew over with sumac and then poplar. Finally oak and maple returned. The jack pine in the swamps spread up shallow banks to hillier areas, and a mixed forest emerged, holding little memory of the lumber camps or failed farms.

Through the decades of transforming landscapes, the double Sapphire lakes remained the same: large, edged with broad sandy beaches, and fed by fast-moving trout streams. The lower lake flowed in the upper one, which in turn emptied into the Coeur de Lattigeaux river which flowed north to tumble into Lake Superior. And always, the loons continued to sound through the evening wind.

In the distance, the cacophony of the Thread Screaming Loons marching band could be heard. Cynthia Trueheart was still standing in my cafe. She took a wide-eyed lingering look to completely capture the interior space as if trying to decide something.

"Why don't you have curtains?" she concluded. "Don't you think it would be more inviting with chintz?"

"No," I replied. "I want people, especially tourists, to walk by and be drawn in. They need to see people sitting around their tables, enjoying good food and good talk. The Loon Town Cafe should pull people in."

"Aren't you afraid they'll just get scared away? You know, I really like Claire, Bromley and Mr. Packer, but they're a bit weird. Even a New Yorker like you would have to admit that," Cynthia said. She paused, and I pondered how a decade away had somehow made me a New Yorker.

"Don't you just love that music? It's so alive. Loon Fest makes this town jump. So many tourists show up. If only all these old folks who once summered here could come back. Daddy told me how they used to have great cabins on the west side of Big Sapphire. And they'd throw fantastic parties, bringing in bands from Milwaukee and Chicago. Their guests would come up on the train for the weekend. The wives and the children stayed all summer. The fathers would come up for a week or two and the weekends.

They even had servants." Cynthia sighed. "Those old enormous camps are almost all gone. Burnt down, torn down. It depends.

"But when I was little, some of the old folks still shopped in Grandpa's store. Grandpa would let me sit by the counter as he rung up their goods. I'd sit there all day long. They'd come in, buy a few things, and say 'Big John, put it on our account.' and Grandpa would. Daddy won't do that anymore, but Grandpa would. He knew all those people. And they all knew him. They loved him. I know they did. They'd talk about the way Thread used to be. That's when I'd hear about the old parties.

"I like hearing about the way things used to be, because they used to be better, don't you think?" She twirled to the door. "The front of the parade is almost here. Aren't you going to come and stand with me? You'll miss the whole thing standing in the gloom. Come out in the sun with me."

I followed Cynthia out to the radiating heat waves of the sidewalk. The day was going to be a scorcher, with extremely clear blue skies and just a few billowing cumulus clouds on the southern horizon. The sky suggested a change on its way.

Almost the entire square had people fronting the sidewalk. Close to a thousand people were probably in town. In places, people even doubled or tripled up.

In the center of the square, a huge temporary dance stage was set up. Tonight, Jerzy Jerzynski and his Jelly Jesters would be playing their mixture of polka and top 40 rock hits. Colorful red, white and blue bunting saved from last year's festivities decked the sides, masking the rough two-by-four planking that held the level dance floor a good foot above the uneven ground. Some enterprising gardener from the Ladies Guild had cut bundles of red and white gladiola and set them in large buckets wrapped in aluminum foil.

The stores around the square made a token effort to join the holiday spirit. The more thrifty ones followed the town square's approach and simply pre-used Fourth of July garb. Others, like Red's grocery store, took the high road with a loon motif. Black and white birds wrapped in pine greens decked out many a store.

Most of the crowd was in front of Red Trueheart's Piggly Wiggly supermarket. With its parking lot, it took up the entire west side of the Thread Square. The supermarket was the newest building in town. Red took a leap of faith back in 1968 and over his father's objections tore down the

...buildings housing the original Big John's Market. In its place was a less-than-marvelous example of '60s architecture with big plate glass windows making up a long transparent wall. True, the parking lot faced part of the square, and the glass and cement block building didn't quite match the timber and brick of the rest of the square. But the townspeople liked the place's fluorescent brightness.

The south side of the square was also well graced with spectators waiting for the parade. South Square had some of the town's more important businesses, like the hardware store, the drug store, and the hotel (where both Claire and Bromley lived, separately of course.)

On North Square, my side, there were fewer people. Since this side of the square had the businesses catering to the tourists, including the ever popular Little Papoose gift shop, this seemed a bad sign. The Loon Town Cafe was at the west end of this street, close to the glamour of Red's supermarket and the occasional traffic of Highway 17.

On the east side were the fewest people. The only attractions were the defunct railroad station, the bank which had already closed for the day, and the movie theater, long since boarded up, the tattered posters from a 1971 showing of *Cabaret* peeling away.

"I see Claire," shouted a local. "Claire. Claire. Claire." The chant went up. And there was the town's favorite loon, her webbed feet high-stomping to the pallid march beat of the twenty-person Thread Screaming Loons marching band. Claire grabbed the baton from the drum major and took over the lead. "Claire. Claire. Claire."

Behind the band came the town fire engine, followed by the only police car in town, looking a bit forlorn in its black and white markings as it was missing a red bubble on top. Then there was the Cub Scout troop and the Brownie troop, walking in perfect disorder. Some of the out-of-towners in front of the Little Papoose were exchanging glances. They had been expecting a parade.

The highlight of the parade pulled around the corner. It was Red's annual float extravaganza, a wagon pulled by a John Deere tractor, driven by Rueben Cord, the pony-tailed butcher at Red's supermarket. Covered with a year's supply of tissue and crepe paper, the float was graced by four of the high school cheerleaders, in tighter garb than normal.

I turned to Cynthia. "Aren't you a cheerleader? Shouldn't you be up there?"

"Daddy won't let me. He thinks it's undignified."

"But it's his float."

Cynthia shrugged her shoulders.

"I'm going back into my cafe," I said. "I need to officially open, and maybe I'll get some business." Walking back into the place, I ceremoniously turn the sign over. "Closed" became "Open.".

The high school band from Timberton was now in the square, playing with a precision and volume that had always escaped the Thread Screaming Loons High School marching band. Timberton was the only high school that could always be coerced into supporting the Thread festivities. Bromley had some pull with the mayor there, who knew the school superintendent, who in turn could overrule the band director. As for other schools, not only did they seldom venture to participate in the Loon Fest, but they rarely invited the Screaming Loons to march in their summer jamborees. Bromley, Red, and other town leaders took some offense at that, but Big John, the town patriarch, always maintained that the only losers were those who didn't ask, and that Thread could get along very well without their leave.

I was wiping down my wooden bar counter for the ninth time that morning, my feet bouncing along to the Sousa march. The parade was nearly over. Maybe a lunch crowd would soon develop. If the tourists weren't interested, perhaps the locals would be curious.

An older man entered the bar and slid to a seat at the far end of the bar, as hidden as one could be in a cafe with a front wall of plate glass. "What an ass-hole of a town. How I get stuck here every fucking year is beyond me! Can I get a Heineken?"

"Sorry, only got Wisconsin beers."

"Shit. This town's just shit." He paused in his tirade and looked around the place. "What is this place? Reminds me of fucking Manhattan. Who the fuck are you anyway? I don't recall seeing you here last summer."

"I wasn't here last summer. Just opened the place. Today's the official opening, at least for the bar. And while I can't give you an imported beer, how about a nice glass of a California Chardonnay. Something crisp, not too mellow."

"Sure, how about a glass of Kendall-Jackson. Got that?"

"Want a bottle? I don't serve that by the glass."

"Yeah, why not. A bottle. Since you have some decent stuff, I might as well drink it. I definitely do not feel like going back to the compound and dealing with my wife and her mother. By the way, the name is Henry Van Elkind."

"You the guy with that huge estate on the other side of Big Sapphire Lake?" I asked.

"My wife owns it. It's about the only big place left in this god-forsaken crap heap. She sends her mother up here for the summer, and I get dragged up for too many weekends. They still live in the Thirties. They have to 'summer.' Hell, I'd summer too if it were Cape Cod or the Hamptons. But here!"

"Don't come then."

"Easy for you to say. Besides, I have my plans for this place. Just wait and see. You got here just in time. You don't know it yet, but you'll see that we're kind of like partners."

"Mr. Van Elkind," Cynthia shouted as she bounced back into the cafe. "We didn't know you were up for the weekend. Daddy would love to see you again. You and Mrs.Van Elkind should come over." She turned to me. "They have the most beautiful place, and the roses in the yard are fantastic. They're in full bloom right now. Mrs. Rabinowicz is a wonder with them, isn't she, Mr. Van Elkind."

"A wonder, yeah, that is exactly how I would describe my mother-in-law."

"Hey gang, how about some Leinies?" shouted the headless loon as she waddled in. Claire had removed the mascot's head, and her small-featured face encircled with gray hair beamed. "Did you see me lead the parade, Hank?"

"It's Henry. Henry Van Elkind."

"Oh, you'll always be Hank to me. Hey, Bromley, Mr. Packer," she shouted out the door, "come in and sit down. I'm going to buy you lunch at this fine new establishment. Wally, send over three fish fries to the corner table."

"Fish fries," said Henry Van Elkind with a raised eyebrow. "Maybe this place isn't as Manhattan as it looks."

"Then how about a toasted baguette with Wisconsin sharp cheddar and applewood smoked bacon?" I countered.

"Sounds good. I'll give it a try."

Cynthia gave me a wink and formed an A-OK sign with left hand.

"The Loon Town Cafe is officially in business," she said.

For some reason, I immediately wanted to be back in Manhattan.

CHAPTER TWO

My new life began several months earlier with a wintry return to Thread. On the bobsledder's chute of a road from Timberton, the high white banks of snow gleamed a bright yellow in the skittering catch of my rental car headlights. I had decided to return to Thread and open a cafe. Who cared if it was the middle of February? Time was wasting.

The car swerved on an unexpected patch of darkly gleaming ice. I turned back into the spin to control the car. I had been gone too long. Winter roads seemed a stranger.

The hilly road meandered from Timberton to Thread, crossing the continental divide that separates the Great Lakes basin from that of the Mississippi River valley. It all fell within the great snow belt that winds from near Syracuse across the continent to Duluth. Along this geographic arc, each city, each hamlet, on the south shore of a Great Lake shares heavy and frequent snows.

But in Thread the snow belt is at its worst. Wintry northern winds rush from Canada, fleetly skip across Lake Superior with warmer unfrozen waters beneath its ice. As the air warms, it holds more water according to the unbending laws of physics. It sucks moisture from the lake until the very wind becomes a water-soaked sponge ready to be squeezed dry at the slightest change in pressure.

The wet winds head inland across northern Wisconsin. The remnants of the old, worn-down Porcupine and Penokee Mountains slightly push the air level up, compressing the air sponge and cooling the winds. In the rush of condensing air, the water vapor quickly turns into snowflakes which drop. And drop.

After flights from New York to Milwaukee to Timberton, I listened as the guy at the rental car counter told me that the snow count had already raced past two-hundred-inches. Over sixteen feet of snow. And it was only February. Luckily undergrowth prevented drifting in the woods and kept the compressed snow to a man's waist. Still, there were no sidewalks to be found on the scattered outskirts of Thread. The residents always gave up on shoveling by Thanksgiving.

I was home, but I didn't know why. Perhaps the horror of that New York mugging had done more damage than I had thought. It was as though that taste of unconsciousness loosened some memory of smells that lingered in my mind at the slightest encouragement: Freshly fried fish. Evergreen boughs. Mixed with laughter and a little bit of cheap perfume.

It was that damned cafe in Thread. I couldn't avoid thinking about it, and I needed an escape.

I would be sitting in Tom's, a small, unpleasant coffee shop near Columbia University, having a quick coffee and powdered sugar donut for breakfast before heading to the office. The memory of the smell of fresh coffee mixed with falling snow would infect my mind.

I would sit down to a business lunch at the Russian Tea Room, ready to interview a celebrity, and instead of blintzes, caviar and sour cream, I would flash to the odor of fried fish.

Dinner with some challenging new companion would begin at an arty cafe near the theater district, in a room rich with wood and fine linens. The lady at the next table would laugh at her date's joke, twist her head ever so slightly, and what would I smell? Not Chanel or Opium, but rather the fragrance of an over-used bottle of Evening In Paris.

And I'd be back in Thread again.

Why reminisce about such a small and inconsequential resort town? Didn't I have everything I ever wanted? Just the week before three people in one night at one party—three people I had never met before in my life knew my name and had read my latest cover story in *Inside Manhattan*. My rent-controlled apartment was a deal. And I had friends, lots of friends. Maybe there was one friend gone missing for good, but wasn't I churlish to want more?

I did, and I didn't know why. But here I was, in the middle of February, in a two-year-old rented Ford with a bad heater, skidding down

Highway 17, rushing into the city limits of Thread.

Technically speaking, Thread doesn't have city limits. In political terms, Thread doesn't exist. Some map companies don't even bother to plot its location on their drawings. Legally, Thread is nothing It's just part of a township called Sisu, a subdivision within Penokee County found in northern Wisconsin. So, it's not a city, not a village, not a county. It just is.

Locals call Bromley the mayor of Thread, but he is really the chairman of Sisu township. Whatever, it was Bromley that I was on my way to see.

My fixation was simple. I would open a cafe. All my adult life, I enjoyed cooking and eating. My friends considered me quite a fine chef. Lording over my own small empire was appealing. Thread deserved a place with food worth eating—in my kind of cafe, a place that celebrated the fresh ingredients of Wisconsin, a location where friends and neighbors could gather, a menu which took the best of the German and northern European heritage that was Wisconsin and combined it with contemporary tastes.

Admittedly I had never worked in a restaurant except as a waiter. That didn't seem a significant hurdle. Not knowing the first thing about cooking in quantity, or managing a business was less important than that I would be my own boss. Free of the rat race and memories of Manhattan best forgotten.

So here I was racing down a snow channel to meet a man I once vowed never to see again. "Wally, my boy," Bromley boomed as I entered the hotel lobby where he dwelled. "So it's back to your roots. Never really expected to see you enter this town again, now that your parents are moved away. Big city lights got you down?"

Five minutes and I was already annoyed. "I'm thinking of relocating. Buying a business here. Returning home."

"Home. Now that's an odd word coming out of your mouth in regards to Thread. Always thought you hated this darn place. Be that as it may. Let's get to the business at hand. What kind of establishment you thinking of buying? Got the money to do anything with? I hear you've always been a bit spend happy back in the Big Apple."

That was the problem with Thread. Everyone always seemed to know everything about other people's lives. Or so they thought. I had actually been quite thrifty.

A massive Cadillac, an amber pink 1960 model with fins just beginning to recede back toward the trunk, pulled up in front of the hotel. It was loaded with power gadgets for everything: windows, locks, mirrors, seats. A twenty-five-year-old miracle of engineering. Out stepped the real power in town, Big John's son Red Trueheart. Red was fond of vintage cars. He had seventeen of them.

Red stood outside the hotel and motioned me to come out. He was a tall man, a broad man, with unnaturally vibrant red hair. But it was Red's genuine color.

"A god damn surprise when Bromley gave me a call. You know I never expected to see you back in town," he said.

"So I've heard. I'm getting bit tired of everyone telling me how I hated this town," I replied.

"You know you detested the place," Red laughed good-naturedly. "But times change. People too, I guess. Not that I've ever really seen that. To me, people pretty much stay the same. Always ready to screw you. I try to give everyone a fair deal, but it's tough. No one's honest anymore. Always looking out for themselves. But if you're a businessman, you gotta expect it. Goes with the trail. Know what I mean?

"Of course, you know what I mean. You're a smart one if you're thinking of buying into Thread. Things are ready to boom. This town's a gold mine, just waiting to be discovered." He patted his car affectionately. I noticed ice fishing gear in the back seat.

Bromley perked up at Red's words. "What do you mean by that? What kind of a boom?"

Red waved him off, "Never you mind. Such a god damn nosy man, our mayor is. Will get him into trouble one of these days." Red looked me in the eye. "So you're looking to buy something, eh, Wally? You've come to the right place. If it's for sale in Thread, I'm the man who can sell it. Bromley was right if he told you that."

Red's praise of Bromley didn't mean much. Even the smallest school kid in Thread would have told you that Red Trueheart was the real man to see. But everything he had came from his father, Big John Trueheart.

During the Depression, Big John ran the only store in Thread, a combination grocery, dry goods and hardware store that caused most everyone in town to fall into Big John's debt just to scrape by. Big John was always most accommodating, willing to write up their orders and put it on account. "Just pay when you can," was his motto. Eventually, as the bad years rolled along, the day when you could pay became the day when you had to pay. And if the out-of-work lumberjacks and mine diggers couldn't come up with the cash, then Big John was always willing to take out the mortgage on their house, or accept the back forty acres on their useless farms. By the times the Japanese bombed Pearl Harbor, which prompted a new rush of interest locally for iron and copper, Big John owned half the township that surrounded Thread.

Even that day in the thirties when Capone stopped at the Thread Tavern and Big John served him his beer, a priest might have debated which of the two had more reason to confess? Was it the notorious gangster known throughout the country as an outright robber? Or was it the unknown northwoods entrepreneur who slowly bilked his day-to-day customers of their most important possessions?

That was fifty years ago. Now Big John was retired and growing senile, confined to his oversized house on the lake. Red tried to keep his spirit alive in the various businesses he ran: the Piggly Wiggly grocery store, the hardware store, the Quaking Birch Lodge on Big Sapphire Lake and the dozens of rental houses in which half the townsfolk lived. But he didn't really have the old timer's cutthroat spirit.

Red dragged me into the long-boarded-up Thread Tavern. "Always a great bar ," he said. "You know Al Capone once drank a beer here."

"So I've been told." I was going to play it cool and keep my answers short. This was a professional negotiation.

"Lots of history in these old walls. Dad owned this first you know, even before the general store. They used to play a lot of serious poker in here, back in the days when the lumber mills were going strong. Not like up in Timberton where there were eighty-five bars on Silver Street with eighty of them cat houses. You should've seen some of those old places: Swede House, Ole's Place, Wolf Saloon. Only the old Penokee House is left. That was the best place. Or, so Dad said. Oh, it was wild enough. Dad won the store in a poker game at the Penokee House bar. They dealt him a royal flush. You ever see something like that? They accused him of cheating. But it was an honest game.

"The guy who lost never really missed it. The family still vacations over on Big Sapphire. The girl married some Boston snot named Van

Elkind. City sophisticate, know what I mean. My wife thinks they're hot shit. Me, not so much.

"So what do you think of this space?" Now he was quiet, chewing on a toothpick.

What could I say? The building didn't look like much. Some dismal winter light was sneaking through the boards that covered the front windows. Had anyone been in this place in the last decade? Cobwebs and dust everywhere. But beneath the dirt, there were lines, nice lines. The interior was spacious with large windows. It could be bright and inviting. The bar itself, which ran the entire back length of the room, was a beautiful piece of carpentry from the early Thirties. You could see the influence of art deco movies in a rural, hand-crafted way.

"There's an apartment upstairs where you could live. Not much, but you can see the lakes. So, let me show you the kitchen," Red said. "My father never served anything but fish fries here. Neither did I. But the first owners used it as a full cafe."

"That was nearly sixty years ago," I pointed out.

Red gave me a look that implied I was an idiot. "Everything's still here. What more could you want?"

Maybe clean floors, tables with all of their legs, a refrigerator that would pass a health department inspection, a dishwasher of any type, and, of course, customers. A few pieces of china might come in handy as well. But I didn't say anything. I was playing it cool.

Red just chewed on that toothpick. "A perfect kitchen. Just as we left it when we closed down the place ten years ago. That was right before your pa and ma moved out of Thread. Well, what do you say? You want it?"

The kitchen was large, with a huge picture window at the rear that overlooked a small yard separating the rear of the restaurant from the alley. I could turn that space into more parking, I thought, then stopped myself. I wasn't in Manhattan any more. There was plenty of parking on the town square. Instead, this could be my herb and vegetable garden. And in the winter, I could build a snowman every other day while wondering where all the tourists were. I laughed lightly to myself. Both Bromley and Red exchanged looks.

I walked to the back of the kitchen and surveyed my potential domain. The snow clouds had fled south and the flakes had stopped—at least for a while. The sky was a bright and clear blue. Each snow crystal on the ground shimmered with its own diamond brightness. There was barely a track on the snow, just the tiniest of swishes from a field mouse that might have raced across the snow earlier, keeping its eye out for a swirling hawk above. I wanted this place.

"Lot of space to keep your trash back there," noted Red helpfully.

There were no trees in the little yard. The other stores on this side of the Square were less deep than the cafe, so no structure blocked the sun. Plenty of light for a garden. I could picture it now: the steady progression through the spring, summer and fall. First, there would be the tiniest of sprouts from the green onions, the radishes and the leaf lettuce. They would be small, ever so green, flirting with the first signs of spring.

As the days grew longer, and the dusky evenings brought forth long shadows to snake across the yard and through the alley, the tendrils of the green beans and peas would shoot up. The frothy tops of carrots, the broader leaves of red beets, the first wandering vines of cucumbers from their planted hill would sway in the light winds of the evening.

If I planned now, in a few years, that same midsummer light would shine upon the last ferny spikes of asparagus gone to seed, its lace-like filigree tipped with red berries. And off to the side could be the strong red shoots of rhubarb with its broad green-red leaves that were so poisonous.

Then as the summer days began to shorten, the rain clouds would come more frequently in late summer thunderstorms, and the sweet corn would grow, if one were lucky, knee high by the fourth of July. The first potato plants could be pulled and the ground searched for the tiny red nuggets of new potatoes that were best when drowned in sweet creamery butter. The green orbs of heirloom tomatoes would swell each day, gaining a deeper and deeper blush, waiting for the fresh basil in the herb garden to catch up.

Eventually the first hints of winter chill would force their way back into the daylight. The silk on the corn, now as high as me, would be golden. The tomato plants, while withering, would spill red fruit across the ground. The cabbages would grow large. The fight would be on to keep the broccoli from being eaten by the worms. Snaking wildly among the potatoes and corn patches would be golden pumpkins and squash.

A season of eating. All in one back yard. Not just in my mind, but real and touchable, doable. I wanted it.

Bromley was pontificating. "Just put one of those big hinged garbage containers back there, and you'd only have to contract for Jack Manny's trash truck to come by once a week. Once every ten days at first. You're not going to be that busy. Course it ain't really Manny's truck anymore. Well, I guess technically it never was, seeing as how he gave it to the city and all that . . . ."

"Red," I said, interrupting Bromley. "I'll take the place. Let's talk money."

Red smiled. He named his price. It was ten percent more than what Bromley had told me the place was going for. I could do better than this. We hemmed and we hawed.I knew exactly how much I was willing to pay for the place.

So Red wanted ten percent more. What's ten percent when you have dreams? I bought it anyway, and wondered how I would ever find enough money from my limited savings to make the changes that were so essential.

A month later I stood in the wreckage of the Thread tavern and began to take inventory of what I owned.The front room had space to seat forty-five easily, without any crowding. I wanted people to be comfortable, with room to spread out, able to get out of their seats to walk over to some other table to say hello. About ten or eleven tables seating four each could fit in the space and still provide that greeting room.

If I kept the bar as a bar I could seat another ten people there. But I didn't think too many people would come into my Loon Town Cafe just to have a drink. Maybe I should think of it more as a lunch counter—at least during the day, where individuals could have a quick meal. That meant maybe fifty, fifty-five people at the most, in a single seating.

Now if I were really lucky, I could get through a single seating at breakfast, at maybe five dollars a person. That would be two hundred fifty a day. Plus another seating at lunch at maybe another five dollars a head. Another two fifty. Plus two seatings at dinner at ten dollars a person. That would soar the total up by a thousand. So my total possible take was fifteen hundred a day, times six days, since I planned to be closed on Mondays. This allowed for a potential gross of nine thousand a week. With fifty weeks in the year, giving myself a two-week sanity sabbatical each year to a big city, I could potentially gross $450,000 a year.

"Dreaming?" asked a thin man, maybe a few years younger than me, as he walked through the opened door. From his dark, strong features, I suspected he was a member of the Lattigo tribe, whose reservation was about ten miles east of town.

"Just calculating in my head what I might make on this place, once I get it fixed up." I extended my hand "My name's Walter Pearson."

"Mine's Chip," he said, ignoring my outstretched hand. He proceeded to walk into the center of the dusty room giving it a slow and complete, three-hundred-and-sixty degree inspection. "Chip Frozen Bear. Get a good year, you'll clear twenty thousand, thirty thousand tops," he drawled.

"You think I could make that a month?" I asked amazed that he was so close in his calculations to mine.

Chip snorted. "I was talking about a year. If you're lucky. Remember you're in Thread, not the Upper East Side."

"It's not the Couer de Lattigeaux reservation either," I retorted. "A lot of city folk drive through this town and need a good place to eat. If I give it to them, I'll keep the place busy. I'm going to be very unhappy if I don't gross at least twenty or thirty thousand a month."

"Sorry to hear that you'll be so unhappy," he drawled.

I was pissed. "What is this? You waltz into my place, before it's even opened, happy as hell to proceed to tell me my business? What do you know about running a restaurant?" What an arrogant ass.

"Big white man speaks," he mocked. "And by the way, you don't need to call it the Couer de Lattigeaux reservation. We call it the Lattigo. Keep it simple. Just because the French trappers tried to change our names three hundred years ago doesn't mean that we still have to put up with your cultural imperialism.

"And I'll give you some free advice. Get off your high horse and ask a few questions before jumping to conclusions. I know who you are, but it's obvious that you don't know who I am. Just like it's clear to me you know nothing about running a restaurant.

"You want the proof. Here goes. You were a writer in Manhattan. Your business experience is zip. I, on the other hand, have an MBA from the Graduate School of Business at Columbia University. I guess that gives us something in common, eh? We're both ex-New Yorkers.

"But, you see, while you were figuring out clever little stories to write about the latest way for the trendy to spend their money, I was back here with my people helping them get what belonged to them. I'm the business manager for the Lattigo nation. I guess I'm the person who keeps people like you from stomping all over us."

Who was stomping whom, I wondered? His impassioned fury gave Chip a Hollywood air of fascination. This Native American had almost black eyes, dark straight hair clipped close to his head. Just under six feet, thin and sinewy, he had a look that seemed almost French. There were those who believed the seventeenth-century French voyageurs did much more than portage as they made their way from the Great Lakes down the Lattigeaux river, before crossing over to the St. Croix. But as a child in Thread, I had long ago learned you never suggested to a Lattigo that he might carry European blood.

"There's a fundamental problem with your whole operation," Chip pointed out. "This place was a tavern. That means alcohol, and alcohol means high profits. But you're planning to open it as a restaurant, and worse than that, a fancy restaurant. That translates to labor, lots of labor. Extra time in the kitchen. Food that has to be prepared in advance, food that if it doesn't get ordered, ends up being thrown away. Waiters, busboys, lots of cash. And where does the profit come in a restaurant like that? In alcohol, of course. It's like popcorn in a movie theater. You can't make money on just the tickets. But you don't have a liquor license, and you can't get one. Ipso facto, you can't make the big money. The county, no, let's be honest, Big John Trueheart, doesn't want anyone to sell liquor—except for his grocery store and his taverns. So if you apply for a liquor license, you're going to get the same answer our reservation has gotten for the past ten years: this county has all the liquor licenses it's allowed. Go away. Case dismissed.

"Without liquor, you won't get the customers and you won't get the profits. You want to see the financial models. I have a PC back on the reservation. Yeah, we have computers. I'd be happy to run a few 'what-if's."

God, this guy was as annoying as he was handsome. "You don't know what the hell you're talking about?" I replied. "You think I'd buy this place without making sure I could sell liquor. It's one of the first things I asked Red." Not quite true. It was one of the first things he told me after I signed the offer to buy.

Chip laughed. "It doesn't matter what Red says. His father's the person who really owns it all. He'll never let you sell alcohol."

Now I was the one to smirk. "You better go back for another MBA. I already have a liquor license. It came with the place."

"That's impossible," said Chip.

I went behind the bar and pulled out a framed piece of paper. "Look at this," I said. "This place has had a liquor license since the day it opened in 1922. It continued to have it every day it sat closed for the past ten years. And it has one now, a license that's been signed over to me as the new owner of Thread Tavern, soon to be known as the Loon Town Cafe."

Chip's movie-good-looks transformed. "What a lying son of a bitch! Three years. Three years, my people have been trying to open a bar in Lattigo so we wouldn't have to throw money away in Thread. For three years, we've been told it's impossible. And all that while, an unused license has just been sitting there, attached to a boarded up bar. Big John just didn't want us to have it, even though we would have paid him a good profit for it. If the Trueharts think I'm gong to go into business with them after this, they're in for a surprise. Let me get ahold of that fucking fat mayor." The last sentence was barely audible. Chip Frozen Bear walked out

Minutes later, Bromley Bastique waddled into the café. "What were you thinking about? Talking to Chip Frozen Bear that way? Are you trying to start another god darn Indian War?" Bromley was on the warpath himself. "The man's gone berserk. I had to hustle Claire Moon out of my hotel before he tried to scalp her. He thinks this whole town is against him and his tribe. He's beyond reason."

"It strikes me," I said, trying to keep a calm voice, "that he has a reason to be angry. It sounds as though this town's leaders have been lying to him for the past several years."

"Of course we have, but it's been for their own best good. Everyone knows that liquor and Indians just don't go together. We don't want a bunch of god darn drunken braves going on a rampage through town. That'd be lunacy.

"Ever since that Chip Frozen Bear got back from his Ivy League school, it's been nothing but trouble. Lawsuits left and right. Claiming the Lattigo have the right to fish any time they want, without regard to fishing season.They'll destroy the fishing for the resorts. I hear they even want to open gambling casinos on the reservations. Claiming segregation just because we have two separate schools systems between Lattigo and Thread. We're two separate towns. Why shouldn't we have separate school systems?

"Of course, Red 's got no one to blame but himself and that pretty wife of his, Barbara. She's always putting on airs. She came back from Chicago ten years ago just ready to do good. She had this idea that Red and Big John should sponsor a scholarship so some poor little Indian kid could get off the reservation and go to a real school.

"I don't know how she managed to talk the two of them into it, but they finally agreed to underwrite one kid's college education. Little Chief Chip won the competition. I'm sure Red and Big John had in their minds that the winner would go to a state school, like down to Madison. Nothing wrong with Madison, other than that it's a cesspool of drug-smoking hippies. But given that, everyone know it's still a great school. People go there from all over the world. And if that Indian kid didn't want to go to a public school, well there's always Northland College in Ashland. Good little private school. Couldn't complain about that.

"But not our Chip Frozen Bear. He had to go East, all the way to Columbia University. Who would have thought he'd get in? And who would have thought the Truehearts would actually pony up and cover the tuition for a school that expensive. Of course, they only did it for the first year. Not even Red's that dumb. But by then Chip had figured out other scholarship programs. He stayed in New York six years, got two degrees. Now he's been back home three years causing problems.

"You'd think if a person would finally get a fancy ticket out of a place like Lattigo, they'd cash it in and take the first train available" Bromley stopped his rampage to look at me, as though wondering what I had done with *my* ticket.

I had to agree with Bromley that I would have expected anyone who squeezed their way out of the Lattigo reservation would fight to stay out. To reach Lattigo, you take County Road Z off Highway 17. The trek starts out pleasant enough, a narrow, curving macadam road beneath a canopy of beeches. But this picturesque road follows some ancient animal trail that wended its way between slight hills and marshy bogs, always skirting both the inclines and the depressions. During the logging days eighty years ago, this path had been bolstered in its marshier spots by laying rows of tree trunks side to side creating a corduroy road. In the years that followed, blacktop had simply been laid on top of this for a sturdier road.

But as the winter freezes and spring thaws came and went, the old, half-petrified logs heave up, creating new bumps and dips that sorely test any car's shock absorbers.

Bad as the road to Lattigo is, it is in far better shape than Lattigo itself. Northern Wisconsin can be a beautiful spot. Hardwood forests march endlessly into the horizon, broken now and again by shimmering lakes of clear water refreshed by fast moving streams. The land, flattened by eons of ice age glaciers, has no sharp hills and valleys, but neither is it bored by the monotonous sameness of a Nebraskan plain. Far from any cities, the skies are completely free of smog; yet they are never pure blue, since moisture is always blowing in from Lake Superior, often resulting in giant cumulus clouds that create a skyscape far more romantic than the ground below. On other days, wispy cirrus clouds float by in an ever changing menagerie of shapes.

The forests are still lively with deer, raccoons, squirrels, beaver and even the occasional bear and wild lynx. The lakes are well stocked with fighting fish like the giant muskellunge and fine-tasting walleye and northern pike, as well as giant schools of perch and bluegills and sunfish.

Then there are the occasional ecosystems best loved by biologists who know how to appreciate the hidden beauties of stunted flora. Bogs and marshes, whose rising and falling waters kill off new stands of pine trees to leave yellowing stretches of dead tree trunks.

It was in such a bleak depression of land that the U.S. Government in the late nineteenth century assigned the Lattigo to do as best as they might. The Coeur de Lattigeaux River slows down tremendously as it goes through the Lattigo reservation, turning temporarily into a broad meandering. The slow moving wall of water gets lost in marshes and swamps before refinding strength as it makes a last rush through the Lattigeaux Gorge just before falling into Lake Superior.

The ancestral Lattigo birch wigwams centuries earlier may have been healthier shelters than the shacks and shanties that now lined the dirt streets of Lattigo. Built on a slight swell in the swamplands, modern day Lattigo claimed running water, electricity, and a sewer system; yet few of the homes actually had these features. The two hundred or so homes had been built in the Fifties with the help of the Federal government. And time had not been kind.

Even though Lattigo was only a fifteen-minute drive from

downtown Thread, I can't remember ever traveling to Lattigo when I was in high school. The Thread Screaming Loons never played the Lattigo team. No Thread boy ever dated a Lattigo girl, or vice versa. It was as though we were two camps separated by swamps as impenetrable as the briars that surround fairy tale princesses.

But Chip Frozen Bear was slashing through those thickets. Maybe, I should try to get his help in figuring out just how successful the Loon Town Cafe might be.

Bromley was still in my empty cafe, and it was as though he read my mind. "That Chip is not to be trusted," he mused.

Red walked in, an aura of anger bristling around him. "Wally," he shouted. "I fucking went out of my way to help you in every stinking way I can. And you repay me by stabbing me in the back. You got to learn something, kid. Business is business. You don't share details.

"My wife Barbara is going to be heartbroken when she hears how you have broken our trust and confidence in you. That damned Indian kid. If it wasn't for me, he'd still be there on that reservation, with his god damn pretty boy looks, dancing a rain dance for whatever fucking lost-in-the-woods tourists makes the wrong turn down that swamp road. He wouldn't be causing shit for every resort owner in Thread and the whole of Northern Wisconsin for that matter. He's an instigator. That's what he is. A fucking instigator.

"And now we get another hometown boy back from New York City ready to bite the hand that's feeds him. What is it with kids today?" Red's face was matching his name by now.

"I just want to run a cafe," I said. "Do we really need to play cowboys and Indians?"

A rather buxom woman was standing inside the door listening to our conversation. I had no idea know how long she had been lurking there. She wore an amused smile on her face. "Red," she said, "when are you going to learn that you can't control the lives of every single person in this county? If Chip wants to strut about as king of the Indian hill, why don't you just let him? What damage can he do?

"Hi," she continued, holding out her hand and walking rapidly toward me. "I'm Thelma Schmidt, and I'm the most bored woman in Thread. So when I heard you had come home to reopen this old dump, I just thought to myself, how could I help. And it was clear to me. You're going to need a cook. I could be that cook. And maybe life would be a little bit more interesting. For both of us." And she laughed, a hearty laugh, that began deep in her stomach and rushed out to fill the room, echoing from side to side before it died down in a series of small chuckles.

I remembered that laugh from my high school days. When the Thread Masquers managed to pull together a few would-be thespians and a few dollars to pay the royalties on some silly high school comedy from French's, they were always guaranteed at least one resounding laugh at every joke, no matter how old. And that laugh would be like a spark among dried-out leaves in the fall, jumping from leaf to twig to branch, resulting in a bonfire of guffaws that threatened to engulf the Thread High School auditorium in totally unwarranted hilarity. With that laugh, you were always guaranteed a hit. All thanks to Thelma.

"And why should I hire you?" I asked smiling. "What are your credentials?"

"Well Wally, I'm the person who taught your Ma to make her famous red velvet cake. Put that on your menu and you're sure to draw in old Red here. What do you say Red?" and she was off on another laugh.

"The truth is, Wally, that I've been cooking nearly fifty years, ever since I was eight, and if people eat it in Wisconsin, I know how to make it. Maybe I've never been a cook in a restaurant, but when I was younger and my Fred was still alive, I used to cook Sunday dinner for his entire family. There'd be thirty if there'd be one person at those dinners. And you know how those German dinners are. It's not enough to have just one meat. You'd have to have roast beef, ham, and a turkey. Three kinds of salads. mashed potatoes and dressing. Vegetables, relish tray. Two or three pies. And if it wasn't all on the table at the same time, all piping hot, then you just weren't a good housewife.

"If I was one thing, I was a good housewife to my Fred. And I figure if I could keep all those Bohunk relatives of mine happy every Sunday, then how much more difficult could it be to keep a bunch of tourists, used to simple city food. Give them the real stuff, plentiful and hot, made with good meat and fresh produce. They'd have to be happy.

"Besides that Wally, I'm just plain bored since Fred died. I need something different. You can understand that, can't you?"

"Thelma, you're hired," I said.

One decision down. Maybe Thelma's laughter and the need to still make another ten thousand decisions would keep me from dwelling on the memories that drove me home.

CHAPTER THREE

My life as a restaurateur took a turn on its eleventh day. Years later, after the earthquake and with my advantage of hindsight, I could easily identify that the moment Danny Lahti walked into the cafe looking for a job was an instant that changed everything. So easy from the vantage point of time to recognize how that troubled teenage boy contained more than a litte of myself, framed a person who wasn't willing to stare back at himself in the mirror and accept life for what it was, in short, a cypher only he could solve.

But isn't it always easy to look back and reflect on what you should have seen then? The trick is to see it in the moment and not be distracted by the warped reflections of the funhouse mirrors of life. To be fair, my life in Thread had more than its share of carnival moments and crazy midway barkers, twisting my mind with stories that made little sense, but were much beloved by those who told them.

Danny Lahiti walked in, looking both young and far too old. He asked a simple question. "Are you Mr. Pearson?" The boy looked to me, and there was something dangerously appealing in his voice that gave him an added dimension, as though the usual three were simply not enough to deal with all of the unhappiness that seemed trapped within him.

It was too beautiful a July morning for dealing with that. Outside on the town square, a dozen cars were parked. Small groups of tourists were already strolling the square, stopping at the Little Papoose to pick up a few postcards, checking out the abandoned train station, peering at the peeling posters for *Cabaret* below the marquee of the Thread Theater.

In the distance, revving motors sounded from the big power boats that were already skimming the top of Big Sapphire Lake to tug along struggling young water skiers. The breeze was slight, still cool from the morning mists. A somnambulant air hung over the people making their morning rounds. Even here inside my Cafe, each sipper of their coffee cups seemed contented, satisfied with life, on vacation from trouble and fear.

Danny's mere presence made a lie of it all.

But I get ahead of myself. A few days before I hired Danny, I had hired Cynthia as a waitress. It was at a point when I was still optimistic, believing in my calculations and not considering that the spreadsheets once proffered by Chip Frozen Bear might prove a more accurate predictor of the year ahead. I was feeling good. So far I had managed to avert tragedy. Loon Fest had come and gone. Business was so-so and yet two weeks in business it was already clear that Thelma and I weren't enough to keep up with the flow. I occasionally had Thelma's cousin Gerta in to help as needed, but I felt success would require more.

Already the cafe had its traditions. Each morning, my faithful trio appeared: Bromley would waddle in; Claire would soon follow with some tale of visitors in the early morning; and then Mr. Packer, always wise, always dignified, even with his long beard and missing arm.

Each had settled into his or her own peculiar routine. Bromley would start with a black coffee, then decide he needed cream, and maybe a little sugar, maybe a lot of sugar. Then a caramel roll, better make that two. Might as well have a rasher of bacon. As long as he was making a special day of it, it wouldn't hurt to have a couple of eggs, scrambled loose. Maybe put a little grated Colby cheese in those eggs. And, oh, by the way, could he have some butter to go with his caramel rolls? No, he always added, change that to margarine since he had to watch his health.

Claire, on the other hand, liked a cup of tea with a little bit of lemon on the side, a toasted English muffin, with wild strawberry jam. Each morning I would tell her that I didn't have wild strawberry jam and if I did, I would probably have to charge her $2 a serving for it. In that case, she would pleasantly reply, "Plain strawberry jam would be fine." It was just that she liked to stay close to the wild, natural things that grew in the area. Her little men that only she could see had taught her that.

Claire and Bromley would already be on their second cups when Mr. Packer would stroll in.

"What's new with the world?" Bromley would always shout out.

"Great things," Mr. Packer would reply as he would ask for a cup of coffee, black. "I love coffee," he would often say. Once he told me, "Learned to adore it in Paris, in a little cafe on the Left Bank after the war, World War I. There was a lady I went to see, a wonderful lady, a true lady. I wanted to befriend her, but I never really succeeded. Her children learned to love me, but she never did. So all I am left with is my coffee and memories. There are so many things I like to save, but those memories of her . . . they are one thing I would like to lose. Sometimes when I drink my coffee, I hope the steam might rise up through my mouth and my nose, seep into my brain to loosen those memories and let them float away. Never works. Still, I can try each day."

Then there was Henry van Elkind. More days than not, he would stroll in for lunch. There was a middle-age dissoluteness to his blonde, lankish look. His orders always conveyed a condescending sneer. I didn't understand why he wouldn't eat lunch at that big house of his on the lake. It was as though he preferred to sit at my table, staring out my windows, surveying some kingdom that wasn't even his. This sunny morning, my breakfast three were sitting at the bar, serving its planned double duty as a breakfast counter. Cynthia Trueheart walked in.

"Mr. Pearson, I want a job,' she said. She was so much more direct than Danny would be a few days later. But it was always easy for people to misjudge Cynthia. Her bubbly enthusiasm and her easy willingness to like almost anybody surrounded a sturdier spirit that often knew exactly what it wanted.

"Isn't that sweet?" said Bromley. "Now why would a beautiful young lady like you, with a father who will give you anything, want to work at this place? Don't get me wrong, Wally. It's a fine place. No doubt about that. Wouldn't want to disparage it. But no high school sweetheart should spend her last summer before senior year catering to god darn old fools like us." Bromley looked at me. "Sometimes, I think this girl is simple."

"You're not old fools," Cynthia said without a single sign that she found Bromley's comment offensive. "I like being around you."

"And why is that?" asked Mr. Packer.

Cynthia seemed stumped for a moment. Her reflective silence stretched on and on. Claire squirmed uneasily on her stool, looking at Mr. Packer. She opened her mouth about to say something. But some look was exchanged, and she remained quiet.

"Because you like me, and I like being liked. I want to be around people who like me. Working here would be fun," she ended.

"You sound like Jack Manny, needing attention," Bromley snorted.

"That's a mean thing to say," she said, this time with hurt in her voice.

"Who's Jack Manny," I asked.

"You remember, Wally," said Claire. "He was here when you were a kid. Always hanging around, wanting to be noticed. Finally got it, I guess. Like a bear gets noticed when it steps in a trap." And thus begun one of those stories that seemed to keep me from recognizing what was going on around me.

Mr. Packer smiled indulgently. "Jack Manny. Now there was an odd duck," he noted. "He never quite felt at ease. Wherever he went, whomever he was with, he always lurked with that disquieting sense of not belonging. I guess that's why he used the fifty grand his mother left him to buy Thread a new trash truck."

Bromley broke in, "That god darn truck was the start of his troubles. If he hadn't bought the town a truck it didn't need, Amanda would have paid him no attention. And his life would have been fine."

"But Amanda did pay him attention," Mr. Packer replied. "Jack was like a hummingbird, always flying around trying to feed on the attention anyone would pay him. And he put such energy into it that he always needed more. Of course, that's why he fell so for Amanda."

This story was starting to sound familiar. My mother had recounted it more than once on my visits home during my college days. Amanda came to Thread shortly after old lady Manny died, and just after Jack had donated the dump truck to the town. Jack was living in his mother's house. Quite a nice place. Old Mrs. Manny knew how to save her pennies. Amanda was quick to tally Jack's merits: that meticulously maintained five-bedroom house on the lake, the expensive donation of the new dump truck as well as the new basketball team uniforms. What could she do but fall in love? Mom always said Amanda trapped Jack into a quick marriage, but it seemed to me more that Jack's foolish generosity had ensnared Amanda.

Mr. Packer noted, "A lot of people find Amanda larger than life. When she wants to be, she's a vivacious one. She has a talent for dressing and makeup. In those day,s it made her look special, not cheap. So it didn't take much before Jack had proposed and married. Jack fluttered through town in those months with the happiest countenance he ever had. He never asked a soul for their opinion on how he looked or what they thought of him."

Claire added, "But remember when Amanda's kids appeared? And then she discoved Jack was broke, after he spent every last dime on the wedding and honeymoon. She was as shocked as a loose wire in the rain by those kids," murmured Claire.

"They were a surprise to all of us," agreed Mr. Packer. "Amanda didn't look a day over twenty-five, so no one expected her to have two attractive teenage kids, practically identical twins, except for their being a boy and a girl."

"When I first met them," Claire broke in, "I thought they were both girls and that one just liked to wears jeans and t-shirts. If it hadn't been for what happened later, I would still say they were two peas from the pod."

Now I remembered why I left Thread. Everyone knew everything about everyone. And they told the same stories over and over. Over the years, I had participated in enough phone calls with my mother and read enough of her many letters to know all the details that would follow: how Amanda finagled Jack to mortgage his house to fund her redecorating business; how everyone thought she slept with the banker to get the loan; how the townspeople always thought those two kids were a litte strange, a little too close. This town was like a tar patch, trapping you for all eternity. And then making you hear about it, over and over. I was so glad my parents had left town, or everyone would know the full story of what had happened to me in Manhattan.

"They've always seemed such nice kids," Mr. Packer was on a roll. "Polite, hardworking, good students. Back then, Johnny had a lot of promise as a basketball player, and Francine was even more beautiful than her mother. She never would have needed a bit of makeup to look wonderful. Shame that only Amanda stayed in town.

"They were always together, the two of them, inseparable, like lovers. Neither ever paid one bit of attention to Jack. For that matter, once Amanda found out that Jack's only assets were the house, she didn't pay him no attention either—except when she had figured out a new way to try to squeeze him for a few extra dollars.

"He was a sad little thing to watch after that, even more desperate for the slightest bit of attention. Pitiful really to watch him in the corner of a restaurant or bar, trying to screw up the courage or the wisdom to say anything that would cause one of us to say something to him other than hello or goodbye."

Claire broke in excitedly, "One day he even had the gumption to say that he had been visited by men from outer space. Imagine, thinking he was visited by my men." Claire was in a clear huff.

Cynthia was becoming fidgety, looking away from this group of oddballs she professed to like so much. Finally, she burst out, "You're all too mean. Francie and Johnny were good kids. And Jack Manny only wanted people to like him."

"They were good kids," Mr. Packer agreed. He turned to me, "You know, Francie became a cheerleader. Brought a bunch of Chicago cheers with her to liven up the Screaming Loons. Not that it helped much. They still kept losing.

"And Johnny was playing on the team. Only five foot nine and thin-boned, with that long blonde hair always falling in his eyes. His teammates didn't like him much. But he was good. What a jumper. Haven't had a jumper like that since. Several of the players were six foot plus, but that little Johnny could play rings around them. Fast on his feet, quick into the air, a good eye for aiming, and quick decision.

"It hurt Jack that he couldn't claim Johnny as his son. After all, he was Amanda's husband, so shouldn't that make him the father of the best player on the team—on the team that was still playing in the uniforms he had bought? He thought so. But when he went into the hardware or grocery store, no one ever slapped him on the back and said, 'What a game your kid played.'

"Everything was fairly stable as the season wore on. The team was still losing, but Johnny was getting better and better. The other players were holding him back. They didn't like being shown up by the newcomer. That Gunderson boy was the worst of the lot. And they didn't like the fact that Johnny's sister wouldn't go out with any of them.

"All this time Amanda carried on with her own world that didn't seem to include much of Jack. Most days nobody even walked into that decorating shop of hers. Who in town had a need for anything she had to offer? Sometimes the banker checked in on her, worrying that if this business didn't take off, the total mortgage on that Manny lake house was going to have to come out of Jack's bus driving salary. And being on the school board as he was, he knew that there wasn't enough money in that lowly salary to pay for a house mortgage. But she found the money somehow.

"It was about that time of the year when the lakes are frozen their thickest that folks began to notice that Francine was developing a little tummy, and not from her mother's food. The girl was clearly pregnant. No one acknowledged it. Not a word was said about who the father might be or whether she would keep the baby."

"Well, we all had our thoughts of course," Bromley noted. "There was the basketball captain, what was his name. He had taken quite a shine to her, always mooning about her. And she was a cheerleader, riding the bus with those boys on the away games. It takes two hours to get to Mandarin, you know. And Mrs. Limpit never was a very good chaperone. I bet you top dollar some pretty nasty things take place on those basketball busses. That's my theory." Cynthia turned a furious red at this notion. Didn't Bromley remember that she too was a cheerleader?

Mr. Packer simply ignored the interruptions. "Life went on that winter as it always does. Amanda kept her secret smile. Francie grew inch by inch. Johnny continued to nudge the Loons closer to victory but remained a loner. And Jack managed to put a happy face on it all.

"The more the snow piled up along the roadsides as it was scraped there by the road graders, the more Jack managed to find something special in all of this. He had a wife and she was a beauty. No one could deny that. There were two great-looking kids in his house. He had a job that he was even getting kind of good at. His wife had a career and lots of rich friends. The school team was playing better than ever, thanks to his boy and no doubt to those smart uniforms he had purchased for the school. And every week, everybody in Thread had to acknowledge his generosity when they saw that gleaming dump truck at the end of their driveway gathering up their weekly debris.

"By the time basketball season wore its weary way to end another year of complete losses, Jack had managed the impossible task of mentally levitating himself to the top of the world. The only sorcery that remained was convincing everyone else in town to acknowledge the good fortune of Jack Manny.

"After thirty years of ferreting out every compliment and positive remark possible about his sorry life, this was no challenge for Jack. He became a braggart. One night, near the end of winter, he just got carried away with his euphoria. Over at the Northern Nights, across the Square. A bunch of guys were there heaving boiler makers, talking about the ice fishing, and how pretty soon the ice would be breaking up, and then there'd be the fish spawning season with the game wardens all out. No good fishing could happen then you know. It was just the usual guy stuff.

"Jack decided to get into the conversation, although no one wanted to listen to him. There were only so many times anyone could say how great the uniforms looked, or how nice it was to have your trash picked up in such a shiny truck.

"Maybe Jack realized that night that it was time for a new subject. So all the talk was of Amanda and her beautiful children. He wasn't content just to tell the lies that Amanda wove, he had to embroider them into some even greater finery. It wasn't long until Amanda was the greatest decorator there ever was, and that the Loons would have won every game that season if just one other kid in town had played as well as his Johnny, and next year, the homecoming queen was bound to be Francie because there was never a more beautiful girl in Thread than his Francie, and was there ever anybody in the entire State of Wisconsin that had ever been more blessed in life than Jack Manny?

"Sam was tending bar that night, and I bet to this day he wishes he had thrown Jack out after his fourth beer. Jack never could hold his liquor, and it was just the beer talking. But old Emil Urho, who certainly was always ready for another drink, was fed up with Jack's braggadocio. Emil never did stop to think what his words could do. Just popped out with whatever bubbled up.

"'Jack, you are one fucking lucky man,' he started. The rest of the guys in the bar, sensing danger, stepped back a bit. 'One lucky man, indeed. We'd all have to agree with that.

"'Inherit a beautiful house and thousands of dollars, letting you fritter away the money on goddamn stupid asshole things like a trash truck, for god's sake. Who the hell said this town needed a new trash truck? A fire engine, maybe, a cop car, yeah. But a trash truck!

"'Well, we all love you for it anyway. And we're so happy that it's brought you such joy in your life.' At this point, Sam tried to pull Emil away. But Emil's nearly six foot four and a heavy man, after working in the woods all these years. He was on a verbal roll, and he wasn't about to let Sam put a stop to it.

"'All that money, and what do you have to show for it? A beautiful wife. She's the only person in town who fell in love with that dumpster. You want to know why? Because she thought a man had to have millions to be stupid enough to waste some of it on giving a town a new dump truck.

"'She don't love you. She's screwing every rich Chicago businessman that comes into town, hoping to get one so wrapped up in her cunt that he'll drag her away from this shit hole. And you're too fucking stupid to realize it.

"'"Oh, my beautiful wife.' You can say it again and again. But it's just a fucking joke. And those kids. That boy's so pretty, he has to be a fag. And your little Francie. She ain't so little anymore, in case you haven't noticed. If she ain't pregnant, I ain't a Finn.

"'And you come in here, night after night, wanting us to say how wonderful your life is. It's wonderful, Jack, just wonderful. Sure wish it was mine. Like hell, I do.

"'Give me another beer, Sam. I ain't drunk enough.'

"Jack was horror-stricken. He just stood there, his eyes moving from face to face, trying to get someone, anyone, to look him into the eye and say, 'It ain't so.'

"In his heart, he must have known it was all true, long before Emil ever uttered a word. But everyone in that bar that night knew Jack would never have faced it. That baby could have been born at the kitchen table and he would have thought it a miracle. A miracle given especially to him by God.

"He stood there for a moment. The only sound in the bar was the jukebox. His eyes began to well, his face getting red, then pale white, the tears beginning to stream.

"Emil never knows when to stop, so he kept on talking. 'Your pipes certainly are flowing. But you need a plumber to clean out the pipe to your brain. It's clogged with fuckin' stupidity.'

"Emil didn't get to say anything more. Jack turned and walked out of the bar. What happened next no one really knows for sure. He went back to the house on the lake, that much we know for sure. An hour or so later the town siren are blaring. Sam at the bar rushes out because he was one of the volunteer ambulance drivers.

"The call came from the Manny place. Amanda made the call. Sam walked into the kitchen. There was a lye-vomit-like odor everywhere. Jack was on the floor, curled up like a baby, jerking here and there, moaning piteously, kicking an empty can of Drano now and then by him in his throes of agony. The caustic chemicals were eating through his esophagus and stomach.

"Amanda, Francie, and Johnny hovered like three angels looking down on Jack. Each were in pale silken pajamas Sam said, as though angels awakened to take Jack on his way. They just watched, huddled together, but with the light of the kitchen on their white silk and golden hair, they seemed of another world.

"The ambulance crew rushed Jack to the airport in Ashland and flew him straight to a hospital in Milwaukee. Jack never did do anything right. Not even suicide. They saved him, if you call it saving. The pain made him go crazy, and his insides were all eaten up. No way could he ever eat again or lead a normal life. He's still there in a hospital bed in Milwaukee, fed through tubes, watched over by nurses day and night. And maybe he's happy, never alone, never unattended." Mr. Packer stared into his coffee, letting the steam rise up into his nostrils.

Cynthia was sitting at the counter, tears streaming down her face. "I'm not like that man. I just wanted to work here because I like you. I'm not like any of those people."

I walked over to her. I didn't care whether she was right for the job or not, whether her father Red would protest, whether I could even afford another worker. I felt sorry for this girl, and I made a decision. "You have a job. You can start right now. The Loon Town Café needs you." I glared at my dining trio to see if any one of them would dare to suggest otherwise. Only Mr. Packer even seemed to have noticed I had just hired a new waitress.

Danny came on board a few days later, and I think I would have suffered another of the town's stories. But somehow Danny's mere presence kept it from being told. To this day, I don't know whether it was to protect Danny, to avoid their own embarrassment, or simply the ease with which they could be distracted.

It was about time for my lunch crowd to appear, god willing, even though the breakfast crowd wasn't completely gone. Claire was still drinking her tea. Cynthia, already into her waitress mode, was pouring a fresh cup of coffee for Bromley. Thelma and her second cousin Gerta were in the back.

Van Elkind had decided to grace my cafe again for lunch, but this time he was walking through the door with a teenager in tow. The kid was almost as tall as his father but skinnier and sneerier. Apparently, all the van Elkind money wasn't enough to give the kid a good haircut or a clear complexion.

"Wally, come over here," said Van Elkind, "and meet my son Kipbert."

"Kip, Dad," the boy said with a sullen air.

"Kip. Kipbert, it's all the same"

"Okay, Dad, I'll call you Hank."

"Children, so annoying," Van Elkind said. "Mr. Walter Pearson, allow me to introduce you to my son, Kip Van Elkind. Happy now, Kipbert?"

Kip ignored his father. He had spied Cynthia. He signaled to her to bring two coffees. I expected Cynthia to smile in return, as she did with everyone. Instead, she pretended not to notice.

"Wally, I brought my boy along today. He needs to get to know the town. His mother and I want him out of Chicago and away from some shitty influences. So he's staying with his grandmother at our compound. Maybe if it works out, we'll have him stay longer and keep his grandmother company at the camp, because she's decided she won't come back to live with us in Chicago."

Kip jumped in. "Hank, there's no way I'm staying in this shit hole. You hate it yourself. So don't go bullshitting me into thinking it would be great thing. Just because you and Mom convinced that judge . . ."

"Yes, well, Wally is not interested in all of that. But, Wally, you may be interested in a small business proposition." I had guided them to an empty table, and Van Elkind motioned me to sit. With Cynthia now on staff, I thought, "why not?" I noticed Kip was back to ogling my new waitress. She was continuing to ignore us.

"What do have in mind? Buy the town together?" I joked.

He seemed quite startled. "Don't be ridiculous. My wife Rita is flying up on Friday to spend a few weeks with the old warhorse, you know her mother, Regina. Rita thinks we should throw a party for her Chicago friends she's bringing along, as well as the few people we like in Thread."

Dinner at the Van Elkind camp. Now that could be fun, a bit like my old entertaining days in Manhattan. I heard that Regina Rabinowicz had the real money, not Hank or Rita.

"Rita is very fussy about such things, with the very best of taste. Of course, she'd love to make everything for this party herself, but she simply will not have the time. As I am sure you can imagine. So I told her about your restaurant and how it is the one decent place in town. To make a long story short, we want you to cater our party. So much more sensible than flying in caterers from Chicago, and so much more authentic too, don't you think?"

Kip muttered, "Cheaper, too."

My entrance to the jet set of Thread had been so quickly trashed by Kip. "Henry, didn't you tell me once that Thread was a rathole? Why would you care if the dinner was authentic?" I already knew he was the kind of person who would care if it was cheaper.

Van Elkind didn't answer. He was intently watching somebody across the street. His son noticed his father's intense concentration and strained to see who was being watched. Chip Frozen Bear was walking into the hardware store on the opposite side of the Square. At his side was a beautiful woman with the same striking features as Chip. Long luxurious black hair flowed down her back. It must have been Frozen Bear's sister.

"That damn Lattigo," muttered Van Elkind.

Kip smiled at his father, "Yeah, but can you introduce me to the woman?"

"Stay away from that girl. And stay way from her brother. They're trouble for us. Don't get within one hundred feet of them. Do you hear me?" Van Elkind snarled to his son.

He turned back to me with a practiced smile, "So, you interested in the job? It's a small dinner party, twenty-four people. We are happy to throw ourselves into your capable hands. Serve anything you want, as long as it is not beef. Rita can not abide beef."

"Sure, I'll do it. Say, thirty dollars a head." That seemed an outrageous price that would be well worth it, if he accepted, which I hoped he wouldn't.

Van Elkind turned to Kip. "See, son, cheaper than Chicago. And it will drive your mother crazy."

Back to me. "A deal. Call me when you work out the menu, just to make sure we agree."

I walked by the bar and whispered under my breath, "Why do I dislike that man so much?" Mr. Packer with his keen hearing overheard. "You don't want to know. You surely don't."

That same day, and only minutes later, Danny walked in. I was about to add another employee. I remember that at that moment Claire was once again repeating her never-ending, day-long quest. "I'll have wild strawberry jam with that toast."

"I'm sorry, Claire," I replied, "but we have no wild strawberry jam today, like every other day."

"But I need it. My little men tell me to get closer to nature. It is very important to them. It's why they make me eat at this cafe, because they know you feel the same way." She nodded her head sagely. "Just bring more hot water. I've nearly drunk this pot of tea. I don't know why I'm so thirsty every morning. I'm like a duck out of water with no nest."

"Perhaps it's because you were down at the lake with Reverend Willy last night," said Mr. Packer. Claire's flush spread from her fleshy neck up into her worn and wrinkled face. Thelma who was working with me on the day's menu gave a hoot.

"Such an idea, Mr. Packer. If you weren't so old, I would . . ." She stopped in mid sentence and looked at the door. She closed her mouth and took on her prim demeanor, normally reserved only for out-of-town and elderly tourists. I turned to see who was so honored. It was a young man, no more than sixteen or seventeen, with the faintest of blonde fuzz on his cheeks and upper lip. Tall, at least six feet two, but uneasy at standing above the rest. He scanned the room tentatively, as though he wasn't certain what he was looking for, and even if he did, he wanted no one to know he was looking. Of course, it was Danny Lahti.

"Now, Mr. Packer," whispered Claire intensely, "No more talk of the Reverend Willy while Danny's here."

"Are you Mr. Pearson?" Only I seemed to sense his unhappiness. In fact, it was as though the others perked up.

"Danny, what's that handsome father of yours up to these days?" asked my cook Thelma. She turned to me, with her usual infectious laugh, "His father Toivo is quite a looker. A widower you know. A bit rough on the edges, but I like my men that way. A good man, your father, ain't he, Danny?"

"I guess so," he replied too politely. "Mr. Pearson, I wondered if maybe you had a job of some kind. I kinda am looking for something to do this summer. To make some money you know for when I go to college next year. I mean after my senior year. When I graduate. I've worked in restaurants before. Well anyway, I was just wondering," he wandered to a quiet stop.

Cynthia came bounding out of the kitchen, heading toward the table where Henry Van Elkind was eating. "Here's that fresh cup of coffee, Mr. Van Elkind," she said. Then she noticed Danny and she finally smiled, even allowing it to fall over Kip. "It's great coffee, Mr. Van Elkind. I just made a fresh pot, and it's that special blend that Mr. Pearson's bought. Really rich. You'll like it." All the while she talked, she never took her eyes off of Danny. And he never noticed that she was watching.

Everyone else noticed. I glanced about and saw that Mr. Packer, Van Elkind, Claire, Thelma and even Hank were watching Cynthia gaze at Danny. Unlike his unhappiness, in Cynthia there seemed a totally unfettered innocence and joy. Then she blushed. No explanation. The silence was awkward.

"So Claire," began Henry, "what were you saying about the Reverend Willy?"

Cynthia gasped. Danny looked strickened. Mr. Packer hemmed. Kip snickered. Claire pulled herself up straight. "There's nothing for me to say about the Reverend Willy. He's not my type of man."

"Who's this Reverend Willy?" I asked.

"So you have any work?" Danny broke in rapidly.

"Oh, he needs a busboy . . . and a dishwasher," jumped in Cynthia. "You do, Mr. Pearson. You know that you do. Gerta's too flaky. Hire Danny."

"I want to know who this Reverend Willy is," I said. The town may be too in love with its stories, but they weren't about to leave me in the dark.

"No you don't," Claire pronounced. "If you don't already know, you don't need to know. Enough said about that."

Cynthia rushed to take over. "Danny, come with me into the kitchen and I'll show you the dishwasher. It would be real easy for you to work it. And once you see it, I know that you'll be able to convince Mr. Pearson to give you a job, because he really does need another person here. Even if it isn't that busy right now." Cynthia walked to the kitchen with an imploring look cast back towards Danny, seeking his acceptance of her offer. He followed, with a glowering look back aimed at Thelma but encompassing us all.

"So who is this Reverend Willy?" I whispered.

"Well, we don't need to talk about that," Thelma said. "With that Van Elkind job you just took, we could use another person in the cafe. Why don't you hire the boy."

"Shhh!" hissed Claire. Her wrinkled face floated up and down in waves of frantic control. "They're coming back out."

"Mr. Pearson, Cynthia showed me the equipment in the kitchen. It's just like the dishwasher I used at the resort last summer. I really want a job in town. To do something. Something to get me out of the house. What do you say?"

"Okay," I gave in. Cynthia let out a whoop. "Start tonight. And Cynthia, I don't want you mooning all over this boy when he's here."

"Mr. Pearson," she drew herself up into a straight line that pierced the air. "Danny and I are just friends. You have nothing to worry about."

Danny didn't even hear Cynthia. A big smile transfixed his face, causing his tension and unhappiness to simply vanish. "I'll see you tonight, Mr. Pearson. You won't regret it."

I waved him off. "See you then."

Another expense added to my accounts. Van Elkind looked over, with a condescending smile on his face. Claire had become engrossed in the careful placement of her domestic strawberry jam to ensure its exact boundaries and knifed-out thickness on her muffin. Thelma muttered something about needing to begin work on the specials for tonight's menu, because it took a long time for the stock to cook and that was the secret of the sauce. Cynthia was sunnily strolling with her coffee pot back to Van Elkind's table. Kip gave her a leering smile, and she quickly retreated.

"Thanks, Mr. Pearson," said Cynthia as she sidled up to sit beside me and pulled me out of my reverie. "Danny really needs that job. You won't be sorry."

"Things are tough for him, huh?"

"It's not like that. It's his father who never really has any time for him. We all like Danny at school, but he never seems to notice us. Always seems lost in himself. I don't mean he's stuck up or anything like that. I don't know what I mean. I just like him and I feel sorry for him." She pulled out a cloth from her dress pocket and began to rub the bar counter down with ferocity. "I better go pick up the order for table four," she said and rushed back into the kitchen.

Thelma came out of the kitchen. "What did you say to that girl. She's in there with tears streaming down her face."

I shrugged my shoulders. "Danny," I said. My new waitress did seem to have quickly changeable moods.

"Poor thing." I didn't know if Thelma meant Danny or Cynthia at first. "That girl's got a heart of gold, but ain't got no common sense. Such a crush on that boy and he don't pay her no never mind. Danny's not a romantic like his father. Not at all."

"Oh, his father's a lovely man," piped in Claire.

"I used to think so, but not since Lempi's died. Toivo Lahti's a different man now that they moved into town from that little farm they had over to Deep Lake. He just mopes."

"Who is Lempi?" I asked.

"His wife," Thelma said. "They're both first-generation Finns you know. Carry that dour streak all the Finns have. Never did know how to show emotion. Won't hug you or kiss for love of money. It's no wonder that half of them turn into drunks during the winter.

"But Danny's father Toivo never was that way. His emotions are out there for all to see. Was a romantic even as a boy. I'll always remember how he used to come over to our house when my ma was making doughnuts. I probably was in middle school then. He was about to go into first grade. My ma made the best doughnuts. I think I learned everything I know about cooking from her. I wish I was half the baker she was."

Claire looked at me and wagged a finger. "And Thelma's mother could make the best wild strawberry jam. It was delicious. And her white bread had the finest crust I've ever had. It's the crust that makes the difference in home-made bread. Thelma's pretty good as baker, but I'm afraid her white bread just doesn't have the crust. That's why I always get an English muffin. Maybe if you had wild strawberry jam, I'd feel a little bit different about the bread. Oh, Thelma, I do miss your mother."

A brisk wind was picking up from the mid-morning sun and

causing little dust eddies in the Square. I thought about going back into the kitchen to begin work on a new recipe I was going to put on the menu tonight, a German dish, rouladen. But to make it distinctive, I was thinking of rolling the thin layers of beef around a mixture of ground liver and fried onions instead of the customary bacon. The pickle in the center I would leave out, maybe substituting slivers of oven-roasted vegetables.

"Toivo didn't care that much for the bread," Thelma continued her reflections, "but he did love Ma's raised doughnuts. The smell of them would waft through the air, especially in the summer when the windows would all be open. Things were simpler then. No one worried about locking doors. No one ever feared that any of the summer folk would steal from us.

"You know that smell never failed to lure out Toivo. Minutes after Ma would take the first doughnut out of that cast iron pot of hot fat and roll it in granulated sugar, Toivo would be at the screen door, looking in. You could see all over his face that he wanted to be invited in. And he would eat those doughnuts with such pleasure. It made you happy just watching him.

"That's how he was when he met Lempi. Lempi told me once her name meant "love" in Finnish. And did that man ever love her. Sometimes, I wondered if he even noticed that he had a son, he was so wrapped up in Lempi. He took it real hard when she committed suicide. Never understood why she did that. But if he don't look out, he's gonna lose that son too."

"Do you remember how Lempi used to dance in the St. Urho's Day festival up in Timberton. She was quite a beauty. Like a princess in a fairy tale," said Claire. She stood up and waddled to the window. "I don't like the looks of that wind. It's going to get hot, real hot today."

"After Lempi died, Toivo was beside himself. He couldn't stand to live in the same house anymore. Sent Danny off to work at a resort last summer. Had to sell the place and move into a little house in town. Dragged Danny with him, and from what I hear Danny always loved that farm, especially the little beach that was right past the farmhouse on Deep Lake. But now the two of them are stuck in that little house. Toivo still works in the woods on the lumber crews. It's only when he's working that he seems normal, from what I hear.

"But not for long, because when the day is done, he goes to her gravestone every day to bring her flowers. Sometimes you see him there in the cemetery for hours, talking to her I guess, not letting go, sitting beneath those trees he loves. A strange Finn. Ain't sensible or right for the boy."

"I guess that's why Danny looks so sad," I said. "Must be tough living a life like that, always around a man tied to his past, not letting go."

"No, that's not why he's sad," said Thelma. She bustled back into the kitchen.

I was fed up. "Thelma and Cynthia," I called out, "look out after the place. I'm going for a walk." Who needed all the mysteries people were trying to send my way?

Stepping out of my cafe gave me a strange sense of freedom. I had only been in Thread since February, but already I was beginning to be snared in a sticky web. But the question was: who were the spiders and who were the files in these gossamer threads?

I turned right as I stepped out of the Loon Town Cafe and headed east on the Square. Across the street was the park in the center of town, its grass badly in need of its weekly mowing. The summer had been a wet one, and the grass always seemed too long. Since school was out, they had hired the town's latest school bus driver to do the mowing but he didn't seem too interested in the task. It was harder than driving the school bus, and there weren't any little kids to boss around.

Next to the Loon Town Cafe was the Little Papoose—the one-stop shopping spot for everything no sensible person needed. Did anyone need an anatomically correct ashtray that said "A Butt for Your Butts?" Or a T-shirt that said "Not the end of the universe but you can see it from here." Or a precious heirloom plate with a man rushing to the wooden outhouse carefully handpainted on it. These were the treasures of the Little Papoose, which took American Express, Visa, Mastercharge, but no wampum please. At least that is what the little sign said next to the cash register. I had heard a delegation of the Latttigo had demanded that Myra Collucci, the Little Papoose manager, both remove that sign and change the name of the store. They called it degrading. She called it good business and ignored their complaints.

Next I came to Sven's Barber Shop. No Sven had been the barber at Sven's for sixty years.The original Sven had been a crackerjack lumberjack in the days when they went after the hardwoods. That was back

55

in the Twenties, but then he had made one mistake. A huge maple came crashing down and pinned his legs, breaking both of them. He walked with a distinctive limp ever after and took to barbering, even though he only knew one way of cutting your hair.

The current barber is named Harry and he pretty much only knows one way to cut hair too—and that's badly. People who can afford the time head up to Timberton. But Bromley, Red and many others in Thread give Harry their business anyway.

Bromley was sitting in the barber's chair as I strolled by and he gave me a wave. "What's new with the world?" he shouted out. Harry didn't wave or say anything. He hadn't stepped into my cafe yet either. Claire had told me confidentially that I until I went to Harry for my haircuts, I wouldn't get the time of day from him. The town had to stick together.

Two giggling teenagers rushed out of Lil's Fashions. I couldn't hear what they were whispering to each other, but having looked at Lil's store windows more than once, I guessed that these big city teenagers were amused by the backwardness of small towns. Of course, most women in Thread responded with equal astonishment to Lil's merchandise. In reality, most of Lil's customers were matronly summer women who were carried away by nostalgia or a summer giddiness. They bought clothes that they would never wear again once they returned to the big city. Yet they made grand entrances into my cafe night after night wearing the most bizarre outfits. It gave the Loon Town Cafe its own peculiar and eclectic look. I was tempted at times to snap group photos of everyone dining, and then travel to Chicago's North Shore, grab passerbys at random and asked them to identify which of the diners were from Chicago and which were locals. I would guarantee you that most of the tourists would be dismayed by the results of that poll.

I turned the corner onto East Street, the former power strip of Thread. The theater, the railroad station, and the bank were all lined up in a row on East Street. Now it was the targeted redevelopment zone—should any redevelopment appear on the horizon.

The Thread Theater had stood empty since 1972. It sputtered into its last showing not long after the last train of the Great Lakes Rail Road had made its farewell run. The Great Lakes train schedule stood curling near the old ticket window of the depot. The only sign of life on the entire

East Street this morning was in The Old Candy Shoppe that occupied a small store front carved out of one corner of the theater's street frontage. The balancing corner was the catalog storefront for Sears, but the owner had posted a sign that he had to run an errand and wouldn't be opening until noon.

After the depot were the solid pillars of the Great Northern State Bank, chartered in 1890. The bank was the only substantial building in town, clad in marble and three stories high. It had been built when optimism for the town had run high, and speculators from the East had surveyors mapping out whole cities at any potential railroad stop. There had been no end foreseen to the lumbering, and the cut over land would surely support great farms. Rumors of enormous mineral wealth further captured the heady imagination of many a distant investor.

Great towns need great banks, and so the Great Northern was chartered and built. The third floor had long since stood empty. The second floor was home to the few professionals who could pull a living out of Thread: a lawyer, an accountant or two, an insurance agent, a dentist. The bank itself was only open in the morning, run as a branch office of the Timberton bank. But they kept the marble floors nicely polished.

To the right of the bank was a small gravel path that crossed over the abandoned railroad track and led two blocks to Big Sapphire Lake. I headed to Homestead Park on the Big Sapphire. As I approached the lake, I could see a familiar tall figure sitting on a park bench. Waving to the man with the long beard, I yelled out, "Mr. Packer."

"Wally, is business so slow that you can depart to perambulate to the beach?"

"I need fresh air now and then," I said.

"Yes, I understand. Just thinking myself that I should have stayed in town for another cup of your fine coffee. Need something dark and rich. But there's something so pleasant about a warm summer day, children playing in the water. Serenity. All's right with the world. Why don't you and I recline here for a moment and regard the children."

I sat next to Mr. Packer and gazed out at the small beach. There were maybe a dozen children in the water. They acted as though they all knew each other and were about the same age, maybe nine or ten.

"Where's the lifeguard?" I asked.

"No lifeguard at this beach," Mr. Packer replied. "At least not on weekdays. The town can't afford it. They have one at the beach at Little Sapphire Lake since that's where most of the tourists go. Easier to find a parking spot over here though. This park is more for Thread. All those children down below reside in Thread. I know who they are. I know their parents."

"Do you know everyone in town?" I asked.

"Most likely do," Mr. Packer replied.

"What can you tell me about the Reverend Willy?"

Mr. Packer looked up, slightly startled and slightly concerned. Just then a scream came from one of the small girls. All of the children came rushing out of the lake, water spraying everywhere as they churned through the water in a slow-motion run.

"I felt him!" shouted one of the girls.

One of the boys chimed in, "I could see the shadow. He was there. He was huge."

Mr. Packer and I walked over. "What happened?" I asked.

"There's a giant muskie in the lake," shouted one of the girls. "And every day when we go swimming, he comes swimming in close by, like he wants to play with us."

"Or eat us," said the first girl.

"Muskies don't eat people," said the skeptical boy.

"Muskies don't grow seven or eight feet long either," said another.

"Let's go back in. Maybe we can catch it."

The horde of children rushed back into the lake, water splashing everywhere.

"A giant muskie? Really?" I asked Mr. Packer.

Mr. Packer was quite amused. "We should call the Milwaukee and Chicago papers. Imagine the headlines. Giant muskie in Big Sapphire Lake. We'll get more fisherman in one week than have descended on Thread in the past fifty years. They'll all be trying to catch the big one. Bromley will be on the phone in a minute if he hears of this."

"But what if there really is a giant fish in these waters? Would you want to see it caught?"

"I'll tell you what," said Mr. Packer. "Let's just head back to your fine cafe and have some coffee. We can talk to Claire about her aliens. I'd rather see one of them caught and put on display."

As always, Mr. Packer was the voice of reason. I had a cafe. I had a staff. I had customers. And the town already had Claire and her imagined aliens. Who needed giant muskies or any new stories?

CHAPTER FOUR

My work family had grown. Thelma in the kitchen managed to make my crazy menu ideas actually work. Cynthia charmed the diners out front to forgive the often slow service. Danny pitched in where needed. Gerta worked a few shifts to give Thelma time off. I was host and bartender, and having a blast forgetting Manhattan.

But I was worried about the dinner party I had commited to cater for Henry. I needed to have someone come with me to make it work. "Danny, ready to help out at the van Elkind event?" I asked.

Danny, his hands in the soapy water of the kitchen sink, gave a startled, frightened look. "I don't think so," he said.

"Why not?" I asked, not really seeking an answer. Danny was my enigma. He was never late to work, always dressed just right, and did every task both correctly and completely. He was courteous and polite with the diners. Yet asking him to do anything new was like slapping him in the face with the impossible. I was delighted that Cynthia had convinced me to hire Danny, but he could be tortuous. I wanted to help him be happy, but who knew how.

"Danny, do it," begged Cynthia. "The Van Elkinds are fascinating. I just wish I could go along."

"Cynthia," I broke in, "why don't you? You were invited with your parents. Henry specifically mentioned that Kip was hoping to see you there."

"Kip is too weird," Cynthia shuddered. "Even if I was invited, I need to be here on Saturday night."

"But I would have given you the night off," I persisted. Thelma and Cynthia had talked me into keeping the lights on for the night, with Gerta on as temporary help.

"But Claire would have been so disappointed. She depends on me for her fish fry on Saturday. You know how she has to have the fish placed on her plate just so, with the tartar sauce in a certain spot and the lemon wedge on the left edge. Otherwise she won't eat it."

"It's Wally's own problem," Thelma broke in as she stood by the stove. "You could have told Claire the very first time she asked for a fish fry that they were only available on Fridays. Now every Saturday she comes in and orders her perch. Then there's at least one other customer who wants the same thing, and you won't let us give it to them. Either you have a fish fry or you don't."

"I shouldn't have one at all," I said. "This isn't a tavern. There's no reason to have a Friday night fish fry, except this damn town has its traditions. God, this cafe wasn't even open for years. Where did everyone get their fish fries then?" I knew the answer. They got their fish fries wherever they wanted, since there wasn't a place within five counties that didn't offer a Friday night fish fry. Even the fancy Penokee House up in Timberton offered one, complete with a hefty price.

Danny retreated during this hullabaloo back to washing his pots. He was always so intense and careful, never a spot on his pots and pans that wasn't properly scoured and rinsed. Glasses, plates, cups, flatware were correctly placed in the dishwasher, no unpleasant banging from carelessly stacked dishes. Yet when you looked at Danny there always seemed something a bit forgotten, a lock of hair out of place, a collar turned up— nothing to complain about, actually sometimes attractive, but definitely not planned, just overlooked.

"Danny, don't you want see the Van Elkind place," Cynthia pursued her sales job for me. Cynthia was Danny's protector, helping him cope. He never seemed to notice how beautifully perky she could be. "There's a lot of cool houses over there. They say Dillinger once stayed at one."

"Did every crime lord from the Thirties come to this town?" I asked in mock disbelief. Somehow, though, I liked the idea of Henry dwelling in a crime hangout.

"Not all of them," Cynthia replied in total seriousness, "but

Dillinger did. Grandpa John told me about the time he was here."

"Didn't your Grandpa cause a couple of those hooligans to get shot? That's what I recall," Thelma said.

"That's not the way it happened at all. Grandpa John has never done anything to hurt anyone." At that, Danny and Thelma simultaneously rolled their eyes.

"He didn't do anything wrong. He was just making money," said Cynthia. Her large brown eyes seemed ready to rain with tears. "Anyway, I probably have it wrong. Dillinger hung out in a different place."

A glorious afternoon in July. Thelma and I, were headed to Timberton for van Elkind dinner party supplies. Making good time on a back road that Thelma chose, we were enjoying open touring in her 1965 cherry-red Mustang convertible.

"Ain't it grand?" she said, "Riding under blue skies. And just smell that air. It's summer at its best."

I inhaled deeply, as much to pull in fresh oxygen to calm me down from the speed of Thelma's driving as it was to quench the desire for clean country air. Then it hit me.

"Stop the car!" I demanded.

A wine-like aroma hung in the air, as though we had stomped through a field of overripe fruit. "Wild raspberries," I said. "I'm swimming in the smell of black raspberries."

"Big deal," Thelma said, but she pulled to a stop.

I bounded out of the car to walk the ditch, smelling out the berries. Tall orange Indian bushes and a low spread of white Queen Anne's lace blanketed the shallow trough. "There," I said, pointing about one hundred feet behind the car. "See those brambles. I know you got some empty pails in your trunk. Let's go berry picking. It'll be raspberry cobbler for dessert tonight."

"Wally, I'm happy to pick some berries. Just recall you still have a lug of ripe peaches back to the cafe. Remember your plans for peach pies a la mode with that crazy maple syrup ice cream you've been fooling with."

"We'll offer both," I said.

"You expecting some land rush in business that I ain't heard about? You know, Wally, running a restaurant requires some common sense planning. Peach pies and raspberry cobblers won't hold up after the first day. And you know as well as I do that home-made ice cream is only good the day it's churned. Once you put it in the freezer, it just never feels right again. You might as well dish up the store-bought stuff."

"I know all that," I countered.

"And I know you know all that," laughed Thelma in return, "but I also know what my eyes tell me. Every night you're throwing away perfectly good food because you won't serve anything that ain't fresh, and you can't keep from overcooking like a darn fool."

"People want fresh ingredients.That's what keep's them coming back."

"It ain't enough for them to like your cooking. You gotta make some money. Wally, I like this job. God knows why, but I'm getting kinda fond of you and Cynthia and Danny. Even Claire and Bromley coming in every day are starting to be fun. Hank, not so much, but I'd hate to see it all go down the drain. I know you know this, but if you don't make good money during the summer, you're going die during the winter. There just ain't enough snowmobilers and skiers to keep this town from skidding through the winter."

"So you want me to leave these berries here to rot?"

"Wally, God surely has other plans for these berries if we don't pick them up. But you like picking them, so I'm not saying we won't pick some. I'm just saying, we got peach pie for dessert tonight. Put the berries in the cooler for another day. Use them for dessert at Hank's big dinner party out to their lodge. Use God's plenty to make a little more profit. He won't mind." Thelma started walking briskly down the road, two white plastic gallon ice cream buckets in her hands, each bumping against her fleshy thighs.

"I don't know, Thelma. God might not mind, but I'm pretty sure Henry Van Elkind would. He and Rita were quite particular. Like with the appetizers. They didn't want the smoked fishes, because they think sturgeon is an endangered species. Piroshki with wild mushrooms was too Russian. They couldn't have beef, but somehow veal was just fine."

Thelma had shifted focus to berry picking. Her fingers quickly purpled as they moved from place to place, sntaching only the ripest of fruit. "Taste one," she said. A thumb-sized berry at eye level tauntingly begged to be picked. I popped it into my mouth. The flavor was intense, sweet and rich, almost alcoholic in intensity."Careful, now," warned Thelma, "don't get your clothes caught on these briars."

"How can we leave these raspberries until tomorrow? They need to be eaten today. They're perfect."

"They'll wait. Believe me. Just serve them to those rich folk. They'll think they died and gone to heaven. Trust me on this. They take what you give them, just as long as you make them think they've gotten their way. It's up to you to know what you're willing to give them."

"I have a great raspberry cobbler I could make with these, or maybe a creme pie. What do you think about that, Wally? We'll put a nice vanilla custard down as the base, made with whole milk and a little cream, so it's nice and smooth and rich. Then we'll mix these raspberries with fresh whipped cream and a little vanilla and sugar and pile it high over the custard."

"Henry has a cholesterol problem," I pointed out.

"So we'll add a little more cream to the custard," Thelma suggested with a wicked guffaw.

"Maybe we could put a little melted white chocolate into the whipped cream?" I suggested.

Thelma sighed. "Can't leave things simple, now can you? Always having to go too far to show how special you are."

"Thelma," I said in my best cafe-owner way. "The white chocolate will add texture and firmness to the whipped cream topping. That will make it easier to assemble it ahead, plus it will add a undercurrent of flavor to complement the ripeness of these raspberries. Remember, these are snobs who think they're sophisticated, and their original request was for a white chocolate mousse. We'll just change it to a white chocolate mousse with raspberries, served with a Wisconsin cream custard."

The sparkle was back in Thelma's eyes. "Just keep it rich, Wally, they'll love it. But you better start picking and stop talking. We still have to get to Timberton to pick up your veal chops."

Thelma was moving into the tangle of shoots and vines, nearly half-hidden in the raspberries thicket. "Shouldn't you stay at the edge?" I asked.

"If you want good berries, you gotta risk a few scratches," she shouted back.

"I wanted to serve lake trout at the party," I said loudly so she could hear, "but Henry warned me the kitchen was small. So I figured they wouldn't have enough broiler space. Henry probably wouldn't have agreed to it, so it's just as well. He wanted real meat, even though Rita vetoed beef. I'm giving them veal chops baked in parchment paper. God, I hope that order of veal came into the butcher shop, or I'm in deep trouble. It would be so much simpler if we could depend on getting these things through Red's grocery store." I looked up from my berry picking but I could no longer see Thelma. I started walking toward some motion in the thicket ahead.

"I'm surprised they think they can get away with veal and not sturgeon. Won't their environmental friends be as concerned about the mistreatment of poor little calves as endangered fish? Thelma, can't you answer me once in a while."

A black snout broke through the raspberry bracket, exactly in the spot where I had expected to see Thelma. There emerged an adult black bear, several hundred pounds at least. It waddled by to plod ahead one paw at a time, then rambled through the ditch and onto the roadway. It looked back for a second as though to see just what it had passed by.

"Thelma," I whispered, frozen where I stood.

The bear stopped, cocking its head back with a quizzical look. A reddish purplish stain encircled its snout, like lipstick on a smiling clown.

"Speak up," Thelma shouted. The bear, now startled broke into a gallop, racing into the woods. Thelma came out of the berry patch and looked at me with concern. "Did you see a ghost."

"No, a bear. A black bear. A big bear. A gigantic bear."

"Is that all? Where are you from, boy? Nothing to worry about a bear during berry season. She's fat and happy. If she's got cubs, then they're already big enough that any old she-bear is already letting down her guard now and again to worry about better things to do, like get fat for the winter."

"That may be," I said trying to prove my reasonableness and not take offense, "but a bear is still a bear. Caution sometimes is a sensible thing."

Thelma set her pail into the grass and lowered herself to sit on an old stump. "Indeed it is," she agreed. "And you should have more of it. Listen to Thelma: Watch out for the people in this town and stop worrying about the bears. People are harder to predict than bears. You think everyone in this town is a hick and a quaint hick at that."

Thelma held up her hand, seeing I was about to protest. "We all see this. We like you, Wally, but you've been gone too long in that big city. You think we're like some cute television show. But it ain't that way. Watch out for the people in this town. It's not just Hank and the other summer folk. It's all of us. Every one wants something. We're all after some thing or some one. Look out for Red. He's still his father's son, you better believe it. He couldn't have grown up with that old miser and not learn a few of the old man's tricks. I know he holds a second mortgage on your place. That was the only way you could swing the cafe after the way he gouged you on the price. And don't think Bromley didn't help him do it. And that Indian kid, Frozen Bear, you be careful there too. He don't care that the Truehearts are the ones who lied to him about the liquor license. He blames you because you're the one who ended up with it."

"Thelma, has the sun has gotten to you? I've not seen Chip Frozen Bear in my restaurant except that day I hired you."

"It doesn't mean he isn't talking."

"Talking about what?" I demanded. "Never mind. And don't bother telling me what you're after. I don't want to know. Just let me make peach pie and a raspberry cobbler in the same day if I want to. Just let me be happy."

We drove the half hour to Timberton in silence. Thelma was wrong about me condescending to the people of Thread. Maybe I was that way while I lived in Manhattan. I threw fabulous parties in my old life. I knew how to regale my guests with stories of life in Thread: the characters, the small scandals, the outlandish events. I nurtured each story until it had grown into some strange shadow of what had really occurred. I could pause at just the right places to elicit that chuckle. But I never thought of these townspeople as quaint hicks. How did Thelma get such a loony idea?

Thelma turned her car left, back onto 17, looking ahead, still driving in silence. We were a few miles south of the main intersection in Timberton. Old wood frame houses built at the turn of the century lined the highway. Each stood closely to the next, with barely room for sidewalks between them. Ninety years ago, Timberton had been a boom town and the speculators had laid it out with expectations of growing into a major city. There was no land to spare in their greed. Each lot had been a tiny forty feet by eighty feet. The original settlers could only build up, at least two stories, if not three, capping each house with Victorian accouterments, now all badly weathered and in need of paint.

"Did this town ever look healthy?" I asked Thelma.

Thelma cast a glance at me, as though deciding to a truce. Her eyes turned back to the road, but she allowed one hand to move from the steering wheel and gesture as she answered. "My grandma always said it was a magnificent city when she moved here. That was back in the 1890s. There were at least four times as many people as today. The woods were still being cut, and the iron and copper mines had just opened. There was money to be made.

"Grandma came on tour with Sarah Bernhardt. Yes, that Sarah Bernhardt. She played at the old Alcazar Theater on Silver Street. Grandma had been Sarah's personal maid, but she fell in love with an old Swede, got swept right off her feet, and forgot all about the theater and Sarah so she could stay with Ole. She became a cook for a while at the Penokee House in its heyday. I wonder what she would think if she knew her kin came around full circle. A cook again."

"But not at the Penokee House." I pointed out.

"Thank God for that. The Penokee has a reputation it don't deserve. Back during the Depression it was rotting hulk traded for a million used stamps, worthless boxes of canceled stamps on envelopes. Not worth the cost to burn them probably. It only took some licked stamps to buy a place that cost $100,000 to build back in my grandma's day. But the hotel was just a white elephant. Who needs a wooden-frame hotel covering a whole block when no one comes to town? No one wanted it. When I was a girl, only tramps stayed then, and they didn't appreciate the Honduran mahogony walls. And then it stood empty until the late Fifties."

"What happened?" I asked.

"Some New York art dealer who vacationed over to Emeryville heard about it. Anyway he went on a Sunday drive one summer and saw this run-down building, bought it on a whim, and spent his entire fortune in restoring it. There's a hospital down in Emeryville that was fit to be tied when the old man died, because while his will left all the money to them, there wasn't a penny left. It had all gone into this hotel. So the hospital got stuck with the hotel. Took them four years to find anyone willing to buy it, and then they didn't get very much for it. So if you get sick, don't go to the Emeryville Hospital."

"The hotel sure looks beautiful today."

"But it's still just a white elephant. If city folk hadn't started skiing up here in these hills, it'd be a derelict again. And the food . . . expensive junk. People are paying outrageous prices because they're in this great old building, or because they're too stupid to drive thirty minutes and have our food at the Loon Town Cafe. I guess you're not the only fool in these north woods."

I let Thelma rant about the unwarranted cost of meals at the Penokee House, but personally I would have liked to have seen more of Timberton restored to the same state as the historic hotel. Timberton's famous Silver Street, once known throughout the nation for its wildness and nightlife, was a discouraging hodgepodge of turn-of-the-century brick store fronts interspersed with cheap steel-pole construction buildings with plate glass fronts and parking lots at the side – much like Red's Piggly Wiggly back in Thread. Where was the architectural consistency?

By air, the Timberton airport was only an hour from Detroit, Chicago, Minneapolis, or Milwaukee. The town could have easily been a weekend trendy getaway if the city's fathers hadn't allowed its past to rot away.

"Let's just get to the butcher and to the fish market, and then head home," I said.

"Don't think I'm criticizing you," began Thelma, off on a new train of thought. "I'm trying to warn you. There's no one who don't like you. But this ain't New York. Don't trust people to mean what they say. Television makes people think small towns are somehow different. We're only different in that we ain't ever surprised by what happens. Maybe we pretend we don't know what's going on with each other, but we know—even when we don't talk about it. How can we not know? And how can we pretend that people aren't complex beings, with some good and some bad thrown in? Sometimes we like the mixture more than other times. But unless we're willing to be hermits, we know we gotta accept one another. But live and let live don't mean that you don't keep your eyes open.

"I knew there might be a bear in those berries. Knew it probably wouldn't bother us. So I picked some berries, and I let you pick some berries. Always danger in the world, you know. For every pleasure, there's something you gotta watch out for.

"It ain't just raspberries and the bears. Picking wild strawberries for Claire last month in the ditches to the highway was just as bad. I could have found myself in the way of one of those 18-wheelers that come barreling up

17. Or next month, when the blueberries ripen in the bogs, I could make a false step and find myself in an unexpected pool of water, maybe even get tangled up in a submerged branch, unable to pull free, stuck in the woods, with no one knowing what you're up to. Few days go by and it's fodder for the coyotes.

"But I still go and pick the berries. I still crouch for hours in the ditches picking those tiny little wild strawberries. Then, I spend hours more, huddled over the kitchen table cleaning out all the bits of grass and leaves and twigs, because when you're done with it all, there's nothing more flavorful than a bowl of wild strawberries or a little bit of frozen wild strawberry jam spread with fresh butter on good white bread fresh from the oven. Claire ain't the only one who likes wild strawberry jam."

"Thelma," I interrupted. "I don't know what you're trying to say."

"I'm saying this. I've seen Red and Chip Frozen Bear together, talking about liquor licenses, and your name came up. And I've seen Red and that rich Hank Van Elkind huddling together, talking big dreams. They're all up to something. And Bromley trying to get in on it. I'm not saying to stop enjoying berry picking. Pick some raspberries. Eat wild strawberries. Make some jam for Claire. But we gotta keep an eye out for the trucks. They can come from nowhere damn fast, and if you don't jump out of their way, you ain't getting to taste no more wild strawberries no matter how good they are."

"That all?" I asked.

"Ain't that enough, Wally?" she answered.

"Turn here. Onto Clearwater Road," Danny said, pointing at the blacktopped road that wended its way beneath arching white birch. "You know, that's the way the G-men went by mistake when Cynthia's Grandpa rented the cabin to Dillinger."

"So what was that story all about," I asked Danny. "Why did Cynthia get so upset?"

Danny was smiling and for once seemed relaxed and free of worry out here in the middle of the woods. "Everyone says her grandpa gave the cops the wrong directions on purpose, you know how everyone thinks Big John was connected to gangsters and ran liquor down from Canada during

Prohibition. They say he was just protecting Dillinger. But the cops didn't know they had been sent to the wrong cabin. So they staked out this regular fishing cabin and ended up killing three business guys from Chicago. Cynthia doesn't want to think anyone ever did anything wrong. Didn't you ever hear that story before?"

I hadn't, but I was beginning to understand that there were lots of stories in town still to hear. It was late afternoon. Danny and I were on our way in a fully loaded car to set up the catering for the big dinner. I would be meeting Rita Van Elkind for the first time. The Van Elkinds, given no choice, had agreed to a slightly improved menu. The raspberries had proven too perfect to not use.

The narrow wood lane widened into an avenue bordered by maples, stretching tall and evenly spaced, obviously planted after the first cut off of white pine a hundred years earlier.

"Is this the Van Elkind place?" Danny asked. "I've never been down this road before." Some nervousness has crept into his voice.

This was clearly a private road, because nothing so grand and so well maintained could have been the responsibility of Bromley's town road department. It led to a gatehouse and two imposing, but open, iron gates. Past the gates, the stately maples retreated from the roadside, creating a broad parkway. Rose bushes, resplendent with midsummer blooms, sat between the pavement and the forest on both sides.

"My Dad told me this place was built by some lumber baron in the nineteenth century. He owned all the land up here, practically ran it like his own kingdom, using it as a hunting camp. Dad says the first place burned down sometime around World War I, but was rebuilt grander than ever. Mom always wanted to come out here and see it, but Dad said it wasn't ours to show off. She never got to see it." Danny grew quiet.

I had only heard of the camp before today. My Dad, who often went fishing on Clearwater lake, had described the place to me because he had a favorite fishing spot that was a hundred yards off the Van Elkind dock. Neither his descriptions nor my long-distance glimpses had prepared me for its grandeur.

This northwoods summer palace was no more a camp than the mansions of Newport, Rhode Island, were cottages. The drive crossed a field-sized lawn of carefully mown grass. In the middle sat an oversized wonder, an English half-timbered Shakespearean manor built of life-sized

Lincoln Logs. Its three stories were topped by steeply pitched roofs pierced with dormers. The house rambled this way and that as it moved towards the woods, back toward the lake and then again toward the road. Ivy clamped the logs to the earth. Small clumps of shaking aspen were planted here and there on the lawn. And roses were everywhere.

"Man, this is bigger than the high school," Danny whispered.

So it was. But the high school, which also contained classrooms for the middle and elementary schools of Thread, only housed 200 students in total. Even a modest mansion could eclipse it in size. But this place must have encompassed 20,000 square feet.

"Dad told me once that the property taxes from this place is howThread can afford to keep the school open." Danny sat upright in the car gazing forward.

My own father's stories had not prepared me for this estate. It must take a small staff just to maintain the grounds. By the time you finished mowing the lawn on one side you would have to start over on the other side. Looking at all the leaded glass windows scattered higgledy-piggledy within the stacked round logs—I didn't even want to imagine the effort in keeping them washed.

Few who lived in Thread year-round had wealth. To the degree such money existed, it was usually kept hidden. Everyone suspected Red and Barbara Trueheart had enormous resources, but they lived simple lives. Their house was only slightly larger, slightly better maintained, than the rest of ours.

As for those summer folk who visited each year, we knew at least in our hearts that many of them had far more money than any of us would see throughout our lives. And enough people in town were employed as handymen and cleaning women to get a good sense of the quality of their summer cabins. But even these homes, which after all were second homes, were relatively modest. They hinted at a lifestyle within reach.

But this camp suggested a world I seldom entered, even in Manhattan. Could any other camp on any lakes within fifty miles approach it in grandeur? If so, why I had never heard of them, why I had never seen them, why didn't the entire town envy and gossip about their owners?

"It's only a house," I said to Danny, "let's go in and get set up for tonight."

The front door opened. A dumpling of an old woman trundled

out. Her cheeks were as ample as her bosom, although more flushed. She was wearing heavy black wading boots and her hair was tied up in a colorful old world kerchief.

"Are you the food people?" she asked. "I'm Regina. Regina Rabinowicz. Welcome to my home. Hank likes to call it his. But it's really mine. Casimir bought it years and years ago. My husband, you know, dead for so many years now. God rest his soul.

"Are you the caterers?" Once again, she didn't wait for an answer. "Just follow me. Let me show you where to set up. Oh, it's going to be a big wingding tonight. That little weasel Hank's got something up his sleeve. Never know what he's plotting to do. But who cares? It's great to see the place filled with people. Casimir wanted it that way. It reminded him of the estate his father had in Latvia. That was before Casimir ran off to America. Didn't need his father's money. Made his own fortune. Meat packing. Used every part of the pig but the squeal.

"Are you the caterers? Well, let's get going."

"Mother, dear, are you out here," a younger, much thinner and more stylish version of the old woman walked out the doorway, her hands folded. She saw us and walked forward. "I'm Rita Van Elkind. Forgive my mother. She gets so excited whenever we do something out of the routine.

"Mother, weren't you on your way to tend to your roses. There's no need to dally here. I will escort these gentlemen to the kitchen."

"Casimir used every part of the pig but the squeal. He left that for his daughter. And Casimir used a lot of pigs," Regina began to laugh heartily. Her mirth shook her entire ample body. It was like watching a jolly Jell-O mold walk toward the roses. "Every bit but the squeal." And the laughter erupted once more.

"Mother's getting old," said Rita with a thin smile that sought our understanding while condemning the old woman. Regina was now clipping fully opened roses, laying them gently in a gathering basket. "You must be Walter Pearson. My husband has spoken of you only with the highest of praise. He so admires your restaurant. He would hear of nothing other than your catering this party. I do try to humor my husband. He so seldom has an interest in our entertaining. Usually, his only concern is to save money, to find the less expensive alternative." Another thin smile. "Why don't you pull the car around the back and I'll let you in the kitchen door. It's just that way." She pointed with a half motion, keeping her arm close in as though she feared letting us too near. We were graced with yet another small smile as she closed the door.

"I wish my mom could have met the old lady. She seems neat," said Danny. Then he looked at me more forthrightly than he had ever done before. "But it's not going to be much fun tonight, is it?"

We got back in my car and drove around to the rear entrance. It was an odd experience to sense you were making a real journey as you drove from the front door of a house to its rear door. The journey covered more than mere distance.

The back door was already opened. We walked into the largest kitchen I had ever seen in a private home. It was as large as my entire restaurant. "Mr. Pearson, I thought you were worried about space," Danny whispered.

Rita Van Elkind overhead Danny's sotto voce remarks as she walked in. "Blame that on dear Henry. I don't think he even knows this room exists. There is another kitchen off the breakfast room, a butler's pantry really, but it's the only one we use when we're here alone. That kitchen most assuredly is quite small. But for parties, I always have the caterers use the main kitchen. This kitchen lives up to lumber camp origins of this place.

"Why am I telling you this. You live here. Surely you know the town's quaint history better than I. It is so romantic and so colorful. This house is redolent with its past.

"Oh, here is Stephen, our major domo. He does takes care of us so well when we summer here. Well, whenever we're here, of course. He can show you where everything is. He will arrange for the setting of the tables. I don't really like strangers handling my china. You understand of course. It's been in the family for so many years. Such sentimental value."

"Is that china from the Latvian Rabinowiczes smuggled from behind the Iron Curtain? Or is it the Boston Van Elkinds taken out of pawn?" I asked trying to make a joke. Stephen's eyes widened, his lips slightly twitching as though he wanted to smile.

Rita looked at me, without blinking, without her thin smile. "Henry told me how amusing you were. I meant of course that we have had the place settings in Chicago for decades. Other pieces were with the house when Daddy bought it. The man who built this was quite wealthy you know, one of the pillars who created this part of the country, who civilized it.

"This camp was his retreat, the kitchen in particular. He had been a cook's helper in the early days of lumbering; his mother had been a cook in the camps. He overcame his poor beginnings and used his intelligence to become one of the most powerful men in the Midwest. I've heard a famous Jewess once wrote a thinly-veiled story of his life. In the Thirties, I think. Have you ever read it?" She didn't wait for an answer.

"By then, Daddy owned this place. The original family had to sell it during the Depression. The paper business wasn't doing well, and I've heard there were family troubles. The son wasn't nearly so talented as the father. Daddy bought everything from the son, or perhaps it was the daughter-in-law. I think there had been a divorce—or maybe a tragic death. Who can remember such details? The wife had furnished this camp with so many beautiful things that she bought while in Europe in the Twenties. She had true taste.

"So you see Mr. Pearson, this camp, humble as it may appear, is very important to me. I don't want you to think that I am being unnecessarily fussy or untrusting when I ask Stephen to help out in this affair. It really is his job, after all, and it truly is better for all us. You do understand, don't you?" The thin smile was back.

"Yes, Mrs. Van Elkind," I replied with a thin smile of my own. I might be as unhappy as Danny by the time this dinner was over.

Large pairs of French doors, cut through the thick log walls of the main living room, opened to a terrace that cascaded in broad stone planes to the edge of Clearwater Lake. An early evening breeze softly rustled through the immense room. Like the loft of an old country barn, the room soared nearly thirty feet in the air, the space above crisscrossed by immense hand-hewn beams. At the far end of the room, a fire crackled in a fireplace built of enormous boulders.

The dozen people, with their clinking drinks, were nearly lost in the cavernous space. A piano player was playing Barry Manilow tunes. Kip Van Elkind sat in one large chair near the fireplace, scowling at the others in the room. Rita Van Elkind stood with her back to the door, letting the soft glow of the early evening sun reflect off the lake to shimmer through her hair and the slight fabric of her long white cotton skirt. She laughed, and the group around her laughed in unison.

I motioned to Danny to move into the group with his tray of canapés. I hung back, drinking in the glamour of the room, knowing that I needed to return to the kitchen to prepare the appetizers. Danny's back was straight, and he looked handsome and worldly in the white dinner jacket that I had forced him to wear. He seemed a guest, not the server.

Red Trueheart walked in from the patio with his wife Barbara at his side. They had arrived in his overpowered speed boat. Clearwater Lake was connected to Big Sapphire Lake by a wide, but slow flowing stream. Red saw me lurking in the dining room doorway, and gave me a thumbs up and big smile, as though to say he had found me this job. I returned an acknowledging nod.

I retreated into the dining room. Stephen was fluffing up the napkins, each folded into a Napoleonic hat covering large Villeroy Boche servers. Even though the table was set for twenty-four, it seemed uncrowded, as did the room. There should have been footmen in a setting like this. Danny and I would have trouble serving the food promptly. I felt daunted by the sheer scale of this room. As though reading my mind, Stephen said, "Mrs. Van Elkind may not have been clear, but I am at your service for the evening. In whatever way you may need my assistance, just ask. Perhaps it would help if I were to serve the wine before we sit down. For the moment, I think everything is in place here and fully up to Mrs. Van Elkind's satisfaction. It wouldn't be a bit of trouble to help out."

Danny came through the doors, his face flushed, his trays empty. "People just keep arriving. They're like locusts, man, eating anything they can get their hands on. It's crazy. I don't think you have enough food, Wally."

"It's Wally now?" I said, amused, "I'm no longer Mr. Pearson?"

The flush turned to a blush. "It sounded so stuffy when Mrs. Van Elkind called you Mr. Pearson, and you've always told me to call you Wally. Did you know there's a senator here, our Senator to Washington."

"Mr. Van Elkind is very close to Washington. People of power intrigue him." Stephen said.

I wondered how Thelma was doing back in my restaurant without me. In this enormous kitchen, I felt small and insecure. The Van Elkind party began to loom as the greatest of misfortunes. The people in that cavernous living room were precisely the people that I most needed to start frequenting my cafe. They would order the appetizers, the desserts, the expensive wines and fancy cocktails that spelled profit. They might even compliment the cooking. Without them, I would be just another small town cook catering to locals who barely had the cash to spring for a cup of coffee.

"Man, what a fucking bore." Kip Van Elkind slouched into the kitchen. "Got to get away from those old assholes. And where's Cynthia? Dad promised she would come to help you out? That's the only reason I told the old lady we should hire you. She wanted those freaking caterers from the North Shore. But I stood up for Dad because I wanted Cynthia here. She's got great tits. Instead you bring that pansy."

"What!"

"You should see him out there. Can't take his eyes off that fucking Indian Chip Frozen Bear. Like he's good looking, I suppose, but Jesus Christ, he's a guy. Why isn't Cynthia here?"

"Cynthia wanted to stay in town. Maybe she didn't want to be admired for her breasts all evening," I said. From the first day Kip had walked into my cafe with his father, I had found him dislikable. In his eyes lingered a dull meanness, a longing to put firecrackers in anthills, to tear wings off flies, to dissect live frogs, and to drown cute kittens.

"I'd rather look at any girl's tits, than have to be around some queer. But I guess you don't feel the same way, huh?" He smirked.

"Don't be such an asshole," I erupted.

Kip moved around the counter to where my white chocolate raspberry tarts, all twenty four of them, were laid out in a neat row. All that I had left to do was garnish each with some plump, perfect raspberries and frame them with white chocolate molded leaves. "Oh, I'm sure Cynthia dreams about me. I certainly dream about her. Very satisfying and wet dreams. Maybe I should start coming into the Loon Town more often for lunch. Let her think about what I have to offer. It's something big."

I rolled my eyes. "Just get out."

He dipped his finger into one of the tarts, through the whipped cream topping interlaced with melted white chocolate. He withdrew it and sucked on this fingertip, his dull eyes meeting mine. Suddenly, he spit on the ground. "What the fuck is this? You got raspberries in this fuckin' dessert."

"It's a white chocolate mouse mixed with raspberries over a Wisconsin cream custard." I explained calmly, remembering my conversation with Thelma about the dangers of deviating from the agreed-upon menu.

"That's not what Dad fucking ordered. I hate raspberries. You're not going to serve this shit in my house!" Kip swept his arm across the counter in one grand motion that flung all the tarts to the floor. Raspberries, custard, and whipped cream splattered across the tiles and up the oak doors of the cabinets. He turned and stalked from the room. The dessert remains resembled a murder scene of some bizarre extraterrestrial victim with custard for brains and raspberry puree for blood.

The room was fragrant with the smells of the dinner that would soon be served. Moments earlier, I had finished sautéing minced basil, parsley and shallots in the drippings of freshly cooked bacon. Then I had quickly seared on the grill twenty-four veal chops, thirty seconds on each side. Each chop had been placed onto a square of parchment paper, topped with a spoonful of cooked herbs and bacon, and then each sheet was carefully folded into a small paper envelope for baking. A timer binged. The appetizer in the oven was to be replaced by the veal. The smell of the havarti cheese brushed with Wisconsin ground mustard and baked in individual puff pastries mingled with the fragrance of veal and bacon. It made me hungry.

But I had to act. Each cheese pastry had to be placed on an individual plate with slices of apple. When Kip had walked in, I had been taking the slices from a bath of acidulated water. The appetizer had to be served. The splattered desserts seemed to taunt me from the floor. Now, I had no dessert and there was no time to make a new one.

Danny walked into the kitchen with an empty tray. "The canapés are all served. That butler has been great about serving drinks. And believe me those people can drink. They're getting quite a buzz on in the living room." He noticed the gourmet murder scene. "What happened?"

"Kip" was my single word answer.

"What are you going to do," he asked.

"He doesn't have to do a thing," old Mrs. Rabinowicz said as she trundled through the swinging doors that led from the butler's pantry. She shook her head and titched. "That boy. He needs a good spanking. Never too old for that. Discipline from his father. He never had it. Never will either, will he? Ha!" she laughed.

I just looked at her.

"Go, go," she said, waving her hand toward the dining room. "Those drunks need to get some food into them." She went back through the swinging doors into the pantry, and came out holding a big bag of Oreo cookies.

"We can't serve cookies for dessert," I said.

"And I said, go. Go. Don't you worry. I will take care of this. They'll be the happiest people ever. Rita won't know the difference. She's already had three glasses of wine. I counted. My own daughter, but that girl needs a spanking too. But I'm too old to give it to her."

I shrugged, motioned to Danny for help, and decided to power through. Quickly, we placed the nicely browned rectangles of puff pastry encasing melted cheese on the porcelain plates. Each pastry was encircled by slices of apples. "Set them out Danny. By the time they're done spreading their cheese on their fruit, the veal will be a perfect medium rare and ready to serve."

Mrs. Rabinowicz came through the swinging doors once more. This time she held four jumbo boxes of Jell-O instant pudding and pie mix. I grimaced. "Mr. Van Elkind is expecting a gourmet dessert," I protested.

"Gourmet, shmormet. Hank's had more to drink than Rita. You could serve him a cowpie and tell him it was chocolate mousse, and he'd think he had died and gone to heaven. He's a happy man tonight because he's finally got that Injun on his side."

Stephen came into the kitchen. "Shall I call the guests into the dining room?" and then he noticed the newly decorated floor. "I see Kip has been helping out."

"Not to worry, Stephen," said Mrs. Rabinowicz, "I'm making a new dessert for this young man to serve tonight. It'll be better than anything you ever served back in that fancy house in Chicago."

"Yes," I said to Stephen, harking back to his earlier question, "we might as well call the guests in. Danny's already laid out the appetizers."

Stephen came back into the kitchen in a few minutes. "They're seated and I've poured them new wine. Not that they should be allowed it. Except for Chip Frozen Bear, they're all inebriated. Especially that local. Red Trueheart. He'll run his prized powerboat aground if he tries to steer up the channel in his current state.

"Enough of that. I'll get a mop and start cleaning up the mess. Where did Mrs. Rabinowicz go?"

The old woman came out of the walk-in cooler with two large containers of Cool Whip. "Wait a minute," I said, "just what are you planning to do with this hodgepodge of junk food?"

"Didn't I tell you to just serve the dinner and leave dessert to me?"

"Yes, but . . ."

"All right, I'm going to tell you. I got these cookies and I'm rolling them out into crumbs. Mix them with a little butter and mold it all into a crust. Won't even bake it. Just line these custard bowls with it. Mix up this pudding and in two minutes we can pour it into the shell. I got a couple of pints of raspberries in the cooler that I picked this morning. I'll mix it in with Cool Whip and put a heap of it on top of each bowl. It'll taste as good as what you made, and I didn't even taste what you had. Just saw it on the floor." She had a rolling pin and was tackling the cookies in earnest. Oreo crumbs were flying around the kitchen. "Stephen, melt me some butter," she commanded. "You got to react fast in this world."

My timer buzzed. Danny walked in. "They're ready for more," he said.

"Well, we're ready for them. Clear the tables." I began pulling down the serving plates. On each I placed a serving of a wild rice and mushroom pilaf that had been baking for the past hour. Next to it, I placed a delicate carved tomato rose. From the oven, I pulled a parchment packet for each plate. The paper had browned from the heat of the oven. Juices from the veal had mingled with the herbs and bacon. Tiny wisps of fragrant steam escaped here and there from small air vents.

Mrs. Rabinowicz was finishing lining her custard bowls, and had already poured the pudding mix and milk into a big Mixomatic. "Danny and Stephen," I said, "I want your help on this. After we set the plates in front of each diner, we need to go to each plate, with a small scissors, cut a diagonal line across the paper and pull it back to expose the baked veal chop. Quickly but neatly. Ready? Let's do it."

We entered the dining room and began setting down the main course. Henry Van Elkind was at one end of the long table, Rita at the other, with eleven guests on each side of the long table. Three large silver candelabras were filled with lighted candles, their flames wavering in the breeze. Large French windows at one end opened to the same stone terrace that fronted the living room.

Snippets of conversation slipped into my mind during the frenzy of serving.

"It's an opportunity to transform the region," said the Senator, "how could I not support it . . ."

" . . . she's getting so old. What can we do with her? She hates Chicago . . ."

"Tell us, Kip, what are you planning to study? Medicine? Law?"

"Buzz off!"

"Reagan won't let the stock market drop. This is the time to make investments like these. . "

" . . . so amusing, this town. Have I told you about the character they call the Revered Willy?"

"It would be betraying my tribe . . ."

"We should get Kip and Cynthia together. Like old royal times. It would cement the bond. . . "

Back in the kitchen at last. Stephen and I had made the rounds, serving Chardonnay to some, a delightful pinot noir to others. If it had been my cafe, I would not have served another drink out of fear they would kill someone on the drive home and I would be stuck with the liability.

"I need a cup of coffee before serving them dessert," said Stephen as he slid into a chair. "Mrs. Rabinowicz, how are those desserts coming along?"

"Finished," she said. Indeed they were. Twenty four custard cups, each topped by a cone of artificial whipped topping. Only the raspberries met my standards. I could never let Thelma know about this.

"Wait a moment," I said. "They need one thing." I went into the cooler where I had stored my garnishes. "Kip didn't get these." On top of each cone, I placed one perfect luscious raspberry, and from either side I stuck a delectable leaf molded in white chocolate.

"They look great," sighed Danny.

"They do," I agreed. "Let's see if they're ready to have us clear the dinner plates and bring in dessert. You didn't drink all the coffee, did you, Stephen?"

All twenty-four custard bowls were placed on a single tray. I marched in, holding the tray aloft smartly. Stephen followed with two silver pots, one holding caffeinated and one with decaf coffee. Danny brought up the rear with a tray of after-dinner liqueurs. The group broke into applause. Admittedly, the desserts did look grand.

Back in the kitchen, we collapsed onto pressed wood oak chairs around an old oak round table. Mrs. Rabinowicz was already there, a shot glass in her hand, and a bottle of schnapps to the side. Suddenly, it occurred to me. Why wasn't she a guest in the dining room?

Henry walked in. "Walter, I must talk to you about the dessert."

Fear rose in me. He wasn't too drunk to notice the dessert's shortcomings. Visions of the Loon Town Cafe sinking into the water of Big Sapphire Lake flashed before me.

"Damn good dessert. Best I've had in years. Like a childhood ambrosia. Even Kip loved it, but then he's always loved raspberries."

The bastard.

CHAPTER FIVE

My car headlights pierced ahead through the dark outlines of tall trees stabbing the night. Above us, the sky was top-heavy with diamond-sharp stars. Inside the car, our wheels battled noisily with the town road potholes once we left the smooth pavement of the Van Elkind camp. In Danny, there was a disquietude unusual even for him.

While still in the lodge's kitchen, I asked him if something was wrong. He just shook his head and aggressively polished Mrs. Van Elkind's precious silver forks. The butler Stephen caught my eye as he put away dried china and simply shrugged his shoulders.

It had been an evening of success for my food and my cafe. The extravagance of the flowers and the meal—despite the reasonable rate I gave Henry Van Elkind—combined with the jewelry and fine clothes of the guests suggested more money that I had made all summer at the cafe. Admidst the plentitude and chatter, you could feel the spark of being in a place of importance. For me, the aura of the dinner elicited a nostalgia for those nights in New York when I was someone, when I was still with someone. Yet a glimpse of Rita or Hank would remind me of my place. I was nothing. They didn't even see me, nor did their guests. I became a nothing, a ghost, a non-existence even as I filled their glass with wine or served them dessert. I was just a piece in their jigsaw backdrop for a festive evening in Thread.

Had Danny felt that? Or was it something else? As Danny cleared the dinner plates, he was close enough to hear some whispered words among two guests. His face reddened, and I thought he would tip the plate with its greasy parchment still surrounding a gnawed-upon veal bone onto the Yves St. Laurent peasant skirt of the Senator's wife. But he caught himself and went on, yet his face burned brightly for many minutes.

What did he hear? So many things it might have been. Ghosts can hear, and this one had listened to the meaningless gossip of the night. The belittlement of the town. The challenges of isolation. And the more personal jabs, like tittering over Reverend Willy or a laugh at a townsman who so missed his dead wife that he spent each afternoon at her grave. I hope it wasn't that Danny had overhard his father's love turned into an anecdote. Whenever I thought of Toivo, I liked to focus on how he and Lempi for years had walked each evening along Highway 17, hand in hand. Until that day that for some reason she chose another path. If I learned that Henry or Rita had joked about Danny's father in any way, I vowed I would never work for them again. No matter how much they paid. No matter who their guests might be.

The car bucked through a particularly bad pothole. I looked over at Danny to check on him. In the glimmer of starlight, I quickly looked away from his face scarred with silent anger.

"Tell us all about the party," Cynthia demanded breathlessly. "Wasn't it just grand?" On this stormy Sunday morning, my faithful coterie gathered within the cafe's warmth. Mr. Packer, Bromley Bastique and Claire Moon sat at the counter with their respective morning beverages. Officer Campbell, the town's sole police officer, made it a sipping foursome. He had taken to frequent visits at times he thought Thelma might be about. Outside, dark clouds were rushing across the skies. A brisk wind whipped up small eddies of dust in the square.

"Tornado weather," declared Officer Campbell. "Reminds me of that time twisters came through and cleared a path halfway from here to Timberton. Back in '66."

"No, the cyclone was in 1965," stated Mr. Packer. "Came within one quarter mile of the Van Elkind camp. Too bad it didn't just blow the place away."

"Mr. Packer, you don't mean that," said Cynthia. "Danny, please tell me about the party. I would have gone, but I can't stand that Kip."

"Cynthia, warm up my cup of java here. And forget about that party," demanded Bromley. "Couldn't have been much of an event. They didn't even bother asking me."

"But the senator was there," Danny broke in. He had arrived for the morning shift on time, but his outlook seemed as troubled as the stormy skies outside. Yet as the morning went on, the cheerfulness of Cynthia seemed to uplift his mood. Even if he normally paid her little attention, he was always positively affected by her lack of gravity.

"If the Senator was there, he must have dropped in unexpectedly. I obviously would have been invited otherwise. As the mayor. . ."

Claire looked up from her muffin. "You're not really the mayor, you know. You can't have a head without the table."

Mr. Packer added. "Bromley, for there to be a mayor, there must be a city. And to be quite accurate Thread is not anything. You only head the township, and that makes you chairman, not mayor."

"So what? That makes me the head of something bigger. All the more reason I would be invited."

"Where's my wild strawberry jam?" Claire asked.

Cynthia slammed the coffee pot down on the counter. Just then a loud clap of thunder reverberated through the town. Everyone but Cynthia laughed. Cynthia was running out of patience. To protect my business, I was going to have to describe the event. There was no way that Danny would ever give her any details. But there seemed to be a righteous anger building in her. Her desire to be liked would only go so far, before being overtaken by her need to tour an imagined romantic life.

Officer Campbell looked at Cynthia with affection. "Girl, forget about those rich summer folk and their fancy ways. I got a project for you. It would make up for the time you broke the police light at the prom."

Cynthia suddenly looked abashed. We all knew the reason why. A year ago, she had convinced her classmates that, after eighty years without such a fete, the school needed to host a prom. She selected the theme, designed the decorations, hired the band, and pretty much told everyone they were going to attend. The highlight of the decor had been an eight-foot tall lighthouse, constructed of old two-by-fours, chicken wire, and dozens of boxes of white tissues. Its crowning glory had been a rotating red light borrowed from the town's only police car, because her dad Red had the power to make such things happen, a power that didn't turn out so well when the light fell in the middle of prom's king and queen dance and broke into a myriad of pieces. Officer Campbell still didn't have a new light for his car, because Bromley wouldn't buy him one.

"Forget your old parties," said Officer Campbell. "Help me figure out what to do with that giant muskie down to the Sapphire lakes."

"You're smoking dope," Bromley scoffed. "Just like those kids who claim a nine-foot muskie is trying to attack them! Nonsense!"

"You know," I broke in, "a few days ago, Mr. Packer and I were at the lake when a group of small kids dashed out of the water claiming they saw it."

"Group hysteria," Bromley replied.

I had an idea that I thought Bromley would like. "Mr. Packer suggested that publicizing the fish would lure people to Thread. Think of the challenge we could promote: reel in the world's largest muskie."

"Not exactly what I said, young Pearson," Mr. Packer noted, then took another sip of his steaming coffee.

My mind was on a creative burst. "We could be the Loch Ness of Wisconsin. Sponsor a festival. I could have another grand opening of this cafe. Serve muskie as one of the main courses. That could be fun. Eat the fish before he eats you."

"Interesting idea," mused Bromley. "God darn interesting."

"You betcha," said Officer Campbell. "These kids ain't making this fish story up. There's something big in that lake."

"Well, I will just ask my little men the next time they visit." Claire paused, as if frightened by her thoughts. "Oh, what if my men accidentally dropped one of their fish into the lake? It could be an alien fish. What if it's still a baby?"

"Stop talking nonsense!" shouted Cynthia over Claire's din. "None of you people listen to me. I'm always listening to you. It's not fair. I want to hear about the party. Danny, please tell me everything." She ignored the rest of us.

"Don't badger the boy," Officer Campbell said. "I think you should listen to your boss here. Plan a festival. Get your Dad to fund it. It would be good for the town. We should get Thelma out here to tell us what she thinks about our giant muskie."

Another clap of thunder, and the rain started down in fierce sheets. With a rush of damp air from the opened door, Chip Frozen Bear dashed into the cafe, his clothes dripping wet, his dark black hair plastered back against his skull, giving him a particularly ominous, if handsome, look.

"Talk of a giant muskie?" He seemed amused. "Don't you think we should honor our land and the spirits that live within it? Perhaps this giant fish has been sent as a sign that we must live in harmony with nature."

"What B.S.," Bromley said. "Your reservation's a god darn dump!"

Frozen Bear held up his hand as though to stop an expected protest. He had very strong hands. "Bromley, please. You're happy as can be to keep us there. Don't deny it. You know the state wanted to combine the Thread and Lattigeaux school districts. Both districts are too small to serve our children well. But together, they would make a better high school and a less expensive one to run."

"We don't want our kids to travel so far," said Officer Campbell.

"Nonsense. Some kids are already bussed twenty miles from resorts way back in the woods. Distance and time has nothing to do with your decision. Only the color of our skin.

"To the Lattigo, muskies are virtually sacred. Don't make a mockery of this giant fish, or, you never know, we Lattigo might claim it as our god." He smiled broadly, his white teeth perfect. Cynthia momentarily forgot about Danny and the party.

A lightning bolt pierced through the sky and a giant peal of thunder shook the town. The rain pounded against the windows like the tom toms of war.

"Who are you? Chief Thunder Water?" laughed Bromley. "Anyway, it's our god darn town. We can have a festival if we want one."

"Of course you can, I just came by to compliment this man on his food at last night's event." He held out his hand, "Wally, I know we had a rough meeting once before, so let's start fresh. Thanks for bringing a great restaurant to this town." His handshake was warm and his grip was strong. It was all better than a peace pipe.

"And, Cynthia, while I'm here, can you bring me a cup of coffee and a cinnamon roll? Might as well try the place out."

Cynthia beamed. "You got it. And then you can tell me about the party last night, because Danny won't."

Danny suddenly erupted. "Because the party was shit, the people were shit, the night was shit. The only thing that wasn't shit was Wally's food. So be glad you weren't there. Just forget about the god damn party."

Danny rushed into the kitchen. I could hear the big pots being banged around the sink.

"The boy's probably right," Mr. Packer said. "That camp has always been filled with unhappiness."

Cynthia, who had momentarily been caught between the excitement of Chip Frozen Bear and the dismay of Danny's reaction, perked up. "What do you mean? Are there some stories I haven't heard? Have you ever been there?"

"Oh, yes, I used to be a frequent guest," Mr. Packer paused. For a second it seemed to me that he grew younger, as though in reflecting on his past, his own youthful appearance reemerged. The scraggly beard, the missing arm, the unwashed body transformed in a momentary shimmer to a younger, handsomer man who hadn't yet become a town eccentric. "In those days, it was still owned by the family that built the camp, by the daughter of the old lumber baron. A beautiful woman. Her life was a tragic one, as the family's life was filled with tragedies and tied to the very woods of this area."

Cynthia was thrilled by a potential romantic story of the past, completely ignoring Chip's order. "Mr. Packer, you have to tell me about this."

"No, I don't think I will," he replied.

"Why not?" she pouted. "Well, Grandpa John can tell me. He knows everything about everyone in town."

"Not everything," said Mr. Packer enigmatically. "Go ahead and ask him."

Thelma came out of the kitchen, "What happened to Danny?" She stopped suddenly, seeing Officer Campbell was at the bar. Her ample cheeks were flushed.

Somedays, I felt as though I ran an amusement park for the people who worked for me. Did the restaurant exist to make money so I could pay both them and me? Or was its reason for being simply to give everyone in town a stage on which to parade for one another?

"He got mad because I wanted to know about the Van Elkind party. And Mr. Packer was just about to tell us a story about the Van Elkind camp, back in the old days, when some mysterious family still owned it.".

"Would that be the Oxfords from down south?" asked Thelma. Mr. Packer raised his coffee cup in admiration toward Thelma. Cynthia looked at the cook with round eyes.

"What do you know about the Oxfords?" Cynthia was happy, sensing another source for this mysterious story.

"Who cares about these old families anyway?" asked Bromley. "None of them are going to help us pay the bills around this town. We should get back to our big fish and do something about it."

Claire broke in hurriedly, as though she didn't want anyone to continue talking about the Oxfords, whoever they might be. "I could have my men radiate the lake the next time they visit and kill the thing."

"Now why would you want to do a god darn thing like that? Who's going to come to Thread if the thing is dead? Claire, where's your brains?" Bromley had gotten up and was starting to waddle around the cafe in excitement. "You know I like young Wally's idea here. Let's make this fish an asset to this town. Who needs a giant loon? We could have a giant muskie."

"Doesn't Hayward over to the west already have a giant muskie outside their town limits?" asked Mr. Packer.

"Well, that's a god darn fiberglass fish. Ain't no more real than our wooden Claire de Loon out on 17. I'm talking about a real fish. A monstrous mystery fish that no one can capture on film. Imagine that!"

"All right, if you don't want him dead," Claire went on, "I could have my men capture him and put him in a giant baggy and set it down in the town square."

Bromley Bastique gave a major sigh that only the girth of his body would permit. "You do that, Claire, and I'll have to have Officer Campbell here post guard all night long so no little hooligans come out and punch a hole in that baggy to let the water out and kill our prize."

"Good idea," agreed Claire, "except for one thing." She hesitated and gave the officer a quick glance. "I don't know if Officer Campbell is the best man for the job."

"What do you mean by that?" the officer huffed. "I'm a damn good officer." He puffed up his chest and took a stance designed mostly to impress Thelma.

A storm was brewing inside to match the external thunder and lighting that was now accompanied by a major rainfall. Huge drops of rain slammed against the plate glass windows. I thought of the little garden I had planted in back in hopes of growing some fresh greens for the cafe's salads.

With this rain, it would be washed out. Completely.

"You know, I think a twister could be coming," said Officer Campbell in a bid to change the subject. "Maybe I should get out in my patrol car and make the rounds in case something bad does happen."

"You stay here," Bromley commanded. "I'm the town chairman," he said with a sneer as he looked pointedly at Mr. Packer, "and I think we should pursue this idea of promoting our giant fish."

Frozen Bear seemed amused by us all and broke in. "You people are crazy. There's no giant muskie in any of these lakes. Why don't you tell this girl the stories she wants to hear?" Cynthia look at him with thanks. That annoyed me. "In fact, I'd like to hear about these Oxfords myself. Did you know them?"

Mr. Packer gave him an appraising look. "I've known a lot of people in my years."

The door opened. Wrapped up in our conversation, we hadn't noticed that someone had been struggling with the door against the strong winds. But with the door suddenly open, the full force of the storm was obvious and a spray of rain flew in.

"Close the door," I yelled. It was Kip van Elkind, with his stringy hair and a cigarette dangling from his lips. Was last night's party all going to show up here?

"Got any raspberries, man?" and he laughed. He was in worn and dirty jeans, frayed at the knees and on the seat, all of it held together by a safety pin at the crotch. His stained t-shirt was overlayed by a heavy flannel shirt. Every bit of it was wet, and it stank. The room was quiet. Cynthia turned to go back to the kitchen.

"I'll get you some more coffee, Mr. Packer," she said.

"What about my coffee and roll?" reminded Frozen Bear. Cynthia awarded him a smile.

"Cindy baby, bring me a cup too," Kip said. He got no smile, and she was through the kitchen door.

"Cute ass, don't you think?"

Officer Campbell stood up and strutted over to the table where Kip had taken a seat. "You're not in Chicago now, young man. You need to treat people better in Thread. Keep that kind of language you've been using out of public. Do you understand?"

"Yeah, I understand. You keep a real tight lid on this town. I guess that's why the Reverend Willy attracts such a congregation."

The cop seemed torn as to what he was going to say. He started to speak, then closed his mouth, started again, stuttered to a stop. Then as he looked at Bromley instead of Kip, he said, "First of all the man's no preacher, and second of all, he ain't hurting nobody in town. So we just leave him alone. He ain't hurting nobody, so I don't want you go bothering him either. Understand?"

"Sure man. I'll leave him alone. But maybe then you better go check out another a problem. I hear some guy's trying to raise the dead out at the old cemetery. He's there every day casting a spell. I hear people been seeing a ghost at sundown. Check that out, sheriff."

In the kitchen, a huge clatter arose as though the entire table of pans had tipped over. Danny came out, his face glowering, his eyes focused right onto Kip. But he didn't say anything. He only turned to me and said, "I'm sorry."

Laughing, Kip walked to the door, without waiting for any coffee, "See you later, assholes." Then he turned abound to look at Chip Frozen Bear, "And you. Stay away from my dad." He paused. "You should all stay away from my dad."

Promontory Park spread before me like a sun-faded, shaggy green carpet brushing against the cool blue marble of Big Sapphire Lake. The sun, lowering behind the treetops, encouraged shadows to encroach onto the lake. I lay back against the tinder dry August grass and stared up into the blue bowl of a sky. Except for the darting sparrows, the sky was as clear as any time during the summer.

It was a commanding view of Thread and the lakes that surrounded it. There was a hint of fall in the foliage, a bit of summer's past in the sound of the sparrows. The lake, still crowded with fisherman cramped in their wooden boats, was placid. The fishermen sat quietly on their seats, protected by bright orange lifejackets half strangling them in the heat, their poles held semi-erect over the water, motionless. Then a bobber dipped into an expanding ring of ripples, and the pole was jerked back. The reel began to be turned and another fish broke through the water in an arcing struggle.

A waterskiier went shimmying over the water, her wake rolling several fisherman. They seemed not to notice. The roar of the skier's powerboat was muffled by distance. High overhead, in the heat of the late afternoon, a golden-tailed hawk rode the air currents, circling the lake. It waited for that fish that would be thrown back as too small.

A slight sound to my right from the thick ferns beneath the old maples. Out stepped a fawn, nearly a deer this late in the summer. Did it see me, lying on my old flannel blanket frayed at its edges? Did it know that a half drunk bottle of gewurztztraminer sat inside my cooler? It eyed me curiously, then bent its head to pluck at the tender shoots of grass that grew in the shade of the glade's edge.

Summer's end. I was avoiding the reality of the Loon Town Cafe. Business had not been good. The summer folk were snobbier than I expected; the Thread residents thriftier than I remembered; and the expenses out of control. Who would have guessed that good fresh ingredients would be more costly here than in New York City? Maybe a Chip Frozen Bear. But not me.

Townspeople were already claiming the good times were over for the year. The tourist rush had come and gone. All that was left was a slow dance toward Labor Day. Oh, to be sure, there would be that quick tarantella of fall colors when hordes descended in late September and early October to gape at the colored leaves. But a night out at the Loon Town Cafe was unlikely to be entered on their dance cards.

And after the last leaves dropped, it would be yet another month until the hunters arrived in November: first the bow hunters stalking the deer; then the bear hunters; and finally the fainter of heart who drove into town with guns for the full deer season. All any of them would want at the Loon Town Cafe was beer, and lots of it.

The fawn moved closer into my thoughts. Little deer, run now before they arrive. No one cares how darling you look or how clever you are. They won't care that your white spots still show like mirages beneath a winter coat. If they think they can convince a game warden that you're a buck, they'll shoot you dead in your tracks. You'll be another venison burger.

It was a rotten day and I had to face it. My life was now tied to the give and take of the summer visitors. Soon most of the resorts would close, pull their floating docks up onto the shore and await another season. The windows of the log cabins would be boarded up, the power and water turned off, the lawns raked for one last time until next May. What of the people who worked at these resorts, who mowed the lawns, cleaned the cabins, served as guides? They would have to scrape by until spring. Just like me.

Where could any of us go? There was no industry. The forest had been depleted decades ago. All that was left was some scrub lumber that headed to down-and-out paper mills. Sure, there were iron and copper mines in the upper peninsula of Michigan but the drive was far too long for any but the most desperate. Some said the local window and woodworking factory was about to expand, focusing on energy-saving, custom-built, triple-paned windows. A few weeks back, a fancy New York advertising agency team had been in the cafe after talking to the plant owner about a national campaign. *Metropolitan Home. House and Garden.* All of that. I didn't have much hope that Thread windows would become the next architectural fad.

Was my life like this town? Depleted and meaningless? Why had I run from Manhattan, unwilling to deal with the emotional aftermath of that mugging? What had I expected to find in Thread? Something to give meaning to a life that had so far meant so little?

Lately I obsessed over watching Danny and Cynthia as they worked in the restaurant. Soon they would cut back on their hours when they entered senior year at Thread High. It would be fine with me. Except for weekends and evenings, Thelma and I, with the occasional shift from Gerta, would be able to handle the cafe by ourselves. But I liked the kids' company each day.

A large orange and black butterfly flitted overhead in a curious projectory toward a patch of milkpod plants. Was it true that Monarch butterflies migrated to Mexico? How did they have the energy? Who knew they lived so long to take a journey like that?

"What ponderings give you such a serious look, young Pearson?" The young deer fled back into the woods, and beside me were tattered shoes of Mr. Packer. "It is a beautiful day, isn't it? But why retreat to this lovely hillside? Searching for your giant muskie?"

I shook my head. "But it would have been a wonderful gimmick for the town to sponsor a giant fish festival. I don't know why Cynthia couldn't talk her father into it."

"Who needs big fish?" Mr. Packer had plopped down beside me, his long legs projecting in a gangly way down the hillside. "It's better this way. More peaceful. We only have those people who really want to be here, who enjoy the town for what it is, not for what it might be, or for what it isn't. They enjoy it for its true essence. A quiet place filled with decent people surrounded by God's beauty." We sat quietly for several minutes.

Mr. Packer leaned over, patted my leg, then used my shoulder as a fulcrum to get back up. He was heavier than I thought. "Do you think that young Cynthia would pour me a cup of good coffee if I were to head down to your cafe right now?"

"I'm sure she would," I said.

"Then why don't you join me in a walk back for a cup of your brewed elixir?"

"Okay," I replied taking one last look at the blue water. I looked again. What was that shadow beside the fourteen-foot Chris Craft? How had it disappeared so quickly? I looked up at the sky to see if a quickly moving cloud had played a trick shadow on the lake. But the sky was clear. I looked back at the lake. There was a giant dark spot a hundred feet aft the boat. "Mr. Packer," I said pointing to the shadowy fish lurking beneath the water's surface.

Mr. Packer kept his eyes on his feet as he walked slowly down the incline toward Hazel Street. "Don't look for things you'd need not find," he said. "Come on, let's get into town while the coffee's still fresh."

.

CHAPTER SIX

Manhattan and its memories were behind me. The promise of a new life in Thread was well underway. Each day I was growing into some new person, even as my wallet slimmed down. It was as though my finances had become a crazy reverse mirror to the garden in back of my kitchen.

By late August, crops in Thread were at their fullest. In the marshlands deep within the woods, one could still find late-blooming blueberries. Apples reddened, hanging heavy from the branches, inviting the picker to take one home. In the gardens stroked by nightly lake fog, the tomato bushes laid low to the ground, seldom properly staked, but always overflowing with thin-skinned and fragrant tomatoes. When sliced, they perfumed the air with their sweet acidity. Zucchini and cucumber vines sprawled across mounded earth, long green vegetables growing with no end in sight, finally becoming too large for good eating and left to yellow on the vine. The patches of sweet corn grown tall boasted hair on each cob that grew darker by the day. Potato plants, once bright green with tiny white blossoms, began to retreat, slowly dying back, shriveling up, while beneath the soil each potato grows large.

Thread gardens held a cornucopia of plenty beneath their surfaces. As word spread through town that I bought fresh ingredients, backyard gardeners began to stop by, trying to sell the best of their lot. Those who sought to unload their shriveled cast offs soon learned that I held no interest in anything but the finest. I vowed to have my life and my restaurant involve only the finest.

So as my bank account shriveled, I felt an enlargement of spirit I had never achieved in Manhattan. It was as though I had planted a seed of myself, and every aspect of my personality burst with flavor around me. I liked to think I could be as wise and thoughtful as Mr. Packer, as quirky as Claire, as down-home sensible as Thelma, as eternally optimisitic as Cynthia, as fulfilled and grounded as I had always wanted to be.

But then there was Danny. Surely there was something I could tell Danny that would lift his perpetual cloud and let him too be a reflection of what I wanted, and not what I feared.

Kip lounged against the dark stone column at the Great Northern State Bank. A cigarette dangled from his mouth. The kid was moored to the spot with no sign of his father or that lifeboat of a car that Henry van Elkind drove. The grass in the square separating the bank from my cafe was dry and yellow, a few unmowed weeds gone to seed. A flick of Kip's cigarette into that mess and it would go up in flames.

The kid just glared in the direction of the cafe's plate glass window. At least it seemed a glare to me, but perhaps it was really a misguided longing stare or leer. Ever since the raspberries desserts were flung across the camp kitchen's floor, I sought to avoid the younger van Elkind. Luckily, he seldom joined his father for Henry's frequent lunches. Yet, he inhabited the square much of every day, doing nothing but watching. His lounging around the square seemed to match Cynthia's work schedule.

Today I stood outside my cafe and watched him watch me. It was an afternoon lull and I had put Danny and Cynthia to work washing the windows. I stood guard, like my old friend Patrice in Brooklyn who always kept a lookout posted as we painted over neighborhood graffiti, as though a lookout could be a magic talisman against evil.

Cynthia was on a stepladder, reaching high to get the top of windows above those arched letters spelling out "Loon Town Cafe." Danny was beside her, bucket at his feet, drying rags at hand.

Mr. Packer ambled over. During the course of the day he seemed to visit every establishment in town. Somehow, growing up, I had never realized that he was the one person in town who truly knew everything that went on in this town. He paused at my side, watching me watch Kip watch us. He said nothing.

Behind us, Cynthia was her talkative self, unaware of any lurking danger. "This will be the best school year yet. I have it all planned out. All the courses I'm going to take. What I'm going to wear the first day. Even where we'll take the senior class trip."

Mr. Packer always found Cynthia's planning for the world amusing. "Don't you think, young lady, that the other students in your class might have a thought or two about where to travel?"

"They always listen to me," she replied nonchalantly, then turned her attention back to Danny. And she was off, informing Danny of every course choice and every reason for every choice. Not that there were many choices. The school was small. The faculty even smaller. The only language choice was French, and if Cynthia didn't want to take that that, her one elective would have to have been either home ec or shop.

"So here's my plan. First hour I'm going to take trigonometry with Mr. Hackens. He's such a strange one, the way his hair is always sticking on end, but I think he's kind of cute. And I think it would be fun to take trig, and it might help when I go to college, although I'm not really interested in math at all. Still it seems the right thing to do. Then the second period, I thought about taking French. I suppose it's kind of silly starting French in my senior year since it really won't do me much good for getting out of a foreign language in college, but you know it's the first year they've ever managed to hire a foreign language teacher, so it would be kind of rude not to enroll. Besides, Daddy said we might go to Paris next summer if everything works out all right with his business deals. He wants to talk to some French people about something or another, so it could come in handy.

"And then third period has to be gym. Do you think Miss Cupid is, well, you know, that way?"

Danny threw his sponge into the bucket. "Cynthia, I don't really want to know every course you're planning to take this year, and what you think of the teachers. Who cares? It's not like we have any choice."

"I could take shop. Build a book case. I could do that." Cynthia flounced her hair and came down the stepladder. Then she pulled out the sponge from the bucket, wrung it dry, and stepped back up the ladder. "And what would be wrong with that? I bet I could build a wonderful bookcase. In fact, I bet I could build anything better in shop than you could bake in home ec."

96

I jumped into the conversation so that the windows would get washed before being shattered. "Cynthia, don't forget. Danny's learning to cook here. Remember how he helped Thelma bake those tollhouse cookies yesterday."

"Anyone can make cookies." She restarted washing the windows. I watched her scrub with incredible energy. All summer long she had mooned over the boy.

"I haven't tasted yours yet," I joked.

Cynthia flung her sponge at me. I ducked. It flew over my head. Suddenly it was thrown back against the window and landed on the sidewalk with a puddle of grey water ebbing out.

"Such a welcome, throwing sponges at me," snickered Kip Van Elkind. "I guess you got a thing for me, huh, Cynthia?"

Cynthia simply stared back. Her look of disdain for the kid was clear.

Across the Square, Henry Van Elkind had just driven up and was locking the door of his beige Mercedes, and noticed his son smirking at the girl. Henry crossed the Square. He glared at Kip, 'What are you doing in town? You're supposed to be with your grandmother. But now, stay here until I get through with Wally."

He then indicated with a furtive gesture that he wanted us to go inside the cafe. "Leave the children outside to play. I have a business proposition."

Cynthia shot me a look imploring me to stay. Danny seemed to shrink inward while at the same he bristled. Mr. Packer moved in between Kip and my teenagers as though to take up my lookout post. I turned to follow Henry in.

"Sit, Wally," he commanded. The cafe was nearly empty as usual on weekday afternoons. Outside the window, Mr. Packer had taken up talking to Cynthia, keeping an eye on a smoldering Danny who seemed incensed by the lolling Kip. Kip was making suggestive comments, not loudly enough to be heard through the thick plate glass windows, but obvious by the way they rankled Danny. Cynthia was pointedly ignoring whatever Kip said, and a gallant Mr. Packer was helping her maintain the charade. Mr. Packer's lanky body blocked Kip from seeing Cynthia clearly without swaying to and fro.

"Pay attention, Wally, what I'm about to say is important," Van

Elkind demanded.

"Another dinner?" I asked. I had learned one lesson already in dealing with the rich. Insist on cash up front. It had taken two weeks to get full payment from Henry after the catered affair at his camp, and then the check had bounced. "A misunderstanding," he claimed. The fact remained that I still had to pay the butcher in Timberton, Danny, Thelma and others. Patrice who had once worked on Cape Cod always joked with me, "Never take a check from a Kennedy." I thought it had just been his Republican-born nature bubbling up. Now I knew that the rich really were different. They didn't know that money mattered.

"That was a great meal, wasn't it?" Yes it was, I thought to myself, but I never saw your friends come into the cafe for more of a good thing. "The Senator talks about it every time I see him. Even Rita admits you were the right choice. Now she insists we will use you for everything we cater at the camp. But this is not about the camp. I need a less personal setting for a more private business event."

Suddenly, Van Elkind bolted up and walked rapidly to the window. The late afternoon sun was flooding through. It caused four distinct shadows: the window-washing silhouette of Danny which even in the distortion of shadows showed off his trimness; a ball-like shadow of Cynthia as she crouched near the ground, apparently wiping dry a corner of the just-washed window; the lanky one-armed shadow of Mr. Packer; and then there was the interior shadow of Van Elkind going into a St. Vitus dance of anger. "Where the fuck is that boy? I told him to stay right here until I was done."

"What's the worry? Kip's what? Seventeen? Eighteen? I'm sure he can take care of himself," I offered. I was just glad he had run off, and I looked forward to the day he headed back to Chicago.

"That's not the fucking point. I tell him to do something. I expect him to do it. I give the orders. He takes them. That is the agreement. I told him to stay in the square so we could leave together. This disobedience comes from his school, filled with nothing but bad influences. Crummy friends. Drugs."

"Imprison him in Thread," I joked. "No bad influences here. The only trouble he can get into is death by boredom."

Van Elkind sat back down. "We've already thought of that. Rita and I have decided that Kip will stay in Thread this school year. He and

Rita's mother can all stay at the camp this winter with Stephen. The old woman and Rita don't get along anyway. This way we'll avoid the battlefields that leave us all bloody. Besides Mother Regina loves the northwoods and her gardens. She will be happier here. And Kip staying with her will stablize her, give her something to worry about. Avoid interfering with us.

"Kip did so badly at school last year that he failed almost all of his courses. He can't get into any college without returning to high school for a year to build up a better record. We can't let him go back to La Salle academy. That would be too humiliating, and he is a Van Elkind after all. A hole in the wall place like this would be a better setting."

I had two hopes. One was that Henry would soon rethink this plan. The second was that that Cynthia never learned I had even jokingly suggested it.

"But back to business. Here's the deal. I want to rent your back room for a private business dinner. Actually, I want you to close the whole restaurant for the night so we have the place to ourselves. Naturally, I would fully pay you for whatever it might cost."

"If you want the whole cafe, then we can set up your party in the dining room. It would be much more comfortable and pleasant than that backroom," I pointed out.

"Don't quibble Wally. I know what I want. I want both privacy and quality. And I don't want that at home or perched up against walls of glass. If we sat in the front we might as well put ourselves on a pedestal in the Town Square and light fireworks in the sky. We would be as much of a tourist attraction as that ridiculous Reverend Willy.

"I just want a quiet place with a good dinner where four of my colleagues and I can have a very private business meal. Your back room is perfect. That way my guests can enter through the alley. How about Monday? You'd be closed anyway. It's a small group, so you can handle all of it. Leave Danny, Cynthia, and that loud-mouthed Thelma out of it. It will be your party. No one else need know."

"Henry," I protested. "I keep the restaurant closed on Mondays because I need some time off." I was flattered at his request. He really did like my restaurant.

"There is a thousand dollars in it for you." He opened his wallet, and counted out ten one-hundred dollar bills. "I knew you would want the cash up front after our small mix up last time. Wally, I'm an honorable man. You do not have to worry about getting paid. It is all on the up and up. In fact, I'd like you to sit in on the whole thing if you will. In fact, I insist you do just that. Your input could be valuable. So, is it a deal?"

Who could say no? I always was a sucker for the rich. At least someone in this town sought me out.

We shook hands and walked to the front door together. Cynthia and Danny were just finishing their window washing. Mr. Packer was walking on to his next event. Van Elkind did a quick scan of the square. "I'm leaving without that fucking kid. Let him find his own way back to the camp." He got into this Mercedes and left with a squeal of the tires.

"How'dya like him for a father?" Danny muttered as he walked in.

"The only thing worse would be to have Kip for a brother," Cynthia said, "I can't wait for the whole bunch of them to return to Chicago. That'll be the best thing about the end of summer—seeing the last of Kip"

I kept my silence.

The best of the summer's produce was available to me as I thought about the Elkind dinner. I planned to create a memorable meal. I only had to pick and choose from the freshest of product to blend something that would please the Chicago gourmands. Normally, I turned to Thelma for advice, as she was a good check on my overreaching ambitions. More than once she vetoed a menu that surely would have undone me with its complexity.

But Van Elkind had been adamant that I involve no one else in his catered dinner. The customer is always right. So I sat alone in the kitchen on the following Monday afternoon, surrounded by the splendor of my larder, unable to decide what to make.

Each course I thought of seemed momentarily perfect, and then transformed into a dish either untrue to the season or simply a pretentious fantasy. The dinner should be simple. He asked me to join the meeting— whatever the meeting was about. I would not be able to do that if the meal was so complicated that it kept me in the kitchen every minute.

I had to start with the tomatoes . My lovely red Big Boys and golden heirloom tomatoes were so different from the usual commercial tomatoes. Just walking by the window sill where they sat in a row, each growing still riper in the heat and light of the summer sun, you caught the odor of true tomato essence, hinting of what a tomato sauce could be. There was a reason why Europeans first thought these fruits were aphrodisiacs.

Keep it simple. I repeated my mantra. Slice the biggest tomatoes into thick slices that drip with ripeness. Alternate the red and gold in a semicircle of rounds. Drizzle the slices with fine olive oil, freshly ground pepper and sea salt, and sprinkle with minced basil from my back yard garden. Then take thin slices of Thelma's French bread, drizzle with the same oil, and top with freshly grated Parmesan cheese. Lightly broil the bread as toast, and arrange the rounds in a second semicircle. Top the presentation with a sprig of basil atop a small pile of fresh Colby cheese curds, milder than any mozzarella, so young, made just that morning by the Thread cheese factory, that there has been no chance to age, the essence of milk captured as solid, so fresh that it squeaks as you eat each curd.

And the main course would be roast chicken—those beautiful spring chickens now four months old and range fed by Danny's father Toivo. I had convinced him to sell me a dozen of his birds. The richness of their flavor was almost wild, so unlike the timidity of commercial chicken. Some oil and wine, some fresh herbs like parsley and rosemary, a spoonful of good Wisconsin ground mustard, some cloves of garlic. I'd throw it all together in a blender until it became a fluid paste. Then I could use a spoon to go in and under the tender yellow skin of the young chicken, loosening it from the firm flesh, creating a pocket just underneath into which I could insert that fragrant paste. Roast the bird for 40 or 50 minutes at a high temperature, the fluid causing the bird to self baste in fresh herbs, causing the skin to crackle into a crisp brown papery covering that kept in the steam of the moist meat.

And what about vegetables? New potatoes boiled with some cut-up baby turnips, riced to remove all lumps, and then mashed with lots of butter, heavy cream, and no stinting on the garlic roasted in the oven. Aromatic and flavorful potatoes bathed in rich yellow gravy blended from the roast chicken drippings. With some fresh green beans cooked slowly with bacon, the southern style, not so they're crisp, but so they have full flavor and richness.

It would be simple and easy and I could do it.

That only left dessert. With a bushel of the seasons's early apples sitting in the larder, the choice was an obvious one. A deep dish apple pie with a Pennsylvania Dutch brown sugar streusel topping, and freshly made brown sugar and buttermilk ice cream. Van Elkind's guests would forget about their business when they ate all of this. They surely would elevate me to a culinary genius.

Later that evening, just past seven, with the evening light still bright, a car stole up behind my alley entrance. Henry Van Elkind got out of the passenger's side carrying a large circular container, the kind that contains architectural plans. Three others also stepped out of the late model black Cadillac. Two of the three I had never seen before. The third was the handsome and always brooding Chip Frozen Bear. I opened the door for the group.

"Wait for Red Trueheart to show up, then lock the door and join us in the back room. I'll show these three where we're meeting and begin pouring the wine. You do have the wine out?" Van Elkind asked without awaiting a reply.

I looked back into the alley and saw Red walking toward me, still wearing the white apron that he normally wore when he worked in his store. "Good evening," he said to me as though reciting a secret code. "Strange to see you working on your night off. Mind if I come in for a cup of coffee."

I let him in, then locked the door behind. "Who do you think would be spying on you?" I asked of Red. "The others are already in the back room. You can join them there. I'll bring in the first course."

When I came in with tomatoes, they were already seated, chatting about the weather. They ignored me as I placed the plates in front of them "Wally," said Van Elkind. "We have decided we will eat first and then get into business when dessert is served. So plan to join us then. Just keep the food coming and the wine flowing." Without saying a word, I left a serving of the tomatoes at the place setting that was intended for me.

No one seemed to relish the delicate ripeness of my carefully chosen tomatoes.

Red looked questioning at the curds of cheese on his plate. Wait for the chicken, I thought, then I'll hear some sighs of satisfaction.

There were none. Yet their mothers would have been happy, since they cleaned their plates and asked for seconds. But no one complimented me. I started the coffee and heated up the pie in the microwave.

I set out the desserts, poured the coffee, and was about to leave. "Wally, I told you to stay for dessert," Van Elkind said. "Sit. We're about to review our plans and I want you to hear them. I think you could be useful.

"First, the introductions. I'm sure you know Red and Chip. So let me turn to the two new faces. This is Jonathan Webber Oxford. His great-grandfather helped tame these woods, even built the camp that I live in now. Jonathan has broad business interests, access to great amounts of capital, and is not too fond of these woods that make his family fortune."

"But it wasn't these woods that my great-grandfather cleared," Oxford said in a squeaky voice that seemed at odds with his heavy face. "When he was here, this was all virgin timber, massive woods just waiting to build America. It's nothing but crap wood now, not even good for high quality paper."

"Whose fault is that?" Chip Frozen Bear leaned across the table. "Who clear cut these woods and never replanted them? Who hunted the bear and the moose and the lynx to extinction after you had already destroyed most of their habitat? You and your fellow robber-barons—none of whom hold legal right to this land. It belonged to the Lattigo. Your families stole it and destroyed it." Chip caught my eye and winked.

Oxford stood up rapidly. The dishes on the table rattled, coffee spilled into the saucers. Oxford's own fatty rolls jiggled as much as the dishes. His blue eyes flashed with anger. "Henry, you assured me when I agreed to come to this meeting that I would not be subjected to remonstrances such as these. My family no longer has anything to do with mining or lumbering these woods. We simply have land investments retained from earlier days. I do not care if this ill-educated, ill-mannered young man thinks my great-grandfather was a villain. He no doubt was and he no doubt deserved the untimely death he met. None of that has anything to do with me, and I do not care to be insulted by Mr. Frozen Bear, especially when he seeks to be my partner."

"Let's just be clear," Chip broke in. "I don't want to be your partner. I am just keeping watch, preventing you from raping my tribe. Your land investments, as you so lightly put it, cover fifty thousand acres of undeveloped second growth woods, and you control the mineral rights to another fifty thousand acres. With your family's various trust funds, corporations, and legal monkeyworks, you control half this county.

"And what you don't control Red does. Leaving my people stuck in a swamp." Frozen Bear sat down and dipped into his ice cream. "Hey, this is good," he said, "just like the whole meal was. Wally, your restaurant's really quite fine. It deserves better than the people you're serving."

I smiled in satisfaction. Van Elkind sighed and motioned for Oxford to continue with dessert. "Wally, as you can see, we have a delicate situation, but one that holds great promise. Let me also introduce Mr. Tesla Haligent." He motioned toward the man who had been silent through much of the meal. "I don't know if you have ever met him, but he is the president of the holding company that controls both the local bank and the window factory. Tes is very interested in the future of this region, even though admittedly most of his company's holdings are outside the region."

"I'm always interested in new business opportunities," Mr. Haligent said, "especially when I can get an early play." He was short and thin, slightly balding, although he appeared not much older than I. Throughout dinner he had held a bemused smile, seldom talking, but fully connected with the conversation. "This country is quite beautiful. I think it would attract many, if they only had an inkling of what it could offer."

An odd collection. What brought together these five individuals: Red Trueheart, the town's official power broker who so many thought owned most of the township; Jonathan Oxford, the man who I now learned actually owned most of the place; Tesla Haligent, the absentee owner of the bank that held my mortgage, a man whose name I had heard from time to time since he was known to run the company that owned the bank and factory, but as far as I had heard, had never visited either; Henry Van Elkind, the ostentatious vacationing millionaire who was just another of the summer folk who passed through town; and finally, the most unlikely of all, Chip Frozen Bear, an MBA-wielding native American who could have made a fortune on Wall Street but had come home to be angry.

"I think it's time we told young Wally here what this is all about. We are the primary stockholders in a new land development and entertainment company, soon to transform this corner of the world through a great re-creation of Penokee County." Henry unrolled a large poster that he had brought in with him. "Introducing American Seasons –

an amusement park par excellence and resort for the entire family.

"There's Winter, home to fast-paced snowy fun such as tobogganing and thrill rides like the Avalanche.

"There's Spring, with Mardi Gras in New Orleans and Spring Break on the Seasons Lagoon.

"There's Summer with a white water ride through the natural wilds of our native lands.

"And there's Fall—where the state fair meets the horrors of Halloween.

"Put it all together with a convention center, resort hotels, fine restaurants, new shopping centers and four intertwined amusements parks that will put Disney World to shame. It's American Seasons." I thought Van Elkind would drown the room with his enthusiasm.

"But why would anyone come?" I asked.

"The billion-dollar question," murmured Taligent.

"That's why I'm here," Chip said. "They need the Lattigo because they want gambling and they think we can give it to them."

"I don't get it."

"Recent Supreme Court decisions create an interesting opportunty," Chip began. "The court has greatly increased the recognition given to Native American treaties and acknowledges our reservations as national entities with the freedom to conduct internal affairs on tribal land. Specifically, several cases now have prevented states from prohibiting tribes from conducting bingo and poker as gambling activities on reservation land. My legal advisors and I are convinced that we can extend this new ruling to all kinds of gambling, including slot machines, roulette, and anything else you would find on the Strip in Vegas. Mix gambling with theme parks and you got the whole family hooked. You have, in a word, the true American Seasons, the lure to attract thousands."

Henry broke in. "Each of us here bring a certain necessary element to move this vision forward. Red and Jonathan control much of the land that we need to pull together for a project of this scope. Tes and I have access to capital and other investors for a project that will involve many hundreds of millions of dollars. And Mr. Frozen Bear, of course, can deliver gambling on the reservation—an insurance policy essential to cementing the loyalty of many potential investors."

"Why tell me?" I asked. "I would think you need to keep this secret." In my Manhattan days, I had learned that people liked to divulge secrets to me. I don't know what it was about my personality, but it made it easier to be a reporter. Maybe people just wanted to see their names in print, and they counted on me to treat them fairly.

"We do and we will," said Chip, "but this isn't like your Manhattan days. We don't need some gossip flack. We want someone local, someone with a base in journalism, but someone who knows everyone in town because those people come in and out of his cafe everyday. We need someone like that to be our partner in good will, to help us plan how to to position this, how to announce it to residents so they support us, to position us with the local government so they provide the needed improvements. A local lobbyist, if you will.

"I did a little research on you as a journalist and as a society schmoozer during your days in Manhattan. You were good, and I think you're our man. And I knew your friend Patrice. I trusted him, so I'll trust you."

"Besides that, it was Tes' idea." Frozen Bear spooned up the last of the melting ice cream in his dish.

"So can we count on you being part of the New Thread?" asked Henry.

Who could say no? I had come to the small town only to become part of the big time. Wealth, fortune, influence had always intrigued me, and now it sat in my back room, beckoning me to the table

FALL INTO WINTER

CHAPTER SEVEN

The early morning sun was already reflecting with a nauseating brilliance off the kitchen pans piled next to the sink. Dishes and stemware remain crusted with remnants of last night's dinner. Inebriated with the audacity of the redevelopment of the entire county, I drank heartily with the businessman. Chip seemed to study me with undue interest as the evening wore on, but I didn't mind being the center of his attention. After all, he understood my food.

After all that, who could be bothered with scullery duties. I knew I could be industrious with the rising of the early morning sun. But a few hours later, as the first rays skipped across the eastern edges of the Sapphire lakes, I only moaned and reached for the aspirin bottle. I had to beat Thelma to the kitchen. She always showed up first to put the caramel rolls into the oven. Henry wanted the dinner meeting to be a secret, and now that they had entrusted me with their vision, I needed to act as a trusted partner. I nearly succeeded.

"What was than Hank van Elkind doing here last night?" asked Thelma as she walked in the kitchen. She stopped suddenly and surveyed the kitchen with the third degree. She looked at me with disapproval.

I wasn't going to own up to anything. "What do you mean?" I could feign innocence. I had learned that skill interviewing socialites in Manhattan.

"I recognized the tire tracks of that fancy car of his in the back alley. Ain't many of those cars in this town. And all those footprints. Did he bring a party with him?" My eyes followed Thelma's gaze, picking up the many clues to the night before. Her eyes stopped first on the ice cream maker, still unwashed and still plugged in. They traveled over to some apple peelings left on the unswept floor. The gaze swept over to her favorite roasting pans sitting dried and cleaned, but on the range instead of their storage racks. It skipped to the trash can with four empty wine bottles from Chateau Montelana. Boy, those whites were good. Thelma's tour reached its final stop on my face, bleary-eyed and a little puffy. "It looks like someone not only met up with a bear, but invited it to dinner." She released a disappointed sigh. "I guess I need to face up to some cleaning in addition to baking this morning."

Instead of mooning over Thelma, Officer Campbell should be taking detective lessons from this middle-aged woman. I was convinced she knew all my secrets, from who the guests were to what I served them. But then, in this town, only Officer Campbell lacked keen skills in discernment. When my breakfast trio showed up, Bromley immediately begain the third degree. "Did you see Van Elkind last night. God darn, if I didn't see him drive through town with Tesla Haligent and that Lattigo kid. You know Haligent's company owns the bank. Why would he be in town and not try to see me? But he has time for Frozen Bear. Not even seeing Claire's men would surprise me more."

Claire seemed to take offense at that statement, but then she focused on spreading her strawberry jam. Mr. Packer took another sip of coffee like he'd heard it all before.

By the time Cynthia and Danny showed up for their lunch shift , I was feeling skittish. I just hoped that Thelma and Bromley wouldn't sit down together and truly piece together the whole evening.

"What was Daddy doing here last night?" Thank God, Bromley had already left. Cynthia seemed really interested in her question. Somehow, it even caught Danny's attention.

"You're closed on Mondays," Danny pointed out.

I was in a quandary. Should I ignore their comments? Should I make up a story? I was relieved of making any decisions by the arrival of a customer, Chip Frozen Bear, who looked quite hale and hearty despite our evening of wine and my fine food. He walked straight up to me.

"Hi, Mr. Frozen Bear," said Cynthia. What was that tone in her voice? She normally reserved that emotion for Danny. Thelma walked out of the kitchen just then, and smiled at the staff and at Chip. Even Danny seemed entranced by the man.

Chip seemed oblivious to their interests. "Great dinner last night. Really enjoyed the company and the food." Everyone now turned their attention to me. But I could say nothing, and didn't. Let them wonder. "Buy more, young man. Stop being penny-wise, pound-foolish," proclaimed the dapper man in a dark suit, white starched shirt, and gaily red polka-dotted, hand-tied bow tie. "No need to fool around with using fresh ingredients. Build up higher volumes on ordering canned goods, and I could get you a better buy on case lots. But a few cans here, a few cans there, it just doesn't give you the volume discounts. Why I tell you, you would be saving two ways if you'd listen to me. First, there's no way you can obtain fresh produce as economically as you can get canned and frozen items from NorthWoods Supplies, and second, you'll end up with lower per unit costs on those things you already purchase. So why not let me put you down for two gross of canned tomatoes? You want those on Thursday or Friday?"

"Mr. Ford," Thelma broke in with a laughing voice. I hadn't even known she had been listening. But after my secret dinner a week earlier, she seemed to gravitate more to the front of the restaurant. While she stayed out of the business side of the restaurant, baking in the kitchen and making wisecracks to the steady customers kept her occupied and amused. "Now, I never met you before, Mr. Ford . . ."

"Just call me Gilbert, sweetie,"

Thelma gave him an amused but still withering look. "You obviously don't know Wally Pearson at all. He won't buy two gross of canned tomatoes from you on Thursday or on Friday. He isn't even going to buy one can as long as the gardens in this here town are overflowing with fresh ripe tomatoes. He don't care one bit if those tomatoes are blemished or if they have a little snail bite out of them. They just got to be bursting with flavor.

"Same thing goes for your creamed corn, your potato flakes, your individually prepared chicken cordon bleu ready after two minutes in the microwave. That ain't Wally. That ain't the Loon Town Cafe. So why do you come in here every week trying to badger him into buying something he ain't never going to buy?"

The town cop, Officer Campbell, started laughing out loud. He had been sitting at a corner table with a cop of coffee and one of Thelma's famous sticky buns. "You tell him Thelma!"

"Am I talking to you Campbell? There are bigger things going on in this town that you should be looking after instead of what I have to tell some peddler. Someone's got to look after this foolish boy Wally. The back room's already overflowing with produce that he'll have to throw away because there ain't enough people coming through to eat it."

I was about to pipe in and protest Thelma's lack of confidence in my purchasing skills, but Gilbert beat me to the pulpit. "Tell me, Wally," he began, "how it can be that I've been dropping by to see you every other week for the past two months, and in all that time I've never had the honor of being introduced to this fine woman." He twiddled his bow tie, setting it off at a more rakish angle, perhaps imagining himself to be a Fred Astaire.

"If I had wanted to meet you, Mr. Ford, I wouldn't have needed Wally to set up no invitation. I'm a grown woman."

"I can tell that," Gilbert said appreciatively, "and I insist you call me Gilbert. I would hate to be on such a formal basis with such a lovely woman." He rose from where we had been seated near the door and began walking toward Thelma, who stood in the doorway to the kitchen.

Thelma's eyes did a quick scan of this middle-aged man. He was of moderate height, slight in build, with ever-so-stooped shoulders. His hair was jet black and perfectly coifed. His clothes draped just right. It seemed to me that Thelma's eyes lingered unnecessarily long in the area of Mr. Ford's crotch.

Thelma noticed such things. One weekend evening after a particularly strong night of business, we had stayed in the kitchen long after everyone had gone. We'd decided to finish off a bottle of good Cabernet from Heitz Cellars. She had told me then, "Women always say they don't care what a man looks like, or that they just look at his hands, or his butt. I suppose those things are nice, but I like a man who's well equipped. It ain't so hard to tell, you know. It's kind of exciting to guess what's underneath all that fabric. I like men who wear boxer shorts and loose pants, because there's a freedom there as he walks. Forget those men in bikini briefs. It just makes a bulge like they stuck a sock there. Men in boxer shorts—that's my kind of man. With a good eye, you can always tell if they're excited to see you. My old Freddy was always a giveaway. I liked having him watch me, and then catch him shifting his pants around."

It may have been a nervous tic, but it seemed to me that Gilbert

Ford hitched his well-hung pants a bit as he walked toward Thelma. She gave him a smile that made me wonder if there was some truth to the old story that Fred Schmidt had died happily smothered in Thelma's bountiful breasts.

"It seems such a shame," Gilbert began, "that you and I haven't met sooner. I truly believe—despite our disagreements about canned tomatoes—that we have something special in common."

Officer Campbell stood up, with a look of fierce protection crossing his face. He swaggered after Gilbert. "Don't go bothering Thelma. She said she wasn't interested."

"I said no such thing, Campbell," laughed Thelma. "Go back to your corner and finish your coffee. And when you're done, leave more than a quarter for your tip, you old cheapskate." Thelma turned her attention back to the man in the bow tie. Officer Campbell stood stunned in the middle of the cafe, not wanting to retreat from his manly duty, but wanting to keep Thelma on his good side. Thelma gave him a dismissing look.

"Gilbert" she said in a pleasant voice that offered the hapless policeman a momentary reprieve from her attention, "please don't take what I was saying the wrong way. I have nothing against restaurant supplies. I just don't want Wally spending his money foolishly, or you wasting your time." Her smile was downright coquettish.

"You are so considerate madam. Surely you must be new to this area, or how could I have missed the enjoyment of knowing you. What is your name?" Gilbert already had his hand extended. An old trick that he had probably learned in a sales class. Almost no one will avoid shaking your hand once you've extended it. Thelma had no reluctance in taking Gilbert's hand. The handshake lasted unnecessarily long, just like her earlier glance below his belt. Officer Campbell still stood in the middle of the cafe, uncertain whether to go back to his table or to seek to protect Thelma.

"My name's Thelma. I'm the cook here, but I've lived in Thread a long time. You should stop by more often. Maybe we would have been introduced sooner."

"Indeed, indeed," he said, "I surely have made a mistake in that, but there's always time to recover. My next visit will have to be sooner. And perhaps if Wally isn't interested in buying a few jars of mayonnaise or some thousand island dressing, then I could convince you to slip out for a little lunch at the park."

Campbell decided to make his move. It was toward the kitchen door where the two chatterboxes stood. Thelma threw a look that stopped him in his tracks. His face reddened to a hue as vivid as Gilbert's bow tie. Gilbert missed the small drama as he pulled out a pocket watch. "I fear I must be going. Another appointment in Timberton."

Campbell saw a chance to reclaim honor. "That's a fine watch," he said, "I noticed the fob and chain earlier and I was just coming up to ask if I could see the piece itself. I'm quite interested in pocket watches." Thelma snorted. Campbell's face remained bright red. Gilbert seemed oblivious to anything but the compliment toward his watch.

I decided to help out Office Campbell, "The watch is quite lovely. Is it a family heirloom?"

"In a way, I suppose it is. There's quite a story behind it."

Thelma leaned forward, "Why don't you tell us." I looked at her in astonishment. She was always the first to head back in the kitchen whenever Mr. Packer, Bromley or Claire had a story to tell. "If I ever get as silly as Cynthia over all these tired old tales," she once said to me, "take me out in your back garden and shoot me. Bury me there, so at least I can fertilize your tomatoes."

"I thought you hated stories," Officer Campbell said. "Whenever Claire wants to tell a story, you yell 'shut up.'"

"Claire! Would that be Claire Moon?" Gilbert seemed to perk up another notch or two. "I haven't see that old gal in years."

"She's been busy with moon men," muttered Thelma.

"I think Thelma asked if you were one of Moon's men," said Campbell. He smirked and walked back to his coffee. Gilbert looked perplexed. Thelma was momentarily at a loss.

"Do you have time for that story?" I asked. I wanted to help Thelma out. I couldn't imagine what she saw in this cocky little bantam of a man, but she was always looking out for me, and there weren't that many available men in Thread. The hunters and fisherman who flowed through the town were interested in nothing more than a vacation experience. Lusty as Thelma liked to pretend she was, I knew she really wanted someone to replace her Fred, someone dependable who would always be there when she went home. Gilbert didn't seem too likely a candidate, but after hearing his story, maybe she'd realize she needed to look elsewhere.

"If I'm late to meet the manager at the Penokee House, I'll just say there was heavy traffic on 17. Ha! That'd be the day." Gilbert sat down at the stool on the end of the bar nearest the kitchen door. He glanced around the room as though some extra patrons beyond Campbell would suddenly materialize just to hear his story.

"This story begins nearly seventy years ago, right after the great war, the First World War. This was still a lumbering area then, dying down, but it retained a few good camps. Mining had picked up a lot during the War. All in all, it was a healthy area, still drew a lot of immigrants to these woods. They would land at Ellis Island, take the train out to Chicago, and then connect onto the Great Northern Railroad right to Thread, Timberton, and all the towns up here.

"The towns were bigger then, of course, much bigger. There used to be a trolley system that ran all through Timberton down here to Thread and over to Amster. An opera house in Timberton. It was a more glamorous place. That's important to this story, because it involves an immigrant with great ambitions and a singer with great talent. His name was Luigi Santoro. Hers was Flora Johanssen."

"My grandmother came to Timberton with Sarah Bernhardt in the 1890s," Thelma said.

Gilbert smiled at her. "It was over twenty years later that Flora arrived. She came to perform at the opera house too, and that's when she met Luigi."

"It was a sweltering Sunday in early August, middle of the afternoon, with a matinee of *The Student Prince* just ending. A Romberg operetta always attracted a crowd. Romance and passion and good music. Luigi would have preferred a more traditional opera, an Italian one by Verdi perhaps. But to him, light opera was better than no opera, and so he would splurge once a month to attend the Ridge Opera House.

"Flora was in the chorus that day, a bar maiden in the beer hall scene. At least that was the first scene where he noticed her large brown eyes that drank him in. The rest might only be a costume, but those eyes! He couldn't be sure that she would live up to those eyes, but he wanted to know. He desperately needed to know. So quite unlike him, he lingered after the curtain fell. He slowly walked up the short aisle to the rear of the top tier of the balcony; then he came down the narrow steps to the first landing, and then even more slowly down the grand steps that led to the entry foyer. The opera hall was pushed back from the street to allow stores

along the main street. Perhaps you've been there. They show movies now."
Thelma nodded her head in agreement. "So you know there is a long hall,
with an arched fresco ceiling that leads to the street. He looked down that
long corridor, seeing the hot sunlight at its end, and he just couldn't will
himself to take the first step back to the humdrum day. All he could think
of were those eyes. He had to meet the woman behind those eyes.

"But he had never been so daring, to simply linger at a backstage
door and introduce himself to a perfect stranger. Such things were not done
in the old country. And to Luigi, the ways of the old country were religion.
He longed to return home. But first he would have to make his fortune, and
he would have to meet a beautiful woman that would make his old mother
forgive him for the pain he had caused her, that he had left home as a child
to make his way, and that he had never written to his mother in the twelve
years he had been gone.

"But that dream was elusive. Luigi scrimped for years. He worked
many hard hours. All that he had was a small bag of gold twenty dollar
pieces that he kept carefully hidden in his small house on the outskirts of
Timberton. He thought of that little house, with its carefully whitewashed
walls, its well-kept gardens brimming that August with tomatoes and basil,
but all he saw were the scuffed chairs, the patched clothes, the little bag
with a few gold coins. What was he waiting around for? Any woman would
want more than him. Disheartened, he began to walk the long hall.

"'Are you waiting for someone?' he heard. He turned. It was her.
At least it was the eyes that he knew and loved from the performance.
Large, brown, beautiful eyes. She wasn't blonde and she didn't have braids
as she stood beneath the chandelier of the Opera House foyer. Short
auburn hair cut in a pageboy, looking very sophisticated. Her dress barely
covered her knees. A flapper, he thought, his mother would never approve.
But then he noticed that the binding she wore wasn't quite tight enough to
hide a voluptuous bosom. He was smitten."

Officer Campbell looked over at me and rolled his eyes in disbelief.
"I've arrested people for smaller bunco than this," he whispered. I
motioned him to be quiet.

Gilbert continued. "Luigi knew at that very moment that the great
dream of America might still come true for him, but first he had to take the
risk. He had to be willing to overcome his cautious self, to do something
more than he had ever done before. He had to tell a woman what he really

thought. 'I was waiting for you. I love you,' he said.

"It was a simpler time. To be back then once more would be divine. She didn't slap him for being forward. She didn't worry that she would be raped. She blushed at the ardor of this northwoods lumberjack. Small beads of dew appeared on her forehead and she fumbled toward her tiny purse to find a handkerchief.

"But before she could find it, Luigi whipped a huge starched white blanket of a kerchief from his side pocket and presented it with a flourish. As he did so, a pocket watch fell out of that same pocket and fell to the ground, having no fob chain to hold it in place.

"Flora quickly bent and picked it up. 'Oh dear,' she said, " I hope it's not broken. I would feel so dreadful.' Then she looked at it more closely. 'What a beautiful watch,' she said. And indeed it was. You can see for yourself. It was this very same watch you all just admired."

Campbell rolled his eyes once more, "I don't think so."

Thelma shot the officer a withering look. "Wait right here," she said, "let me get some coffee and sticky buns and we can have a good three o'clock coffee while you finish."

So we all sat around the table, drinking coffee, as Gilbert continued his tale.

"Love at first sight is a rare thing. Few of us are willing to believe in it today. But it can happen. It happened that day. Anyone who saw Flora and Luigi together would have known that it was true love. So there was no surprise when Flora did not return to the traveling troupe to continue singing Romberg. Instead she took a small room at the old Comstock Hotel that once stood across the street from the Penokee House. Flora could never have afforded the grandeur of the Penokee House, plus both Luigi and she found it more comforting to meet in the small front parlor of the Comstock in the room lined with faded dusty rose wallpaper, with its old horsehair sofas and drooping ferns on tall stands.

"Luigi wanted to do everything right, which is why they didn't marry at once. He insisted that they have a courtship, and so they did. Each night he came to the Comstock after he finished in the lumber mill, usually bearing some small gifts, a fresh flower, a sweet dessert, a new magazine. Soon she began to drop her flapper ways, and seemed more and more the simple country girl that he wanted.

"At the same time, he grew more adventuresome. One day early in

September, he borrowed a Model T from a co-worker and they drove all the way to Thread, rented a canoe and rowed out to a hidden beach. They say she even convinced him to drop all his clothes on the beach, and together the two swam for hours in the all-together.

"When they came back on to the shore, their pale skin sunburned from the out-of-the-ordinary exposure to the sun, Luigi suddenly became quite agitated. He rummaged frantically through his piled-up clothes. 'What is it?' Flora cried out. He didn't answer. He just continued to search. Flora ran up from the beach, her breasts bouncing in the sunlight. 'Tell me what the problem is. What is wrong?' he still didn't answer.

"Luigi got down on his hands and knees and began running his hands through the tall grass, back and forth, crisscrossing the meadow. Suddenly, he fell back against the grass, his legs splayed out against the green, his arm spiking into the sky, with a glint of gold from within the clenched fist. 'My watch,' he said, 'I though I had lost the watch.'

"Flora began to pummel him. 'Why did you scare me so?' she demanded, 'I thought it was something important. You frightened me half to death.' Gradually, her punches became softer, more playful, and he began to punch back like a cat batting at ball of thread. Before you know it, they were rolling across that meadow, burning their private skin to a nasty red.

"It was that day that they knew they truly were in love, and that meeting in the parlor of the Comstock must come to an end. It was time to get married. As they made the long drive back to Timberton, and it was a long drive in those days since the roads were not nearly so good, Flora asked Luigi why the watch was so important. And he told her the story. It had been a gift from his dear mother the day before he left southern Italy. It had been the last gift that he had ever received from his mother. She had made great sacrifices to save enough money to buy the watch. He had always felt guilty that after receiving such a magnificent birthday gift, he was still able to leave his home, without telling his mother, to make his way to America and to what he hoped would be a great fortune. The watch was his only tie back to his past, the only link to his dream that stayed with him as he lay sick to his stomach in the steerage of the slow ship from Naples to New York, his passion as he worked twelve-hour days throughout the harsh Wisconsin winters, the hope that he would meet a woman who would make him happy and create a life of prosperity. Once that happened, then he would be able to return to southern Italy, to tell his mother once more that he loved her, to seek her forgiveness and to tell his dear mother how much the watch had meant to him through all the years in America.

"Flora was touched, as who could not be? 'We will go back one day,' she said. 'We can go back any day you want because as far as I can see, you are the wealthiest man there is. Why? Because you are filled with love and happiness.'

"Luigi shook his head slowly in disagreement. 'I am not even worthy of letting you into my life. We should not get married, but I can not live without you.' He was silent for the rest of the drive to his little home. When he pulled the Model T into the rutted driveway of his little whitewashed cottage, a golden collie came running from behind the outhouse, barking joyously. The dog was named Spot, a name Luigi had chosen because it seemed so American. Before there was Flora, Spot was the only thing that Luigi had truly loved in America. Another animal might have been jealous when a new love had appeared. But not Spot. He adored his master, and therefore he adored everything important to his master. Another woman might have wanted her husband-to-be to give away a dog that had played such an important part of his life. But not Flora. Each, in fact, adored the other. And Luigi adored them both.

"But that night, the wagging tail of Spot and the beautiful eyes of Flora were not enough to pull Luigi from his melancholy. The near loss of his watch made him realize how very little he had in material things. The more he reflected on it, the more uneasy he became. It was wrong to marry Flora unless he had more to offer. Unless he were to make a fortune soon, he would never be able to afford to return to the old country and see his mother one last time.

"He paced the small front parlor, while Flora sat in his one good chair, with Spot at her feet. She petted the dog, who acted concerned over Luigi's behavior. Finally, Luigi went into his bedroom and after much noise and banging about, he came back into the parlor carrying a velvet bag. 'Count them,' he demanded.

"'Count what?' she asked.

"'My gold coins,' he replied. And so she did. It wasn't a large bag. It didn't take long. She did it as slowly as she could. She wanted the count to last longer than it did. But there were only twenty-seven gold twenty-dollar coins in the purse. Five hundred and forty dollars. It was more money than Flora had ever seen. In fact, she thought it a small fortune. She knew that many of the men in the woods only made a dollar or two a day. Yet she sensed that no matter what she would say to Luigi, he would contradict her. She could see in his face that he considered the small count a mark of failure.

'How many?' he whispered.

"'Twenty-seven,' she said in a low voice, unwilling to look into his face, knowing that she should, but yet unable to raise her eyes that fraction of an inch.

"'It's not enough,' he said. 'I have to find a way to make more. I did not come to America to be poor.'

"Flora stared at the small pile of gold coins, the value of it gradually cascading into her mind, and she begin to think of the many despicable characters she had encountered in the rough and tumble lumbering and mining town. 'You should put this in a bank,' she said. 'Does anyone know you have so much money in the house? It's not safe.'

"'It's safe,' he replied. 'There's not enough worth stealing.' Flora remained still. The joy of the afternoon on the shore was quickly receding into a tiny wave, dying out into the tiniest of ripples. They both sat quietly in the room for many minutes, Flora sitting on the good chair, Luigi sitting cross-legged on the braided rag rug atop the golden soft pine floor. Finally, slowly, he began to pick up each gold eagle, looking at it carefully as he dropped it back into his bag. When finally all twenty-seven were once more in the bag, he stood up and went into the bedroom. He didn't close the door. Flora could see him pry up one of the loose floorboards and put the bag below it. He came back into the room. 'It's time you went back to the Comstock, and I need to return the car.' The evening ended.

"It was only a week later, after they had announced in the *Timberton Mining News* classifieds the joy of their engagement, that Luigi came running to Flora filled with excitement. He had finally come into a secret opportunity that would make all his dreams come true. He had met someone at one of the small bars that lined Silver Street who could make him rich, a person with knowledge of a mine lined with copper ore, a vein so rich in copper that its wealth would make everyone who came into contact with it a millionaire. All this new-found friend needed was some money to help him buy the mineral rights to the land and set up the initial cut. If Luigi could provide him with that seed money, then the two of them could become partners. They would roll in the cash that would follow.

"Flora was not a foolish woman. She had worked a few cons in her own tumultuous lifetime. She recognized this tale for what it was—a fantasy for rubes, intended to unknot their pursestrings and send the coins tumbling in the direction of the weaver of the tale. She tried to warn Luigi that the deal could not possibly be true, and that the person would only take his money and never be seen again. But Luigi insisted the man was to be believed.

"They argued late into the night. Spot crept out of the small cottage and hunkered down against the tilled garden dirt of Luigi's prized tomatoes. He whined ever so low. But the cabin was far from any neighbor, and the only people who could hear Spot's anguish were Luigi and Flora, each of whom were determined to change the mind of the other. Neither had time to worry over a dog.

"Finally, Flora gave up on Luigi in dismay. But before she left, she exacted one promise from her fiancé. 'Vow to me on your mother's heart,' she said, 'that you will not spend any of your money with this man whom you only met today until we talk again.'

"Luigi took out his mother's watch, this beautiful gold pocket watch that I have with me now, and he set it into the palm of his hand. He was so nervous that his heartbeat was almost as loud as the ticking of the watch. He believed that on one hand he had waiting for him the beautiful woman he had vowed to meet and love forever. On the other hand, he finally had the opportunity to rise above the poverty that had been with him all of his life. But the two were in conflict. He wanted both. But it appeared he couldn't have one without losing the other.

He held the watch in his unsteady hand, looking straight into the beautiful eyes of the woman he loved so much. 'This watch is like my mother," he said, 'it will never leave my heart. And on this watch, I vow to you tonight that I will obey your wishes. I will not give any of my money to this man before we talk again tomorrow.'

"Flora left, feeling comforted that he had made this promise. She knew Luigi to be a strong Catholic and a man of his word. But late in the night—in fact, it was already near morning and the sun was only an hour from rising—she awoke in a panic of anxiety and thought about the vow Luigi had made. He said he would not give the money, but he had never thought of the transaction as giving the money away. He was investing it, loaning it. Would he still loan that horrible grifter the money he had? And if he did, would he think somehow in his Catholic heart that he had not given it away? Would he still feel secure that he could go to confession on Saturday night, and have no sin to confess? Would he feel he had not in any way compromised his mother? Flora fretted and could not go back to sleep. Soon, roosters, kept by those families who raised a few chickens for eggs, were beginning to crow, welcoming the sun rising in the east. The morning light flooded through the lace curtains of her little room in the Comstock. The faded wallpaper seemed to glow in the early morning rays, and Flora began to fret that she was thinking unfairly of Luigi. He loved her. He would never lie to her, never mislead her. He meant what he had said. There was still time during this coming evening to convince him to avoid the grifter.

"She spent the day with a calm heart, looking forward to the evening, preparing her arguments to convince Luigi to do the sensible thing. More than that, she began to see that it was essential for her to make him realize that he was already prosperous in all ways that counted. He had a small home, a woman who loved him, a nest egg for emergencies. He had so much more than most men.

"She took the street car to the last stop, and then walked down the dry country road that led to his small cottage. It was a beautiful early autumn evening. The roadside ditch was lined with tall purple thistle and goldenrod. Butterflies were flitting to and fro. Evening birds were beginning their night songs.

"She arrived at his cottage. There was something wrong. Spot did not run out to meet her. Luigi was nowhere to be seen. She walked through his small house. He was not there. There was no note on the kitchen table. She went out to his garden, certain that Luigi would be weeding or picking fresh tomatoes from his low-lying vines. He was not there. Spot was.

"Spot was hunkering down over an area of the worked garden dirt, his body low to the ground. The dog kept crying, moaning. She tried to pull him away, but Spot refused to move; he just kept whimpering. She sat down beside the collie, wondering what was wrong. They waited for Luigi to return.

"Luigi did not return.

"He did not return that evening. He did not return the next day. He did not return in a week. He did not return in two weeks.

"During all of that time, Spot never left the garden. He stayed low to the ground, sometimes pawing it, as though seeking Luigi through the dirt. Flora would bring the dog water and food. Sometimes, he would pay attention to her offerings. More often than not, he would only keep his head to the ground. Some evenings, Flora would sit in the garden with Spot and weed between the rows, stake up the tomatoes, pick the ripening corn. She would bring it back with her to the Comstock and let her tears of fear fall over the bounty.

"After that first evening when Luigi had not returned, she became convinced that something horrible had happened to the man she loved. When he had not returned the second day, she became certain it had something to do with the grifter who had wanted Luigi to partner on the secret mine. She wished so desperately that she had pressed Luigi for more details of what the man looked like or where he had lived. Had he taken the gold and then killed Luigi, she wondered?

"She ransacked Luigi's cottage looking for his sack of gold coins. She knocked at all of the floor boards until she found the one that was loose. When she pulled it up, the space below was empty, a few dusty webs and nothing more. But she refused to believe what the emptiness portended. So she yanked up every board, until all that remained were a few boards on which the furniture stood. There was nothing below any of the boards. The gold was gone. As gone as Luigi.

"One evening Flora sat in the dying light looking out the windows of the little cottage, looking at where the garden cornstalks stood in the dim evening gloom. There was a portent of frost in the air. She could see the sorrowing body of Spot, who had not barked in joy in weeks, an animal which seldom left his grieving location for more than a few minutes during the day. Suddenly she knew where Luigi was. In that autumn instant, she knew what had happened.

"But how was she to convince the sheriff that she was right? She was a show girl and they paid no attention to her when she showed up with her fantastic tale of the missing Luigi. Luigi had become frightened of marriage and ran off was their surmise. But, no, she insisted, he was robbed and murdered. He was buried in his own garden. She insisted that was why Spot wouldn't leave the garden. He knew his master was there, buried beneath the soil he had loved. The sheriff just laughed.

"One day, Flora overheard a story of a pawn shop that had a

beautiful watch with an inscription in Italian. Some stranger had pawned it about the time Luigi had disappeared. The people were joking, that it had been Luigi himself, gathering more money so he could run off and avoid marriage. She raced to the pawn shop to see for herself, but the shopkeeper said the watch had been bought by someone from out of town earlier in the week. Flora could take no more. She heard the other guests at the Comstock snicker when she walked in.

"She knew what she had to do.

"She was going to dig up the garden herself. She knew a murdered Luigi had to be buried there. Spot had told her by his loyal actions. She began digging. The driver of the street car could see her digging from the crest of the hill where the street car line ended. When he got back to Silver Street he told everyone what that crazy Flora was doing. But not everyone was amused. Many had wondered themselves if Luigi might not have met a foul end. There were the ones who had seen just how much the man loved Flora. They never quite believed that he could have run off without so much as a fare-thee-well.

"So first one, then another, picked up their own shovel or pick, and caught the street car to the end of the line. They walked up that country lane and past the little cottage. None of them said a word to Flora. They just started digging. Spot began to howl in a mournful way, a way that sent shivers up the backs of all those who were digging. But the townspeople did not stop, not even when the sun went down, and the mosquitoes and chill of the night came out in force. The bites began to swell in their damp sweat and yet they kept digging. But as the full moon rose over the sight, it was clear that the entire garden had been dug and redug, and there was no body. There was no murdered Luigi. Yet Spot still sat and howled.

"Flora fell to the ground and began crying. One by one, each who had come out to help her dig left to return on the same street car that had carried them out.

"Flora never saw Luigi again. Never heard from him, never heard of him. The watch never appeared. The twenty-seven gold coins had vanished into another era. Spot never left the garden. He lived a full year, with Flora bringing him water and food daily. People said that you had never seen a more loyal and frightened animal. Then he died in the garden and Flora buried him in the very place he had guarded so loyally through four seasons. Flora, never married, eventually died too, never knowing why her happiness had disappeared that fall."

Gilbert sat silently for a moment, his tale finished. He took a last bite of his sticky bun and a sip of the now cold coffee. He looked over at Thelma, who looked back at him, her eyes brimming with tears. For once, she had nothing to say and no laughter to ignite the crowd.

Campbell harrumphed. "You just made that whole story up, and you couldn't even keep your lies straight. If no one ever heard of Luigi again, then how did you end up with that watch of his?"

Gilbert smiled, "It's like this, you see. Years ago I bought Luigi's cottage. Of course, it was already many years after he was gone, but just before Flora died. I met her and she told me the tale during one long winter evening."

"But what about the watch," Campbell persisted.

"That came later when I lost my house to a land collapse. You know how they didn't properly buttress some of the old mines, and how time and water has weakened them, until they sometimes collapse in on themselves. That happened to my land. Old Luigi's place had been built on top of a mine everyone had forgotten. One of the first mines. What they say is that it never was much of a mine. But it collapsed some ten years back or so, and took my house with it. The collapse created quite a bowl, and at the bottom a little pond formed. They said it was water streaming out of the old flooded mine.

"That water stayed there most of the summer. But by fall it had all dried up. And I went walking down along the bottom of that little pond now shrunken to a tiny puddle. It was right about where old Luigi would have had his garden. Lots of little things had rushed up with the water when it had flooded out after the collapse. Pieces of wood, old mining bolts and the like. And then I saw a flash of gold.

"It was this watch. It had come up from the ground. Brought it to a jeweler to have it shined and oiled, and it's been working ever since."

"But where did it come from?" Thelma asked.

"The way I see it," Gilbert said, "is that it came from Luigi. I think he got snookered into going into that old abandoned mine by the con man he had met, who probably robbed him of his gold coins and knocked him dead. Probably didn't know that he had killed the man right below the very spot that Luigi gardened. But the dog Spot knew. He knew his master was dead below his feet, even though the body was a hundred feet down.

Somehow the dog knew. And he never left his master's side.

"I only wish Flora had known that Luigi had never left her, that he had been there with her all those nights she sat in the garden."

Gilbert stood up. "I really must go. It's been a pleasure, Thelma, I look forward to seeing you again." Thelma smiled.

I looked out as Gilbert walked out the cafe, across the square, got into his big shiny new car and drove off. "I wonder what the point of that story was," I mused.

"Don't go looking for meanings," Thelma snarled, "it just shows to go you. Nothing more."

CHAPTER EIGHT

At the beginning of September, the days were already shortening with shadows grown long. Chip Frozen Bear invited me to his home and to attend the Lattigo PowWow. I didn't really want to go because I was afraid he would try to talk about the van Elkind business. Yet I was excited to see Chip in his native surroundings.

Dusk was nestling in as I drove into Lattigo. The sickly pines in the marshlands beside the Lattigo trunk road cast spiky narrow silhouettes across the cracked blacktop. The first streetlight sputtered into fluorescence just as I passed the welcoming sign that read "Lattigo. Population: 626." Ironic that Lattigo was a true village in the eyes of the government, warranting an official population count on its sign. Thread, larger and slightly more prosperous, had never managed such official status. Its state sign simply read: "Thread. Unincorporated." When I left Thread for college over a decade earlier, Lattigo had also been in that same netherstate, neither village nor city, merely a collection of houses. When had it changed?

Chip had instructed me to drive through town and turn left at the fork just south of town. I was to pass the sign pointing to the site for the PowWow, and go to the next house. There I would meet his sister and the three of us would take the ten-minute walk through the woods to the dance site.

The village of Lattigo was depressing and had little in the way of business: a small general store, a post office, a cafe, a souvenir shop or two. Not many tourists ventured down the twisty, bumpy road. All the commercial buildings were rundown with peeling paint and an air of unprofitability. Unlike every other Wisconsin village, not a bar was in sight.

After passing through town, I kept my eye out for the fork in the road. I had been warned I might easily miss it. I saw the badly weathered signboard for the PowWow, half-hidden in blazing red sumac. Its letters were so nearly obliterated by time that a casual observer might think they had encountered an obscure message in baby talk: *at go ow ow*, instead of Lattigo PowWow.

But Chip was playing games with me. He had neglected to mention the massive, brand new industrial complex, with a large backlit sign at its entrance that read Lattigo Electronics. What was this?

I turned left at the not-at-all-hard-to-find fork and drove slowly by this unexpected plant with its three separate buildings. There was a two-story, contemporary office building covered in vertical red cedar siding, with four ground-to-roof columns of weathered fieldstone that bubbled up from the ground to anchor the roof. A lush lawn encircled this building, and behind it was a broad expanse of gravel intended for parking. Behind that were two pole-and-steel buildings, typical inexpensive construction designed for manufacturing processes. When had this been built?

Suddenly I was at the driveway of the Frozen Bear property. A graceful curving gravel path led up a gentle hill to a sheltered two-story modern log cabin, in which every window cast a welcoming yellow glow into the growing twilight. A pair of Norwegian elkhounds came bounding to meet the car, their silvery black curved tails wagging furiously to and fro. I stepped from my car, just as Chip walked out of the house. He sensed my admiration.

"Not what you would expect in Lattigo, is it?" he stated briskly, but without his usual sardonic air. "You know I stayed east for a few years before I came back home and I put my Columbia MBA to work on Wall Street. Did pretty well, but like you, I wanted to come home," he smiled.

"And the factory. Is that yours?" I asked.

"Not quite a factory yet. And, as a member of the Lattigo, yes, it's mine. Not personally. It's a tribal investment, with some venture capital funding from people I know in New York, including Haligent who you met. It's a disk duplicating and fulfillment center for software companies, mostly small ones, who want one place to handle the entire manufacturing, inventory and shipping process. With the contracts we have in place, we'll hire about one hundred and ten people over the next few months. A small step to ending the unemployment on this reservation."

I was perplexed. "If you're able to do this, why get involved with American Seasons? It'll destroy this environment. Maybe your people can get rich, but are you creating the right kind of heritage for them?" I had been thinking a lot about Van Elkind and his scheme. Maybe it wasn't such a good thing to be involved with.

"Perhaps you can help me keep that from happening," he smiled enigmatically. "Come into the house and meet my sister. We need to leave right away, or you'll miss the big opening dance."

The living room was spacious with an open-beamed ceiling. The furniture was low, plump and substantial. Large plate glass windows looked over a small stream near the base of the hill. "This is one of the few spots on the entire reservation that isn't a marsh," he said quietly.

"So why did you come back?" a calm voice said from behind me. If Chip were a casting agent's dream of a handsome Indian brave, then his sister was simply that same agent's finest fantasy. Tall, slender, with clean lines. Dark long hair, dark eyes and controlled self-confidence.

"I'm Jacqueline Grant," she said, extending her hand. "You must be Walter Pearson, and I'm delighted that you could come." I took her hand, but said nothing. I didn't know what to say. "I really don't understand why Chip wants you to see this PowWow. He hates them and finds them degrading. Or so Chip says. He believes we must be true to our heritage. That's why he calls himself Frozen Bear, instead of Grant. Even though we have been Grants since the time of Ulysses S. Grant. My great-grandfather met President Grant in the 1870s and was so impressed by the man, he decided to call himself Grant. But Chip doesn't prefer to honor that part of the heritage. I guess the ancestors involved aren't ancient enough."

Chip looked indulgently at his sister. Clearly, they had had this conversation before. "Great Grandfather Grant sold out our tribe at the same time he sold out our name. He signed the final treaty that stuck us on this god-forsaken swamp."

"What other choice did he have? To leave us with nothing? It was a different world then. We weren't even citizens. We didn't have the right to vote. Northern Wisconsin was overrun with robber barons looking for new worlds to plunder. There were forests to cut. Mines to dig. Lakes to fish to exhaustion. What did a few hundred Native Americans mean to them? What did it mean in the Dakotas? Sure, our people took care of Custer. But

129

then what? The Sioux are on lands no better than this. Worse in fact. They're not called the Badlands for nothing. I say it's time to look forward," she sighed. "Let's get to the dance, or Walter will have missed his reason for coming."

Chip turned to me, "If we were all like my sister Jacqueline, we would simply be frozen into inaction. She wants to be a Native American, and yet she does not. She hates what has been done to us, and yet she accepts it. She wants to reverse it all, and yet she acquiesces. I won't do that. I know you wonder why I cooperate with Van Elkind and his modern-day robber barons. But I won't let them rob us again. Unlike my great-grandfather, I know survival is not found in mimicking the oppressor. You must use their own ways to trap them.

"Let's go to the PowWow." He closed the discussion and opened the door.

"Wasn't it awful?" Cynthia asked the following morning. "The last time I went to a PowWow, the music was dreadful, just a loud noisy steady beat. And the costumes were so sad. Not at all like our costume for Nanoonkoo."

"Did someone mention Nanoonkoo?" Claire piped in. She had shown up this morning with a tiny jar of wild strawberry jam. She claimed it had been left behind the previous evening by a new group of visitors. They were able, she claimed, to create any type of food in a special "transmogrifier." I asked if I could order one of the thingamajigs for my restaurant. She cast a scornful look and demanded a new cup for her coffee claiming there was a lipstick stain on the one she had been given. The stain looked suspiciously close to her own tone of lipstick.

"Claire," Cynthia began, trying again, "it's not about Nanoonkoo. It's about trying to do better. You know that all of us in Thread try very hard to do things the very best way we can. And it just doesn't seem that way at all in Lattigo. Daddy won't even let me go there."

"Didn't you want to go with me when Frozen Bear asked," I reminded her. She had been serving him dinner when he asked me, and she had done everything but insist that he invite her too. He did not take her hints.

Cynthia blushed and walked toward the coffee and hot water stand. "Claire, do you want some more hot water for your tea?" she asked.

Cynthia was right. There had been something unpleasant about the PowWow. I still didn't understand why Frozen Bear invited me. In fact, I didn't understand why he didn't force an end to the tourist event.

Although it had been the Saturday of a beautiful fall weekend, there were only a score or so of tourists in the audience, taking up less than a tenth of the open air amphitheater. The wooden benches of the bowl had not been properly maintained since the building of the PowWow Bowl decades earlier. Many were either half-rotted or split. One quadrant of the theater seemed completely abandoned and roped off. Giant thistles thrust up between the bleacher rows.

The row of theater lights dimmed, then stuttered out. A single pinlight illuminated the very center of the stage. A block of dry ice was opened to the air and a few weak tendrils of carbon dioxide fog snaked across the bottom of the stage. A ponderous voice boomed from a scratchy p.a. system. "Before there was the United States, before there was Columbus or even Leif Erickson, there was" (momentous pause, crescendo of music) "the Lattigo and the PowWow. We invite you tonight to engage in the mysteries of the Indian PowWow." It only got worse from there. The dancers were too few and unpracticed. The dances seemed choreographed out of a bad Hollywood B-movie. The tourists were visibly unimpressed.

As Chip, Jacqueline, and I rose from our seats, we could see the Lattigo dancers streaming out from the small dressing room near the amphitheater. They seemed anxious to avoid Frozen Bear's eye.

"We shouldn't be doing this," he said, "but it's like religion. It serves a principle in continuing traditions and in setting a compass. But like religion it can become divisive and an excuse for not thinking. It cloaks many motives and can hide many truths. Why else does a town as small as Thread need so many churches? In the end tradition can snare us in a degrading trap, and the rope pulls tighter with every move. But why release the trap before you have a safe place to go to? And why release the trap if you can turn it on the trapper?"

"Are you a trap or a trapper, Wally? Don't get too close to Van Elkind and his group. You could get hurt." We had arrived back at the Frozen Bear home. He simply walked in without inviting me to follow or saying good night. Jacqueline looked at me before following her brother through the door.

"He means what he says," she said.

"But I don't understand what he's saying," I replied.

"Does it matter? Just know that he means it."

I survived the PowWow, but I was still pondering Chip's final words as I watched Cynthia bring Claire a fresh pot of hot water. Already there was lipstick on Claire's new cup. And from this angle, I could see a sticker still left on her tiny jar of wild strawberry jam. It said "Knott's." An intergalactic brand, I guessed.

Thelma came out of the kitchen with her hands covered in flour. "Has that Gilbert Ford fellow shown up yet," she demanded. She was wearing blush which didn't seem appropriate to her.

"What's that smell?" I asked. There was a hint of sandalwood and gardenia mixed with yeast and flour as she walked by. "Are you wearing perfume?"

"What's it to you? I just want to know if that Gilbert Ford has shown up yet with my delivery of goods. I need the canned apples for tonight's pies."

"What canned apples?" I demanded. "You're using those fresh apples we got from Door County. What are you doing with canned apples?"

"Canned apples make for a faster pie, and no one can tell the difference," Thelma plumped herself onto a stool by the bar. "Hey, Cynthia, bring me a cup of that coffee. I think it's time for a break from the heat."

"I can tell if we use canned apples. So can our customers." I wasn't about to relent.

"You couldn't tell two nights ago, when I used canned apples in the apple crisp," she retorted.

"What . . . " I began, but Cynthia cut me off, asking, "So Thelma, do you have the sweets for Gilbert."

"Well, he is kind of nice, but there's no need letting him know that," she said with a shake of her head toward me. "He don't understand romance. It's because he's never had it himself. Kind of a gelded calf, you know—always ready to go bucking up his heels in the fresh green grass, but don't really understand the emotions of the heart and all. He's kind of simple in that respect. Sort of like our Wally." I didn't like the way this was going. "Wally thinks everyone's like him. Honest, nice, understanding, trustworthy—all that stuff. And I guess he thinks everyone's like him in that they don't need or want somebody in their lives. Well, I miss my Fred, even though he's been dead four years now. I miss having him in bed at night. I miss turning over, and him turning over too and flinging that big hairy arm he had around my body and pulling me tight to him, even when it was hot at night. And I miss a lot more.

"So when I see somebody nice that I think is nice looking, and who seems to take a hankering toward me, then I want to pay attention. And I want him to notice me. So maybe I do have perfume on. Big deal."

Thelma was wrong. I did have something I missed, someone who once protected and sheltered me. But this town didn't need to know about my mistakes.

Claire picked up her cup and moved to sit at the counter next to Thelma. Cynthia was standing behind the counter with her coffee pot, ready to pour Thelma a fresh cup, just so she could hear every word. I was stranded in the middle of the dining room, feeling attacked.

"You know," Thelma continued, "there's two people in this town who are really sad. I can say this because Danny's not working today. One of them is Danny's father Toivo. The other is the Reverend Willy. The Reverend Willy is sad because he is all wrapped up in himself and his mistakes. Maybe he don't even know how warped he's become. Or maybe he does. Maybe that's why he goes to church three times a Sunday." One of these days I was going to meet this Reverend Willy.

"But Toivo . . . he's sad in a different way. He knows what he's had, and he knows what he's lost. He knows what it means to be bigger because someone has become part of you, and you part of her. Lempi and Toivo are what all of us should want to be. I used to know people who would drive into town late in the evening, just because they wanted to see the two of them walking down the road, hand in hand, like they did every night. Because there was love in their walk, and you could see it. You could feel it. I know it's not good that Toivo can't let go of that love, that he sits there in the cemetery every evening talking to a memory of a woman long gone, a woman who can't never come back. Because you know there's no such thing as a ghost that lingers around to give us comfort. But you know in a way I wouldn't mind being Toivo. I mean I wouldn't mind having a Toivo. Not to replace Fred. Fred can't be replaced. But to have a light in my life again. You can't live without that light. Maybe Wally, you can. I can't."

Cynthia clapped her hands. "That was so beautiful Thelma. I just wish someday that I have a Fred or a Toivo in my life. Instead of that Kip." Her eyes threw daggers in my direction. Ever since school had restarted and she had discovered Kip had stayed in town, she found every excuse to accuse me. But I paid no attention. I was still wondering if I could live without my own light for the rest of my life.

I had left Manhattan to keep from thinking about things. But now in Thread, I had more things than ever to think about. There was keeping the business going, and how to pay Thelma, Cynthia and Danny every week. There was the way I had become ensnared in Van Elkind's business for no good reason. I kept reflecting on Chip's comments on all of Thread's churches, and how they weren't enough to solve the problems of Reverend Willy?

Why did I still not know this man? Was Reverend Willy a nickname for one of the preachers at the local churches? But which one?

There was Our Lady of the Rushes Catholic Church. But that church's leader would have to be a Father Willy, not a Reverend Willy.

Then there was the Holy Rollers Spiritual Church of Christ. As a teenager, I found it daring to sneak by the old log cabin church, built before the rest of the town. For most of the week, the building sat empty, dark and moss-covered, faintly reeking of the decaying swamp from which the cedar logs had been cut. But on Saturday night, lights blazed and rolling organ music fled from the windows. Singing and chanting echoed into the woods. A Reverend Willy could belong there, maybe.

Closer to my life were the three Lutheran churches. Each had its own anemic following. Once there had been only one Lutheran church. But that had proved to be insufficient.

Like so many things in town, it started with the Truehearts. Since they owned the material life of the town, they saw no reason not to own its spiritual life. But when the original Lutheran pastor refused to allow Big John to hold a bake sale years ago for his plan to build the town's first giant wooden loon mascot, the family quickly determined the old curmudgeon was under the control of Rome. There was no alternative but to build their own church. And when the Truehearts build a church, people come to pray and pay. Thus, the Reformed Lutheran Church of Thread was born.

All would have been fine in the Lutheran world if it hadn't been for the Second World War. Since America won, the country was faced with the problem of coping with millions of displaced persons from central and northern Europe. Part of the solution was to ship several score to Northern Wisconsin where they could be conveniently forgotten. They arrived with their kielbasa and kerchiefs and sat appalled in the first Lutheran Church. Where were there conservative traditions? So the next Sunday they promptly trooped to the Trueheart church. Again, they were appalled. And so was born the Old World Lutheran Church.

In a town that had never seen its population hit one thousand, each Sunday morning rang forth with the warring carillons of Lutheran bells at nine, ten and eleven. It would be immensely fitting in my opinion that at least one, if not all three Lutheran churches, were to house the offices of Reverend Willy.

My parents could never decide which of the three churches they should join. We played religious musical chairs, moving from pew to pew, church to church, each Sunday of my childhood in Thread.

That left only one church. The so-called church of the Summer Folk, or more accurately the non-denominational Chapel of the Wooded Glen, governed each summer by yet another soon-to-be graduate of some theological institute back East. The only people who attended its services were the rich vacationers from Chicago and Milwaukee whose wealth had somehow made them grow beyond memory of their immigrant religious roots. I am sure Henry and Rita van Elkind attended this church. Reverend Willy. Yes I could see a Reverend Willy at one of those churches. Perhaps a female Reverend Willy. Maybe that's why everyone was so tightlipped. A babe in the pulpit. A Wilhelmina, perhaps. Sister Willy to some.

There was a chill in the air. "Wally, I hate you!" Cynthia cried out. An ill wind blew dust eddies in the town square. "How could you do this to me?" A squadron of geese flew in 'V' formation high above the town, silently fleeing south. "You know how much I hate Kip. Now he's in every one of my classes." The town's sole school bus headed south on Highway 17, a yellow box getting out of town. Over the past few weeks, Cynthia had become more and more convinced I was responsible for Henry's decision to leave his only son in Thread. She was always at her most accusing right after getting out of school and coming to work.

"I'm sure Wally didn't mean to do it," Danny said, wincing in expectation even as he tied his apron and edged back into the kitchen doorway. He looked more and more tired as each day of his senior year passed. I was worried about the boy.

"Didn't mean it?" Cynthia countered in a near scream. She collapsed into an empty chair at the bar where Bromley, Claire, and Mr. Packer were finishing their three o'clock coffee. She set her head in her hands and rested both hands and head on the counter. She broke into heavy sobs. Coffee sloshed over the edges of the cups. Claire looked anxious.

"Kip?" Bromley demanded. "Is he one of those god darn Indian kids. Keep trying to integrate these schools, but I tell you it's no good. Washington knew what it was doing when it set up these reservations. There's no need mixing. You know," he began in a near whisper, "I hear those redskins are up to something sneaky down there in Lattigo. My friends in Madison tell me the Lattigo have been spending a lot of time down there with the state attorney general. Don't know what they're up to, but you can count on me to keep my eyes open. I'll keep this town safe."

It didn't seem worth the effort to remind Bromley that Kip was the Van Elkind son. That would only set him off on some other theory about Henry Van Elkind. Anyway, Cynthia would soon start to return to her sunny self.

"This morning my men were telling me that," Claire said, "they might begin to execute that plan they've been working on for so long. You know to invade the Earth and take over. It's the fish they want. Especially the giant muskie. It's a delicacy back on their planet. But the fish don't survive that star trip back. And even when they take eggs, they never hatch. So they have to catch them here, freeze them and transport them home. That's why the fishin's getting worse, you know. Don't you go looking at me like that Mr. Packer. I know what I'm talking about. And if they do take over, they're going to put people like you on a reservation. Mark my words. They'll be no fishing from the top of a spaceship."

Mr. Packer just picked up his coffee cup. Cynthia suddenly stood as she presssed her fists onto the bar. Bromley's cup tipped further, spilling hot coffee into his expansive lap. He yelped, quickly rose and headed to the restroom. "What about Kip and what I was talking about. None of you care about me!"

"Cynthia," I said, "I never meant for Van Elkind to have Kip spend all winter in

Thread. And since when does Van Elkind ever listen to me? We were just talking one day and the idea sparked. That's how things work."

"Your idea's for real now," said Danny. "Kip's here for the duration. He saunters through school like he owns it. Just because he's richer than everybody else don't mean he's special."

"I feel slimy," Cynthia said, "because he never stops looking at me. And if I try to glare at him to make him stop, he just smirks. He looks like he has a cigarette dangling from the corner of his lip even when he doesn't."

"And it looks like he stuffs a sock in his pants," Danny joked.

"It sure ain't real," yelled Thelma from the kitchen. It was a rare day when Thelma didn't have the time to keep up with a conversation in the dining room even as she prepared for the dinner time crowd, such as it was.

"What are they talking about?" asked Claire, looking straight at Mr. Packer and ignoring Bromley back from the rest room and still muttering to himself about Indians.

Cynthia stood suddenly and walked toward the door. "Pastor Mall," she said, with some alarm. "No one saw you come in."

The man in the white collar ignored Cynthia but spoke grandly to all of us, "I wanted to stop by and introduce myself. I'm Pastor Paul Mall." I thought perhaps I should ask him about Reverend Willy, but he was apparently new to town and no doubt had other things on his mind.

"They tell me you serve alcohol in this establishment."

Of course, I did. It was the secret to my success.

"The demon drink must stop. I've been called to the Old World Lutheran Church here in Thread, and I'm deeply offended by all I see. Such sin. Such degradation. And so many Catholics. Not enough true Christians. There are those who think the Pope is the Anti-Christ. Now, I am not one of those people. I am an open man, but when a town has more sins . . . "

For the first time, the man looked around the cafe and he spied the mayor and his cohorts. "Mayor Bastique! I am shocked that you would be sitting in a place that serves alcohol." Bromley twisted in his seat, although it may have been more the result of the drying wet spot from the coffee spill, then from the pastor's disapproval. Although it may also have been the presence of some ladies from the Old World Luthern Church having a late lunch in the corner. Bromley liked to keep everyone on his side.

Claire stood up and waddled over to Pastor Paul Mall. "I'm Claire Moon," she said, extending her hand.

"I've heard of you," he muttered, ignoring the proffered hand.

The man was of middling height, heavy, and triple-chinned. His hair was cropped close to the skull, almost military in style, and gone silver with years. He appeared to be in his fifties, but it was hard to tell because there was a childish softness about him, as though made of clay stretched to whatever size and shape was needed. Although dressed in black slacks, with a black shirt and white clerical collar, something about his manner seemed better suited to pumping gas or handing out shoes at a bowling alley.

"This is a resort town," I began.

"Indeed it is, but that is no excuse," he replied.

"Please let me finish," I complained.

"No need to," he said. "I know what you're going to say before you say it. You're going to claim that because this a resort town, people are here to have fun, to relax, to enjoy life a little.

"But God should be your relaxation. God and hard work. When I heard that the synod had sent me a calling to a little town in the northwoods, I was distressed for a moment, but only a moment, because then I realized that God was testing me. He was sending me to a place where they did not know Him. Oh, you may think you know Him, but you can not know Him as I know Him."

"Knowing God. Do you mean that in the biblical sense?" asked Mr. Packer, without an ever-so slight smile on his face.

During this exchange, Chip Frozen Bear had entered the cafe and had been standing near the entrance listening to the Reverend. "As a child, I was told God made this country for my people," Frozen Bear said. "And I prefer to continue to believe that. And a town this size needs every business it can get. I'm not so sure about the churches."

Mall sidled to the door, staying as far from Chip as he could, looking at him as though he were dressed in full warpaint and attack regalia. "Don't think you can avoid this." He pointed his finger at me as he walked out into the street. I watched him head toward Happy's Northern Nights on the other side of the square, no doubt to continue his crusade. If Happy Thorp were in, the Reverend Mall would be thrown back into the square within ten minutes.

I had heard that the Old World Lutheran church had a great deal of trouble finding someone to take their call. They were, after all, a very small and not very generous congregation. The intelligent thing might have been to merge with one of the other two Lutheran congregations in town. But the old immigrants came to the predictable conclusion that the other two churches were still too liberal. They kept looking until Pastor Paul Mall appeared. Through Bromley and Claire, I knew there had been resistance to Mall. He was a single man who had divorced his first wife early in his career, and his second wife had run off with another man only last year.

Thelma came out of the kitchen, "Who was that awful man?"

Bromley took center stage. "I wish you two hadn't been quite so harsh with him. Every minister is one of the leaders in the town, and it's never wise to get them angry at you . . . "

Frozen Bear broke in, "Bromley, what do you think Red would do if he were forced to stop selling liquor at his Piggly Wiggly? Do you think he would be a very happy citizen? And what about Happy Thorp, if he had to close down his tavern? And think about all of the resorts that have little beer bars on the premises. Do you want every business in town to board up like the old theater?"

"Of course not. But politeness and moderation always has its place."

"Aw, get off of it," Thelma said, "I just want to see Mall's face when he finds out Reverend Willy is part of his congregation. Let him fix that man." Claire twittered.

"The Reverend Willy is a very god-fearing man," Mr. Packer said. "I'm told he never misses a sermon in town. He attends all three Lutheran churches in a row each and every Sunday, the Old World Lutheran at nine, the Faith Lutheran at ten, and the Reformed Lutheran at eleven. They say he even goes to midnight Mass when they have it at the Catholic church."

"He goes to the Holy Rollers' church on Saturdays too," Claire piped in. "He's very fond of church."

"If he's such a god-fearing man, why won't anyone ever tell me the Reverend Willy story?" I asked.

"If you're really interested, I'll take you to Reverend Willy's Sunday for one of his performances, and you can see for yourself," Thelma said with a sad smile.

I noticed Danny standing in the doorway, listening, watching. His face turned ashen, and he backed into the kitchen.

"Not to change such a fascinating subject," Frozen Bear interrupted, "but I did stop by to see Wally about some business matters."

Bromley jumped in. "What's this I hear about you and Red hanging out together? I can't much imagine that, don't know what you folks and a Trueheart would have in common." When Bromley said that, Cynthia flashed a look of disdain at him. Then she turned her full attention toward Chip Frozen Bear, with quite an admiring look. Thelma frowned; I think she was still hoping to get Cynthia and Danny hooked together.

Bromley was beginning to wind himself up. He already had had too much coffee. Caffeine made him jittery, but he couldn't stand the taste of decaf coffee. While Pastor Paul Mall had paid his visit, Bromley had assiduously avoided all opportunity to speak up, but continually sipped from his coffee, refilling the cup twice from the carafe on the table. By now all two hundred and sixty pounds of him was jolted into action. "There's been funny things going on in town. The senator comes and visits Van Elkind, and I don't get an invitation. I'm practically the mayor of this town, and I don't get an invitation.

"And there's been people coming and going. I swear I saw Tesla Haligent himself here in town just the other day. He's never been here before in his life, even if he does own the bank. I only recognized him from pictures in magazines. What would he be doing here?

"And something's going on with buying land around here. The county clerk's never seen so many people checking on so many deeds as she has these past couple weeks. The county courthouse is a regular revolving door she says."

"A little land boom is desirable, isn't it?" I asked, doing my bit at planting good public relations for the American Seasons venture, and looking at Frozen Bear, who was refusing to meet my eye. "Isn't prosperity what everyone wants?"

"I just like to know what's going on?" Bromley replied. "Like why are you and this Indian becoming buddies. He wanted the liquor license that you ended up getting. Is he trying to buy it from you? Don't you sell, you hear me. You can't trust a god darn Indian, and they don't need any bars on the reservation or anywhere near it. Get a bunch of drunk Indians, and who knows what will happen next."

"Wally," Frozen Bear said, pointedly ignoring Bromley's racism, "I stopped by to ask you to give me some thoughts on how we might update or replace the PowWow for next Summer. Now that you've seen it."

"Oh, I'd like to give you some ideas about that," crooned Cynthia. She was always up to planning a new event. Bromley flashed her a look of disapproval.

I was pleased by Frozen Bear's invitation, but I thought he was going to want to talk about American Seasons. Since the dinner a few weeks earlier, I had heard nothing from any of the participants. Red had been as silent as Van Elkind. For all, I knew, the plan for the big amusement park was already dead.

It was time to change subjects. "So who's going with me and Thelma to see the Reverend Willy Sunday night?" I asked loudly. Mrs. Hutchinson, head of the Ladies' Aid at the Old World Lutheran Church, stood up suddenly and threw down a few bills on her table, and walked out in an unexpected huff.

"I think it's just the two of us, kiddo," said Thelma.

On Sunday evening, we were finally on our way to the Reverend Willy in Thelma's cherry-red sixties Mustang. "I'm sorry," I said, "that I joked about Gilbert Ford the other day. I'm also sorry he didn't show up."

"Not your problem. I was feeling foolish for getting so excited at my age about a salesman. But there's a twinkle to him that I like," she said, keeping her eyes on the road.

We were headed south on 17, past the end of Big Sapphire Lake and then out on Jackrabbit Road. The road was narrow and the trees grew right to the edge of the lane. The tree branches from either side met high above the road, creating a green tunnel through which we drove at a speed more moderate than usual for Thelma. Here and there stood a house with a lawn that rolled down to the road, green grass covered with a smattering of fallen leaves. The sun had dropped behind the horizon. A break in the tree canopy would occasionally surprise us and the first stars of the evening could be seen in the purple sky above.

"Doesn't Danny live down this road?" I asked.

"Yeah, he's a neighbor to the Reverend Willy. Only two houses are on this end of the road."

"Gotta turn off the lights now," Thelma said. "Nothing happens when he sees car lights, even though he knows we're here. Every Sunday, it's the same story. So they say, anyway. Don't know for sure. If there's no one here, how do we know? It's like a tree falling in the forest."

"What are you talking about . . ."

"Sshh! I'm turning off the engine, and we're coasting the rest of the way in." Thelma cut the ignition, and we coasted in the darkness down a slight incline. She turned the wheels to roll onto the grass of a small field. Two others cars were already there, their lights off, their engines cooling. All three were pointed like hunting dogs to a small house at the edge of the clearing, its doorway open except for a screen, lights on in the room behind. A figure moved into the light.

"I know him," I said. "That's Pete Sullivan. He used to own the theater, but why do you . . ."

"Sshh!"

Pete stood in the doorway of his house, leaning against the door jam, a sideways silhouette. Pete was a bit slow of speech, but earnest, good natured and good looking. He probably wasn't yet fifty. He was surprisingly muscular and trim, something I didn't remember from the few times I remember going to the old theater years ago.

"He started doing this about two years ago. No one knows why."

Framed in the doorway, he was bathed in the light, a little bit like an angel in a Renaissance painting, with the room's lighting providing a glow that came from behind. In turn, the small house was framed in the clear dark night filled with stars. He looked out toward the road. To me, it seemed he knew we were there. Then he turned out all his lights, and I heard the screen door bang as he walked out. Suddenly a beam of light hit his garage door. He had started a movie projector. The scratchy, jerky images of a silent movie were projected on the screen. The logo of D.W. Griffith appeared. The title appeared as "Way Down East" starring Lillian Gish.

The Reverend sat in a lawn chair watching the movie. We were there watching him watch the movie, but soon I had forgotten him and was watching the movie myself and feeling connected to the shame of the Gish character, and then her fear as she floated on the ice floe down a wintry river.

"Everyone knows that Pete always loved his movies and that closing the theater nearly killed him. But no one knows why he started showing these old silent movies outside. It's like a penance that he wants us, or someone, to see."

We sat in the car watching actors probably long dead work through their sad story. Then the final images sputtered to the end, but the projector's light still shone. Willy stood up bathed in the light looking out at us. Even from our distance, we could see there were tears streaming, tears that seemed totally unrelated to the old film. "The sermon's over," he shouted out. Suddenly, the light was gone. We heard his screen door bang, and then his interior light came on.

"It's one of his calmer nights," Thelma said. "Just the movie. Sometimes, after the movie, he starts to rant and rave. There's times he even shows up naked. That's probably why some of these ladies hang around through the whole film, just to see if Pete will show his willy at the end."

Each of the cars started its motor and backed up from from this strange drive-in movie. For the first time I noticed that there was a house on the other side of the field, behind us. It was Toivo's house, Danny's house.

I caught a glimpse of someone looking out of the second story gable window, then quickly letting the curtain drop back into place. It was only a glimpse of a face, but I was certain I had seen Danny, and that he had seen me see him watching.

I turned back to face the small house. The front door was closed. The lights shone from the front room. It was just a little house in a clearing in the big woods.

"Like he said, sermon's over," Thelma said, turning her head to the side as she backed out onto the road. "Every Sunday for the last two years, maybe more, he shows a silent movie, and he always cries, even if he has nothing else to say. He's gone crazy, caught up in God and movies. I suppose it's harmless entertainment for people to watch, even the night's he naked, but there's something a little dirty about it at the same time. It's like we're watching his confession. None of us know why.

"We shouldn't watch other people's woes, but sometime you just can't help yourself. And then you have to turn it into a joke to keep it from hurting yourself."

CHAPTER NINE

From my bedroom window vantage point atop the cafe, I could look east toward Big Sapphire Lake. My gaze skipped across the autumn patchwork of tree tops. Heavy with browns and golds and an occasional steeple of evergreen, the trees marched across the landscape. Only the crystalline waters of lakes here and there broke their stride. The early morning sun was bright and clear. Each object on the town square cast a sharply etched shadow on the drying grass of this early October morning.

A black BMW pulled in front of the cafe. The heavily detailed chassis gave a little buck when its front wheels met the concrete curb. Out stepped Van Elkind, dressed in blue jeans, a denim shirt and black leather boots. Even from my second story perch, I could see that he was unshaven and generally rumpled. He walked up to the cafe door below me and began pounding noisily.

"What do you want?" I yelled down. "We're closed on Mondays."

He looked up, his eyes bloodshot and his face grim. "Please open up. I need some decent coffee."

For a reason I couldn't quite fathom, I felt compassion. "I'll be right down," I grumbled.

Close up, Van Elkind looked no better than he did from my second story. "Are you fleeing from the law?" I asked. "You know Capone once stopped here to have a drink."

Van Elkind looked up tiredly. "Kip's disappeared. Regina is frantic with worry at the camp and demanded that I come up. I drove from Chicago overnight. There's no flight up here until a 10 o'clock on

145

Northwest into Timberton, and it was fully booked. Who the hell is coming up here this time of the year?" He shook his head, not really caring for an answer. "She tells us that Kip's been gone two days. Frankly, I wouldn't care, and it wouldn't be the first time. But Rita and Regina insisted I come up here and look. Didn't want to call the police. No reason to get them involved."

The coffee grounds were now in the automatic drip machine and I turned it on. I didn't see any reason to respond. A smarter man wouldn't have even acknowledged the knock on the door.

Van Elkind had followed me into the kitchen. With all the chairs perched atop the birch tables, legs pointing toward the cafe's pressed tin ceiling, the front dining room looked alien. The kitchen while eerily quiet seemed more comforting. Then the gurgle of the coffeemaker as it heated up sounded a quiet warmth through the room. Van Elkind grabbed Thelma's stool. She was fond of half sitting when she stirred her soups or rolled out pastries. Van Elkind slumped on the tall stool with no energy for anything else. The pot stopped gurgling.

He grabbed eagerly for the freshly poured cup, drinking hurriedly, barely grimacing when he scalded the top of his palate with the hot coffee. After a couple more hurried swallows his back grew straighter and he began to look around the kitchen. "Any chance of making some toast. Maybe some of that cardamom bread Thelma bakes?"

I sighed and pulled a loaf out of the storage container. With a long serrated blade, I slowly sawed through the hard-crusted loaf, exaggerating each cut back and forth, hoping to make clear my desire that Van Elkind leave. "How about some wild strawberry jam?" he asked.

I turned, holding the blade out and mockingly thrust forward. He laughed hysterically, then even louder, slowly grinding into strangled sighs. "That damn kid. We leave him up here to stay out of trouble. Still in trouble."

He reached for the pot and poured himself another cup of coffee. "Got some cream?" he demanded. I went to the glass-front refrigerator and pulled out one of the small creamers. I handed it over wordlessly. The slice of cardamom bread popped out of the toaster. I walked over, pulled it out, and passed it back from hand to hand to cool and then dumped it on the counter beside Van Elkind. Before he had a chance to ask, I walked backed over to the refrigerator and grabbed a bowl of butter patties. "No wild strawberry jam," I said.

"Now I have to head out to the camp and face that ogre Regina. Hate that fucking old bitch. She's supposed to take care of Kip. Why'd she have to lose him and then call up Rita and scare her half-to-death. And involve me. The old bat isn't good for anything."

"She's over eighty years old," I pointed out.

"She liked you. Why don't you come out with me? She won't go off like some fucking old world witch if you're around."

I sighed, "It's my day off."

"So? Consider it part of our new work alliance? We can take some time during the drive out to talk about American Seasons. I can bounce around some new ideas. Figure out the way to introduce them, publicly so to speak. Make sure no one sees it the wrong way, if you know what I mean. Got to handle everything the right way, put the right spin on it. Keep the story positive."

Always the obliging sort, I soon found myself dressed and sinking back into the capturing grip of the Recaro seats of Van Elkind's BMW. He backed into the town square far too fast, nearly hitting Bromley who was on an early-morning inspection of his domain. Van Elkind turned right onto Highway 17 and headed out of town toward the camp road.

It was a beautiful fall morning. A slight mist clung to the hollows of the ground. There was a crispness to the dried blades of grass. The sumac bushes were bright red. Sunlight broke through the gaps of birch boughs overhead. Spots of bright light shook and shimmered across the road ahead as the speeding car sent shockwaves of air through the trees tops, shifting the long morning shadows and patterns of light falling before us. The camp was only a few miles west of town, so we were soon pulling past the gate and through the stately avenue of carefully tended maples. The rose bushes that Regina Rabinowicz so carefully tended had long since stopped their summer blooming. Most were already trimmed back to canes in preparation for the winter ahead. Carefully mown fields of lawn lay before us as a Persian carpet of yellows and golds and greens from the first leaves of fall floating down to cover the grass.

Smoke curled up from the main fieldstone chimney, and from another that I knew was in the breakfast room. Vases of cut flowers could be seen in the living room windows that faced the front lawn. Because the curtains were pulled back, one could see all the way through the long living room to the French doors that looked out to the stone terrace that stepped down to the lake. The camp seemed warm and inviting.

Van Elkind pulled up to the front door. As he stepped out of the car, I could hear unexpected cries of loons, echoing across the lake, plaintive and low. Stephen opened the front door, "Welcome, Mr. Van Elkind," he said, but looking at me with a cocked eyebrow.

Regina Rabinowicz came running to the door. Her voluminous chenille housecoat and big furry slippers made her seem even bigger and floppier. Her hair was in tight pin curls. "About time you got here. Kip is gone without saying a word. Maybe he went fishing and drowned. I'm sure it's something terrible."

Stephen coughed discreetly.

Mrs. Rabinowicz looked at him sharply. "Stephen, Kip's a good boy. He just hasn't been brought up properly."

"Mother Regina," Van Elkind began tiredly.

"Don't ma Regina me," she snapped. "If you and that daughter of mine had paid the least bit of attention to the boy when he was growing up, he wouldn't be in the trouble he is all the time. I don't know why I called you first or why I listened to you when I did call. There's no sense waiting for you to get up and look for him. If he's in trouble, he'll be dead by now, caught underwater when his boat tipped over, or lost in the woods after hiking. Who knows what could have happened."

Van Elkind had another explanation. "Kip has not gone fishing or hiking in five years. If anything, he's passed out from drinks or drugs or in some bed he shouldn't be in. There's no reason to call the police."

Stephen coughed discreetly once more, "Perhaps if Mr. Van Elkind and his guest would like to sit on the terrace, I could prepare some coffee and breakfast and provide added details about Kip's behavior over the past few days. I have suggested to Mrs. Rabinowicz that there is no real cause for alarm. But, as you can see, she doesn't agree."

"You're as bad as Hank," Regina wagged. "You think I'm too old to know anything. Hank's just waiting for me to fall over dead, you know, so he can get his hands on my money. But you got a long wait coming, Hank, because I'm not about to shuffle off. Just remember it's my money, not yours. Not Rita's. It could be Kip's. Yes. It just might be Kip's, if you don't watch out! At least Kip likes me. You exile him up here with this old woman so you can have a carefree life in Chicago. Someday you may come to regret that." She walked up the broad steps to her bedroom with her slippers flopping at each step.

Van Elkind looked at me as though to say, "What I put up with." I thought to myself that I must start to say "no" when people asked me to join them on family errands. Stephen motioned us toward the terrace. Once there, we sat at a small cast iron table. The lake water lapped gently at the lawn's edge a hundred feet away. The loons were gone.

"Smell the air," said Van Elkind. "So fresh, so green, so alive with the rightness of it all. That is what will lure people to American Seasons. We can not lose this air. Admittedly, we can't make the sky look perfect like this everyday. It rains and snows too much. And we can't keep the quiet of this lake. Not if we want thirty thousand people a day. But the air, the smell of the air. If we can keep that, then we have it."

"Don't you think several thousand cars, and thirty thousand hot dogs and hamburgers grilled in fast food shops will make the air smell just like downtown Chicago?" I questioned.

"No, this country is too big for that. This air is fucking bigger than that."

Van Elkind was deluded. A project as big as American Seasons would require widening Highway 17 to four lanes. A new route would surely bypass the center of the town. The town square would become even more forlorn as thousands of travelers sped along the bypass to spend their vacation dollars at Van Elkind's fantasy with its special 'air.' And how long would that last, as they built a new airport to handle the jumbo jets that could never land safely at the current airport in Timberton? Maybe they'd even restart the old train service from Milwaukee and Chicago. Whatever they did, I had trouble imagining the air big and clean.

Stephen returned carrying a set of Wedgwood cups and saucers, a silver antique coffee tureen and a Lalique glass platter filled with fresh fruit, marmalade, jam and croissants. I took a croissant, still hot, and definitely not Sara Lee. The jam was imported and French and tasted of wild strawberries. Stephen retreated into the house as quietly as he came. As he exited he cast a backward look, giving me a supportive smile. Maybe Regina wasn't my only ally in the house.

"American Seasons will transform this place in the best of ways. We lured away a couple of the top designers from Walt Disney Imagineering. Brought along some fucking big ideas. Everything is coming

149

together as four lands, four seasons, just like in those preliminary plans. Each with that special theme and touch. And it won't matter if it rains or snows, because each land will be under a dome. Get it. It will always be all four seasons at American Seasons. Big idea, huh?" I nodded. I was still trying to imagine how he thought the air would stay so big.

"Every season will have its own hotel and casino built right into the land. Once we get the suckers there, they can't leave.

"First there will be Spring. We're giving it a New Orleans, French quarter look. This one will have the Hotel St. Printemps. Chicory coffee, beignets, king's cake in which everyone gets a baby, jazz and all that stuff. Get the picture? A little wrought iron on the front, a little desolate, like those cemeteries above ground in New Orleans. The big attraction will be a great aquarium, and shows to go with it. There will be a Mardi Gras parade every day. We will plant everything with hothouse daffodils and tulips. Or something with the same look. It'll always look like spring. What do you think?"

"Sounds good," I said.

"Wait until you hear about Summer. This is going to be more of a family retreat, a return to the end-of-the-century elegance, sort of like the Grand Hotel at Mackinac Island. We will call it the Grand Island Resort. There will be roses everywhere, fake if need be. And there'll be the convention center and the big shopping street. Some great rides too. We got this idea for a whitewater rafting ride, but built into a giant flight simulator. The movie is all around you, some water splashing up at the right time, but you never move. It'll be big. And we can run it during the winter. We will also have a beach and some water rides under a protective dome. So people can go to the beach even when it snows. Got the idea from some parks in Japan."

"Big touch," I murmured.

"I bet you're thinking 'Where can we go from there?' But this whole concept is really big. Fall is even better than Summer and Spring, because we're going to mix in the county fair and the Halloween horror house. We have this dude ranch kind of hotel called The Barn at Cornucopia Farm. The whole hotel shaped like a giant barn, and the silos house the special suites for big spenders. We'll have a State Fair Midway year round."

"What about a ride?" I asked. "You got to have a ride."

"We do—a boat trip through a simulated forest with all of these animated animals. But here's the truly big idea. I don't know how yet, but somehow we're going let riders in the boat hunt some of them and rack up big scores." I rolled my eyes. Van Elkind didn't see that big gesture.

"That leaves Winter. People can stay at the Hibernia Lodge, sort of a ski lodge, and there will be a giant rollercoaster themed as a bobsled run, and there'll be ice skating in the lobby of the hotel. The decor will be evergreens and poinsettias, always Christmas. Red and green. Every celebration, every land, every day of the year."

"What more could one want," I said tiredly.

"Casinos. Don't forget them. That's why we got to have the Lattigo. That is the tricky part in site placement, to let the casinos be on Lattigo land while the rest of the park is controlled by us. But I'm confident we can do it. Keep the best for us."

Van Elkind reached for another croissant. The sunlight reflected off the heavy diamond in his wedding ring. His hands were soft and well-manicured, with the slightest tufts of hair on each knuckle. The gold on the wedding band almost matched the color of light as he sat in the autumn morning glow of the terrace. He spread a thick wedge of soft butter across the croissant, and reached for the French marmalade. Glints of sugared orange rind mixed with butter. "Have more," he said. "It's here for the taking."

How would I ever get back to town, I fretted. Wrapped in the comfort of his vacation camp, Van Elkind had lost all urgency in finding his errant son.

"Perhaps we should look for Kip," I ventured.

He waved me to be quiet. "I have to tell you the best thing about this deal for American Seasons. These shitty locals aren't going to get a damn thing. Oxford's got it all figured out. Perfect scam to get the land cheap. But we need your help."

"How's that?" I asked. Van Elkind in his big business mode was proving quite tedious.

"Oxford's great grandfather owned most of this land back at the turn of the century. Go back and review all of the land titles, and it's all about one man: Oxford. Cheated it out of both the Indians and the railroads according to family gossip. Now, he was a businessman. Even when he sold the land, he retained full mineral rights. Anything beneath this ground still belongs to the Oxford family, even in this camp they used to own. At the time they thought there would be iron and copper here, but none of those veins went much further south than Timberton. Miles from here. But here's the beauty. After all these years, the mineral rights still belong to the Oxford family trust."

"So?" I didn't see the point. "The mineral rights won't help you get the land to build on. And if there's no iron or copper below us, then the mineral rights mean little to Jonathan Oxford." Nothing would give me more pleasure than to know that such rights were worthless to fat Jonathan Oxford. After our unpleasant meeting in the back room of my cafe earlier in the summer, I had seen him twice during his summer weekends at the Van Elkind camp. Both times he came into the cafe for morning coffee with Red Trueheart.

One time, the two sat morosely over their coffee, engaged in desultory to and fro that passed for conversation. Having had more than one experience in attempting to negotiate with Red, I suspected he was simply aping the personality of his counterpart in an attempt to have Oxford lower his natural defenses, thus opening him up for a quick feint from Red.

Oxford appeared however to have sparred with the best of them. He simply spooned another bit of sugar into his coffee cup, then stirred it, without speaking to Red, without even looking at him. Outside, it was raining. Oxford sipped more of his coffee, then removed a silver cigarette case from his jacket pocket. He flipped open the case, and removed a cigarette, without offering one to Red. He returned the case to his jacket, without saying a word. He lit the cigarette, inhaled and then let loose a small cloud of smoke in a direction that could evoke no offense to anyone.

Red yanked his wallet from his hip pocket, and pulled out a ten dollar bill, and casually tossed it to the table, while jamming the wallet back into his rear pocket. He said nothing to Oxford. He said nothing to me, but simply walked out into the rain, without an umbrella, without a hat. Oxford continued to smoke, the cigarette decorously clutched between his fat fingers.

"Sans une parole," murmured Mr. Packer that day.

"What did you say?" I asked him.

He waved me off. "I was just reminded of an old French poem," he replied, "and of a woman I once knew in Paris."

Van Elkind broke through my reverie. "Yeah, the mineral rights are worthless in and of themselves, but they can serve other goals. That's the fucking genius of Jonathan Oxford. He's sending up his mineral company scouts to do full testing throughout the area for the possibility of open pit copper mining."

"But you said there wasn't any copper."

"There isn't"

"Then I don't get it," I responded.

"If there were copper, and I am not saying that there is, but if there were, then it would belong to Jonathan. And if the copper were his, he could do whatever he needed to get at it. The mineral rights allow it."

"And what do you mean by do anything he needed to?" I asked not really wanting to know.

"Dig a pit, a really big, ugly pit," Hank smiled, "Of course, eventually, he would have to restore the land to its original state. But that could take decades, leaving the land scarred and open. You know. No trees. No lakes. No wildlife. Just a mine. Not quite the vacation investment, is it?" He grinned.

I got the picture. "So what did you do? Line up dummy companies to buy this land once the word of the mining gets out." Van Elkind was reminding me too much of some of the people my friend Patrice once knew on New York's upper east side.

"Well, the land would be worthless, if the mines were to be dug."

"But they won't be dug," I said.

"But they could be," he countered. He slapped his knee in glee. "With the land Red already controls and tribal lands of the Lattigo reservation, we can amass the property we need for a fraction of what it's really worth, even before the casinos."

"And what about the people you cheat."

"Who's cheating them? No one putting a gun to their head and forcing them to sell. It's a free world. Anyone who cared could take the time to find the land surveys dating back over a century and know there's no iron or copper here."

"But they won't look," I pushed back.

"So who's at fault?" Van Elkind sat back and took another bite of his butter and marmalade-laden croissant. The flaky golden crust crumbled in his bite and tiny crumbs fell to the ground. A tiny sparrow swooped in to eat the falling nuggets.

"Excuse me, sir," Stephen had a remarkable ability to move quietly across the stone. I looked up at this butler, or whatever he was—tall and in his mid-thirties, looking far more fit than his employer. How could he stand working for Henry? Stephen noticed my glance and looked at me as though to ask a similar question? "Mrs. Rabinowicz would like to see you. She has awakened from a short nap in quite some terror."

"One of her fucking old-world dreams," Van Elkind muttered. He pushed himself up from the chair, stopped to pick up the last croissant and stuffed it into his mouth. He waved at me to follow him. I looked at Stephen as though to say, what can I do but follow. The butler's eyes gave no free pass.

Van Elkind walked up the broad oaken staircase as reluctantly as one would scale the tall ceremonial steps of a Mayan temple to have one's heart pulled at the altar from a still quivering body. "What's the old witch dreamed up this time?"

The grandeur of the second story of the old camp building was far more engaging to me. The lower rooms had the scale of great ceremonial and public spaces. Upstairs, the hallways and the bedrooms were more discreet, although still grand. The interior walls were thick, hand-plastered walls with carefully crafted moldings. Heavy carved doors with well-varnished woodwork opened into a succession of rooms.

"Seven bedrooms, eight baths, and a study up here," Van Elkind said, as he noticed my sightseeing gaze. "The third floor's for servants. But only Stephen is there anymore. Keep telling him he should hire a live-in maid. Might have a little fun then, but I'm not sure he is into female fun." We stopped in front of the last door in the hallway. "Get ready for a different kind of fun," he warned.

He opened the bedroom door, "Mother Regina, have you had another bad dream?"

Regina sat at the foot of an old-fashioned brass twin bed. A huge stack of thick feather pillows hid the headboard. All of it sat in the middle of large oval rag rug that was precisely in the middle of the room. The positioning seemed odd, and then I realized that by sitting in the bed, one was perfectly positioned to gaze out the small casement windows onto a well-framed view of the lake and forest beyond. The entire house might have been constructed around this small entrancing view.

Regina noticed my gaze, "It's my peace and pleasure, young man."

She turned back to Van Elkind. "Yes, I had another vision. I could see Kip in great pain, alone, surrounded by flames. He reaches out to me for help, and I try to hold on to him. But I can't, and then I fall and keep falling. I wake before I crash, but my last thought is of Kip. I'm his grandmother. I must help."

She seemed tiny as she sat in her anxiety, sinking into the soft mattress, with the fluffy down comforters wrapped around her weight. She looked up at both of us, her face double-crossed with lines of worry.

"It's just a dream," Van Elkind began.

She cut him off. "Don't tell me that. The week before Casimir died, I woke up in the middle of the night with such a feeling of dread weighing me down that I thought I would never be able to sit up. But I did and I saw this large box falling through the sky. I woke up Casimir and made him hold me until I fell asleep. I was so scared, even though I didn't know what it meant. The next week when the officer showed up at my door and told me that an American Airlines flight has crashed trying to leave O'Hare, then I knew what the dream had meant. But it was too late. God had given me a sign to take better care of my Casimir. But I was foolish and thought only of myself, seeking Casimir to hold me when I should have been holding him back, refusing to let him travel during the holiday seasons. And then he was gone forever, too late. It's always too late.

"But not this time. I have had this dream three times. Kip needs our help."

A discreet knock at the door from Stephen. "The police just called, ma'am,"

Regina broken into an unearthly cry. I thought of the loons that morning. Van Elkind just stood there, astounded by her wails. I rushed to the bed side and held onto her, much as Casimir must have done that week before he had crashed to the earth. Stephen joined me at her side, "Please Mrs. Rabinowicz, please, listen. Kip is fine. He is not hurt. They called to ask Mr. Van Elkind to bring the boy home. There's nothing to cry about."

We both cradled the terrified woman. She had seemed strong and large the first time I met her, but I realized she was really quite frail.

An impatient cough. "I hate to interrupt this love fest," Van Elkind said, and I felt Stephen straighten in anger, "but if I need to go bail out the kid again, I want to get started. What did the police say?"

Stephen resumed his professional stance. "The call was from Officer Campbell He found Kip sleeping off an enjoyable evening near Sapphire Falls."

"Yeah, I bet that's just how he phrased it."

"To be specific, he said Kip was drunk as a skunk. But he did request that you arrive as soon as possible to take him home. He appears to washed up on the banks of the falls without any of his clothes."

"I guess your dreams were wrong again, old woman," Van Elkind snapped. "You might as well come with me Wally, so I can drop you off in town after I get the kid in tow. Stephen, get some clothes for Kip."

"They're already on the hallway table," Stephen replied. "A pair of jeans and a shirt, as well as a robe, should it prove difficult to dress him more fully in his current state."

"Thank you for your ever complete thoughtfulness," Van Elkind said dryly. He turned and walked down the hall toward the stairs, the front door and his BMW. I shrugged my shoulders and smiled a bit sheepishly at Stephen and Mrs. Rabinowicz as I followed my ride.

As the BMW sped through the stately avenue of maples, Van Elkind's mood seemed to brighten. "I won't have to put up with any of this once we get American Seasons underway."

I broke in, "Speaking of American Seasons, not that I wasn't honored to be asked . . ."

"We need your p.r. sense and local touch," Van Elkind broke in.

"Be that as it may," I said, "the truth is that I'm a bit uncomfortable with the whole scheme. I'm afraid you will ruin this area and everything that's great about it. And if I were your communications person, I would certainly counsel you to start planning things differently."

"What do you mean? Give me an example."

Why did I start this conversation? It was just this kind of talk that led up to Kip's staying in town. "First of all, stop sounding like a god damn Wall Street robber baron. Don't talk about what's in it for you. Instead, focus on how you're bringing jobs to the northwoods, describe the steps you'll be taking to save the environment, be excited about redeveloping the Lattigo and bringing new opportunities to America's most oppressed minority. God, I don't know. There's a million ways you could position this so it would sound good. But cheating old retirees out of their hunting camps with rumors about fake mining actions is definitely not the way to do it."

Van Elkind was so excited he could hardly keep his hands on the steering wheel. "You're right. You are absolutely right. We got to look at the big picture. I love your idea. We will save the land from being raped by evil mining companies and we'll build an ecologically friendly resort that will restore this depressed economy. It has everything for everyone."

"Wait a minute, that's not what I said at all," I protested.

"Yes, it is," Van Elkind countered. He turned into the Sapphire Falls parking lot. The lone Thread police car was there, still minus its top light. Officer Campbell hearing the rumble of the BMW's tires as they spun over the loose gravel of the lot walked up from the banks of the short stretch of river that ran from the lake to the falls.

"Good to see you, sir," Campbell began. His eyes were averted and his voice had an obsequious tone. "A bit of a problem here, with your son and all. Public drunkenness and public nudity. Kind of frowned on in this town. Normally, I'd just send that kind of problem on home, but the boy's a little too far gone for that. I don't want to say he's taken any kind of drugs, but he's in some kind of stupor. Now if call a county ambulance and have him taken up to the hospital in Timberton, well then if he has taken any kind of illegal drug, then you know, I'd have to arrest him, and I know we talked before you left for the summer how you wanted me to keep an eye out for Kip, and how you would be grateful if I did. Anyway I wanted to call you first."

Van Elkind brushed the officer aside, "Let's just get him in the car."

"Well, it may not be so easy sir. Like I said . . ."

"Just shut up."

Van Elkind strode to the water's edge. We followed. I was getting good at that. Kip lay sprawled at the water's edge, face to the sky, looking like he had been flung up to shore after a midnight skinny dip. His long stringy hair drying in clumps. I noticed a swastika tattooed right above his pubic hair, and was embarrassed to have noticed. Van Elkind was at his son's side, half in the water, half on the shore, toeing Kip in the side with his shoe, "Get up, you damn jackass. It's fucking time to get home. I got better fucking things to do than drive all night to tuck you into bed."

I came down with the terry cloth robe, and laid it over him. "We should get him to the camp and call a doctor. He could be suffering from exposure. It was below 40 degrees last night." I looked back to Campbell. "Are you sure we shouldn't call an ambulance?"

Kip's eyes fluttered open. I wasn't sure he really saw us. "What the fuck," he muttered. "Is this heaven or hell?" His eyes flopped back close.

"Well, at least he's alive," I said tentatively to Van Elkind, "but I'd feel a whole lot better if you get him home. The two of us can carry him to the car. I'll take his shoulders. You take his feet."

Who knew such a skinny kid could be so heavy. Van Elkind grunted as he lifted up his kid's feet, but I had the heavy end. I prided myself on not huffing, and it gave me pleasure to make Van Elkind walk backwards up the slight incline from the shore. We inched our way toward the car with Kip's head and feet held just high enough to keep his ass from scraping the ground. The robe slid off. It was like we were carrying a naked trophy we had just hunted down in the woods.

"Sir, I think he's saying something," Campbell said.

"We're carrying him. You listen," Van Elkind said impatiently. The car was another hundred feet. I thought about Cynthia, who would kill me if she knew I was making this effort to save her nemesis. The kid's body looked undernourished with his ribs rubbing up against the skin, exaggerated by the way we were carrying him. The swastika by his cock was only one of several tattoos, all looking hand drawn on the kid's body.

At last we reached the car and let the kid slump to the ground. Even as we regained our breaths, Kip seemed to revive a little.

"What ya doing here Pop?" he asked. "Couldn't even let me kill myself could you? Had to come and save me. Why bother? No one likes me here. Cynthia won't go out with me. But you keep coming back. And back."

And he was out again. Campbell came back with the fallen robe to put over Kip. "It's time to take him home, sir." I wasn't sure if Campbell meant the camp or Chicago. I would have recommended Chicago, and to take Kip and all of their family's problems back.

Under bare fall branches and in the morning sun, we began the drive back, at first in quiet, with only the occasional moan or grunt from Kip in the back seat. But it was on that cool fall morning in those twenty minutes back into town that I got my first glimpse of this millionaire's real self and that in return I exposed just a small part of myself.

Was it the smell of the freshest of cold river water mixed with the odor of unwashed hair all wrapped up in damp terry cloth? Knowing that

that combination represented yourself in your only son and that somehow you were failing him, that you and your wife would rather leave him to his opinionated grandmother who loved him in a way you couldn't, that you could try to build an entire city even though you could save family—perhaps all of that became embodied in a smelly, gaseous, bombed-out bundle in the back seat and that made one honest for at least a moment.

Henry didn't talk about Kip. He didn't even seem to acknowledge that he had come to the aid of his son. Rather, all the talk was about what was driving him to build American Seasons. It became clear that he needed to prove himself and build a fortune in the way that his in-laws had and live up to the legacy of earlier Van Elkinds who had once created a fortune. In that quest, he seemed alone in that Rita was only interested in the spending of money, not in creating it. Yet I sensed that it was ultimately only a game to Henry and as in any other game he might play, he wasn't particularly concerned about following the rules.

But it was clear he was lonely and that for some reason he thought of me as an ally. I wanted to repay that touch of humanity. I wanted to tell him of my worries for the cafe. I felt a compulsion to recount in detail that horrible day in Manhattan when Patrice and I had been so brutally mugged, to explain like I had to no one yet why I felt compelled to flee the city and return home to establish a different life. But I had no drugged-out son beginning to whimper in the back seat crowding me into honesty, and I decided not to cross that barrier. I didn't need a friend, not even a rich egotist like Henry Van Elkind. I had a cafe, and that was enough.

.

CHAPTER TEN

"What a morning! Brisk enough to nip at the tits of a witch," blustered Bromley as he entered the cafe and allowed the brisk November wind to whistle through the packed cafe.

"Close the fucking door," snapped Red Trueheart. Cynthia looked at her father with alarm. Whenever he ate in the cafe, she tiptoed through the day prepared to be mortified. For someone so easily entranced by my regular cadre of codgers, Cynthia seemed to find no such fascination in her own father.

"Why such a foul mood? It's just a nice cold snap to get us ready for winter. And after the best god darn fall color season we ever had. And you're growling like a hungry bear at the town dump." Bromley was up on his favorite stool at the bar. "A big cup of java, Cynthia, to welcome a day like today." Red simply ignored it all and returned to the financial pages of that morning's state edition of *The Milwaukee Journal*.

Red's inattention irked Bromley, so he walked over to sit at Red's table. Claire quickly began spooning more strawberry jam on her muffin. Mr. Packer leaned across the counter to whisper, "A ritual we must endure each year. Bromley loves the cold. Red can't abide it. You can always safely predict that once the edges of the lake are covered with a thin pane of ice in the morning that these two will break through it."

Claire inched closer. "My men warned me about today. They said, 'Claire, stay home.' But did I listen? No, I did not. Something told me that today Wally would have wild strawberry jam, and I didn't want to miss out on that. But now I'm here, and there's no way out of this but to sit through it. You got to take your medicine and lick it."

Bromley took an enormous swig from his mug, then leaned back against his chair and released a self-satisfied sigh. Another customer entered the cafe. The quick rush of icy air swirled around the cafe creating momentary mini-tornadoes of the steam that rose above each coffee cup. "A great day indeed. Can't ask for a better one, could you Red?"

Cynthia came up beside me with her ever-present pot of coffee. "I know Bromley needs a refill, but I'm staying away. Daddy's in a really bad mood, and Bromley's just torturing him."

Red laid down his paper to look straight at Bromley. Red had always been a big man, and not one who paid much attention to his appearance. He hadn't yet shaved and his red stubbly beard nicely matched the nubbly old plaid flannel shirt he wore. "What are you jabbering about?"

Thelma stepped out of the kitchen. Lately, she had taken to wearing a fanciful hair style and paying a new-found attention to makeup. Today was the scheduled visit from Gilbert Ford, her favorite traveling salesman. She had been a bit giddy all morning. "Those two at it again," she murmured, "One of them owns half the town. The other supposedly runs it. Should have better things to do than act like a couple of little cocks fighting in the ring."

"More the size of bears," said Mr. Packer.

"Bears are nicer," whispered Claire.

Bromley perked up, "Did you say something Claire, dear?"

"I said fairs are nicer. We were talking about carnivals and festivals," Claire dug back into the jam and butter. She lowered her voice to a true whisper. "Stupid old goat. Never did like him. I tell my little men they should use that one for their experiments. But do they ever listen?"

"Fairs are like amusement parks. Both can be a pleasure indeed." Bromley was off and rolling once more. "One of my fondest memories is visiting Disneyland in 1963. Those were still the good years. Wouldn't it be wonderful if we had our own Disneyland here in the northwoods? Wouldn't that be a wonder? What do you say to that, Red?" He held up his coffee cup as though waiting for a toast, a smug smile crossing his flabby face.

Red's face darkened beyond the color of his stubble. He picked up the paper and folded it into a long narrow strip which he then slowly tapped on the table. Bromley just smiled.

"It is a glorious day. The frost is on the pumpkins today. A regular harvest farm out there, wouldn't you say, Red?"

Danny stepped out of the kitchen. Both he and Cynthia had arranged school schedules that allowed them to work the breakfast hours. But Danny needed to head off for his first class, and he was already out of his work clothes. Over the summer, he had filled out his lanky frame. With the new clothes he bought with his job earnings, I understood why Cynthia continued to moon over him. "What's everyone doing out here?" he asked.

Cynthia waved him close, "It's Daddy and Bromley again."

"Oh," he said, understanding immediately.

"Building a park. Now that would take big bucks. And influence. Someone who really understood the politics of the area. Wouldn't you say that, Red? Someone like me, maybe? Hypothetically speaking, of course. Just an exercise in imagination. That's all we're talking about here. Couldn't be anything more, could it?" Bromley raised his hand languidly toward Cynthia, waving her over with the coffee.

Red tried to pin me like a deer in the spotlight of his gaze. I wasn't primed to be shot for something I hadn't even hinted at, and I gave my head a shake back and forth.

Red thrust up from his chair with the force of a shock wave. Officer Campbell shifted uneasily over at his table. Knowing that Thelma was in the room, he wanted to act bravely and intervene. Still Red and Bromley were his bosses, so he stayed put.

Red dropped his paper to the floor, sounding a soft thwack. "Listen to me, you big asshole." Cynthia grabbed Danny's hand. Thelma leaned back against the wall. "Here it comes," she said.

Bromley continued to smile, "Now, Red, it's just the first frost getting to you. Don't do anything you'll regret."

"I regret the day I let you become the town chairman, and wipe that fucking smile off your face."

Aaawooogahh! Aaawooogahh!

Officer Campbell stood immediately. "That's a fire call. Everyone to the station."

Aaawooogahh! Aaawooogahh!

Red pointed his finger at Bromley, "You're just lucky I'm a volunteer fireman or I'd have your ass for breakfast. But don't think it's over yet. We got some things to talk about."

Officer Campbell cut in. "Red, stow it. We got to get going, even though it's probably just some chimney fire. First really cold spell when people light up their furnaces, there's always a chimney fire." The officer rushed out.

"Campbell's kinda of cute when he gets riled up, ain't he?" Thelma laughed. "But things were just starting to get interesting around here."

"Where you going, Danny?" I yelled out.

The boy turned around as he exited the door, a rare smile flashing across his face. "I became a volunteer last month. It'll be my first fire!"

The cafe was emptied of men—except for Bromley, Mr. Packer, and me. I felt like I was the only able-bodied man left in town during the war. Packer was excused because he was missing an arm and was well over eighty. Bromley was too fat to be of any use. "Hey, I have to run the restaurant," I said defensively.

"We could watch it for you," said Mr. Packer. "You know it's important up here for everyone to stayed joined together. I think it's a legacy from our forest fire days, when a lightning strike at the right time could erupt into enormous devastation. I saw it happen once, back in the Thirties. Bad days, back then. Everyone was out on their luck. The market for lumber was very poor. But there were still a few lumbermen hanging on. All that was gone into ashes within a day. Gone like that. Fire's like life. We all need to be prepared for it"

The town alarm stopped, and the lone fire engine had already rushed north on 17. "Jack Manny should have bought the town a new fire truck instead of that god darn garbage truck," muttered Bromley. "A new fire engine would have looked better in the Loon Town Parade."

"So few men. So many beautiful women," Gilbert Ford exclaimed as he walked in on his weekly sales call. Pans were being moved frantically in the kitchen. Any moment Thelma would likely appear to announce some desperately needed item.

"Hello, Gilbert," I said. "The fire alarm just sounded."

"We were telling Wally that he should become a volunteer fireman," said Bromley. "It would be good for his business, and it would keep people from thinking he was one of the summer folk."

"The dreaded summer folk," laughed Gilbert.

Bromley stepped up to the counter. "I love them dearly. Without them . . . well, without them, this town would not exist. But just the same, it would be nice if we didn't need to deal with them."

"I don't know why you say things like that," said Cynthia. "You're the one who's always trying to think up new ways of getting more tourists here. Remember how you were trying to invent that story about a giant muskie in Big Sapphire Lake."

"I saw that fish," I said.

"Now you sound just like one of those god darn summer folk," laughed Bromley.

Mr. Packer fingered his long beard in amusement. I had yet to hear Mr. Packer acknowledge that he too had seen that long shadow in the lake. A fish like that could attract new tourists, even if they were a different class of tourist from those that so entranced Cynthia when she recounted past glories.

Maybe at one time the tourists had been different. It wasn't hard to imagine a different world when you boated around some of the long-settled lakes and saw the big camps with their grandiose log cabins sporting fieldstone fireplaces large enough to roast a side of venison. Sometimes when I had trouble sleeping, I would take a canoe out to the lake and just silently paddle in the wake of the moonlight, letting myself drift in the silvery glow, sliding by the old cabins, their windows dark portals.

Tall pines guarded the cabins from the night sky. And when the moon was in retreat, thousands of stars emerged in the blacky ink, provoking tiny reflections in the dark lake waters. I felt encased in a hall of mirrors—the stars above, the lights below. In those magical moments of calm and quiet, I could imagine the strings of violins warming up for an evening ball, and I could picture the large windows of the wealthy camps alive with candlelight, and the chattering sound of the relaxing rich lilting across the water to mix with the cries of loons.

But had it ever been that way? I didn't think so. Only Cynthia and I imagined it so. In reality, these grandiose places had been hunting camps—stomping grounds for men who wanted to get away. They probably smoked cigars and drank whisky while they played poker. There were no summer night balls. There were no grand feasts. There was only hunting and fishing and good-natured cursing.

The true pleasures had likely been in the smaller cabins and the little resorts that ringed the less desirable lakes, in the city masses who disembarked the train from Milwaukee and Chicago. Husbands with wives and children with parents that fished together, swam together, told stories together around campfires. And young lads from the boy's camp probably canoed across the lake to the girls' camp to carry on clandestine romance and midnight skinny dips.

It didn't seem that way now. Powerboats raced across the lake. Fisherman used radar to track down schools of minnows. Kids stayed in the cabins to watch television and play video games. There didn't seem to be much joy. Maybe that was why no one in town really like the summer folk. They were supposed to be having fun and they weren't.

"Things used to better, " said Gilbert, as though he were reading my mind.

"Why is that?" asked Thelma, bending forward to hear Gilbert's reply. How was it possible for her breasts suddenly to appear so large?

"There weren't so many rules. People could do what they wanted. People were treated as though they had individual responsibility without every decision being made for them," Gilbert was on a roll. "Now, everyone is told what to do and no one knows how to have fun."

"When I was a kid we didn't need any laws regarding drinking or smoking," Bromley said.

"What are you talking about? There was Prohibition when you were a kid," Claire contradicted him.

"I'm talking about those years after Prohibition. You didn't have to be eighteen or twenty-one to have a beer. Why did they pass that stupid law? When you were fourteen in those days people treated you like you were an adult."

"They did indeed," mused Claire.

"And they should have treated you that way. Because you were expected to be an adult. Times were tough. I know lots of kids who left home at fourteen or fifteen and got a job and became self-supporting. You couldn't do that today. And what do you get? Worthless scum like that god darn Van Elkind kid. Parents won't even take care of him. Drop kids like that off on us, and expect Thread to take care of them." The way Bromley was going on, I thought he was preparing a speech for his next election. "You're a romantic thing, Cynthia, what do you think?"

"Kip is a creep and always following me around asking me out for dates when he knows I'll never say yes."

"I meant what do you think about the difference between now and then?"

Cynthia turned to Mr. Packer for support. "I know it was more romantic then, with people more interesting and real stories in their lives. I wish my life could be more interesting!"

"Don't go looking for an interesting life," Claire piped in. "Someday I'll tell you everything I've been told by my little men and all the things they've done to me. If you knew what I knew, you'd think life was a little too interesting."

Thelma settled her ample self on a stool next to Gilbert. He spread out his catalogues and order forms across our counter to prepare for the big order. "Wally, my young man," Gilbert began to inch forward. "Why gamble on getting the right ingredients fresh just when you want them. Be prepared with a fully stocked larder, and leave the risks to the gamblers."

Cynthia interrupted. "I can't stay around to hear this, even though I want to. But I have to get to school in time for my trig class." She took off her apron and threw it to me. "Whatever anyone says, I believe the old days were better."

"They were better then, that's for sure. Because the Indians knew their place." Bromley said.

"What?" Cynthia stopped in her tracks with her hands to her hips. "What do you mean?"

"Don't get on a high horse. You know as well as I do that those Lattigo are nothing but trouble."

"What!" Cynthia commanded.

"You seem awfully sensitive about this subject today. Could it be because your daddy is doing business with the Lattigo?"

"I don't know what you're talking about."

"Your father's just turned into another Indian lover. He'll be sorry he lined up with them."

"Bromley," Claire said peevishly, "don't get started."

Cynthia's face was flushed, and her need to get to class forgotten. "American Indians have been wronged by this country. We broke our treaties with them and we brought diseases that killed them in the millions. And that was after stealing their land!"

Bromley snorted. "And now they're all lying drunk in the streets. If not the streets of the reservations, then they're in their own little ghettos in cities like Minneapolis and Milwaukee. At least we kept our schools from being consolidated with those greasy Lattigo."

Mr. Packer stepped forward and put his one hand onto Bromley's shoulder. "I thought you enjoyed the cool weather. Let's go enjoy it together."

"How can you say such horrible things?" Cynthia was getting emotional again. "What about someone like Chip Frozen Bear. He's done wonderful things for the Lattigo. And he's smart and good looking."

"Maybe you're in love with Big Chief Frozen Bear?" Bromley started laughing.

"I'm late for class." Cynthia was out the door.

We were all quiet. Gilbert was looking at his sample books. Thelma was staring back into the kitchen. Claire was looking sadly at Bromley, and for a moment, I wondered if the old rumors about their being brother and sister were true. Mr. Packer's hand still rested on Bromley's shoulder. "Let's take that walk."

"What the hell is going on?" I wanted to know.

"I just want to sell some canned goods," said Gilbert. "So what can I interest you in?"

I wasn't in the mood to choose a case of cling peaches or debate the price of mayonnaise. "Let Thelma do the ordering," I said. I walked to the door and stood there, looking out over the square.

The skies were dark and cloudy, and the wind had not died down. It looked like it might rain, and then I corrected myself. The temperatures were below freezing, so it would be snow. The seasonal cycle would continue. If the past were any predictor of the future, I had five months of almost daily snowfalls to anticipate. A bleak thought for the beginning of November. I thought of the earlier fire alarm. Maybe, someone had set their house on fire on purpose just to escape to warmer climes.

Now the town ambulance pulled through the square heading north on 17. It was silent and slow moving. "Isn't that odd," I mused aloud, "they've called out the ambulance but they aren't bothering to put on the emergency light. Or was that the rotating light that got broken at Cynthia's prom?"

"Wally, It probably means the person's already dead so there's no need to hurry," Thelma replied. She quickly turned back to Gilbert, "And I think we should get a carton of the canned peaches."

167

Already dead, I thought, and she suggested it so calmly. More interested in buying some peaches from Gilbert. "Wait a minute," I turned back to the order-happy duo, "no one's buying any more canned fruit for use in this restaurant. Next thing I know you'll be asking for a crate of Velveeta cheese."

"I guess you better cancel that order too," Thelma said. Then she laughed. "Don't worry, Wally, I only ordered what we really need. Gilbert won't take advantage of me. After all he wants to keep our business."

"Certainly I want your business, but don't be too quick to think I wouldn't take advantage of a lovely woman such as yourself," Gilbert said, fingering the tip of his polka-dotted bow tie.

"Such a flirt," Thelma responded, "but no time for any of that foolishness. My bread dough in the kitchen needs punching down."

"To be kneaded by your hands. Ah, what a delightful pleasure that would be."

"But could you rise to the occasion?" Thelma asked with a raised eyebrow.

"Should I leave?" I asked.

"Not at all. I must be going myself," laughed Gilbert. "Appointments to keep and all of that. But before I go, I must ask this wonderful cook if we could arrange to meet for dinner on her night off. I could cook for her my ambrosial pleasures."

Thelma giggled, and said, "I'd be delighted."

"We're closed on Mondays," I said. "She can see you then." I found Gilbert's ways smarmy, and I wished that Thelma wasn't so easily entranced. He walked out the door with a wink and a smile.

"What is going on," I said again.

"Can't I go on a date?"

"That's not what I mean. Everyone so edgy today. Cynthia never gets upset. Bromley is always trying to curry Red's favor. Did the universe get re-ordered overnight and someone forgot to tell me? I don't get it."

"Wally, remember when we were picking raspberries this summer? And I told you that people in this town were more complicated than you thought. Well, you're finally discovering that not everyone's some simple twit in a story you've written. You can't make them do whatever you want so your life will be just so. Just remember that when you left your magazine in Manhattan, you gave up being the author. We write our own stories, and sometimes the endings ain't going to be the ones you want."

"Now look at Red who's up to something. I don't know what it is, but I know that he's ensnared you somehow. And Bromley's dipped his toe into it and is testing the waters because he don't want to be left out of the boat. And when that old blubberboat knows he won't drown, just watch how quickly he swims into your hullabaloo.

"And that Chip Frozen Bear has been around Thread a lot more than any Indian I've ever known in the past. You've seen how often he's in here. He's a good looking kid, and since Danny won't pay no never-mind to Cynthia, she's been watching Frozen Bear like she used to watch Danny. She's a romantic kid, and Indians can be romantic figures.

"I don't know how you don't notice these things. By the way, those people at that table in the corner needs some fresh coffee. Maybe you should take care of our customers. I got to attend to that bread dough."

Put in my place again, something Thelma did time after time, leaving me to wonder who was really running the cafe.

Another blast of November air from an opened door. Red was back, his skin so pale that his hair seemed an unearthly blaze. "What is it?" I asked. "Where was the fire?"

"Campbell got it right for once. It was a chimney fire out to the Gunderson place. You know the Gundersons? Their son Josh was your age, I think." I shook my head to the contrary. "No? Well, maybe he's closer to Cynthia's age."

"So is everything okay?" I asked.

"Not much of a chimney fire, was just flaring, still in the chimney, and we had it out in five minutes. Amazing the neighbors even noticed it to call it in. Didn't do any damage to the house. Just burned the creosote that had built up in the chimney. Didn't look like either of the Gundersons were home, so we nearly packed up and gone on our way. But then we noticed that their car was in the barn they use as a garage, so we got worried that no one had answered the knock and searched the house."

Red sighed. "Looked like they were sleeping, but they were dead. Anna Gunderson was in bed, all peaceful like. Found Bernard Gunderson in the bathroom, fallen off the toilet, shower water running, but him naked and dead. Ain't fucking dignified, dying like that."

"What happened," I wanted to know. "Were they murdered?"

"You could call it that, I suppose," Red gave a weird laugh. "If you

169

wanted to put god damn bats on trial. Fucking ugly things."

"Bats?"

"Bernard and Anna had bats in their attic and in their chimney. Fuckers lived everywhere and left so goddamn much shit everywhere that it sealed their chimney shut. Fucking tighter than any damper."

"Is that why the chimney caught on fire?"

"No," Red replied sadly, "but when Bernard turned on the heat today, probably for the first time this season, the blocked up chimney forced the carbon monoxide back into the house. And Bernard was such a frugal bastard. Damn fool. He had the best insulated house in Thread, so it was like being in a sealed garage with a running engine. They probably passed out without knowing what happened. And then they died. In a house full of bats.

"Bats. God damn bats."

We all looked at floor, caught in the tragedy of bats.

CHAPTER ELEVEN

A stark day. Dead leaves untethered from the trees lay sodden in listless piles, trampled by the rain. The still air held the threat of turning colder. A thin line of dark clouds hanging above the northern horizon portended a sleet storm. Dark clouds from the north were conquering the skies above the Town Square. By afternoon, the sun had disappeared in the murk, and it seemed to be early evening even though it was barely three o'clock. Not a customer was in the cafe.

"I've been thinking," I said to Thelma, as we both leaned against the counter looking out across the empty tables, through the glass plate window and across the deserted square, "maybe I should go to that funeral today." The Gundersons were being buried later, and I thought it could be good for business to make an appearance.

Bromley walked out of the hotel on the opposite side of the square. Claire ran after him. They both were dressed in their Sunday best. They headed briskly in the direction of the Old World Lutheran Church.

"Now why are you thinking that?" she asked. "I could hear that old windbag Paul Mall was in here earlier. Did he make you feel guilty?"

"Nothing like that. I've just been thinking about some of the things you said to me the other day, about how I'm not in touch with the town, how I want to manage this town like a story I write. I know I don't have much contact with anyone in this town except for what goes on in this restaurant. I go to movies in Timberton. Most of what I hear in Thread gets filtered by the people who come into my restaurant. Do you think I'm isolated?" I noticed Mr. Packer was leisurely heading in the same direction as Claire and Bromley.

"I think it's just fine if you want to head on over to the Lutheran Church. It don't look like no one's planning to spend any time in this place." Thelma started to remove her apron. "I'll tell you what. We'll both head on over to that funeral. I guess I can stand a dose of Pastor Paul Mall today."

The church was packed. Thread did enjoy its funerals. Thelma and I sat in the very back pew, which was all for the better, since being so far back made it harder to hear the sermon of Pastor Paul Mall. I hadn't been in this church for nearly twenty years. After I had been confirmed, I never wanted to attend Sunday services. I had forgotten the naked little cherubs that were painted on this ceiling, their tiny bare butts pointed here and there.

I tried to count the separate pieces of glass in the stained glass windows, but I lost count as I moved into the nativity scene. I had always mixed up the numbers when I was a kid too. I looked around the room to see who was in attendance. There was a lone young man in the front row. That must be the Gunderson son, Josh. Thelma told me that he had flown back from his current home in Los Angeles.

In the pews behind him were two solid rows of men. They were mostly men from the window plant in town, probably Gunderson's co-workers pressed into duty as pall bearers. It took quite a few when you had two people to bury. All of them seemed to be listening attentively to Pastor Mall. Thelma elbowed me, "Can you believe this old windbag?"

Thelma's jab made me think back on Mall's visit earlier that day. I was always a glutton for punishment, but there was something about the pastor that I found intriguing even as I detested him. Maybe my youthful memorization of Luther's Catechism made me an easy mark for Pastor Mall's extreme confidence in his own worldview. It was almost as he sensed my fascination and so he did more missionary work in my cafe than in any of the town's bars, which arguably had the more damaged souls. So when he asked, "Will I see you at the Gunderson funeral today?" the question struck home in a way that didn't really make sense. The Gundersons never once set foot in the Loon Town Cafe. I'm not sure I would have even recognized them. "Why would I?" I responded.

"Why? The Lord has taken back two of His precious lives to serve

Him. We must honor Him by celebrating the reunion of our dear friends with His spirit, as they prepare to bathe forever in the glory of His pearly gates."

"They were smothered because of bat dung," I pointed out.

The pastor had the look of a man slapped. "They were my parishioners, and I was their shepherd here on earth. It does not matter how they died. What matters is the hereafter, not the here and now." He looked around my cafe as though it were a fly-infested, open-air meat market in a third-world country. "Why should I expect you to understand or appreciate this mystery of life, given what you do." For God's sake, I wasn't a murderer or pimp.

But at least once a week Pastor Mall attempted to convert me. Other bar owners had their visits too, but I was the favored target since the records at the Old World Lutheran Church disclosed that my parents had once been parishioners. Mall was determined to pull me back into his fold. Not that there was much chance of that. A major turning point of my adolescent years was the distressing discovery that most people actually believed in God and the Bible. In some youthful deluded way, I had always thought that everyone simply pretended to believe. This revelation created quite a rift between my boyhood friend Tommy and me. He never truly trusted me again. It never seemed important to me that there be a supreme being in whom I could place my trust. I would trust myself and let the chips fall where they might.

On the other hand, Pastor Mall was concerned with everyone's chips. Once he had been called to Thread, he found plenty of fertile soil in our citizens' vibrant lives and managed to plant his little seeds of disapproval into most every public setting. Wherever a group of citizens gathered to make a decision, the pastor was there. His silver-haired, close-cropped head would bob up and down as he tried to grab the spotlight. He'd stand up, his ample stomach stretching against his black shirt, his white collar straining to pop out, his eyes bulging and the tirade would begin.

No activity was too innocent to escape his scrutiny. Why staff lifeguards at the park; swimming simply encouraged nudity. Abolish basketball; putting skimpily clad athletic boys next to bouncing cheerleader girls with skirts hiked to forbidden regions was just asking for bastard babies. The town's festivals only attracted big city tourists with big city ways.

But his biggest issue was with drinkers. Why should a town of 743 souls require eight places to buy alcohol—nine, if you included Red's Piggly Wiggly? It was no use to argue that most of these places catered to the tourist trade since in his mind tourists were simply part of the devil's plan.

A few at the Old World Lutheran Church were giving Pastor Mall a chance. They pointed out his hard past, what with divorcing one wife and having another run off with a traveling salesman. If he could find the right woman, maybe then he'd settle down and be a good preaching man.

"Listen to me, Mr. Pearson," the pastor was swinging into a new pitch, "come to the burial to honor the Gundersons. I'm sure your parents knew them and would want you to do them this remembrance. Besides It would help atone for your moral decay."

"What!"

"It surrounds you. That young man who works for you. His father invites in the devil, sitting in the cemetary every afternoon talking to the grave of his wife instead of accepting God's will. And your waitress's family. Consorting with the Indians, I hear. Plus they go to that blasphemous church. And your cook, the way she flirts with that traveling salesman. Officer Campbell has confided to me his concerns about her behavior. It would do you good to stay on the right side of God." His collar popped open, and his triple chin wobbled like a Thanksgiving turkeys wattle.

"Maybe I'll see you there," I gave in. Actually it might be good to be more involved with the community. Like Henry Van Elkind said once, I should be in touch with the pulse of the town. I could help guide the way it thought. Instead of this pompous pot-bellied man.

"Do come," he said sternly. "Perhaps my final words for the Gundersons will help you take the path to salvation for your own soul."

Thelma nudged me and said again, "What a windbag." I returned to the moment.

"I'm not paying attention," I whispered back. I continued to survey the church. Of course, my cafe trio was there: Bromley, Claire and Mr. Packer. Mr. and Mrs. Trueheart were sitting near the front. Amanda Manny who still ran the decorating shop was midway back, and probably wishing it were her Drano-drinking husband who was occupying one of the coffins. Rueben Cord, the butcher at Red's Piggly Wiggly. Several school teachers. Officer Campbell. Some high school students. I didn't see any of the summer folk, like the Van Elkinds. But then why would I? They had all left for the season. Even if they had been in town, none of the local people mattered to them. The locals were just the people who mowed their lawns, repaired their plumbing and guided them to the best fishing holes.

Nor were Chip Frozen Bear and his sister Jacqueline in the church. I was starting to like Chip as much as Cynthia was beginning to adore him. I still didn't understand what he hoped to accomplish by being part of the American Seasons deal. I wondered if he even knew about Henry's strategy to scare townspeople into selling their land cheap.

The pews were filled with people who were likely targets of Van Elkind and his crowd. Most of them just scraped by, living from season to season on what they might eke out of the summer crowd. Some had been born here and never left. Others fled to the area because they couldn't deal with pressures of metropolitan life. And then there was me. I had escaped and then I came back when I needed a new escape.

I was becoming uncomfortable with this funeral. The last funeral I had attended had been in Brooklyn, and I didn't like being there either.

Pastor Paul Mall kept glancing over the congregation. At first, I thought my fidgeting was capturing his attention. Then I realized he was looking at the Gunderson boy, Josh, with clear signs of displeasure. At one point, I thought he would stop the sermon and direct some chastisement directly to the boy. God only knew what Josh could be doing to get the pastor so upset. Probably chewing gum.

I continued my survey of the congregation and reached the back row on the opposite side. There was Pete Sullivan, our very own Reverend Willy. What was he doing here? I guess he really did try to attend every church service in town—including the funerals.

Another poke in the ribs from Thelma just as the organist began a mighty dirge. "Stand up," she whispered. "We're walking across the street to the cemetery."

A light sprinkling of sleet was falling as we departed the church. A thin layer of ice formed on the flight of exterior steps that led down to the street. The procession of two coffins, each supported by six men in black, was descending the steps. One man slipped on the ice, momentarily losing his footing and causing his end of the coffin to bob, setting in motion a curious undulation of coffins as each of the pall bearers strained to see what had happened while striving to hold up their lot.

The sky was completely dark with storm clouds. The little pellets of ice stung as they fell, flung against our faces by a wind just strong enough to make its point. The empty branches of the maples were swaying. The evergreens at the edge of the cemetery were already dusted with light ice. As the sleet hit the recently mounded dirt, freshly spaded from the earth, it melted into tiny puddles of water beside the two graves.

Pastor Mall stood between the two graves with a coffin on either side of him. The crowd divided onto two sides, with only young Josh Gunderson standing at the foot of both graves, looking solemnly at the two gaping holes.

The women pulled out their scarves and wrapped them around their hair. Out of coat pockets, men pulled stocking caps and put them on. The temperature was dropping even as Pastor Paul Mall began his final words. "From ashes to ashes," he began. He looked up, seeming to notice for the first time how evenly the crowd was divided between the two graves. On the right hand and the left. There was nothing to distinguish on which side each congregation member had gone. Somehow, Thelma and I had ended up on different sides. Only Josh, stood alone, by himself.

Indecision flitted across Mall's face. He looked at Josh, who looked directly back at him, Josh's head held high and bare in the sleet, his clothes better suited to a trendy street during a Los Angeles rainy season than to a Wisconsin November. He smiled.

The young man's smile seemed warm, friendly, but totally wrong. He looked far too healthy, too pleased for a man whose parents had died so tragically. I looked at him closer and I saw the artifice. He was wearing makeup. The mascara around his eyes was beginning to run in the sleet, creating black icy tears that conflicted with his smiling lips. Shiny, silvery glitter reflected from his eyelids.

The pastor looked as though he had downed a dozen lemons. He stared again at the division of people on his left and his right. I could tell he was thinking of Revelations and the Final Judgment, and desperately seeking in his mind some way to discuss that in a manner that only damned Josh. But he couldn't solve the puzzle. So he looked back at his prayer book and continued the service.

Pastor Mall's indecision had taken only a moment, and most of the attendees had not noticed anything. They had kept their heads and eyes lowered, not only out of respect, but out of a desire to avoid the elements. Josh continued to look forward and I followed the line of his gaze and saw that he wasn't looking at the pastor, but at one of the pall bearers. It was focused on Tony Masters, a young man was married to the town's nurse, whose beauty caused many a young lad's heart to flutter when they had to visit the town clinic for their annual high school basketball physical. Masters was staring back at Josh, not with belligerence, but maybe with a kind of hunger.

I looked down embarrassed. I wanted the ceremony over. I was freezing. I was uncomfortable. And I didn't even know these people.

I looked back up. Josh and Masters were continuing to look into one another's eyes across the emptiness of the graves. Pastor Paul Mall was finishing up a prayer. Everyone else was looking down at their feet with proper reverence. Except one person. Danny Lahti was also watching. Watching Josh. Watching Josh watch Masters. Watching me watch Josh watch Masters. He saw me watch him. He didn't blush or look away as he normally might. He seemed to sigh and let his eyes drift down to the funeral program in his hands.

Earlier in the day, during my exchange with Pastor Mall, Mr. Packer had been sitting quietly at the counter drinking his coffee. He harrumphed at its end. There was no other word to describe the sound he made. It was clearly a tone dismissing worthless chatter. Pastor Paul Mall looked over in Mr. Packer's direction. "Is there something on your mind?" he asked even as his tone implied that nothing important could flow from a man of Mr. Packer's unkempt demeanor.

"I was listening to your ruminations on the private lives of everyone you encounter, thinking to myself what an intelligent man you must be to be able to know exactly what each of us should or should not be doing."

"It does not take great intelligence when you follow the words of the Lord."

Dennis Frahmann

"If you say so," Mr. Packer smiled.

Pastor Paul Mall stopped, a scowl forming on his face. He sensed that he had stepped into a trap. But he couldn't quite figure out what the trap might be. "You should take a bath old man," he went on the offensive, "instead of trying to debate theology."

"You know, Wally," Mr. Packer said to me, deliberately ignoring the fuming pastor, "I'm reminded of another fellow from Alabama who used to come through Thread each summer. We called him Petey the Peach Boy.

"Petey was a good-natured boy, kind of dim-witted, but his heart was always in the right place. In those days, you could keep a calendar by when Petey would show up in the Town Square driving his dilapidated 1939 Ford flatbed truck. The back of it would be piled high with bushels of peaches, all freshly picked from orchards down south. He'd set up shop for a day or two, sell the best peaches you ever tasted from the back of that truck, and then he would be on to the next town, just traveling down the road till the last peach was sold.

"And there was no one who loved a peach as much as Petey. He was one of those lucky people who loved his work. You asked him how the peaches were, and he would just reach into one of those bushel baskets and take out a peach without even looking at it. He'd bring it up to this mouth, and sink his teeth through that fuzzy yellow red skin, letting his mouth close around the soft luscious flesh, and the peach would be so ripe that its golden juices would just flow around his lips and over his chin and drip to the ground.

"There would be this smile that would animate Petey's face, just took over every inch of his cheeks and his eyes, until that entire face was animated like an angel's. 'That's a peach!' he'd say, and then he would keep on eating that peach, slurping at it. There was such pleasure in his simple face that you would have paid a fortune to get a hold of some of those peaches.

"But you didn't need to pay a fortune. A couple of dollars and the bushel was yours. And when all the housewives had paid their visit to Petey the Peach Boy, he would take down his sign and his little canopy strung to the wooden rails on the flat bed and he would be on his way to Timberton, and then to Ashland, and wherever else his trails took him. But we were left with the treasures of the best peaches there ever were, and we knew how to

178

enjoy them." Mr. Packer had a wistful look as he reached for his coffee cup.

"A very nice story, but I really must be going," Pastor Paul Mall gave me a look that suggested he thought Mr. Packer was as dim as Petey the Peach Boy.

"Hold on just a second there, Mr. Mall. I'm not finished with my story." Mr. Packer took another sip of coffee. He looked out toward the empty town square underneath now graying skies, then continued. "We must have seen Petey every summer for ten, fifteen years. Then he stopped coming. We had to rely on getting our peaches at the Piggly Wiggly. I heard tell some minister down there in Alabama got Petey religion, convinced him to give up on all his passions, including his passion for peaches.

"I don't know if that's true or not, but I miss Petey. It's been over twenty-five years since he showed up with that truck, and I still miss seeing him eat a peach. I never saw a man happier than Petey was when he had a peach in his mouth. I hope he's as happy with his religion. I hope so, but I wouldn't bet on it." Mr. Packer put a dollar on the counter and gave me a half-hearted salute. "It's time for this old man to wander on. Don't want to overstay my welcome.

"And Mr. Mall," he said as he walked out the door, "for God's sake, let people eat their peaches." He was out the door.

Pastor Mall finished his prayer, the coffins were lowered into the grave and then he sprinkled a handful of ice-covered dirt across each grave. Josh did the same, but the pastor ignored him.

"Ooh boy, it's cold. Let's get out of here," Thelma was pulling me along as she moved back toward the church. She had on a heavy ski parka and thick woolen mittens. If anyone was warm, it should have been her.

"Back to the restaurant?" I asked.

"Don't be silly," she replied. "The Ladies' Aid is having a potluck supper. Anyone who doesn't want to cook tonight in this town is already here. We might as well keep the cafe closed and enjoy the food here. What do you say?"

Who could say no? We descended into the basement of the Old World Lutheran Church, where several of the older members of the Ladies' Aid were busily setting out the town's specialties.

"Now this is what I call real eating," said Thelma.

"Thanks a lot," I replied. There wasn't one menu item along the entire length of two long tables that I would even consider serving in my restaurant. But I was hungry, so I grabbed a plate and began working my way through the offerings.

First, there was the boring stuff. Sandwiches made with sharp cheddar cheese on rye bread with butter, or with Wonder bread and a ground bologna combination that included sweet green pickles and lots of Miracle Whip. Miracle Whip seemed to be an essential ingredient to many of the items here.

Canned soup was almost as important as Miracle Whip. As incredible a baker as Thelma was, she had an unusually strong loyalty to Campbells. She believed that virtually anything could be improved by the use of a can of condensed soup. Spread before me was a range of evidence from some of the best kitchens in Thread. Here was that old standby—the ground beef hot dish. A casserole made with a pound of hamburger browned with onion and mixed with sliced carrots and sliced potatoes and, of course, a can of cream of tomato soup. After an hour in the oven at 400 degrees, you had a tasty hot dish suitable for any funeral.

The many hot dishes at the funeral supper attested to the popularity of the Gundersons. There was the green beans and onion ring casserole made with cream of mushroom soup. Next to it was scalloped potatoes and ham bound by cream of potato soup. And here was another cream soup concoction, this time tomato pulling together curly macaroni and browned ground beef. And what was the secret ingredient in the tuna hot dish? Could it be cream of celery soup?

In truth I loved all these dishes, but I wasn't about to let Thelma know that. Nor could I eat too much, because there were still the salads and the desserts to be sampled. A big bowl of fruit ambrosia beckoned me. A simple thing to make, really. Empty a can or two of fruit cocktail, thicken the juice with cornstarch, and then mix it with a container of frozen whipped topping. Why bother with whipping cream just because you're in the dairy state? Here was another funeral fancy: a fruit salad made with unadulterated cherry pie filling used to bind together canned syrupy cling peaches, canned pears, and a jar of maraschino cherries.

Those were the salads, of course. Time to move on to the desserts. Apple pie, cherry pie, black bottom pie, maraschino cherry cake, lemon cake with poppy seed pudding icing. I half expected to see the Gundersons walk through the door, because if they were on their way to heaven, then this surely had to be a stopping point for their journey.

"Disgusting spectacle," moaned Pastor Paul Mall as he stopped by our table unwanted "The boy's a Sodomite. If his parents were alive, they would disown him. To have to look at his mascara eyes as I gave my sermon. I'm a Christian man with feelings for sorrow, or I would just have thrown him from my church. It's an affront to God to behave that way. And at one's parents' funeral!"

"I think the boy's kind of cute," said Thelma.

"We'll see what the Lord says on Judgment Day," huffed the pastor and he went to the next table. Josh didn't seem concerned about upsetting the spiritual leader of his dead parents. In fact, he was holding a small court of his own in the far corner of the church basement. I noticed that both Masters and Danny were among the circle of people who were listening to a very animated Josh. Peals of laughter floated out. Then there was quiet as everyone at the table leaned in closer as Josh began another story.

"He probably has a colorful life back there in California," I mused.

"Probably," Thelma agreed. "Are you done pigging out? Ready to head back to the restaurant? See who shows up?"

"I thought you said no one would come in tonight, and that there was no sense in opening the place," I pointed out.

"Well, I do recall that Gilbert mentioned he might be driving through Thread tonight, and if he did he was going to stop in. It's a nasty night out there. Don't want to make the poor man get out in the cold for nothing." Thelma stood as though there could be no argument about returning.

"Fine," I said. "Might as well see if we can make a few more bucks."

"Great to see you here, Wally," I heard Red's voice boom out as I felt a heavy hand slap me on the back. Red leaned in close to whisper. "It's a damn shame about the Gundersons. But they say every cloud has its silver lining. Bernard and Anna own two hundred acres of swampland right in the middle of parcel we need to put together. Should be able to get it for a song from that one. Fucking city boy." He tilted his head dismissively toward Josh.

I returned a half-hearted smile and looked over toward Thelma, who returned a dismissive look. "We should be going," she said.

"Don't let me stop you," said Red. He was on to the next table, shaking hands and smiling.

Another loud peal of laughter rushed from Josh's corner. I looked over and Danny who was giggling and rocking in his chair. His entire face was animated.

"It's nice to see the boy happy, isn't it?" said Thelma.

"Yes," I agreed.

"It would be nice to see you that happy once in a while," she added.

"What do you mean by that?" I asked.

She just smiled and waved me to follow her. I looked back at the corner with Josh and his admirers. The circle of followers had grown. They were having entirely too much fun for a funeral. Pastor Mall was standing with several of the leaders of the Ladies Aid near the doorway. They too were looking in Josh's direction. "I always liked the boy," said one of the ladies. Pastor Mall turned on her rapidly and began a new sermon.

"Let's get out of here," said Thelma. We stepped into the cold evening. The sleet had turned into full snow, but the steps up from the basement were still dangerously icy. Once up on the street, we could see a landscape transformed by the ice and snow into a wintry wonderland. The lone streetlamp flooded light through the nearest ice-covered branches in a shimmering glow. Beyond that, the icy white glimmered in the shadows.

"Stop," I said. Was that a bear at the edge of the cemetery? It should be hibernating. Then I saw the movement again and I resumed breathing.

"It's Toivo Lahti," said Thelma. "He must have waited until the funeral was over before he visited his wife's grave."

"Does he really go there every night?"

"Every night," she replied, "for an hour at least. When Lempi was still alive, they would walk for an hour every evening, hand in hand. I guess it's the closest he can get to her now, and he just can't let go of that hand."

We stood there quietly for a moment watching the crouched figure in the shadows, his form up against the granite gravestone, the fluffy snow gently falling to land on him and on her memory. We turned and began walking toward the town square, toward the warmth of my cafe. But I was drawn to look back, again and again, to stare after that sad figure, tied to his love, trying to hang onto a disappearing happiness in the cold reality of the falling snow. And what could I say? We all need to find our own way of letting go of lost loves.

CHAPTER TWELVE

As the weather grew colder, the Loon Town Cafe menu begged for a transformation. The lower temperatures of fall and winter demanded substance in your stomach: warm porridge in the morning, hot soups in the afternoon, hearty roasts at night.

"So what should I add to the menu?" I asked Thelma. My faithful trio perked up.

"If you ask me," began Bromley, even though I hadn't, "I would vote for potato pancakes. Not that many can make them like I want them. Too many people think they should be a pancake. Flour and eggs and all that. God darn nonsense. No, what a potato pancake needs is lots of grated potatoes."

"With fresh apple sauce," Claire burst in, "you know the kind where the apples are still all chunky and it's warm and you just let it flow all over the pancakes."

"I like mine with sour cream," said Cynthia.

"No," Claire said firmly, "it has to be home-made apple sauce, made from Macintosh apples, not those tasteless Red Delicious. All Red Delicious are good for is a crunch."

"What about Granny Smiths?" asked Thelma.

"What about sour cream?" protested Cynthia. She flounced her hair and marched off toward the kitchen. "You never listen to any of my ideas."

Over the last few days, Bromley had been trying to curry the good favors of the Trueheart family, and Cynthia's reaction gave him pause.

"Poor girl," he said. "School must be getting to her what with that Kip Van Elkind always fawning about."

"Back to potato pancakes," I said, "They could marry well with roasted pork loin. Maybe grate a lot of potatoes, mix them with a little minced onion, some flour and egg and fry them crispy brown."

"Sounds more like hash browns to me," pointed out Mr. Packer.

"Nonsense," broke in Bromley, "he's describing potato pancakes just the way I like them. Add them to the menu and I'll be here every night." In the five months since I had opened the cafe, Bromley had yet to come for dinner, and I didn't expect potato pancakes to be the winning lure. Of the regulars, only Mr. Packer ever bought dinner in my place. Perhaps Bromley and Claire frequented some other spot, or maybe they huddled over a hot plate in their barren rooms in the Thread Grand Hotel.

The two of them lived a strange life. As long as anyone could remember, each had been a tenant at the hotel. Often, their two rooms would be the only ones rented in the deteriorating building. The hotel never had been very elegant, but by now, any town larger than Thread would consider it a flop house. The shabby lobby that faced the town square had two large bay windows above the street. In each window, overgrown but sickly maidenhair ferns sat on high Victorian carved plant stands. The lobby also held some late 1950s sofas upholstered in the favored indestructible fabric of the era, with a few cigarette burns here and there to show the passing of the decades. At times, Bromley gave the impression that he owned the place. But it actually belonged to Red Trueheart, like nearly every other business in town. Claire, they rumored, had once been a chamber maid to the establishment, as well as the town floozy. Now both she and Bromley survived on small Social Security checks, along with Bromley's occasional real estate commission.

Mr. Packer's story was more of an unknown. He lived in a large house one block in from Little Sapphire Lake. Every room was filled with items that Mr. Packer had collected. He liked to find items of value in people's trash and bring them home, turning his home into a bulging stuffed pinata of other people's discards.

Loud laughter at the door signaled the entry of Josh Gunderson and Kip Van Elkind. Josh was short, dark-haired, slim and slender. He had the looks and moves of a model. His clothes were stylish and distinctive, and he carried himself with a certain peacock self-assurance. Kip moved with a dull slowness. He had acquired a strange pumped-up look as though he had been working out without regard to what he built up. Unlike the neat cut of Josh's hair, Kip's was stringy and in need of a wash. As usual, his clothes were dirty and tattered, pinned together more for value than for any punk look. Josh's eyes sparkled with wit; Kip's burned dully. A more unlikely duo was hard to imagine, yet in the days since Josh's return, he had befriended the outcast rich kid. And already Josh seemed to know more about the goings-on in Thread than even Bromley.

"Wally man," Josh called out, "you got any champagne in this place. I feel like celebrating. I got two people bidding on that worthless swamp my folks left me. I might just be able to head back to Los Angeles with real cash in hand."

"Maybe it's a little early to start celebrating," I said, thinking of not only the time but the likely bidders.

"It's nearly noon," he replied. "Why don't you have that cute young waiter of yours . . . what's his name . . . Danny, yeah that's it. Let him bring it out."

"Nah," objected Kip with a goofy grin, "I want Cynthia."

Josh smiled expansively, "You heard the man. Let the lovely Cynthia deliver."

Kip was stoned, and Josh was amused. Eleven o'clock in the morning and both were out of control. "Sorry," I said. "You have to be twenty-one to drink in this state. And since Kip can't have any alcohol, I think it would be best if I didn't serve either of you." Josh smiled his acceptance of my verdict.

"Tell me, is that Danny here? I'd like to admire his looks before I have lunch?"

Kip flopped down by a table that hadn't yet been cleared. "You're such a fag. You just can't help yourself." He started giggling. Cynthia peeked out from the kitchen and quickly beat a hasty retreat. Cynthia wouldn't want to leave the kitchen until Kip was out of the room, and Danny hadn't yet shown up for his shift. I guess I would be handling this table. "But don't help yourself to me. Don't even try. Only Cynthia's gonna get to see what I can do."

For my benefit, Josh raised his eyebrows. "So much for trying to convert Kip. Takes a few favors, but his true colors always shine through. What's a guy to do?" He sat down next to Kip and clapped him on the shoulder. "You're a good man, Kip. Wally, can I see the menu?"

I deposited a menu and began to clear away the remnants of the earlier breakfast crowd. The funeral glitter was gone from Josh's eyelids as was the mascara. He looked like a clean-cut young man, good-looking in fact—not at all the flirtatious, mourning son of the funeral. One thing for certain, Josh's appearance brought some life into town. Pastor Paul Mall had thundered from the pulpit on Sunday about big city's sins and man's depravities. His eloquence painted a seething lake of brimfire in hell reserved for anyone who dared to think of any acts between those of the same sex.

"He's too hard on Josh," is what Officer Campbell had told me later that day relecting on the sermon and the funeral. "The boy has had a tough life. And he was always trying to shock his parents. Why not do it one last time?"

And as long as you were doing it, you might as well shock the whole town. Unfortunately for Josh, few in Thread were really shocked. Everyone had pretty much deduced that Josh was gay by the time he was a sophomore in high school. It was probably a draw as to who knew it first— Josh or the rest of the town. Always prone to flamboyant overstatement with a flair for the dramatic and a keen ability to tell a funny story, Josh was always well-liked. He still was. The town folk didn't care what a fussy pastor had to say.

"Sit down with us, Wally," Josh said. "The place is nearly empty. Besides if you're not working, Cynthia will have to come out of the kitchen and take our order. We're just helping my friend here achieve his fantasy."

"She wants me, but she won't admit it. The bitch is playing hard to get." Kip's mood was shifting.

"Maybe she's interested in someone else," I said.

"Yeah, who? Show me the son of a bitch who would try to take my girl away from me. Someday, she'll realize it."

"Delightful town, isn't it?" Josh said to me. "I can see why you left a dull place like Manhattan to move here."

"It has its attractions," I replied.

"I think I could recite them all to you. First, good old Claire. I think they put a bat in her belfry every time she slept with someone. She still does, you know. Her little men probably tell her to."

"She does not," I protested.

"Wake up, Wally boy! Even in Thread, she couldn't live on her Social Security—at least not as long as you make her pay for breakfast every day. My father said she was the first person he ever went to bed with. Back then, it was rather like a senior class trip for all the boys to head down to the hotel for an evening with Claire. Sort of like *The Best Little Whorehouse in Texas*, except I don't think the boys ever danced naked in the showers as they got ready. Now that would have been a tradition I would have enjoyed." Josh noticed Cynthia taking another peek out of the kitchen. He waved comically, and motioned her forward with his index finger.

"I think you're exaggerating," I said. "People in this town develop reputations which have nothing to do with reality."

Cynthia walked up to the table, looking straight at Josh and deliberately avoiding eye contact with Kip. "Would you like something?" she asked with no sign of her usual happiness.

"Just some coffee for my friend and me." She turned. Josh yelled after her, "Thanks."

"Man, she don't even look at me," Kip moaned. He thought for a moment. "She's so fucking hot for me, I drive her crazy."

For a moment, I wished that Chip Frozen Bear was eating here today. I was convinced he had started eating at the cafe just to help promote rumors about the mining companies coming into the area. But last week, he had come to Cynthia's defense when Kip had been in a particularly offensive mode. On the other hand, it seemed Chip was mimicking Bromley's tune and catering to Cynthia's moods to somehow influence her father.

"Take Kip's reputation," continued Josh. "Is it an exaggeration to say that he is a dim-witted little hoodlum? A petty thief who would be in jail today if not for the money of his extremely wealthy father?"

"Leave my fucking dad out of this."

Josh raised his shoulders, spread his arms out, palms forward as though to include the entire town. "I rest my case."

"You have a quite a reputation yourself," I said.

He laughed. "And quite deserved, I assure you. I work hard at it. Any sensible person knows not to wear mascara in an ice storm, but I was going after my Tammy Faye Bakker look. I thought a famous preacher's wife would appeal to the Reverend. I guess I was wrong. Such a sin."

"So why are you sticking around?" I wanted to know.

"Why not? I'm a land tycoon with property to sell. My father always wanted to turn his swamp land into cranberry bogs or wild rice marshes. He never had the money to do it. Maybe I should hold on to the spot and realize his dream. On the other hand, my father believed in life insurance. Mom and him have left me quite comfortable. It doesn't really matter what I do."

"I don't think you're sticking around just to sell that property. Barbara Trueheart is a realtor. She could handle it for you," I said.

"Wouldn't that be like having the wolf protect the sheep? I think the Truehearts are behind one of these insistent offers to buy. Besides Barbara has such atrocious taste. I could never do business with her. The only person in town with poorer taste is Amanda Manny.

"Now, there's another example of a reputation that's totally deserved. She drove Jack Manny to attempt suicide. Too bad he was too stupid to do it right. Did you ever wonder who pays those hospital bills for him? He's in a private hospital you know. Still can't eat a thing after all these years."

"No," I replied, "I never wondered."

"Kip," Josh turned to his greasy friend, who was looking vacantly in the direction of the kitchen, apparently awaiting the return of Cynthia, "I hear your father is very philanthropic about paying the hospital bills of some of Thread's poorer citizens."

"What ya talking about?" Kip asked, not turning to look at us.

"That seems unlikely to me," I replied. "And quit trying to avoid telling me why you're hanging around. Why not take the money and run?"

Rueben Cord, the butcher at the Piggly Wiggly, walked in for lunch. He waved over to our table, and said, "Hi Josh. How ya doing?"

Josh waved back. "I like being the big fish in the little pond where everyone knows your name. Isn't that how it goes? I've only been gone six years. I've done a lot in Los Angeles. Sold real estate. Designed dresses. Even worked as a stand-in for Charles Nelson Reilly. What a crazy guy. But I'm nothing special in L.A., just another gay boy in West Hollywood. Here though I'm something special. A unique commodity. A flower in a field of weeds. Why not stay?"

Cynthia was walking over with a fresh pot of coffee and new cups. As I cleared away the old dishes, she gave me a look of disdain that made me feel like a Nazi collaborator in World War II. "I'll get all of this out of your way," I said.

She set a mug in front of Josh and poured a cup. Then she did the same for Kip. Kip reached out to grab her wrist, "Don't run away," he said.

"Let go right now," she said, "or I'll pour this entire pot in your crotch." He let go.

Right then, Danny hurried into the restaurant. Josh looked up. "Maybe I'll stick around for lunch."

"Sorry, I'm a little late Wally. Class ran over." Danny looked at Josh and smiled weakly. "Hi." He walked into the kitchen, just as Cynthia was rushing out.

"Now that's Danny here, I got to be going," she said.

"But you're supposed to be here another hour," I said.

"No, I'm not," she said emphatically with her eyes giving a sharp dart in Kip's direction. "I told you I had to go over and see my father before my fifth period class." Like that, she was out the door, across the square and into the Piggly Wiggly.

"Man," Kip moaned, "that girl will do anything to avoid me. No way I can get her to pay me any attention. She just don't know how much I want her." Kip opened a couple of packages of sugar and poured them into his mug of coffee. Morosely, he stirred and stirred, waiting for it all to dissolve.

Bromley, Claire, and Mr. Packer had all swiveled around on their stools at the counter to watch our table. Bromley, sensing an opportunity to pontificate, raised his ample girth and waddled over to the table.

"You know Wally, I was thinking about your desire to change the menu for the winter months, and I'd like to recommend that you add a few more desserts. Can never have too many desserts."

"I was going more in the direction of adding some dishes with wild rice or cranberries, sort of to go with the season," I replied.

"Wild rice and cranberries. What kind of dessert would that make?" Bromley said.

Danny came out of the kitchen, already wearing his apron and ready to take over Cynthia's role. Josh motioned him over. "What you guys talking about?" Danny asked. He looked at Bromley and me, avoiding the eyes of both Kip and Josh, and yet he seemed hyperaware of Josh. "Something interesting, I bet."

"Could I have more coffee?" Josh asked.

"Wally's got same damn fool idea about making a dessert out of wild rice and cranberries. He asks me my advice, and I give it to him, and then he turns it around into some type of foolishness. Cranberries and wild rice. Sounds more like god darn medicine," Bromley was attacking his own mistaken idea with all the fervor of a political campaign.

Claire came over. "What are you boys fighting about?" She looked Josh up and down slowly, almost disdainfully. "Is this young one telling tales about us that just aren't so. He's got quite the imagination."

"No, ma'am, I'm not," Josh replied.

"It sounds like Wally's going to make leipapurro," Danny said excitedly. "I haven't had it since my mother died."

"Lumps of poodle . . . that sounds good," Kip pretended to stick his finger down his throat. Danny blushed. Josh stared at Danny intently. I was confused

"Now that brings back memories. Remember Bromley how that old Finnish woman who used to work at the hotel made it every winter." Claire seemed more certain of her memories than usual.

"What the hell is leipapurro?" I demanded to know.

Danny was excited. "It's a Finnish dessert that my mom used to always make for my dad. She called it a whipped air pudding, and she only made it in the winter and it was Dad's favorite. I offered to make it for him, but it's like he thinks only Mom could make it. Maybe if you made some, he'd try it here." Danny had been trying to convince his father to come into the restaurant for dinner ever since he started working here.

"So tell me about this Finnish dessert," I said.

"It sounds kind of weird when you describe it," Danny made a face that caused Josh to smile. "But it's really good. It's like you make a really thin version of cream of wheat using cranberry juice and sugar instead of milk or water. Then you beat it for half an hour with a Mixmaster. It gets thicker and thicker, bigger and bigger, like a big cranberry snow bank."

"Think of it as a dull pink cloud with little specks of wheat in it," suggested Josh.

"And this is good?" I asked skeptically.

Claire was enthusiastic. "Oh it is. You pour some heavy cream over the top of it and it's wonderful. Remember, Bromley, at the hotel, how you used to poke a little hole in the center of your pudding and would pour the cream as slowly as you could, and it would soak all the way through and come up from the bottom of the bowl, loosening the pudding and the whole thing would float like a big pink iceberg."

Despite the enthusiastic reminiscing, I watched Kip's reactions. I liked to try new foods on the menu, but I didn't want to fall into the same mistake I made last summer when I added to the menu quenelles of walleyed pike with kasha dumplings. I thought it sounded great. The few adventurous souls who ordered it never cleaned their plates. And because forming those stupid quenelles was a lot of hard work, Thelma never forgave me for that menu addition. Kip didn't look like he would even consider trying a cranberry porridge for dessert.

"Oh, Kip, lighten up," said Josh. "You have a look on your face like we're talking about poison. You'd love it if you tried it. Wally, add it to the menu just for Danny's sake. It would make his father happy." Danny cast a big smile in Josh's direction.

Kip was on another track. "I don't care about any fucking food. Why am I still in this town? No one likes me. I might as well just die. Me and Grammy. We're both just outcasts. Because no one wants us bothering them in their fucking fancy lives in Chicago."

What was this? "Your father sent you here because he cares about you and wants to keep you out of trouble. You're here because he loves you." I was pretty sure I didn't believe anything so positive about Henry Van Elkind, but I wanted to get back to the food.

"None of them fucking care about me. Barbara and Hank would just as soon I off'ed myself. It would be one less thing for them to fucking worry about." Kip's high had completely vanished, leaving a more morose Kip that was no more appealing than the belligerent one.

Kip lived on an island of his own making. Some afternoons, the cafe would be filled with kids from the high school. Most came because in such a small school, there could only be a few cliques, with the basketball team and cheerleading squad being the most prestigious circle there was, and Cynthia was the queen of this group. She reigned alone. A couple of the boys on the team, Jack and Alex in particular, were definitely knights in waiting, but all bowed to Cynthia. I wasn't sure whether it was due to her natural innocence or her father's position.

No clique was associated with Danny, although he seemed well enough liked. Kip was another story. He led his own small—very small— circle of admirers who saw in him the big city embodiment of bad. But these were mostly seventh and eighth graders who just liked being in company of a senior. In a larger school, they wouldn't even have been in the same building as Kip. The couple of truly bad teenagers in town had quickly sized up Kip as an unpleasant pain in the ass; they avoided him as much as Cynthia did.

If Kip had ever taken the time to find clean clothes or wash his face, you might have felt sorry for him. He had been banished by his parents from his natural kingdom. He had grown up getting whatever he wanted and now he was stuck in a rambling log cabin estate with a woman in her eighties and a condescending servant, dealing with a crush on a girl, who while she knew he existed, would just as soon he didn't.

"I bet you think I'm making it up," Kip snarled.

"Making what up?" I asked.

"About trying to off myself. It was last summer on the beach at our camp. With one of Dad's shot guns. I sat there, had a few beers, watched the sun set, and I aimed that gun right at me."

"But then you couldn't do it, right?" Josh asked. "When the time came to pull the trigger you knew life was worth living."

"Fuck no, it wasn't worth living. Not then. Not now. You better believe I pulled the trigger. I just missed."

"You missed! You point a gun at yourself and you miss!"

"Hey, you fucking fruitcake. It ain't so easy pointing a gun at yourself. Try it sometime."

"I'd rather not," Josh said smartly.

"I'd rather not," Kip mouthed back in an exaggerated emotion. "I bet you don't even believe me."

"We believe you," I said.

I'd believe anything the kid said. I regretted ever telling Van Elkind that I would keep any eye out for the well-being of Kip. The kid was beyond well-being. When I thought back on it, I regretted damn near everything I had ever said to Van Elkind. He got me involved with that big dinner at his place last summer and nearly stiffed me on the bill. He conned me into getting involved with this stupid American Seasons project. And he tried to make me buy into being the guardian of his schizoid kid. The next time I saw him I was going to let him know exactly what I thought of him.

"I don't believe him," Josh said. "If someone wanted to shoot themselves, they'd shoot themselves. How would they miss? You put the gun in your mouth and you pull the trigger. Any moron can do that."

"I didn't want a gun in my mouth," Kip muttered.

"So?" Josh replied, dragging out the word.

Kip looked at him sullenly. "So," he said, dragging out the word just as much, "I pointed the gun at my heart and I pulled the trigger and I missed. The bullet went through my shoulder. I didn't know there would be such a kick."

"Uh, huh. Sounds tough. Danny, could I get some more cream?" Danny rushed to Josh's side with a new pitcher.

"You don't fucking believe me. Well, let me show you." Kip stood up, facing the plate glass window looking out onto the square. He began to unbutton his greasy plaid shirt, pulled the shirttails out from the pants and let the shirt fall off his shoulders. Underneath was a tattered, once white, thermal undershirt. He began to pull it up over his head, exposing a swastika tattoo right below his navel.

"Wow, a strip show in Thread! I'm impressed." Josh emitted a low whistle.

"Josh," I whispered, "leave him alone. He's a fucked-up kid. I know he's tried to kill himself at least once before. That time I helped his father carry him home."

By now, Kip had his undershirt completely off. To me, it looked as though he had carved a few more tattoos since the morning Van Elkind and I had found him naked by the lake. He had also put on some bulk. But he wasn't interested in showing us either the tattoos or his muscles. "Look at that," he said pointing to a purplish round scar, just below the shoulder, above his biceps. "That's where the bullet went through."

"Looks like it healed nicely," Josh said smartly.

"You are one fucking asshole," Kip grabbed his shirts and walked outside without saying another word. We all watched him stand in the snow of the square and the twenty-degree temperature putting his two shirts back on. Then he strode off in the direction of the Piggly Wiggly.

"I hope he's not looking for Cynthia," I said.

"Wally, I don't know how you managed to grow up in this town and remain the way you are. Kip's not your worry. Cynthia's not your worry. This climate makes us all crazy. And this town is exactly why each of us is crazy. And no one is going to stop you from acting out your crazy destiny, whatever it might be. This is the most free place on earth." Josh was not trying to be West-Coast clever. Each word he uttered he believed.

Bromley harrumphed. I had forgotten he was there. "You young people. I don't know where you get these ridiculous ideas. This town is no crazier than any other. In fact, I take that back. This town is saner than any place I know. Nothing strange ever happens here. Never has and never will."

Josh started laughing, and it grew within him until he was rocking back and forth in his chair. "I could list strange things all day long. There's nothing normal that ever happens here. It's like God takes all the weirdos and rolls them down Highway 17 until the cart quits rolling, hits a bump, and overturns to drop its load of wackos here. It doesn't matter if you're from a small town or big town. If you hang around here too long, something strange will happen. And no one will ever figure out why."

"That's ridiculous. There's not a god darn mystery in this town that I don't know the answer to."

"Okay, Mayor Bromley Bastique, you tell me why everyone is so interested in buying my parent's swamp. And who's really trying to buy it? A hunting club from Sheboygan? I don't think so."

Bromley looked at Josh for a few minutes before answering carefully, "I just might know the answer to that question, but even if I did, I wouldn't necessarily tell you."

"I see," said Josh, "how many other solutions to mysteries do you keep locked up for you to know and the rest of the world to find out? Do you know why Kip is so unhappy? Do you know why my parents died in such a grotesque way? Do you know why I'm gay?"

Bromley remained silent.

"And how about real mysteries. Who actually runs this town? Is it Red Trueheart? Or is it Tesla Haligent? Isn't he the person who actually owns the bank and the window plant and millions of dollars worth of other assets all around this state? And isn't it true that Red and Haligent get what they want?"

"I wouldn't know about that," Bromley said quietly. He had been slowly retreating back to the counter and was maneuvering a return to his stool. Claire was fidgeting in her drawstring purse digging out some change to pay for her tea.

Mr. Packer, who had been unusually quiet all morning, decided to speak up. "The boy does bring up mysteries, does he not. Mr. Haligent, so

195

much a controlling factor in our lives, and yet he so seldom appears.

"Ten years ago he used to be in town a lot. Yes, he had a cabin then on the Coeur de Lattigeaux; of course, he still does, so that's not the reason why he came so often in those days. There were some who thought he came so frequently because of a woman. A young married lady, as I recall. Of course, Mr. Haligent would have been married then as well. But it was the aftermath of the Sixties. Free love was in vogue, and Haligent was a young millionaire.

"Still the young woman thought Haligent would marry her. No one ever heard her say so, of course. Just one of those things that we all seemed to know. Her husband, though, was a bit of an obstacle. He was such a strong Catholic, and refused to believe in divorce. His name was Phil, wasn't it?"

Bromley and Claire were casting looks at Mr. Packer that were clearly commands to find a new subject. He didn't seem to notice. Or, perhaps he didn't care.

"People weren't quite sure if Phil knew what his wife was doing. He was the kind of man who might have pretended to have never known. As long as the words were never said, it would have been easy for him to deny his wife's philandering.

"Of course, we'll never know what he did or didn't know. No one asked him in time. And then it was too late."

"Why is that?" I asked.

"Phil like to hunt. He had outfitted a small but quite nice camper on the back of his pick-up. It had a little kitchen, a table that could be lowered into a bed, another bed built over the top of the truck cab. Even a little shower if you didn't mind being cramped.

"Phil has some forty acres of deer-hunting second growth woods about twenty miles north of here. He would drive the pickup onto his land, park it there and use it as his camp. That's where they found him that hunting season in 1975. Tragic what they found.

"He was burned to a crisp. Nothing left inside but a charred hand and foot, all locked inside the camper. The entire camper, kitchen, shower, bed, everything was melted inside. The heat of the fire had been intense. Some speculated that his Coleman lantern must have fallen over and started the inferno. Others called it spontaneous human combustion."

"That's nonsense," I uttered.

Mr. Packer shrugged his shoulders. "Who can say what is odd? Life is filled with mysteries. Still I was always mystified by one fact. The camper was locked from the outside. Never could explain that to myself."

"It was an accident," Bromley said. "Everyone agreed at the time that it was an accident."

Mr. Packer shook his head in agreement. "Still," he said, "it was odd how it was locked from the outside. Difficult to imagine how Phil could have done that, or why he would have done it.

"Phil's wife of course was quite the grieving widow. We all expected her to pack up and move to Chicago or New York, or wherever it is that Haligent lives. She didn't. It turns out he never invited her. Or so they say. Others say he only wanted to play with her as long as she wasn't free. It added to his pleasure."

"Haligent is a very powerful man," Bromley warned. "You should be careful the kind of stories you repeat. You could be sued for slander."

"And what would they do with an old man like me. I'm only telling stories. I've lived a long life. I've encountered many rich people and shared their lives. It seems fair that I should pass some of that knowledge along."

"So what happened to this woman?" I asked.

"She moved away. Alone. Thread lost track of her. And now we must go on without her and just ponder our tale." Mr. Packer took another sip of his coffee.

"There nothing to ponder," Josh said, "it was just an accident."

"If you say so, young man, after all, Phil was your uncle. Tragedy does flow in your family, I'm sorry to say," Mr. Packer tipped his hat toward us all and left the cafe.

Josh remained behind, silent and grim.

CHAPTER THIRTEEN

Winter was deep upon the town. Dogs howled in the woods, crows congregated in the Town Square and everyone talked of the tragedy of Tony Masters. What caused him to do such a horrible thing? He had been so normal at the Gunderson funeral a few weeks earlier. Many theories existed for his snapping. Bromley, Claire, Mr. Packer and Thelma clustered around young Josh Gunderson who claimed the full story direct from Mrs. Masters.

"The snowplows went out early that morning," Josh began, "and by ten, Highway 17 held only a thin, but packed, layer of snow. By eleven, the combination of light traffic and a bright December sun had melted even that. The black macadam glistened under a clear sky as the sun reach its noon peak. Black crows cawed and flew from bare tree branch to bare tree branch, looking for something to scavenge." To me, Josh seemed overly dramatic, but he captured everyone's attention. Cynthia walked out from the kitchen to listen.

"In Timberton, a dozen Harleys revved up their motors in unison. Black leather jacketed lawyers from Milwaukee prepared for the next leg of their road run—an all-day cruise south on 17 heading home. This mad dash by motorcycle to Lake Superior and back home was an annual event. One day up, one day camping, one day back, at seventy miles an hour through bone-chilling weather. In the compartments of a few riders were brightly wrapped gifts, secret Christmas gifts picked up along the way to surprise those left at home.

"This year was better than most because the snow came early and heavy this far north. The skies were clear. Bright sunlight played across the crystalline powder, putting everything into stark relief. At the riders' overnight camp at the foot of the Couer de Lattigeaux River gorge, they what they did each year: playing cards, drinking beer, ignoring the roar of nearby snowmobiles, and exaggerating their legal triumphs. Their brightly colored arctic tents, their down-filled sleeping bags, and the deep blue sky were the only disturbance in an otherwise leafless landscape of snow, black icy water, and men in black leather on bikes."

I had dabbled in my own rituals at a different camp the night before. Heat billowed from the Van Elkind's massive fireplace where gigantic natural boulders framed a fire big enough to roast a bear, should one have been foolish enough to have wandered into the camp. A twenty-foot noble fir stood near the stairs, the angel on top failing by several feet to touch the peaked ceiling of the living room. The tree's irregularly spaced branches drooped with Czechoslovakian blown-glass ornaments. Hard-to-find bubbling electric candle lights marched in steady rows from branch to branch.

Henry Van Elkind leaned back against the heavy upholstery of his Morris chair. His lightweight Merino woolen pants and his cashmere sweater were slight variations of the same deep tan. Only the kelly green of the dress shirt peeking from the v-neck cut of the sweater provided any color. He swirled the deep ruby cabernet in his heavy Waterford goblet. The shadows of the flames shimmered through the cut facets and reflected red across his sweater. "Merry Christmas," Van Elkind said. "I am so glad you all could be here."

Coo. Coo.

"What the hell is that?" scowled Red Trueheart. His dress-up for this special dinner invitation resulted in an overzealous knot of a green and red striped tie that appeared to strangle him.

"They're the four calling birds," pouted Amanda Manny, pointing toward an ornate Victorian cage near the tree. She wore a long midnight-blue velvet dress, cut close to her bosom. A large piece of costume jewelry festooned her neck. Companion pieces dangled from her ears. Whenever I saw Amanda walk out of her decorators shop, always thought of Jack

Mandy in his hopsital bed. Rita Van Elkind was not in sight. "When Walter refused to cater this dinner tonight," and a stabbing glance was thrown my way, "well," she shrugged, "Hank said I could plan the dinner, and I thought since it was the fourth day after Christmas, that I would have a theme to the party. That's why we have the four calling birds. And the soup tonight will be a consommé made from three French hens. And each of you will get squab for dinner. They're like turtle doves, don't you think?"

Van Elkind smiled at her tenderly, "Of course, they are."

"Does that mean we're having a partridge for dessert?" I asked.

Amanda trilled a charmless laugh. "Don't be silly. What kind of dessert is that? We're having a pear tart. With a tiny chocolate partridge on top."

Chip Frozen Bear started laughing. Van Elkind glared at him. "I was just thinking," Frozen Bear said, "how much nicer it would be if this meeting were tomorrow. Then we could be given five golden rings."

"Stick around past midnight and maybe you will," winked Amanda.

"And what is Amanda Manny doing here?" demanded the banker who had been standing quietly by the large French windows. The moonlight flooding across the frozen lake silhouetted Tesla Haligent in the window. "I thought we agreed that this was a business meeting. You already got Pearson here for no good reason."

I didn't like his tone, even though I didn't want anything more to do with American Seasons – Van Elkind kept pulling me in. He cleared his throat. "I hired Amanda as a personal consultant for when we get into the design phase. I trust Amanda's sense of style."

"Just don't let her put any white carpet into the hotel lobbies," Frozen Bear joked. At the mention of carpets, Red instinctively took a guilty glance at his feet for any telltale signs of tracked-in mud. Everyone in town knew Amanda had redecorated the Trueheart entry using a plush white pile that was quickly destoryed by Red's unwillingness to remove his waders after any fishing run. Haligent gave Van Elkind a look normally reserved for an irresponsible child.

"Very well," Haligent acceded. "I'm sure you haven't gathered us in this unpleasant spot to look at carpet swatches. So why are we here?"

Stephen walked in with a platter of deviled eggs, each garnished with a big spring of fresh parsley and a strip of pimento. The tray was wrapped in evergreen branches to form a small nest, and on one edge of the tray was small stuffed toy goose.

"Let me guess. Six geese a laying," I said to him. Stephen smiled weakly.

"I didn't think anyone would get it. I'm so happy." Amanda clapped her hands.

Van Elkind motioned Stephen to leave the tray of deviled eggs on the large coffee table and waved him on to leave. "The reason we're here is because I felt it was time for us to assess progress in person. More importantly, there's someone new I want you to meet. She's getting dressed now, but when you meet her . . ."

"They don't need to wait, Henry," said a tall, stately and quite robust woman at the top of the stairs. She walked down the stairs on her stiletto heels with a royal elegance suitable to twelve lords a leaping. "I am here, and ready to meet them."

In the cafe, Josh continued, "In Thread, Tony Masters woke up that Sunday morning in an ornery mood and ready to meet his maker. His wife Nancy had to go into the clinic to help stitch up some kid who had a hand snapped in a muskrat trap. When she left, she told Tony to meet her at church.

"He was just sitting there when she left, drinking coffee from his favorite Mickey Mouse mug. They had bought it the year before when they took their only real vacation—a week at Walt Disney World. It had been such a relief to get away from the winter snow. It seemed another planet to be able to lie next to a pool beneath a hot sun, to jump in the water whenever you wanted, and to feel the heat beat into you. Tony had been real happy that week, but it didn't last once he returned to Thread. He grew morose and withdrawn. When he would get home from the woodworking plant, he'd sit and stare at the fireplace, drinking beer, never saying a word. Nancy hated it when he got like that. The winter mood was starting again, and she knew she had four months ahead of her.

"Nancy has no idea how long he sat there, drinking coffee from Mickey's head. But the coffee pot was empty when he left, and he was a slow drinker. He never changed his clothes. When they found him, he was still wearing the oil-stained blue sweat pants he was so fond of and a white thermal-knit undershirt. He had on heavy woolen socks and his snowmobile boots and a plaid hunter's cap with big furry ear flaps. But he never bothered to find a coat before he jumped in his car that morning and started driving north on 17.

"Up north in Timberton, the biker lawyers finished their Sunday brunch at the Penokee House. They left a really big tip for the waitress who was cute, young and chesty. No one could believe they were a brief of lawyers. They mounted their bikes, did a few checks and rode off in unison. South on 17.

"Now how did it happen? It could have been an accident. The sun was awfully bright, but it was directly overhead, so no one was riding into the light. Besides, the road lies north and south.

"On most days, you might blame the wind. It happened by Chissum's clearing. The wind can pick up loose snow there and slam it across the road. But Sunday was calm.

"No, Tony wanted to do it. As he came over the ridge heading toward Chissum's clearing, he was at the highest point on the road where the continental divide sign is. He could have seen that pack of bikers even if they were miles away.

"The motorcyclists must have looked like a rack of ten pins driving down the road toward him, and he wanted to be the bowling ball that would score the perfect strike. So he crossed over to the other alley.

"Pow! They scattered like falling pins across the blacktop. He downed them all—and himself.

"By the time the ambulances and police arrived, they had to station one man in the middle of the road to drive off the crows. So much blood and gore. It attracted the scavengers like a scene out of *The Birds*."

"Gentleman, and Amanda, it is my pleasure to introduce you to the newest executive member of the American Seasons team, Priscilla Jouer. Until yesterday, Priscilla was the director of new attraction development at Walt Disney Imagineering. Today she is one of us."

"I am pleased to meet all of you," Priscilla said, extending her hand as she walked toward each of us in such an inviting manner that it took every bit of one's will not to respond by picking up that extended hand and kissing the enormous rings on her fingers. A single look pulled each of us into her circle ensuring us it would be an incredible delight.

Outside, we heard the howl of wild dogs. As I looked out across the snow-encrusted terrace, I could see the dark shapes of a pack racing across the white. The full moon shone down upon us all.

"This is such a delightful change from the tedious sunshine of southern California and the muggy heat of Florida," Priscilla's hand moved broadly to encompass all of northern Wisconsin. "The challenge is to open this enjoyment up to millions."

Van Elkind broke in. "Priscilla led the team that designed most of the world pavilions at EPCOT. It's quite an extraordinary place, captures the essence of the entire world in one small spot. There's really no need to travel anywhere else, once you have been there. If she has succeeded so well there, I have the utmost confidence that she can recreate all four seasons of America here in Thread."

Frozen Bear stood up, walked over, and extended his hand in greeting. "I'm sure Priscilla will prove to be an extraordinary addition to our little gang of five. Excuse me, with Wally and Amanda and you, our gang of eight." He smiled slightly. "Priscilla, let me tell you what fascinates me about theme parks. You create a simulacrum of a real place and time. We visitors get immersed in a re-creation that is somehow more tantalizing and enjoyable than the reality. Perhaps because it has been simplified.

"And what do we do? We walk around with cameras, or what's worse, these new video cameras, whirling away, looking for the best shot, viewing this reflection of a reality through a distorting lens that crops it and miniaturizes it still further. When do we finally enjoy this world of ours? Months later, we sit in front of a photo album, listlessly paging through poorly composed snapshots that are a second-hand cousin of a fancifully interpreted and rebuilt reality. In the name of pleasure, we have removed ourselves from the real world."

Priscilla was looking out the window. "What is that?" she gasped. Her regal poise jittered in her fascination with the outside scene. A young red fox stood on the terrace, a bloodied white rabbit hanging from its jutting jaws. It looked into the light for a moment, transfixed by the wonder, and then it bounded into the darkness of the green pines.

"If only we could put that into an animatronic tableau in one of our winter restaurants," Priscilla gushed. "Imagine the excitement, the sense of anticipation."

"It would make me sick," said Amanda.

Frozen Bear walked toward the French doors that opened onto the terrace. He stood there quietly before the glass, the coldness of the night air outside pulling heat from his body even as he gazed out at the fleeting tracks of the fox. Already an eddy of wind was dancing powder snow across the tracks. He looked up and across the lawn toward the lake, toward the moon, toward where the wild dogs were disappearing. He said nothing, but his shoulders seemed to straighten.

Priscilla pooh-poohed Amanda's reaction. "We wouldn't have any blood, of course. That would be distasteful. And just before the children thought it all was doom, we would let the rabbit wriggle loose from the fox's mouth and bound away. The music in the background would swell, and everyone would be happy."

Stephen walked in. "Dinner is served."

The mood in the cafe should have been somber. After all, a man had committed suicide by killing others. For some reason, I could not erase my mental image of Josh and Tony Masters laughing in the basement of the Lutheran church just a few weeks earlier. What was it with Josh that he seemed to attract this macabre combination of levity and tragedy?

I was tired of hearing about Tony going crazy. Soon it would be a new year, but all anyone could talk about was Tony ripping into the lawyers. And Josh had spent too much time in Los Angeles, repeating this tragedy with all the drama of a Hollywood screenwriter. "I think you're making this all up."

Bromley was over it for another reason. "It won't do much for the town's reputation. That's all I can say. Who's going to want to vacation in a spot where they run you down like a mad dog? I don't know what that Tony was thinking," Bromley rambled on. The fiasco threatened his plan to convince Red to fund a new advertising campaign in the big city papers. Red Trueheart felt it would be better to hold off on the campaign. After all, he knew that soon enough he would be promoting a very different kind of destination story. In fact, both Red and Hank had been expecting me to help brainstorm some of the messaging that we could start now without giving away the long term plan.

Claire had her theories though. "It's because of all of the sawdust he breathed in at the window plant. It clogged up his mind like autumn leaves in a gutter. That's what my men told me. Tony was one of their experiments, just like me. Though they only come for him in the winter. Not like me. They check me every day when they fly over the hotel and just hover, pulling me up from my bed with a blue light. I go weightless and float right out the window and up into their ship. That's when they put the needle in me. Right before dawn. Every day." Claire grimaced and fell silent.

We all fell silent for a moment, perhaps surprised by Claire's unusual level of detail about her men. "So," I said, "I hear some type of Hollywood producer's in town buying Tony's life story from his wife."

"I know," smiled Josh, "I called him and gave him the idea. We're going to do lunch. Could we do it here?"

"Why did you go and do a god darn fool thing like that?" Bromley demanded. "The last thing this town needs is to have a movie made about poor Tony. It wouldn't be good publicity. Not good at all"

"But they might film it here, and they'd probably need to cast some of the local townspeople as extras," Josh stuck a big chunk of a sticky bun into his mouth and chewed. Bromley perked up as he considered the possibilities. Josh smiled at him for a moment before a new distraction appeared.

The Van Elkind holiday dinner was served in the enormous dining room where I had catered my first dinner. There was something strangely captivating about enormous wealth and power so casually enjoyed. In Manhattan, I had often interviewed the famous and the powerful. Both Patrice and I had been invited to the parties of the rich. But as a caterer that night that now seemed so long ago, I gained a new perspective on privilege. Instead of enjoying the hefty bouquet of a great cabernet, I was pouring it into bulbous stemware, counting up in my mind, the cost of each bottle, and the markup I was charging. As the total grew in my mind, I began to think what the thousands of dollars being spent on the wine could have bought. Once the mental cash register began totaling, it could not stop. The silver and china, hundreds of dollars per place setting. The hothouse flowers, flown in from Holland, even though Regina Rabinowicz grew beautiful roses right outside the camp's front door. The expensive designer label dresses worn by Rita Van Elkind and her other guests. The jewelry—tens of thousands of dollars. Then to imagine the checkbook capabilities of each person in that room. We were into the millions of dollars.

Yes, there was an intoxicating allure to the camp and its seemingly infinite riches. On slow nights at the cafe, when only a handful of modestly-dressed locals would be in, ordering the cheapest things on the menus, I would stand behind the bar, and let my mind wander through the many rooms I imagined at the camp. Tonight, back, but as a guest, I felt again one of the invited chosen, intended to provide some sparkle and intellectual mix to the evening.

A beautiful pattern of Villeroy and Boche china was set on the white damask linens. A green silk runner traversed the table. In the center was a tall arrangement of white roses with just a small sprinkling of holly leaves and red berries. Simple crystal and elegant silver sparkled in the light of the many candles.

"My compliments," I said to Amanda. "You set a beautiful table."

"It's okay, I guess. That stuck-up Stephen refused to listen to my ideas and insisted on doing it himself. I don't know why they keep him. He has the easiest job in the world. The family's hardly ever here, and he just does what he pleases." She suddenly turned her attention toward Van Elkind. "Hank, don't sit there. I want you here next to me."

"Where do I sit?" said Regina Rabinowicz. The portly woman walked in wearing a bright pink flannel robe and was clearly unexpected. "I hope you don't mind that I didn't dress up. But no one woke me. I didn't even know there was a party going on. Hank, where's my place? Hey, where's my Rita? Too stuck up to be here with her mother over the holidays?"

Van Elkind was patient. "Rita stayed in Chicago. She has social engagements there. Besides this is a business meeting, Mother Rabinowicz. Why doesn't Stephen prepare a nice plate for you to enjoy in your room. I think *Dallas* is on tonight. I know how you love *Dallas*."

"It's not on tonight," scoffed Regina. She looked over at Amanda, taking a long look up and down that trim body. "Who's this? The entertainment?"

"This is Amanda Manny. She owns a local business. Where is

Stephen?"

"I'm right here sir," Stephen walked in with a steaming tureen of soup. "It's time for the consomme of three French hens."

Van Elkind was red-faced. "Just give that thing to Wally. Let him serve the soup. Stephen, take Mother Rabinowicz up to her room. She shouldn't be down here with us. And where the hell is Kip?"

"I wouldn't know, sir. He's your son." Stephen gently held Regina's arm and directed her toward the staircase. She whispered something in his ear, and he chuckled appreciatively. She looked back over her shoulder and winked at me. I looked around the room at my dinner companions, as I held the soup tureen in my hands. With a feeling of deja vu, I ladled out the soup.

"Let's sit," Van Elkind commanded. "Enjoy."

"Hank," Red began, looking around the room and toward where Regina has just left. "I think that your personal life is distracting you from our project." He ended his gaze around the room by lingering on Amanda.

"I've heard you have had an affair with every woman in town," Van Elkind laughed, "and you're concerned about my batty mother-in-law. That's why we have Stephen here, to look after her."

"It's not just the old woman," Red groused. "It's your son too. He's nothing but trouble. Tell that asshole to keep away from my daughter."

Haligent tapped his fork against his water glass, "Gentleman, while this is all most interesting, let's recall our purpose tonight. Henry has already given us two surprises, most pleasant surprises to be sure, the wonderful additions of Miss Jouer and Mrs. Manny to our enterprises. Let's get to the point of this rendezvous and hear what I hope is equally good news on the status of the land acquisition."

"It should be good," said Frozen Bear, "Hank's been a master at rumor mongering in town. Everyone seems to be hearing about the mining. Of course, Wally's cafe has been most helpful in that regard, sort of like Grand Central for gossip." I squirmed. Van Elkind ignored our interchange. "Please. Let's enjoy the meal first."

Frozen Bear walked into the cafe, momentarily causing us all to forget about Tony Masters. "Who's that good looking guy?" Josh whispered.

"Hello, Wally," Chip said to me. "What's up?"

"Talking about Tony," I said, as though that was all anybody was doing in all of Wisconsin.

He gave a look that suggested such talk of highway mayhem should be beneath me. "I'm here to meet Caleb Wheeler, who I believe you know. He mentioned you had once interviewed him for a magazine story back in Manhattan. When he shows up, don't disturb us. We have some business to discuss." At hearing the name of well-known financier Caleb Wheeler, Bromley's ingrained dislike for Frozen Bear was overcome. He moved one stool closer, dragging his coffee cup along the counter.

"Wheeler's in Thread?" Bromley asked nonchalantly.

"No, he's not in town. I'm just waiting here in case the man should suddenly materialize in this spot from the ether. Could I have some coffee?" Frozen Bear spoke without looking at Bromley, directing his words toward Cynthia.

Cynthia had been hovering nearby ever since Frozen Bear had walked in. She placed a cup on the counter and poured it to the brim. "Some cream, please?" he asked with a smile. She took the creamer that had been in front of Bromley and carefully placed it near his cup. Cynthia smiled brightly and walked back to the kitchen, casting a coquettish glance over her shoulder as she exited. Bromley frowned.

Frozen Bear was becoming a more frequent diner, usually around the same time Cynthia arrived from her afternoon classes. Sometimes he'd order a late lunch, sometimes just a piece of pie and coffee. He almost always sat at the counter, and didn't talk to me. But his eyes often fell on Cynthia, and she knew it, and they seemed to chat about more than the menu.

At first I thought he came into town to talk to Red about American Seasons and then stopped by to see me. That would make sense. Not that I actually ever saw Frozen Bear and Red together, but no doubt they were working earnestly on plans for American Seasons. But then I began to fear he was just using Cynthia in some way as part of planting the growing rumors of a western mining company surveying land outside Thread for an open air, low-grade iron ore mine.

"You're from the reservation, aren't you?" Josh walked over with his hand extended and a big smile on his face. Frozen Bear ignored the hand. It seemed to me I had seen that trick before.

"I'm a Lattigo, if that's what you're asking."

"Well, no, I wasn't asking that, but I'm glad to know it. I was really wondering if you lived on the Lattigo reservation, because if you do, I have a question for you. Can we start over?"

Since Josh's parents' funeral, he had been in my restaurant nearly every day. He punched away at Bromley's pomposity; he gave credibility to Claire's fantasies; he sought to mine information from Mr. Packer; and he enticed smiles out of Danny. Only Thelma was resistant to his charms. "That boy is bound to be trouble," she'd say.

Nothing Thelma could say would repress the energy and playfulness of Josh. It wasn't surprising that he didn't get put off by Frozen Bear's coldness. "I was wondering if anyone had been talking to your tribal council about wanting to buy any of the reservation land," Josh said.

"If there had been such inquiries, would I tell you? Is there some reason all you white people think you have the right to know every bit of our lives?"

"Not at all," Josh replied. "I though we could compare notes. My parents have owned some land butting up against your tribal lands for nearly twenty years. No one ever paid the least bit attention to it. Until now. It's worthless swamp. Couldn't even sell it as a hunting land before. Has some good blueberry patches here and there, and that's about it.

"Now out of the blue, I get this insistent big city realtor who has a deal that she says I can't pass up. She claims she's representing a hunting club that's trying to patch together a good-size private tract for their camp. Maybe I've lived in Los Angeles too long, but I think I'm being sold a story. Did you ever see *Chinatown*? Someone knows something that I don't. I don't like that. I don't really need the money from the sale, so I'm just going to hold on to the land."

"My advice is to take the money and run," said Frozen Bear, looking at me instead of Josh. A little smile teased the corner of his lips. "My guess is that somebody thinks they know something, but they don't. Or more accurately, they don't know the whole story."

"What are you hinting at, young man?" demanded Bromley.

"Are you part of the hunting club?" Frozen Bear asked dismissively. "If not, why do you care?"

"So someone has been trying to buy your land?" probed Josh.

"I didn't say that."

"Well, I've heard rumors about this mining company," Josh began.

"That's stuff and nonsense," Bromley interrupted. "If anybody was planning to survey this township for possible mineral deposits, they'd have to go through the town hall for the appropriate licenses. No one has done that. There is no prospecting going on anywhere in this county. I'm certain of that." He even pounded the counter for emphasis. The coffee cups rattled in their saucers. Cynthia rushed out of the kitchen with a new pot of coffee, then stopped, confused.

Like a cat playing with a wounded bird before going in for the kill, Frozen Bear replied. "Maybe it's like the time I was told that there were no more liquor licenses to be had in the county, and yet it turns out that there was a piece of paper attached to this place, just sitting here unused for years. Someone didn't think it was worth telling a poor injun drunk about that. Maybe no one thinks it necessary to tell a fat old man about prospecting rights."

Bromley sputtered. Josh jumped in. "So there is somebody prospecting. I knew it. Someone's trying to buy my land because it's going to be worth a fortune when that mining starts. Someone's trying to cheat me."

"On the contrary," Frozen Bear said, "someone cheated you and every landowner in this township a long time ago. Do your title searches and see who owns the mineral rights to your land. It won't be you. It was all kept by timber companies at the turn of the century when they sold their cutover lands to whomever was stupid enough to buy these raped lands."

"If there's gold underneath my two hundred acres, you're telling me I don't own it. Is that what you're saying?"

Frozen Bear shrugged his shoulders. "It's not me who's doing the telling. It's the courts. The only people who have both land and mineral rights in this whole region are the Lattigo. They were part of our treaty rights. They are ours and ours alone."

Josh slumped despondently. Bromley looked at Frozen Bear suspiciously. A look of comprehension passed over Cynthia's face.

"That's why you're in the catbird seat, like Daddy said. If someone wants to open up a mine, they're going to have to come to your land. All of the Lattigo will be rich. Won't that be wonderful? I'm so happy for you." She was bubbling with enthusiasm.

"I'm afraid not. Rich white men are seldom so generous." Frozen Bear crossed his arms over his chest, and leaned back. "We're the last spot in the county that the mining companies would approach. They can buy the mineral rights to the rest of the county without worrying about buying the actual land. The rights undoubtedly still belong to some large anonymous corporation leftover from an old lumber baron. When they acquire those rights, they can dig on your property and extract their iron, as long as they promise to restore the land to its natural state. We all know how quickly that would be. They could turn this entire township into a big ugly open wound, and there's nothing you could do about it."

"We'd get some good jobs," Bromley said earnestly. "Economic development is always good."

"Sure, and I have a bridge to sell you if you're interested," Frozen Bear turned back to Josh. "You see, if someone is trying to buy your land because they think the potential iron ore will make them rich, they'll soon wake up to a very unpleasant fact. They don't own anything of value. So sell. Sell big. Screw whoever is trying to screw you. It's a dog-eat-dog world."

"I don't think anything you've said is true. It's just a god darn lie you've cooked up for some purpose of you own. That's what I think," Bromley was quivering with rage, as though he had been attacked personally.

Frozen Bear remained calm. "I think you will find that nothing I have said is untrue," he said, and although he was responding to Bromley, his eyes remained focused on me. "Everything is true. I do not lie. It's just all in a day's work. Right, Wally?"

Stephen walked in with a large tray and set it down on the side table. He efficiently and quietly cleared away the soup dishes, and in exchange deposited a new plate with two small birds, delightfully roasted, their skins a crackling brown, with a pilaf of wild rice, walnuts and cranberries to the side.

"Looks like bird food," Van Elkind said, motioning toward the rice. "I thought we were having scalloped potatoes."

"Bird food seemed more appropriate with all these fowls being served, don't you think?" and Stephen was out the swinging doors. Each of the American Seasons principals had before us a beautiful plate of food.

Van Elkind grimaced at his food. "Let's talk about land purchases. Progress has been excellent. We have transferred significant portions of Red's land to the new corporation, as well as Oxford's major timber holdings. With the capital infusion from Tes' sources, we have been quietly buying small parcels needed to round out the boundaries of the land and to connect with the Lattigo reservation.

"At this point, we have offers out on approximately eighty per cent of the acreage we are seeking. In almost every case, our offers have been accepted. In fact, I am pleased to inform you that we are significantly below our planned budget for acquisition. We have been going in with low offers initially, and they are being accepted. As a result, the base price of land county wide has dropped nearly ten per cent over last year. We should be able to pick up the remaining acreage at equally advantageous terms."

"Don't you feel guilty?" I asked.

"What does that man mean?" asked Haligent.

"I mean you're spreading these lies about an apocryphal mining company that's planning to rape the land. People want to get out before it's too late. Most people don't realize how many other people have already sold their land. If they did, they wouldn't be buying this cock and bull story about the mining company. They would know something was up."

"I may be wrong, Mr. Pearson, but I was under the impression that you had been brought in as our public communications specialist, to help us with a disinformation campaign. No one requires you to be our conscience." Haligent picked up the tiny drumstick from the squab and used his teeth to pull all the flesh from the bone in a single slurp.

"Hold on. I never agreed to do anything. You invited me to one dinner, and you told me stuff I didn't want to know. And I kept my mouth shut. That's more than I owed you."

"Yet here you are again," Frozen Bear noted.

"Please," Haligent said wearily. "You two have gone over this previously. It is of no interest to anyone else. We each have something we all need in order to succeed." Haligent preened as though preparing a major speech.

"American Seasons is about money, and making more of it. Nothing more to it. Mr. Trueheart has significant landholdings that we need for this project. He also has a great deal of influence with local politics. Henry and Jonathan Oxford have additional holdings and access to financial markets. I can leverage capital. Mr. Frozen Bear brings his tribe's legal rights to gambling, the most precarious asset we have, which is why the risk and rewards are so great. And we're willing to bet hundreds of millions on it. Why? Because Mr. Frozen Bear and his lawyers have convinced me that they can prevail in court. And if they do, American Seasons will be a mint for making money.

"Priscilla Jouer is the best there is in amusement park design. But that brings us to you, Mr. Pearson? What can you bring, beside your pricks at our conscience? Henry convinced me we needed someone local who understood local thinking, who had a national perspective and ability to communicate. He thought that person was you. He involved you accordingly—against my better judgment, I might add.

"But don't play holier-than thou with us. My bank holds your mortgage. Red controls the town board that could take away your liquor license in a instant. A few well-chosen, well-placed complaints from Henry and your tourist business disappears. You need us. We don't need you.

"So play along. Encourage your patrons to sell their land if they should mention getting an offer. And when the real news emerges, be enthusiastic. Ensure the town sees it for the benefit it will be. It's in your best interests."

Bromley was fascinated by the entrance of Caleb Wheeler. He bounded forward to address the new arrival. Frozen Bear looked at me and said, "Remember Tes's warning." Then he walked over to Wheeler, shooed Bromley away and led Wheeler to a table in the far corner.

Bromley was moored midway between his usual stool and the business-talking duo. He stood there wavering, his Sansabelt pants pulled tight across his broad stomach, his checked-print dress shirt open at the collar, and a bolo tie left loose around his eightteen-inch-plus neck. Wheeler with a neck just as thick encircled his with an expensive designer tie accompanied by a top-of-the-line Brooks Brothers suit. And then there was the casually dressed Frozen Bear in a well-worn pair of Calvin Klein jeans and stiffly starched Ralph Lauren garnet red shirt.

Bromley made his move. "Wally, come over." His imperious tone suggested he had decided to play the elderly statesman. "There's someone I want you to meet. It's Mr. Wheeler. He is a very famous man, very rich. Don't be shy. Come on over."

Wheeler didn't bother to look up until Bromley and I were directly at the table. A small and unstable square had been formed. Bromley cleared his throat. Wheeler looked up. It was as though he had never seen me before in his life.

Frozen Bear smiled at me, "Bromley, didn't I ask you to leave us alone? Mr. Wheeler and I have business to conduct. And Wally, could you have Cynthia come over with menus. Caleb and I have decided to have dinner."

Bromley pulled me back to the counter and his favorite stool while whispering in my ear. "That Indian is up to no good, I tell you. I hear he's been spending a lot of time down in Madison. Just last week, there was a deputy secretary from the Bureau of Indian Affairs in Lattigo. Something's afoot, I tell you."

"What do you suppose those two have to talk about?" mused Mr. Packer back at the counter. "It reminds me of things I used to study."

"I'm not allowed to tell you," said Bromley.

Cynthia headed over to the table with two menus. Frozen Bear and Wheeler each took one, opened them briefly, barely scanned the selections, and then motioned her back to the table. I was miffed. My menu was interesting enough that it should take anyone, no matter how specialized their tastes, at least a few minutes to decide among the many tantalizing opportunities.

Cynthia was walking back by the counter. "So what are they having?" I asked. Maybe they were going to start with a nice bowl of the chicken soup with spaetzle. Thelma had the magic touch when it came to German noodles, and today the broth was pure genius. Maybe one of them would try my escalopes of Wisconsin baby veal. I'd have to convince them to save room for dessert and try the cranberry-steamed pudding that I was serving with a vanilla hard sauce. It was a perfect end for a December meal.

"Hamburgers," Cynthia said.

"Always a good choice," said Claire.

"But there are no hamburgers on the menu," I nearly shouted.

Claire looked at me like I was nuts. "Neither is a fish fry. You always make me a fish fry when I want it. I know you got ground round in that kitchen. Serve them a hamburger."

"That's not the point." I murmured. "Besides Cynthia is the one who sells you the fish fry. We're only supposed to have fish fries on Fridays. Fridays. Fish. It's a Catholic thing." Josh started laughing.

"Wally, I've often wondered," Mr. Packer began, "why you opened a restaurant. Do you suffer from some internal compulsion to disturb the accustomed rhythms to which we have all danced over these many years?"

Bromley threw up his hands in disgust. "Listen to this man. He lived in Europe once and taught college and now he thinks he's Sigmund Freud. Wally's just running a business. In a business you sell what you got. If you don't got ground beef, you don't sell hamburgers."

"I have ground beef," I pointed out. But I was stuck on Bromley's statement that Mr. Packer had been a college professor.

"Then sell them the hamburgers," Bromley said pleasantly. He seemed to have perked up tremendously after he heard their order. "Josh, do you think Mr. Wheeler might be the person trying to buy your land? Maybe everything that Indian just told you was a ruse because his tribe wants to get the land. The two of them look to me like they're talking money." Cynthia was walking by with a small basket filled with little bottles of catsup and mustard. He drew her over with a conspiratorial shake of his head. "Stay close. Fill up their water glasses or something. I want to know what they're talking about. Your father would want to know too Do it for us."

Josh broke in, "I don't think they're talking about my land. There was something about the way Chip discussed the mineral rights that made me believe him. I'm going to check into it."

"Sometimes truths are only partial, those old lumber barons didn't always know what they were doing," Mr. Packer said enigmatically.

Cynthia was walking back our way. Bromley leaned forward in anticipation and to catch her before she went back into the kitchen. "What did you hear?"

She waved him quiet and looked at me, "Will they get their burgers?"

"Let Thelma make them what they want," I said in disgust.

She went through the swinging door. Several minutes later, she came back out with two platters containing the hamburgers and fries.

Thelma had already started them before I gave my approval.

"I think that Chip is pretty cute," said Josh. "I wonder if he's seeing anyone."

Bromley looked at the young man with bewilderment. "How did your parents raise you? You go off to Los Angeles. You get all these god darn crazy ideas"

"Let the boy date who he wants," Claire said. "I never found it hurt me to have lots of boyfriends. More people to look after you when you get sad."

Cynthia giggled. We looked over to the table. She and Frozen Bear were exchanging some kind of small talk. A broad smile broke through the fat rolls of Wheeler's face.

"I bet they're just trying to confuse her," grumbled Bromley. "By the time she gets back here, she will have forgotten whatever they were talking about. She's not that bright, you know. Was held back a year in school early on. That's why she'll be turning 19 soon. Red's always worried about her good sense."

Whatever the tale, it was taking a while to tell. Cynthia was vibrant and relaxed as she listened. Wheeler had the air of a paternalistic uncle who had just arranged a great deal for his favorite nephew. I noticed a catsup stain on his designer tie. My eyesight was better than my ears. I couldn't hear a word of the conversation. But Cynthia's joy was like little peals of Christmas bells ringing through the air.

She was walking back toward us. "Now we'll find out," Bromley said. Frozen Bear and Wheeler returned to their intense conversation.

"Tell me everything you heard." Bromley was like a little boy who woke up early on Christmas morning and couldn't get out of his crib by himself. He just knew there was going to be a fantastic present at the very bottom toe of his stocking.

"He was describing this raccoon that got into the house his sister and he have and how it knocked over the Christmas tree. The way he told the story, it was so funny. I really like him."

"Not that stuff," Bromley broke in. "Who cares about him? What were they really talking about? What business things? Your father needs to know what goes on in this town."

"Would you say that Chip Frozen Bear is a really handsome man?" Josh asked Cynthia. "Tall, dark and handsome. Everything you'd want."

"Yes," Cynthia responded with enthusiasm.

"Forget about all that junk." Bromley was frantic. "What were they talking about?"

"Just a bunch of words," Cynthia said. "I don't know what any of it meant. Something about a leveraged takeover. And pension funds."

"But did Chip ask you out?" Josh wanted to know.

"No, why would he do that?" Cynthia seemed shocked. "He's much older than me. Why would he want to date me?"

"So you wouldn't mind if I tried to snag him."

Now Cynthia was truly shocked. "Don't be ridiculous. I'm sure he likes girls. He's just too handsome to want guys."

"Thanks a lot," Josh said in mock indignation.

"That's not what I meant at all," Cynthia was looking over at the table intently. She looked Frozen Bear up and down. "Maybe I should go check if they need something else. Make sure they have enough water."

"Wait a minute," hissed Bromley. But Cynthia was already walking over to the table. Bromley turned to the rest of us. "They are up to something. But what? There's something I don't like about what's happening."

"All you don't like is that you don't know what's going on," Mr. Packer said calmly. Bromley looked at him quietly and didn't respond.

The front door tinkled. "Things are looking up," said Josh. Danny walked into the cafe and he was carrying a wriggling blur of silver black fur.

"I wanted to show you my new puppy," Danny said. "It's a baby Norwegian elkhound. I got it for Dad. Sort of an early Christmas present. I thought it would help take his mind off Mom." He stumbled to an end, embarrassed by his own statements.

"What a cute puppy!" Cynthia said. "Where did you get it?"

"You better take good care of that dog," Claire began. "You don't want him running off come spring. I've been hearing packs of wild dogs at night, barking as they run through the streets. There's something about the sounds of a wild pack, especially come spring, that seems to take over the mind of a house dog. They just got to get out there and run. Once they do, you can never get them back. They're lost to the wild."

"It won't happen with my dog," Danny nuzzled the dog. He lifted up his head and the dog yelped as though it wanted more attention.

"What is that?" asked Wheeler from the corner table. "Is there a dog in here? I'm quite allergic."

Cynthia was alarmed. "It's just a little puppy."

"Puppies, dogs, they are not allowed in restaurants. Get rid of that dog this instant." By now he was standing and turning red. Frozen Bear also stood.

"No need to get upset. We can go somewhere else to finish our discussion," and he threw a twenty to the table and hustled Wheeler out the door. As he was leaving, Chip turned and whispered to Cynthia, "Don't worry about this. See you tomorrow."

Danny looked humiliated and the dog was whimpering in his arms. All of the shouting had scared the small thing. "I'm sorry," he said.

"No big deal," I responded. "But maybe you better take it home."

Mr. Packer looked at me as he began to speak. "Lovely puppy. Let's hope he doesn't run with the wild dogs. To race with the big dogs can be very alluring, but when you do it, you end up leaving everything behind. Beware the big dogs, Wally."

He looked at me. I looked at him. I didn't think he was talking about Danny's new dog.

The American Seasons dinner was nearly over when Van Elkind handed over a small envelope. "Oh, that reminds me, Henry, we have a small gift for you."

"Open it," commanded Haligent.

I tore open the gilt envelope. Inside was a certificate for ten thousand shares of American Seasons, Incorporated.

"It's not worth much now," observed Van Elkind with a flush to his face. "But in a year or two, it could be worth a million . . . or more. We didn't want you to think we were taking advantage of you in any way. We want you to have a stake in our success."

They were all watching me. Outside, I heard the cries of another dog pack racing wild through the woods, followed by the sheer stillness of a winter night. Then a loud resounding boom echoed in the silence as the ice in the lake shifted and cracked. A shimmer of crackling light from the still-roaring fire in the adjacent living room bounced off the crystal goblets. No one said anything. Haligent was waiting. Amanda was bored. Chip Frozen

Bear's eyes were the ones to avoid.

"Thank you," I said. I looked down at the congealed juices of the squab, and I wanted to escape with the dogs, to be anywhere but here.

CHAPTER FOURTEEN

Winter dragged on, only slowly inching toward spring. Each succeeding day the sun appeared in the eastern sky a few moments earlier. Each evening it set in the western sky just a bit a later. To many in town the blue shadows stretching across the white snow still seemed too long at noon and too short at dusk.

An occasional Volvo, Saab or BMW, topped with racks of skis, would find its way to the town square and park. Vacationers would tumble out and head into my cafe. For a few hours, the cafe would be filled with skiers on their way to the timid peaks of Michigan's Upper Peninsula. Tired from their long drive from the big cities hours away, they stopped to rejuvenate themselves. Business was best when they were young couples, flush with money, out to prove they could still have a good time before they were laden with the responsibilities of children, mortgages, and planning ahead. They would order appetizers, entrees and desserts. A bottle of wine was never out of the question, and they were always generous tippers. After a full evening of dining and drinking, they would slip and slide as they tried to walk carefully over icy sidewalks to their frosty cars, still facing an hour or more of driving before reaching their resorts. The snowflakes would be flurrying about them, each unique crystal dancing about in the falling light of the street lamps. Sometimes the flakes would so blanket the sky that you couldn't see across the square to find the hardware store. On such nights, only the neon sign of the Northern Nights bar across the square would be a beckoning light. Such couples would often stroll to a halt in the empty square, with their car, transformed into a snowbank, parked just feet away. Caught in the shower of snow, they would turn to each other, say a few words. The wispy steaming clouds of their breath would float out into the icy night. And then they would move in for a long kiss.

Cynthia lived for these moments. She would linger in the dining room, slowly picking up the dessert plates, her eyes captivated by the scene outside. When finally the young couple would drive away, she would sigh, then turn to one of us and sigh once more. Danny would look back at her with the wariness of a kitten you were trying to coax into a bath.

Short days flowed into long nights. The packed snow grew thicker and thicker beneath the always freshly-falling snow. Except on the square, the town's sidewalks, when still shoveled, were treacherous paths of built-up ice and compacted snow. The banks of plowed snow along the road sides grew ever higher. Little kids walked along the ridges like mountaineers.

For the past week, the daytime highs never broke zero. At night the temperatures dipped below minus thirty. Frozen water pipes had burst in some of the best insulated homes. My apartment above the cafe, with its drafty windows and minimal weatherproofing, was a whistling icebox. Each morning I eagerly descended into the warmth of the restaurant. Thelma usually arrived an hour before I did to open up the restaurant and make the day's breads and cakes. By the time I got to the kitchen, clean shaven and hair still wet from the shower, the place would be toasty warm and the hot caramel smell of freshly-baked sticky buns floated in the air. In those moments, I had no thoughts of what I had left behind in Manhattan or what lay ahead with American Seasons.

"I just can't decide what to do about this land," mused Josh Gunderson. The restaurant was ready to close. No romantic couples had shown up this evening to kiss in the ever so lightly falling snow. "Thanks to my folks' life insurance, I have more money than I need. Even my father never dreamed his swamp land and cranberry-growing fantasy would ever be worth anything. Now here's someone offering me a lot of money for some stagnant water. And I can't decide what to do about it."

"Take the money and run," Danny suggested. He was seated at the counter filling up salt and pepper shakers. Lately, Josh had taken to staying

221

past closing and talking as we closed up.

"I would," replied Josh, "except I'm convinced someone is up to no good. I can feel that somehow, someone, somewhere is cheating me. Laugh if you want but I have a sense about when I'm getting the shaft. Believe me, there's been times in Hollywood when people tried to sell me a load of goods. They didn't succeed. At least not more than once. No little hick town's going to win where L.A. lost."

I couldn't help but laugh. Josh glanced at me with an air of dismissal. "It's true My mother could foresee the future, extrasensory perception, and they say it's hereditary. Once when grandma was sick, my mother woke up in the middle of the night, knowing something terrible had happened to my grandma. She had to call right then, and you know what? She was right. Grandpa had died, in the middle of the night, quiet and calm in his sleep. Until the phone rang and grandpa didn't pick it up like he usually did, Grandma didn't even know. But my mother knew.

"The day mom and dad died, I woke up in the early morning with a terrible headache. I knew, so I don't know why Mom didn't get a warning. Does carbon monoxide interfere with ESP?'

"Maybe," Danny said, in a way meant to stop another conversation he found uncomfortable.

The lights of the restaurant were dimmed, the evening linens removed from the table, and the chairs upended on the wooden table tops. I was putting away the last of the liquor bottles. The neon sign spelling out Loon Town Cafe still cast its pink glow onto the snow accumulating on the sidewalk. On the square, a few late-starting drinkers headed into a bar. Amanda Manny teetered on the icy steps of the Northern Nights Tavern, her stiletto heels finding no traction. I held my breath, anticipating a fall.

"What were you boys jabbering about, and now you're all so silent." Buxom Thelma stood in the kitchen door. "You know there's still pots and pans to scour. And why are you here every night, Josh? I thought you worked at the tavern now."

"I switched to days," he replied. "I like my nights off."

"Then maybe you should run off and enjoy your nights. These boys have got work to do. The grease won't disappear by itself." Increasingly Thelma had assumed bossing privileges over me and those around me.

"I could help," Josh said eagerly.

Thelma was already into the kitchen. "The more the merrier. The sooner this is all done, the sooner we can all go home."

Like a little train, the three of us followed her lead. Danny went first, the coal car carrying the final tray of dirty dishes to feed the sink. Josh was eagerly pulled along, like a car full of jolly vacationers who had no worries. I brought up the rear, a baggage car that picked up a nearly full bottle of Heitz Cellars Martha's Vineyard cabernet.

"We might as well enjoy the close of our evening," I said, holding aloft the bottle. "I can't believe that couple from Minneapolis would order a great red like this, and barely drink any of it. Let's say we finish it off."

"Danny's a minor. You could lose your license," Thelma said.

"Who would tell? Would you Josh? Would you Danny? You know, Thelma, when I went to high school here, kids got drunk every weekend evening. I'm sure Danny's tasted wine before."

Danny looked worried. "I better not. I don't want to get you guys in trouble." He looked wistfully at the bottle and at the glass of wine already held by Josh. Instead, he picked up a scrub brush and attacked the sink full of greasy pans.

"Hold on, boy," Thelma laughed. "You don't need to set any speed records. Dirty dishes let you take as much time as you want."

Through the glass of the back door's window, I could see the snow-bedecked features of Toivo, who had just tentatively knocked. Big bushy eyebrows and a full head of hair embellished with accumulated snowflakes.

"Open the door," I told Thelma, "it's Danny's father."

Toivo Lahti walked into the warm glow of the kitchen, and he shook like an old dog that just pulled itself out of the lake, with light flakes of snow flying around the room.

"Dad, be careful" moaned Danny.

"It's a cold night out, son. Didn't want you walking home, so I thought I'd stop by and drive you. The door was locked in front, so I figured I should head around back and make sure I hadn't missed you. I guess I didn't."

"How come you're covered with snow, Dad?"

"Couldn't help but stop by your ma, and tell her how you're doing. I don't get to do it as much as I'd like now that it's winter. It's like when she was alive you know, and we never got to walk as much as we wanted. After all these years, I still wish I could bring her back, you know." Toivo bit at his lower lip. Danny kept scrubbing furiously at the pans.

"Son, slow down a bit."

"I already told him that, Toivo," Thelma said. "Won't do no good. Your son is a stubborn one. When he gets an idea in his head, he won't let go. Like someone else in the family I know. Wally probably wouldn't think to tell you, but we're all real happy with the way Danny works here. You raised a good kid." Danny's shoulders seemed to sink lower.

"Yeah, he's a really good guy, Mr. Lahti," Josh was eager to be part of the conversation. "He's a great waiter, a great busboy, and as you can see a great scullery maid."

Toivo looked at Josh with suspicion, but back at his son with love. Even when his wife was alive, he wasn't one to socialize. He never went to a tavern, seldom kibitzed with Red when he shopped for groceries, and had no time to contemplate politics with Bromley Bastique. He was always quiet, smiling faintly if he thought the story was meant to be funny, but always with a look to his eyes as though seeking the nearest escape path into the woods. Only in the forest was he at home and fully at peace. Before he cut any tree or even climbed one to trim it, he would put his hand against the bark and hold it there for a full minute. If you were to ask him about it, he would look away shyly, or redden and say that he was just taking a rest. But his wife Lempi once told her neighbors what he was really doing. He was comforting the soul of the tree by slowly letting his energy move into the life force of the tree, so that he could feel its life and its will to live, and that it in turn could feel his. He was seeking forgiveness and understanding for what he was about to do. Did the tree feel less pain? Did the forest grow back more rapidly? Or did Toivo merely sleep better? Perhaps Lempi could have told us. She was the only person Toivo had ever touched in the same way that he touched his trees, but his touch hadn't been enough to keep her happy and alive.

"The snows seem heavy this year," Toivo said. "Might get three hundred inches before the year is out. Like back in '79. A hard winter for the deer and the animals."

"You shouldn't be lumbering when the snow gets so deep in the woods. It's dangerous. That's what my husband used to say," said Thelma.

"But you can't stop. You gotta live," Toivo responded. "We can cut them down and then pull them logs out come spring. For us, it's not so bad. For the deer, though, it's a harder thing. They can't find nothing to eat, unless it's the twigs of the branches they can reach from the ground, or the bark. They'll be a lot of weak deer come spring. Some say they saw a wolf up to Timberton last week. You know the wolves, they run across the lake from Isle Royale in winters like this. Seeking out weak deer in the woods."

Danny was rinsing off his last pot. "Dad, I'm done. Let's go."

"I should say something to the Gunderson boy," Toivo muttered. "I was real sorry to hear about your pa and ma. It don't seem fair, no way you think about it, what happened to them. But you got to go on."

"And I am," said Josh amusedly, in the tone he offered back whenever townspeople tried to give him their sympathy. "I will go on."

"Ready to go, Dad?"

"Danny, maybe your father would like some wine before he goes," Josh was already handing the man a glass of the Heitz cabernet. Toivo held the glass uncomfortably in his hand, peering at the deep red liquid inside, watching its firm legs hold to the curvature of the bowl.

"I'm not really a drinker," he said. "Maybe a beer and a brandy chaser at home."

"Try it. Prepare for the winter ahead," Josh persuaded.

Toivo stopped the swirling of his glass and ventured a small sip of the cabernet. He made an unpleasant face. "Think I'll stick to my brandy."

Thelma broke in, "Wait a minute, Toivo, we got a full bar here. Let me get you a Leinie's and a shot of Christian Brothers. No sense your sitting here without something to drink while the rest of us finish off this bottle of wine. Do you want something, Danny?"

"No," he replied quickly. "Dad, we should be getting home."

"Oh, Danny, let your father enjoy his drink," Thelma responded. She was beginning to glow. "I never get a chance to talk to your father. I'd like to get to know him better."

Toivo started. "No, no, the boy's right. The snow's heavy. We best be going. I'll leave this wine drinking for another time." And before you could count to ten, father and son were bundled up and out the door.

"Someone's gotta tell that boy to lighten up," said Thelma. Josh said nothing.

A few days passed. As it had for the past several days, the sun rose in a clear blue sky. The weather was too cold to snow, and there was a crackling crispness to the air. By mid-morning, the Saturday crowd was in place and we all longed for an end to winter. Mr. Packer, Bromley and Claire were savoring their standard fare. Danny was in the back helping Thelma. Claire was looking out the plate glass windows onto the square. A large collie sat in the snow on the edge of the sidewalk, right outside the front door, staring into the restaurant, as though looking for its owner. The dog had been there since Cynthia first arrived.

"I'm worried about him," Cynthia fretted. "He was outside our door when I left home this morning. And he followed me here. It's like he knows me, but I've never seen him before. Have you, Mr. Packer?"

"Never laid eyes on the canine before," he replied.

"He's going to freeze to death. Wally, we should let him in."

"Absolutely not," I replied, remembering the scene with Caleb Wheeler when Danny showed up with his dog.

"I just can't look at him any more," she said and hurried into the kitchen.

"That little thing will freeze to death if he doesn't move soon," said Claire. "It was so cold this week that my little men didn't come at all. When it gets this cold, you know, they have trouble maneuvering their saucer. Once it lost power completely, a few years back, and landed right in the middle of Homestead Park. It left a giant depression that was icy smooth. You remember that time, don't you Bromley?"

"No such thing ever happened."

"I think, Claire, you're remembering the time they tried to flood an ice skating rink in the park," offered Mr. Packer.

"That's Bromley and Red's story. But I tell you that's a cover-up because no one wants to hear the truth. Truth can release the dam's waters before it's filled. You know, there's a reason why the little men come here. They need the minerals." Her voice turned to a whisper. "The same minerals that certain people are now trying to buy up." The bell at the door tingled and we all turned to watch Red Trueheart walk in. Claire lowered her voice to her tiniest of whispers. "And speaking of certain people, I think I'd better be quiet now. Because he knows I'm not crazy."

Red had a scowl on his face, and he slammed himself onto the seat. "Give me the god damn biggest cup of coffee you have, and put a couple of shots of brandy in it."

"A little early to start drinking isn't it?" I asked.

"It's been a god damn awful morning so far. Might as well make it enjoyable. Spent all morning in the back cutting up meat because that damn Rueben Cord didn't show up. Not that he's much of a butcher anyway, and I can't get the guy to cut off his stupid ponytail. Damn health hazard. It's like he thinks he's still living in the Sixties. Today's not the first time he hasn't shown up either. He's fucking irresponsible. I tried calling him, but no answer. The asshole probably went off on a drinking binge."

"It is that time of the year," offered Mr. Packer. "The highest rates of alcoholism are in Scandinavian countries where there are long winters and little light. It might explain why there are so many bars in a town so small."

"The reason there are so many bars in this town is because we got too many drunks," said Red.

"And half those drunks are Indians from Lattigo. They can't hold their liquor. They shouldn't be allowed to drink," pontificated Bromley.

"Don't get started on the Lattigo," threatened Red, "I've just about had it up to here with their conniving ways." I had a feeling he was talking about American Seasons and not Indian drinking habits.

How had I forgotten the underlying racism of this town? Whenever Chip and his sister Jacqueline were in the cafe, I noticed the same reactions. While out-of-towners always seemed drawn to look at the handsome couple, most of the locals simply didn't look at the two, as though if they never made eye contact they could somehow imagine that their paths had not been crossed by the two. Chip and Jacqueline relished their food, and seemed to never notice the snubs.

Threadites were enormously aware that the reservation was only ten miles away. Yet they constantly pretended it didn't exist. Lately, as Indian rights stories were beginning to appear in the big city papers, and the occasional story even made it on the news broadcasts out of Duluth, it was becoming more difficult.

"Those Lattigo are trying to pull one over on us," opined Bromley. "I was talking to Assemblyman Jackson earlier this week about what's going on in Madison. The Lattigo are making all sort of ridiculous claims, tied to some forgotten treaties from a hundred years ago."

"It's a well-established fact," said Mr. Packer, "that the Lattigo and the United States Government first signed a peace treaty in the 1850s that created the Coeur de Lattigeaux Reservation and established the Lattigo as a sovereign nation within the United States with certain inalienable rights. That was reconfirmed when President Grant made his famous visit to the state to pay his respects to the original Uncle Sam bald eagle that came from their reservation."

"You're talking like a Communist," yelled Bromley, "They can't have any god darn rights we don't have. Everyone's equal."

"That treaty was from another century," said Red. His hands were fidgeting as though he would rather be outside doing anything other than talking about the Lattigo. "Time passes. If they haven't been allowed these rights for a hundred years, then they can't have them now. Our whole tourist economy is based on certain expectations—like there will be fish in the water and deer in the woods. We can't have a bunch of wild natives tramping around doing whatever they feel like doing."

"Just what rights are they seeking?" I wanted to know. I didn't think Red could have much cause to complain about any rights the Lattigo might be claiming, since the sovereign nation stance would be the linchpin to American Seasons and its legalized gambling.

"You name it; they want it. They say they can hunt as much as they want. Even out of hunting season. Even doe and fawns. Same thing with fishing. You know how the walleye spawn in the Sapphire Run between the two lakes during the spring runoff. There's thousands of fish there, flopping over one another, fertilizing eggs. Those fish are only interested in one thing: fish fucking."

"Oh my," Claire said.

"Give me a break," Red said. "Like you haven't heard worse things in life. The creek would be nothing more than a lobster tank in a Chinese restaurant if we allowed fishing. I mean you can pick the fish up with your hands at that time of the year. They have to be protected, or all the adult fish would be taken, and pretty soon there wouldn't be any walleye left."

"The Lattigo know that," I said. "They aren't going to destroy the land." I was thinking of the obscene re-landscaping Red and Van Elkind were planning to do as part of American Seasons. Their latest brainstorm was to create a miniature mountain where only swamps existed—all so Van Elkind could add downhill skiing to the resort. Where was Red's outrage when it came to destroying wetlands?

Red wasn't convinced. "That's not the way they talk. And besides fishing and hunting, they claim the same thing about logging and wild rice harvesting. Then they claim they're exempt from state taxes, and selling fucking cigarettes on the reservation for half the price I have to sell them in my store."

Now we were getting to the heart of Red's concerns. "Next thing you know," I said, "they will try to set up gambling casinos."

Red's eyes flashed a warning, but he quieted down. It became one of those lingering quiets that grew more discomfiting each second.

"Sure is cold, isn't it?" Bromley said. "Could freeze a witch's tit."

"That it could," Red agreed quickly.

The silence returned.

We were saved by the tinkling of the bell and the arrival of Josh. Danny walked out with a tray of clean glasses for the bar. He and Josh exchanged glances.

"How's everyone in my favorite cafe?" Josh asked with unfeigned enthusiasm. "Don't you love this snappy cold weather?"

"Only a man selling heating oil would like weather this cold," Red muttered.

Josh slapped Red on the back good-naturedly. "Well then you must be a happy man. I hear that's one of your many businesses. God, I love this cold weather. When I lived in Los Angeles, cold was the one thing I really missed. Everyone else talks about fall colors. For me, it's that sharp cold when you feel like your nose is going to turn into ice. In Los Angeles when the frost is threatening oranges in the back yard, it's just a wet cold that makes you uncomfortable. Here cold puts you in touch with living!"

"You're really weird," Danny said.

"You know what we should do," Josh said. "This cold snap has completely frozen over the flowage. Not only is the Lattigeaux river solid ice now, but because it hasn't snowed all week since it froze, it's perfect for ice skating. You could skate for hours across ice as smooth as . . . well, as smooth as ice."

"You'd freeze your ass off," Red looked at Josh with a contempt that seemed quite undeserved. Red kept an ice-fishing shack in the middle of Big Sapphire Lake and he had been out fishing every day this past week.

"No you wouldn't," Josh countered good naturedly. "You just need to wear a ski mask and a good snowmobile suit. It's above zero during the day, and there's hardly any wind. And it's sunny. What more could you want? Danny, want to go ice skating this afternoon?"

"I got to work," he replied reluctantly.

Claire piped in with a motherly smile. "Wally, let the boy go," she said, "there's hardly anyone in town this weekend. You're not going to be busy, and besides it's a rare winter when you can ice skate on the flowage. I loved to skate when I was a little girl. You know, I had a brother then. Two of them. And a dog. It was a collie, like that dog out there."

"Is that dog still out there?" Cynthia shouted from the kitchen. I was convinced Cynthia had placed bugs in the main part of the cafe to keep tabs on our goings and comings. She walked out of the kitchen and went straight to the front window. The red-haired dog got up from its watching position and stood with nose to window, its tail wagging. "It knows me," she insisted.

"Let's do it, Danny," Josh continued. "I got an extra snowmobile suit if you don't have one."

"I got one," he said. "But I have to work."

I decided to let the boy have some fun. "Claire is right. It's a great day for ice skating. No need to shovel snow from the river. Truly a rare day in January." Besides Danny looked eager for the outing.

Josh smiled broadly. "Let's call it a date. I'll pack a couple of thermoses of hot chocolate. We'll skate up the flowage, build a bonfire, have some chocolate to celebrate and skate back."

"What would you be celebrating, young man?" Mr. Packer asked.

"I unloaded the family swamp land," Josh crowed. I had lately seen the American Seasons maps, and Josh's land was part of the site where Red wanted to build the ski hill using swamp land excavated to create a lake. The acreage had been a pivotal piece of land needed. I looked over to see if Red was smiling. But his earlier scowl had greatly intensified.

"I sold it to the Lattigo," Josh continued. "I don't know what they need with more swamps, but Chip Frozen Bear showed up at my door to convince me to sell the place. Of course, I told him he had to sleep with me before I'd sell."

Claire dropped her tea cup.

Josh smiled broadly. "Hey, I'm just kidding. But I signed on the dotted line because the Lattigo offered a great price. Much better than what the hunting camp people wanted to give."

Another crash of crockery. Red's coffee cup had rolled off the counter and onto the floor. "Sorry," he said through tight teeth.

Cynthia rushed over with a rag to wipe up spilled coffee, but her attention was on the forlorn collie staring in the window.

"There's something spooky about that dog," she said. "It doesn't belong here."

"Maybe it's a spirit from the other side," Josh said with a faked hollowness to his voice. "I've been visited by ghosts before."

"Yes, you've told us before you're clairvoyant," I said, "but that dog looks quite real to me. And damn cold."

Josh was not perturbed by skepticism. "Ghosts can look real. I saw one once in my house. It appeared totally three-dimensional."

Cynthia jumped in excitedly. "So did I. Not in your house. I mean in my house. Remember Daddy?"

Red looked at his daughter with surprising tenderness as though she were about to tell a story he had heard many times. She smiled, "Daddy doesn't believe me. Neither does Mommy. But it really happened when I was five.

"It was one night in the winter, just like this, when it was really cold, and I couldn't sleep. I think Daddy was out of town, and just Mommy and me were at home. I went into the living room and asked if I could sleep with Mommy. She said she would sleep with me instead.

"Mommy can fall asleep so fast. When she lay down beside me in my twin bed, all of a sudden she was sound asleep. I was between the wall and her. I felt really warm, really safe. But that's when I noticed him. He was a little boy about my age, dressed in old fashioned clothes, with ice skates around his neck. And there was a dog. They were very quiet. They walked into the room like it was their room, and he seemed surprised to see me. His eyes were big with astonishment, and I felt he wanted to tell me something.

"But then he noticed my shelves along the side of the wall filled with toys. He went straight to the bottom shelf and my musical jack in the box. He was going to touch it, and I didn't want him to so I sat up in bed to tell him to leave it alone. But I wasn't fast enough. He turned on the switch and the music started, loud circus music.

"It woke Mommy up. She jolted from bed. The boy and his dog ran from the room so she never saw them. She tried to find the music box in the dark and knocked my dolls and stuffed animals off the shelf wanting to get rid of the sound. Finally she found the jack in the box, turned it off, and came back to the bed.

"She wouldn't listen when I tried to tell her about the little boy with the skates. I wanted to tell her that there was no way I could have crawled over her, turned on the toy and rushed back into bed before the music woke her up. No one ever believed me about that little boy and his dog."

Red looked at his daughter tenderly, "Honey, it was a dream. When you were a little girl, you would sleepwalk a lot. Didn't Mommy take you all around the house that night? Was there a boy anywhere?"

"He had already left," she said stoutly.

Claire asked softly but firmly, "What did the boy look like?" Her wrinkled face seemed wet. A sense of understanding crossed Cynthia's face, and for a moment she seemed unable to speak. "He looked like you," she finally said.

"Then it was Arthur," Claire said to no one in particular, but looking at Bromley. "Arthur came to see Cynthia, because he needed her to help him. Maybe he couldn't get over to the other side. That happens with spirits."

Bromley seemed embarrassed. "It wasn't Arthur. Arthur died when you were a little girl, Claire. He can't come back."

"No one ever believes me," Claire said nothing more. She merely reached for the jar of strawberry jam and applied another spoonful to the bit of English muffin remaining on her plate.

Another uneasy moment of silence began.

Josh sprung into action. "Cynthia, I'm sure there was a boy. And I believe you Claire. It probably was Arthur, whoever that might be." With that, Josh twirled his muffler back in around his neck in a most dramatic way."

"Arthur was my brother. He drowned," Claire sniffled. "He never got to say goodbye."

"Claire," Bromley warned, "don't get started."

"It all sounds like a stew of Indian superstition if you ask me," Red said dismissively. "Ghosts, spirits. There's no such things. We're here while we're here. And we just got to do the best with what we got."

Another silence.

Outside, sunlight invaded every corner of the town square, dancing over the blinding white snowbanks, jumping up to glint in the giant icicles that hung from building corners, light particles getting caught in the snow-decked Christmas garlands that had yet to be taken down from the street lamps. Icy golden light everywhere—frozen in brilliance.

Red broke the silence. "I need to get back to the store. Rueben probably still hasn't shown up, so today I'll have to do his job as well as mine."

The bell on the door tinkled its clear cold sound once more. An icy rush of air heralded the entrance of Thelma's favorite, Gilbert Ford. He had on a dark green great coat and a bright red muffler. He loosened the muffler and let it fall to the side. His trademark bow tie, blue with white polka dots, was in its proper place.

"Do I smell freshly-baked caramel rolls?" he asked. He inhaled deeply, and one could almost hear him lick his lips.

"Yes, you do," I replied.

"Well, I must have one of them, but only if it can be delivered by your delightful and beautiful pastry chef." He smiled wickedly.

"Thelma," I yelled out, "your beau's here."

"Wally, watch your mouth! I'm older than you. You should treat me with respect," she yelled from the kitchen. "Tell Gilbert I'll be out in a minute."

Gilbert smiled contentedly. He looked around the room to see if any other of his admirers were in attendance. Cynthia had a certain soft spot for the man, as she did for anything or anyone suggestive of romance. Gilbert caught sight of Red. "I wouldn't have expected to see you here," the salesman said.

"Why?"

"What with all that's happened to Rueben Cord. I just drove up from Emeryville. It's been the talk of the town all morning."

"What's the damn fool done now?" Red wanted to know.

Gilbert seemed surprised. "You don't know, do you? Someone murdered the poor man. They found his body today in his apartment. Water was running from his kitchen sink and flowing out the apartment door. That's how they found him, because of the complaints of the water. Otherwise, he might still be there, rotting away. And they say he wasn't just murdered. They called it a scalping." Gilbert was enjoying his moment in the sun.

"Are you certain we're talking about Rueben Cord, my butcher? I was just talking to him last night when he got off work."

"But let me tell you the interesting thing. He really was scalped. That ponytail of his was missing from the crime site. I heard this directly from the investigating deputy himself. The man was at the hospital cafeteria begging a donut while I was there on a sales call. The morgue for the county is at the hospital, you see."

"Daddy," Cynthia said tentatively, "you should go back to work and let everyone know what's happened. People liked Rueben."

Red Trueheart seemed uncertain of what to do. He stood up, reaching for his heavy coat which he had earlier thrown on the stool beside him. He looked at his daughter and then at Gilbert. "Murdered." He seemed stunned. Red was walking to the door. Gilbert picked up his sample kit and rushed after him. "Red as long as you're here, can we talk about some of the new lines I'm carrying. I think they'd be perfect for your store." Red looked at Gilbert as though he were mad. Red walked out the door, with his heavy coat not yet buttoned and Gilbert snapping at his heels.

Thelma walked out from the kitchen. She had overdone her makeup with fresh lipstick and a heavy dose of rouge. "Where's Gilbert?"

Josh replied wickedly, "He found a bigger fish to catch." Thelma's rouge seemed to pale.

Josh turned to Danny. "Why don't we go ice skating now? If we hang around here, we'll just get depressed about this Rueben story."

Claire suddenly spoke up. "Arthur's trying to tell us something. That's why he came to Cynthia during that cold winter when she was so small. That's why he sent his dog today, on another cold winter day. He wants us to know he's okay."

"Arthur fell through the ice while skating in January when Claire was still a small girl," Mr. Packer said softly.

"He knows I've been worrying all these years. He wants me to stop worrying. That's why the dog is here. It's his messenger from the other side.

"Arthur," she shouted up to the sky, "I know you're okay now, and I won't worry anymore. You can take your dog and go."

Cynthia hugged Claire in an enormous embrace, who then broke into furious sobs. Bromley stood nearby, rocking from foot to foot. Danny and Josh looked anxiously at one another, ready to flee, and I signaled with my eyes permission to leave.

I also noticed something else. The collie was gone, with no sign of a dog ever having sat in the snowbanks, no dog smears of his face pressed against the plate glass, no tracks in the snow.

As though the collie had never existed.

CHAPTER FIFTEEN

The ice spread out before us like a mirrored plane. The sun, already low in the western sky, cast a bluish light through the leafless trees lining the flowage banks. Four figures that might in another setting have seemed prankish elves slipped and glided across the frozen river. Even in his thickly padded, black snowmobile suit, Danny appeared tall and thin. He moved across the ice with a surprising grace. All of the anxiety, tension, and self-doubt that normally encircled him vanished. Somehow, somewhere, Josh had managed to find a suit for himself that captured his puckish spirit. Swirls of color raced around his legs and broke into a garish bloom across his back. No one could help but notice him, however far the distance. His skating might have matched the grace of Danny, except he tried to make each push across the ice as grand and theatrical as possible. Cynthia's baby pink suit, padded and quilted more than the others, managed to make her seem even smaller and more petite. She had bright pink yarn tassels on her skates. I had been forced to borrow from Josh his dead father's snowmobile suit.

After their ice skating the day before, Josh and Danny had convinced both Cynthia and me to join them for a second round. Business had been slow, so I thought to myself, "why not?" Now here I was nearly freezing to death despite wearing the dead man's suit.

With temperatures below zero, skating at any type of speed makes for severe wind chill. The snowmobile suit broke the wind and was well insulated. After all, it was designed to ward off wind chills encountered by people foolish enough to flit across snowbanks at fifty miles an hour. But the thought of wearing a dead man's suit was discomfiting, even though none of the other three seemed to think anything of it. In fact, it had been Danny's idea to call Josh and have him bring Mr. Gunderson's suit. Danny had been so eager for my participation. He seemed to feel that if I didn't go along that this trip would somehow be called off. Cynthia on the other hand would have been happier if both Josh and I had bowed out.

A big fire burned on the bank of the bend. Being the worrier that I was, I made us gather the wood before skating, just in case someone fell in the ice and we needed to get them warm fast. Josh laughed at such fatalism.

"Do you want to race?" Josh asked.

"Sure, I'll race you anywhere," Danny quickly answered.

"I don't think I'll join in," I replied, feeling older than my years.

Cynthia lifted the tip of her foot and dug the end of her skate's runner into the ice, digging a little hole. "You guys can race. I'll stay here near the fire with Wally and practice some figure skating."

Josh shrugged his shoulders, "All right then, we'll race to the end of the second bend. Just you and me, kid. The two of us together."

"And I'll let the winner kiss me," said Cynthia.

"Is that meant to be an incentive?" joked Josh.

Cynthia put on a fake pout. She started the countdown, "Ready? Get set. Go!" And the two boys were off. Quick confident slides. They had a true style and grace. Cynthia began to skate forward, slowly, aimlessly. I sidled up beside her.

"I don't think Josh is good for Danny," she finally said.

"Why?" I asked.

"Because Josh is gay," she said forcefully. "Danny's not gay. Is he?"

"I don't know. Besides it's not important what I think. It's what Danny thinks."

Cynthia turned to me, more serious now. "Has he ever told you he was gay?"

"No," I replied. "Maybe he never will. First, he would have to tell himself. I don't think that's happened."

Cynthia continued skating listlessly in the direction of the racers. "I've always had a crush on Danny, but he's never laughed with me. Not the way he does with Josh. He's never really even noticed me."

The boys were far ahead of us, at least a quarter of a mile or so.

The sun was sinking noticeably in the west. Pools of shadows were forming in the underbrush of the banks. Cynthia and I said nothing to one another, simply skating slowly. I wanted to reach out to Cynthia some way and make her feel more secure. But I didn't know what action to take.

The racers were nearing their finish line, racing at it neck and neck. Suddenly a huge cracking boomed in the air, as though a jet plane had broken the sound barrier. The sound so startled Danny that he slipped. He brushed against Josh, causing both of them to lose their balance. Suddenly they were tumbling down onto the ice.

"Oh no," cried Cynthia.

But then the two were already getting to their feet, wobbling on their skates, and laughing uproariously. Each brushed the snow off one another and began circling around. They grabbed hands and swang one another in a circular ice dance, laughing more frantically as they made one another dizzy. Soon, they crashed into one another and again tumbled to the ice. They just lay there laughing. Their peals echoed in the still air.

"It was only the ice cracking," Cynthia explained. "That's what caused the boom. It happens on lakes all the time. Nothing important. It's not important, is it?"

She stopped. "What am I saying? I think he loves him. I mean Danny loves Josh. And Josh better not be using him. I'm going to make sure Josh treats Danny right." With that, she began racing toward them, and I could tell that she was in fact a far better skater than either of the boys. Laughing, she raced right by the duo.

The two boys tried to gather up some of the thin layer of loose snow on the ice and throw it at her. They missed. The powder sprinkled back to the ice. She rounded the bend and was hidden from our view.

Then came a long, loud piercing scream. The boys scrambled to their feet and raced forward. I followed with as much speed as I could muster. Soon, I too was around the bend and found the three of them standing in a semi-circle looking at the frozen river. I slowed down and skated up to them. Josh and Danny both had their arms around Cynthia. They were all staring at the ice before them.

I moved into their little circle to see what could have upset Cynthia so. Was it a dead animal? A hole in the ice.

Nothing so dramatic. Simply a drawing. A heart in the ice etched in yellow. And in the center were the words "C.T." and below that was signed the name "Kip." There was an acrid smell in the air and the slightest wisps of steam still rose up from the heart.

"I think he drew this by peeing," said Danny in wonderment.

"If he did, he's got great control, and a hell of a bladder," said Josh. "And how did he get here?"

Cynthia said nothing. She was scanning the river banks and the river ahead, trying to see where Kip Van Elkind was lurking, fearing that he was nearby, poised for an attack.

"I hate that guy with every bit of my being," she proclaimed. "I hope Kip rots in hell. Do you hear me, Kip Van Elkind? Rot in hell!" she screamed with all of the frustration of the day.

The week went on, with each day as cold as the one before. On Sunday, the after-church crowd was slim. Those that had dropped in were bundled up in flannels and woolens rather than in Sunday finery. Everyone was ordering the vegetable soup instead of a salad.

By now, my menu had twice given in to Thread customs. The first concession to Friday night fish fries had been a no-brainer. The fish fry was popular, if not much of a money-maker. It brought in the locals, even though they seldom ordered dessert or had much to drink.

My other grudging accommodation had been to create a Sunday dinner menu. For locals, I offered a Sundays-only, family-oriented, all-you-can eat approach. No fancy appetizers. No separate price tag for a salad or soup. The meal started with a big relish tray: carrot and celery sticks, radishes cut as roses, olives, pickled herring, corn relish, pickled beets, and bread sticks. Quantity was the most important element, and I learned to set out a colorful and hearty tray at a modest price. Thelma had insisted that I needed to provide both a soup and a salad. I rebelled at this point. They had to think I was a bit different. So diners had to choose one or the other. On Sundays, there were none of my "city" soups. Cream of wild rice was out the door. It was chicken noodle or vegetable beef. And the salad was a simple one of iceberg lettuce, although sometimes I snuck in some bits of spinach and romaine. The main menu was also slimmed down to hearty meats: roast turkey, roast beef, and baked ham with a raisin sauce. Needless to say, dessert in hefty portions was a substantial conclusion to every meal.

Sunday had become my busiest day. A better businessman might have switched his menu for the rest of the week. But I liked the idea of serving a rabbit and wild mushroom terrine. Besides I hadn't fled Manhattan to serve my Mom's cooking day after day. Even Bromley showed up on Sundays to order a full dinner. Just now, he was attacking his apple pie a la mode. "Thelma makes the best pies in town," he said.

Bromley leaned back from the counter and looked out the windows at the bright sunny day that belied the bitter cold that was awaiting his departure. "Sure is frosty today," he said. "The boiler went out at the school. Couldn't keep up with heating the place. Have to close down the whole place tomorrow, maybe longer. Who knows how long it'll take to get that god darn antique furnace fixed."

"I heard," I said.

"Should've bought a new furnace years ago. But the town can't afford it. The state has got a clutch on this town you know. They don't tolerate little schools like this anymore. They conspire to get us and Lattigo to consolidate into one district. Little Nazis down there in Madison. But as long I'm mayor, they're not going to be bussing our kids to sit with Indians."

I nodded, "So, I've been told."

Bromley motioned me to come closer. "You hear a lot of things in this place, don't you? People like to talk to you. What've you heard about those Lattigo lately?"

"I haven't heard anything," I said quietly.

The blustery overweight man eyed me skeptically. "Could be. Could be that no one's talking much, but a man in my position hears things. Rumors. A lot of property has been changing hands lately in this county and especially in this township. Don't think I'm an old fool who wouldn't notice such things. Sophie Dodge checks things for me. She looks at the documents that get filed with the country clerk up in Timberton.

"All these deeds, now, they seem to be sold to different people. No one you would know. Except for that Gunderson boy. His parent's land was bought by the Lattigo, in the name of the reservation. Strikes me as a bit suspicious."

I rose to return to the kitchen to help Thelma and didn't bother to reply. Things were getting pretty busy. A lot of people had showed up after the Old World Lutheran Church service.

"Stay put a minute," commanded Bromley. "It's not just the deeds. When you've been an important man as long as I have, people know you, they whisper things to you. Those Lattigo have our courts in their back pockets, I tell you. They're getting exactly what they want. There'll be trouble by into. They can't go hunting or fishing whenever they want, and not expect our good people to get upset."

"How much damage would a little extra fishing do?"

"It's not just that. They're stealing jobs from this town. Have you been to Lattigo town since you came back?"

"Yes," I replied calmly, "and the place could use some help."

"Did you see that new electronics plant? How did that get there? And how come all the jobs went to Indians in Lattigo?" Bromley was working himself into a frenzy.

"Maybe because they live there, and maybe because the tribe owns the place," I pointed out.

Bromley hunkered down in a truly conspiratorial stance. "Don't tell anyone I told you this, but they're onto a really big deal."

"Really?" I said. My heart began to race. If Bromley knew about American Seasons, soon everyone in town would know.

"I got it straight from Hank Johnson at the bank, who heard it from Tesla Haligent himself. The Lattigo are planning to buy up the woodworking plant here in town. I don't know how they got the cash exactly, but I hear it's some kind of deal they have with Haligent."

"Maybe it would be better to have local owners who care about the area?" I said. At least Bromley didn't have a clue as to the real goings on.

"And have Indians run our town? You got to be kidding!"

"I need to lend Thelma a hand."

Back in the kitchen, Thelma looked gloriously happy in her big white apron and white chef's cap. She lately started wearing a chef's toque instead of a hairnet because Gilbert Ford had assured her it was sexy. Sundays were Thelma's favorite day at the restaurant, because everything served was her kind of food and it made for an easy day. Since only roasts were being served, nothing was cooked to order. There was only slicing and arranging plates. Whatever meats were left over would be used for the sandwiches in the days ahead. Sundays were also the only days I let her make some of her favorite food–things like ambrosia salads heavy on maraschino cherries or coleslaw dripping with Miracle Whip.

Where Thelma and I competed were in the desserts. A sensible person would have allowed Thelma to serve whatever she wanted, since she was prone to offering apple brown betty, berry cobblers and peach pies—the Thread tried and true. But desserts were my favored experiment. Since everyone who ate on Sundays received dessert as part of their meal ticket, we went through lots of sweets, making the day an ideal laboratory. Once I offered a flourless chocolate cake. I let loose a classic French dessert, floating islands of meringue in a custard. Both were failures, so I decided to return to Wisconsin flavors. How about a flan served with a maple syrup sauce? Only the Saturday out-of-town crowd adored it. After that I gave up and crowned Thelma the queen of Sundays desserts.

Sundays were also the last day of our work week. The Sunday dinner crowd was gone by two in the afternoon, and we closed up until Wednesday morning. I suspected that Thelma lately had an open date for a Sunday evening rendezvous with Gilbert. Although she never admitted it to me, it seemed odd that Gilbert Ford's car was in town every Monday morning.

All in all, Sundays always put Thelma in a marvelously good mood. "Need any help in here?" I asked.

"Danny and I have it completely under control," she smiled and nodded to the boy. Danny was filling small woven baskets with Thelma's famous crescent rolls. They were one item that was a hit with any crowd.

"Done any more ice skating, Danny?" I asked.

"Yah," he blushed, then smiled. "It's just great. The ice is so smooth and the river's still completely free of snow. It's like being in another world. Josh and I saw some deer and a bald eagle."

Back at the counter, Officer Campbell sat down next to Bromley. The two were deep in conversation. I tried to avoid them and make a tour of the other tables. But I wasn't quick enough. Bromley noticed me and hissed for me to come over. "Officer Campbell was telling me about Rueben's murder down in Emeryville."

"They got a warrant out for his girlfriend for murder in the first degree and for theft," Campbell said with a raised eyebrow. He looked particularly silly on this cold day. He was sporting a policeman's uniform several times too large, leaving room underneath for multiple layers of wool sweaters, no doubt covering bulky, long underwear. On his head, he had a heavy cap with large furry earflaps that hung loosely along the side of his head. A big silver star was pinned to the front of the hat.

"It's warm in here. You can take off your cap" I pointed out. "So what was stolen at Cord's place?"

Campbell puffed up with the importance of knowing. "His hair."

"You told me before he was scalped."

"He was. Sort of. Actually just his pony tail was cut off. But it's missing. That's why there's a theft charge as well as the murder charge. He had lots of hair. It would be worth something to wigmakers."

I rolled my eyes.

"Don't you go looking like that, young man," Bromley chastised me. "This is serious stuff. And who would want to take his hair but an Indian? For one of their weird rituals, I bet."

"But Campbell just said the police were looking to arrest Rueben's girlfriend. I met her once. She isn't a Lattigo." I was trying to be patient and sensible.

"She's just a scapegoat. What would his girlfriend want with a bunch of old hair? But to some, it means something." Bromley was getting quite excited and bouncing about on his stool.

"You might be on to something there," said Officer Campbell.

"I think you both are just plain on something," I said. "I'm heading back to the kitchen."

Cynthia pushed by me as I was going back through the swinging doors to the kitchen. "Stupid ice skating," she muttered.

I quickly saw that neither Thelma nor Danny needed my help, so I went back through the swinging doors. Cynthia was coming back at me with a tray full of dirty dishes. "Where's that Danny?" she snapped. "He's supposed to be bussing the tables."

The dining room was turning into my worst nightmare. During my quick dart into the kitchen, Pastor Paul Mall had showed up and was talking Bromley and Officer Campbell. He caught a glimpse of me from the corner of his eye and turned to confront me.

"I see you're still serving alcohol in this unholy establishment," said Pastor Mall.

I didn't acknowledge him.

"There's sin and destruction flowing around us, and yet you continue to feed it."

I remained silent.

"And God is making us pay for it. The Gundersons suffocate in their own house. My own parishioner, Tony Masters, kills himself and so many more in a reckless act of destruction. And now our butcher. Can't you see the pattern?" The pastor was standing tall and gesticulating as though he were pounding out his Sunday sermon. From the looks on some of the diners' faces in the restaurant, it seemed they feared they were back in church.

"Why do you feel compelled to pay me these visits?" Surely he had given up hope that I would return to the church by now. If not, perhaps I need to remind him of Job 13:13. "Hold your peace, let me alone, that I may speak, and let come on me what will."

"I have accepted a calling to save men's souls, and that includes you and all those influenced by you."

"I don't recall being asked to be saved. And enough is enough. Please leave." I led the stringy old man by the arm to the door.

"I know you don't approve of me young man, but don't think I can be put off so easily. God watches and knows what you're up to. You won't be forgiven if you don't give up your sinning ways." His hands were waving as though he were drowning and didn't know how to swim.

The pastor departed just as Chip Frozen Bear and Jacqueline Grant walked into the restaurant. He pushed Jacqueline a bit, but offered no apology. "And a lovely day to you as well," Jacqueline said.

I remained by the door, just in case the Pastor decided to reenter. I braved a smile to Frozen Bear and his sister. "Can I show you a table?" I asked.

"That would be nice," Jacqueline acknowledged. "Chip didn't want to go out today. He said it was too cold. But I convinced him that eating here is always a treat. I love so many of the things on your menu."

"Well you know we have a more homespun menu on Sundays," I said tentatively and with a wince, "But I'm sure you'll like it." I handed them the special one-sheet Sunday menus as I sat them at their table. From the corner of my eye, I noticed that Bromley had stood up and was walking toward us. I had to get him away.

"Howdy folks," he said with political bravado.

Frozen Bear looked at him as though Bromley were one of Claire's little men. "Cynthia will be right over to take your order," I said. Bromley pulled over a chair from a nearby table and sat down.

"I'm worried," he began. "I'm hearing all these rumors, and I don't think they're healthy for relations between Thread and Lattigo. Rumors about your tribe buying land...taking over the woodworking plant...planning to go fishing during spawning seasons. I tell everyone that these have to be just rumors, that they can't be true and not to worry. But you know people. They won't listen to good advice. But I thought if I could get the story straight from you, then we'd all have to believe it. There'd be no trouble. So tell me what's really going on?"

Cynthia walked up looking a bit glum.

Frozen Bear looked up and noticed her gloom. He smiled, "Why the long face, Cynthia? If someone disappointed you, I just might have to go have a talk with them and set them straight."

Jacqueline rearranged her napkin with some level of amusement. Cynthia perked right up. "I was just thinking," she said distractedly. "I don't know, about how cold it is, and what I should do, and things like that."

"It is cold," Frozen Bear counseled, "but on the other hand it is truly beautiful outside. I say take advantage of every day. You never know what it might bring."

Bromley broke in, seeking to hurry things along. "Cynthia, just take their orders so the chief and I can discuss some issues."

"I'm not the tribe's chief," pointed out Frozen Bear.

"I was asking about your tribe's intentions."

"And I don't think it's any of your business," said Jacqueline brusquely. "We're here to eat, and believe me, we feel under no obligation to provide you with any information. And in case you have forgotten, you were the person who wouldn't let me attend Thread High School. Don't invite yourself to my Sunday dinner."

Bromley harrumphed. Cynthia stood there awkwardly, wondering whether she should leave or stay. I wished I had never left the kitchen. It was not turning out to be a good Sunday.

"Cynthia," said Frozen Bear warmly, "come back in a few minutes and we'll give you our order. I have a few things to say to Mr. Bastique."

He waited for Cynthia to leave the room before beginning his attack.

"Bromley, you are an asshole, always have been, and no doubt always will. But my sister is right. You are totally out of line asking questions about what my tribe is planning to do.

"But let me tell you one thing. The treaties have been ignored too long, and we are not going to let them stay forgotten. We have the sovereign right to fish whenever we want, to hunt wherever we want, and to economic self-determination. We know how to exercise those rights. We will decide when to do so. Understand, old man?"

More and more, I wished I were back on that cracking ice, skating into another beautiful day.

CHAPTER SIXTEEN

Kip Van Elkind's stunt on the flowage during the ice skating jaunt did nothing to raise his worth in Cynthia's eyes. Rather, he remained isolated. He constantly said what no one wanted heard and did what no one wanted done. And he wasn't a little boy telling the world that the emperor had no clothes. He was more like a wicked old man telling the little boy that there was no Santa Claus. In the warming cool of a late winter day, confronting Cynthia in my cafe, he once again chose the wrong path.

"Tell me you'll date me," Kip demanded, "or I'm going to kill myself."

"Don't be ridiculous," Cynthia scoffed.

"I'm not ridiculous," as he slurred through another drug-dazed day. "I'm serious. I brought the gasoline with me because I can't live without you. I need ya. Ya gotta go out with me, or I'm setting myself on fire."

"And you think I would care?" Cynthia asked with incredulity.

"I mean it," he said firmly, looking straight at her. Cynthia said nothing. She just stared at him until he finally looked away with the air of a young puppy that can't win a contest of will. He turned brusquely and walked to the door. He kicked at the base of the door, causing it to fling open. He walked out and I saw him pick up a can of gasoline that he had left by the door. He stepped off the curb on to the street. He turned and took a few paces until he could see that he was centered in the windows of the cafe, a magic moment for the camera of our eyes.

Dirty snow covered the town square. Piles of shoveled snow now mishapen from multiple rounds of melting and freezing created a barricade of sorts. He trudged over them until he stood in full sunlight, still centered in the window. He stood there silently focusing through the glass on Cynthia. This time, she didn't even look at him. She started wiping down the counter

"I'm glad he's out of here and that's over," Thelma said. "I got to get back to the kitchen and take care of my bread."

"I don't think it's over yet," I whispered.

Weeks later and Kip as a menace was still far from over. I had been invited to party at Jacqueline's and Chip's home. So had the Van Elkinds and the Truehearts. I would not be able to avoid the subject of Kip, even though I intended to try.

"So," I asked Jacqueline Grant as I looked around her living room, "why hold a St. Patrick's Day party if nothing is green?"

She laughed, "Do I look Irish? Besides, the old Finns in the area also claim the day as St. Urho's Day. Maybe their patron saint scared the snakes out of Finland. And aren't their national colors blue and white? I don't know. Besides who really cares? It was Chip's idea."

Frozen Bear stood disconsolately in the corner of their living room, gazing out the large glass windows at the small ice-covered creek below. In more southern parts of the country, spring might be well underway, but here in Thread the weather was still as chilly as Frozen Bear's demeanor. A strange attitude for a party you had requested.

"Your brother doesn't look too happy, " I noted to Jacqueline.

She smiled sweetly. "Well, he doesn't really enjoy the company. Oh, I'm sure he wasn't referring to you when he said that. Just the rest of this menagerie." She waved her hand to encompass the rest of the odd collection already in the room. Henry Van Elkind was here, along with his snippy wife Rita. For some reason, they had dragged along Kip, who had been forced to wash his hair and wear untattered clothes, but his sneer still lingered.

Amanda Manny was also on hand, flitting about as though it were her party. Her eyebrows had arched in disbelief at the idea of ravioli stuffed with a mixture of wild rice and venison served in a pumpkin puree. Clearly she would have preferred a dish in keeping with the day's theme and to match her bright green silk jumper. It accentuated her perky and quite artificial breasts, although the large glow-in-the-dark "Kiss me, I'm Irish" button pinned near her cleavage was eye-catching in its own right. Rita could barely control her shudder each time she accidentally glanced in Amanda's direction. Van Elkind, on the other hand, was entranced.

Amanda pranced over to my side as soon as she saw Jacqueline move toward the kitchen. She half-whispered, "I do wish Jackie had the sense to ask my advice about this evening's party. It's practically a board meeting for American Seasons, and did you hear what she's serving."

"Sounds quite delicious to me," I replied.

Amanda rolled her eyes. "Yes, I suppose it would, considering what you serve in your restaurant. But this is just too strange. I hear she's putting dandelions in the salad."

"What are you two talking about?" Priscilla Jouer moving into our small circle. Priscilla had been engaged in an animated conversation with two elders from the Lattigo tribe. Perched on her stiletto heels, Priscilla's large body swayed dramatically as she sought to entice them in a tale that neither man seemed interested in hearing.

"Is Miss Mandy giving you entertainment tips?" asked Priscilla.

"If you keep calling me that name," glowered Amanda, "I'm going to start calling you Prissy."

"That would be darling. Prissy is what my first husband called me. I met him at Disneyland, where he was a glib skipper on the Jungle Book Cruise. What a tongue on that man. But he proved bisexual. I should have known when he told me his favorite ride was 'It's a Small World.' But then one should never look for a husband at Disney.

"Now, my second husband was as macho as they come. He was a foreman on a construction crew at Walt Disney World who liked Rubenesque woman. But the man was just so boring under the covers. I really should stop marrying people I meet through work. Although I must admit, I do find Mr. Frozen Bear most appealing. I think there's a strength in the way he moves. Have how you noticed how graceful his hands are."

"No, I haven't," muttered Amanda who quickly walked way.

"How about you, Walter?" said Priscilla smiling.

"No I can't say that I have," I replied.

"Well, if you haven't, I'm sure that she has," Priscilla replied, as she watched Red, Barbara and Cynthia Trueheart enter the room. I was amazed that Cynthia had agreed to come knowing that Kip had also been invited.

Red shouted out, "Where's the green beer?" Kip looked up with a greasy grin, poised like a hyena spotting cornered prey. Frozen Bear turned from the dark glass he had been staring through. An unexpected and genuine smile lit up the room. He appeared younger and more attractive than I remembered.

"At last, the party is complete," Frozen Bear announced. Red flung out his hand for a hearty shake. Barbara stood at her husband's side, and I sensed she was cataloging the Frozen Bear living room against her own infamous white salon. Cynthia hung back a few steps in a bashful glow.

I caught a glimpse of Jacqueline standing in the doorway to the dining room. She was beaming. Suddenly it occurred to me. This party wasn't designed so she could meet her brother's business partners. Frozen Bear had wanted to see Cynthia on his home turf.

"Hey Cindy Baby," Kip lurched forward. Frozen Bear stepped into the intervening space before Kip could touch Cynthia.

"Cynthia, can I give you a tour of the house?" Frozen Bear asked. She quickly nodded her assent. Red gave a thumbs-up to Frozen Bear, happy to have the man protect his daughter from the detestable Kip. Kip slunk back to the sofa and slouched down in the cushions, a scowl spreading from his face to his posture.

"Isn't it cute?" Jacqueline whispered to me and Priscilla. "Thwarted love."

Barbara Trueheart overheard and moved in.

"Don't call it love in any form. I'm just glad Cynthia has her job at your cafe, Wally. It keeps her mind off Kip. Although I do wish she would find someone she could like."

Rita Van Elkind, dressed in a becoming Donna Karan cocktail dress that was totally inappropriate for the casualness of the evening, walked up. "What are you all discussing? Something amusing, I hope."

Jacqueline answered honestly, "We're talking about your son and how much Cynthia detests him."

Rita took no offense, "Barbara, I'm delighted to learn that your child has grown up with more common sense than mine. If he weren't my son, I would detest him as well. But there is that bond between mother and child that just can't be broken." She whirled the ice in her glass of mineral water. A wedge of lime floated near the top. I thought of Rita's mother Regina floating through the halls of that gigantic camp on the lake. What was the bond there? But at least Regina had the comfort and care of their butler Stephen. Looking at the boy now, trying to ignite a match for his cigarette and getting angrier with each match he broke, I wondered if anyone could bond with that young man.

Our circle had grown with the insertion of both Priscilla and Amanda, who were now settled into a truce of using each other's given names. "What tales are being told here?" Priscilla asked.

"Is your son suffering puppy love?" Priscilla had no idea of recent events, but she aspired to be always sparkling. Van Elkind dragged Red into the corner for an animated discussion. Red's face was quite flushed. The Lattigo guests moved into their own corner. Kip sat isolated on the sofa. Frozen Bear and Cynthia were on their tour–a surprisingly long tour for a house of this size. And I was in the circle of these women.

"It's not love," dismissed Amanda. "Everyone in town knows that Cynthia can't stand your son. Why can't he wake up and smell the coffee? How dim is he?"

On that day when Kip truly went too far, his canister of gasoline had glinted in the sunlight, with its bright red and rectangular shape, serving as an ornament to the dirty snow of the square. Kip tried to loosen the top of the can and in an instant had the cap unscrewed and off. He held the can high over his head, and he started to talk. But we couldn't hear him through the plate glass. We could only see mouthing words. "I'm going out to see what he's saying," I said.

Danny followed me as I walked outside. Reluctantly, Cynthia followed, but she stayed in the doorway.

"What are you doing?" I asked. "Put down that can."

"Cynthia," he shouted over me to address his unrequited love. "Go out with me or I'm going to pour this gasoline over myself and set myself on fire."

"Who cares?" she said. She turned abruptly and walked back into the cafe, the door slamming shut behind her.

"I mean it," he screamed and let the gasoline dribble from the can. It trickled in thin waves, a glittering sheen in the sunlight. It splashed weakly onto his oily head and ran down around his ears, falling onto his shoulders. He continued to pour. The gas dripped over his head, falling down upon his dirty shirt. As the gasoline spread through the fabric, it transformed the dyes. In those wet spots, the shirt metamorphosed into a bright scarlet, as though blood were seeping through. The last drops of gasoline bounced onto his head and continued to drip down his body, soaking into the tops of his torn Levis, the wet stain slowly working down his crotch and thighs.

His head looked like he had just washed his hair in oil. His torso appeared to be drenched in blood. And his jeans had the look of a little boy who had peed in his pants. Down around his feet, little puddles of gasoline formed, each growing slowly larger as more gasoline puddled down his skinny body.

"Cynthia tell me you love me, or I'm going to set myself on fire," he shouted at the top of his lungs. Cynthia came storming out.

"If I can't light your fire, then I'm going to light mine," said Kip.

"Do it!" she screamed. "Do me a favor and do it! I don't give a fucking damn." She swirled back into the restaurant.

He stood there. A look of dull astonishment worked its way across his stupor. He shifted from foot to foot. He had voiced his ultimatum and now was perplexed as to what he could do. But just as he felt his words had no meaning for others, he realized they had no meaning for him. A lazy smile swirled up.

"What the fuck," he shrugged. "If she don't care, neither do I. Fuck her. Fuck all of you! I'm walking to the lake and washing this shit off me. Fucking women. Fucking fags."

The tension flowed from my body. A disaster had been averted. Or so, we thought.

At the party, hearing Amanda disparage her son was enought to break Rita's controlled demeanor. "I find that quite a rude statement coming from you. You might do well to consider what else this town discusses before you denigrate my son. If Cynthia doesn't enjoy his attentions, I believe it is as much her loss as his."

Through all of this, Barbara Trueheart looked tired and much older than she was. Over the years, she tried to set the pace for the town's society. She was the first to use the talents of Amanda Manny. She frequently went to Chicago on buying trips. Despite Red's just-one-of-the-boys facade, she spent the money that allowed her to swim among barracudas like Rita. But it was clear she didn't enjoy the waters. For the first time, I sensed that much of Cynthia was derived from her mother.

"I just want Cynthia to find true love," Barbara said. "If it were your son she loved, then I would be happy for her and for him. But she doesn't."

"No, she doesn't love Kip," I agreed. "But how many people find true love? Anyway, who even knows what it is?"

Barbara had a faraway look in her eyes. "My grandmother used to tell me a story about our ancestors. Did you know that my family has been in Wisconsin since the seventeenth century? They were originally trappers and explorers, but even before that they were nobility in France. It was a many, many-great grandfather of mine who gave up his family fortune because of love and in the end he trapped beaver in these northwoods. No one has ever really found true love in our family, however briefly, since those days. Cynthia shouldn't continue that sad legacy." She looked so wistful that she seemed young once more, and I wondered about the state of love between Red and her. There truly was an astonishing amount of Barbara Trueheart in Cynthia.

"If Cynthia were here," I said, "she would insist that you tell this story you're hinting at."

Barbara smiled, "But Cynthia isn't here."

"But I am," Priscilla said, "and I want to hear it." While Jacqueline smiled in agreement, Amanda and Rita were locked in their own small battle of wills and weren't paying much attention.

"I love telling it, so why not." And Barbara began her family tale.

"The first European that we know of to find his way to Wisconsin was Jean Nicolet in 1634. He was a young and strapping man on a mission from the governor of New France. And when he returned to France to his home which was very near the chateau of my ancestor, Pierre DuPellier, he was filled with tales of adventure. Pierre was just a boy that winter when Nicolet spent a week at the chateau and told of the wonders of his discovery of Lake Michigan, of the five thousand Winnebago Indians who had welcomed him at the foot of Green Bay, and of his enormous disappointment when he had to report back to the French Governor Samuel de Champlain that he had not found the northwest passage to China, that in fact the American continent must be far vaster than anyone imagined to have such great fresh water lakes within its midst.

"What was such a great disappointment to Nicolet only excited a boyhood fantasy in young Pierre. They say that as he grew to an adolescent and then to a young man all he could discuss was his desire to explore the vastness of New France and to see these Indians for himself. By the time he was in his twenties, despite his father's enormous objections, he had made his way to Quebec to be a part of New France. And there he hooked up with two young French gentlemen like himself–Groselliers and Radisson.

"The three of them decided to retrace the route blazed by Nicolet. What did it matter, they thought, if this wasn't the route to China? The trail could still lead to vast fortunes. It was theirs to discover, theirs to own."

"When was this?" I asked, sneaking a glance at Jacqueline and wondering what she might think of this tale. I knew how sensitive the Lattigo were about their connection to French voyageurs.

"The year was 1656. It was a wonderful time for all of them. They discovered the Sault St. Marie and made their way into Lake Superior. Think of it. The first white men to do it. My ancestor was on that boat. What a wonderful feeling it must have been to be the first to see that great lake."

"My people were already there," Jacqueline pointed out.

"I don't mean to suggest that they weren't. In fact, this story will be as much your story as it is mine. Just wait." Barbara was glowing. Amazing to think this was the same woman who appeared so tired just minutes earlier.

"They followed the shoreline of Upper Michigan and came to a bay just above Timberton. Pierre's journals talk about what a beautiful sight the islands in this bay were. Well, you know, you've seen the Apostle Islands yourself. The way the water's waves have rushed against the soft sandstone to carve out caves that are more like ancient temples. Giant pillars of rock guarding mysterious entries. And the water and wind as it rushes in and out of those caves creates music."

"Legends among the Lattigo say that one of those islands was our original home at the very beginning of time, and that the sound you hear is that of the Great Spirit himself. For some of us it is the most holy of our places." Jacqueline was begining to enjoy the story.

Barbara continued. "It was near that island that the tragedy happened. Storms are wild and quick on Lake Superior. Everyone knows how the Edmund Fitzgerald just cracked and sank without a trace, and that was a modern ship. What were our Frenchmen's long canoes to do in such a storm? Somehow, and Pierre never was able to explain how, he was washed out of their boat by an unexpected wave and cast into the stormy waters in a day that was as dark as night. Radisson and Groselliers went on their way, perhaps not even knowing at the moment that Pierre had been washed overboard in the storm.

"Storms can end as quickly as they appear. Soon Pierre found himself bobbing in a calm lake on a sunny afternoon. But you know how cold the lake can be–even in the middle of June. It will kill you quickly. He was too far from land to safely swim to shore. And in the chill of that icy lake's water, he would soon have lost consciousness and sunk to the bottom.

"And that is when she appeared in her canoe."

"Who?" I asked. "Who appeared?"

"The most beautiful woman he had ever seen. Pierre had grown up in France and he always thought that angels would have a certain look. His savior did not have that look. Yet he still thought her an angel, even though her skin was dark, her hair black. Her tunic was made of the tawniest of leather and the sun shone from behind, creating a glow that transformed her. She was like no painting in the churches of his youth or in the illustrated books in his father's chateau, yet to Pierre this woman was an angel descended from God Himself.

"She was strong enough to pull him from the frigid waters to the safety of her canoe, strong enough to paddle the two of them to the shore of the mainland. There she built a fire and warmed him, and gave him food.

"Pierre never learned her name. In his diaries, which my grandmother still treasured when she told me the tale, he always called her Fleur. She pulled him from the water and gave him life. Yet he never knew her real name. I remember clearly to this day how I would look at the faded ink in his journal, blotched by water and time, and trace out that finely-written name. Fleur." Her voice was nearly a whisper.

"When he was recovered, Fleur somehow convinced Pierre to travel with her. But what else was he to do? He knew none of her language. She knew none of his. His own compatriots thought him dead. He had no way of returning to the safety of Quebec. So he followed. She brought him to her own village, where her tribe still lived in their winter birch round lodges.

"Pierre stayed with the tribe for two weeks–two weeks that he described as the happiest days in his life. He felt he owed his life to Fleur, and she in turn took tremendous interest in everything about him. The others in her village did not seem to share this interest. They let the two of them wander through the woods. Fleur showed him how her tribe caught the mighty muskie, let him taste the foods they harvested from the woods, introduced him to the dark grain we now call wild rice. It all seemed so much more wonderful to Pierre than his predictable life in France.

"He knew he was falling in love with Fleur, and he sensed that she was falling in love with him. The whole village could see that this was happening. And even without a shared language, Pierre and Fleur soon learned to communicate their love for one another."

"So what happened?" Priscilla wanted to know. "Did he stay? Did he marry her? Are you part Native American?"

The business dealings of Red and Van Elkind off in the corner of this modern home receded from our minds. Today's Lattigo tribe members became just another part of the evening's background. Every one in the circle surrounding Barbara wanted to hear how love had emerged across culture and difference to blossom in the summer of that long distant year.

"Love was not to be," said Barbara. "Pierre was torn by the duty he felt. Duty to the other explorers who by now thought him dead. Duty to Champlain who governed New France from Quebec and had given his imprimatur to this exploration. Duty to his father in the far distant Loire valley who had given his blessing to his son's trip to the New World only after extracting a vow from this son that he would return.

"Pierre knew he wanted to stay. Yet he knew he had to return.

"Somehow, and I can't imagine how, he found the courage to let Fleur know that he must return to his homeland, that he must leave her. Somehow, he convinced the tribe to give him both a canoe and sufficient provisions to make the long trek back across the Great Lakes and up the St. Laurence. He needed to start while the summer was still young. If he did not reach Quebec by winter, he would be unlikely to ever make it.

"It was the dawn of midsummer's night when he was finally ready to leave–the longest day in the year. Fleur and others from her tribe traveled with him to the banks of Lake Superior to wish him off. He settled into his canoe at the first breaking light, balancing upon the misting waters as the sun rose over the ancient Penokee hills and skipped across the waters. The lake was unusually placid. The other tribe members retreated into the woods. Only the woman Pierre called Fleur remained on the shore.

"There was no wind that day. Only sunlight on a cloudless day. Only blue sky over blue water with one small canoe and one brave man. And another brave woman standing on the shore. Pierre paddled away,

256

unwilling to look back, fearing that if he did then he would be unable to continue paddling. He knew it was his duty to return–duty to his family, to his friends, to his France. A duty that impelled him, but a duty that he hated.

"As he turned around a bend, he knew that if he did not grab hold of one last look at that moment, that he could not retain her image for all eternity in his memory, but he was afraid she was already fading. He had to take that look. He had to turn around and retrieve one last glimpse of Fleur.

"I have imagined it so often. He sees her. She is there in the distance, standing on the edge of the lake, her feet wet in the gently lapping waters. She stands watching him. A small tower of strength at the periphery of his vision.

"He froze that image in his mind, and he turned back to his purpose. He continued to paddle throughout that long day. He wrote nothing in his journals about what he thought, about the regrets that must have played through his mind on that windless day. He left it to me to imagine. And I have imagined it many times."

Unlike Barbara, I have imagined that earlier day in the square with Kip many times, but never with a wistful longing. At first, Danny and I leaned back against my cafe window in relief, certain that Kip had come to his senses. "Should we go back in?" I asked Danny.

Then Kip reached into his shirt pocket and pulled out a package of Camels. He stuck one cigarette in his mouth, but it apparently had been drenched in gasoline and he spat it out. He tapped the pack and drew out another. This time he left the stick dangling in his mouth. He reached into his pants pocket, and pulled out a Bic lighter.

"What is the idiot doing?" I asked. Danny took off in a flash.

Kip brought the lighter up to the tip of his cigarette. He pressed down on the lighter. The flame burst forth. It jumped to his shirt. Kip erupted.

Danny lunged from the edge of the park, and at the same time, Frozen Bear appeared out of nowhere. Together, they tackled Kip so the burning boy fell to the ground, where they quickly rolled him in the dirty snow. The flames were out within moments. A smell of charred cloth and burnt hair wafted by.

Kip sat up and smiled goofily. "I guess I should have waited for a smoke" and then he tumbled back unconscious.

"Call an ambulance" I screamed to anyone listening inside the cafe. Cynthia had emerged from the cafe during the fracas, and she stood just outside the doorway staring across the square at Kip's prone body in its burnt clothes with disgust. She turned and walked into the kitchen without making the call. Both Danny and Frozen Bear looked with more concern at her than at the scorched boy in the snow.

"Please tell me this Frenchman saw his Fleur again," implored Priscilla.

Barbara sighed, "Duty is powerful and can catch any of us in its demands. He reached the safety of Quebec. He returned to France. His father had died while he was in the new world. Now as the heir to a vast fortune and master of many who lived on his lands, he had responsibilities: his mother to care for, his sisters to marry to suitable husbands, his younger brothers to obtain appropriate commissions from the King. Yet he thought of Fleur. In the years that followed, he never married. He always said he would return to America to find once more his Fleur.

"In France, they thought him daft to want to marry a native. But he was rich and so they tolerated his fancies."

"But he did return, didn't he?" Priscilla pressed. "He came back and found his angel."

"Yes, Pierre came back. Over twenty years had passed before he could free himself from the binding ties of his duties. By then, trappers were throughout the region. Wisconsin, Michigan, Ontario. There was even a small settlement and French fort in Green Bay. The trip was much easier this second time, but it needed to be, because Pierre was nearly an old man.

"Much, of course, had changed. There had been many Indian wars. In the intervening years, the Potawatomi, the Iroquois, the Menominee, the Fox and the Lattigo had made warring incursions on one another's territories many times as they tried to adjust to the westward pressures of the greedy Englishmen from the colonies along the Atlantic.

"Finding Fleur after all that time could only be an old man's fancy. A dream that only a demented man would have followed.

"No, Pierre never found Fleur. Yes, he did marry here, and he fathered two children before he died. It started a new generation that has led to me and to Cynthia. But his remaining years in Wisconsin were bitter ones. As a young man, Pierre had chosen duty over love, thinking he could find love again, that love would wait for him."

Rita broke in, "But love never waits, does it."

Amanda sighed in agreement.

"I think it's a perfectly marvelous story, even if it didn't have the happiest of endings," declared Priscilla. "In fact, it could be the basis on an attraction at American Seasons."

"What's that?" jumped in Jacqueline. Amanda quickly tried to change the subject. Rita seemed eager to help. Barbara was merely confused.

In all of the interaction of these women, I was the only one who glanced out the window and noticed moving shadows on the snow-covered lawn that were cast from the bedroom on the second floor. Two people standing by the window above us with a lamp behind them were casting their shadowy images to spill out the window and across the snow a story below.

Two shadows, a man and a girl supposedly on a tour of a house, but actually standing in the bedroom, with their kisses stretching across the snow into the darkness of the wooded night.

CHAPTER SEVENTEEN

Spring was nearing. And all of Thread could sense it.

Little trickles of water began to form in the snow beneath the heat of the rising sun. These merged into tiny capillaries which slid into the small arteries of streams that formed in roadside ditches. At dips and hollows, the tiny rivulets gurgled as they fell through the metal culverts, then streamed into the true creeks which eventually reached the Lattigeaux. Eventually, a mountainous rush of frothing water crashed through the Lattigeaux Gorge on its way to Lake Superior.

Dead leaves transformed by winter snows emerged from beneath the snow as a fragrant mulch promising new potential. Warmed to unexpected highs of forty or fifty degrees, the sunlit days beckoned like a tropical isle after so many months of freezing temperatures. But winter reclaimed each night. Temperatures dropped back below the freezing mark, and thin layers of translucent ice, as fragile as handblown ornaments, crusted the little streams, only to disappear again with the rising sun.

In the stands of maple trees, the changing temperatures sent a primeval signal to the roots of the trees, whispering "It's time." The stored energy of the sap stirred in its subterranean lair, and the tiny branches at the tip of the tree, like little children with many straws into a malted milk, pulled the tree's leaf-giving nectar up from the roots to the light of spring and the birth of eventual maple leaves.

A few enterprising farmers tramped through the woods with their wood augers and silvery taps, drilling a single hole into each tree, sticking it with the metal channel to divert a fraction of the sugary maple drip into their clangy buckets. With the snow still heavy in the woods, the tappers were forced to break paths through the thick snow grown dense with water.

From the air, the crisscrossing doodles created by the itinerant farmers' paths grew deeper with each passing day, as they took down one pail and replaced it with another. A gallon of sap or two from each tree combined with a gallon or two from each of its neighbors and all hauled back to the central site. Into a huge open pan six feet in length and a foot deep, the farmers poured the buckets of sap. As the sun dropped in the western sky, and the pan filled with the day's collection of sweetness, the farmers lit a giant fire. For several hours, in the deepening dark of the night gone cold, they stirred the bubbling liquid. After many hours, the gallons and gallons of sap condensed almost magically into a thick stickiness and was poured into smaller containers, where it was brought into their finishing shed for the final boiling. At day's end, one hundred gallons of sap were transformed into less than a dozen quarts of maple syrup. But each quart carried a beautiful amber color and a wonderfully sweet consistency.

If people paid as much attention to their breakfasts as they do their dinners, there would be a blue-ribbon society of maple syrup lovers. It would the butternut amber of Wisconsin syrup versus the molasses brown of commercial Canadian syrup. People would talk about the good years for syrup, the undertone of berries one year, the tang of earthiness the next. Small-plot maple syrup would be as prized as the award-winning wine of a vintner who produced only one hundred cases of a great cabernet. For like any natural element, maple syrup reflects the quality of its maker and the environment from which it has been taken.

This spring, I acted like an oenophile thrown into the Napa Valley. I discovered each of the small farmers who still made syrup the old fashioned way, driving from dilapidated farm to dilapidated farm, tasting syrup, selecting the best of it, and buying several gallons for use in my restaurant.

Spring was coming to Thread. In each of us, an energy was rising. Yet we held no focus. The snow had grown too icy for downhill skiing. The lakes had become dangerous with pockets of rotten ice. Snowmobilers soon learned to proceed with caution over the packed snow that lay heavy and damp in the woods. There was no longer exhilaration in the speed of racing. At the high school, basketball season was over. The Screaming Loons again slid into the basement of their league rankings, although they had won two games. The short winning streak gave some townspeople hope, only to be quickly dashed. Few tourists appeared so late in March. And the news on the American Seasons front was as mushy as the snow outside.

All that was left was love. Love was blooming all around me in ways I could hardly anticipate.

Mr. Packer was at the counter with coffee cup in hand. "Keep your dogs tied up at this time of the year," said Mr. Packer. "Their natural instincts emerge and they want to return to the allure of their hereditary packs. Perhaps the deer throw out some scent of their rutting that touches the dogs' limbic memories triggering their wilding instinct to pack and to kill."

"I think they're just interested in the she-dogs," said Thelma in her no-nonsense way.

"That could be another explanation," acknowledged Mr. Packer.

"According to Danny, that cute little elkhound he bought for his father bounded off into the woods. And I say that little dog was looking for love." Thelma was having a romantic view on life these days.

"Do you remember that collie that sat outside the cafe in the snow bank a while back?" asked Claire.

"I do," said Cynthia breezily as she rushed through the room to deliver a plate of waffles and another of pancakes to a two-top near the window.

"Has anyone see the little thing since?" Claire asked with some trepidation.

"Who cares? Why do you want to think about that god darn dog, Claire? Something doesn't seem the same with you lately. Aren't you feeling well?" Bromley stopped looking at his caramel roll, paused for a moment, and then yelled over to Cynthia. "I changed my mind. I think I'll have another caramel roll. And give me a rasher of bacon. Oh, what the hell, it's nearly spring. How about adding in an order of scrambled eggs?"

"Got it Bromley," smiled Cynthia as she waltzed back into the kitchen and shouted, "The usual for Bromley." Then she came back out the swinging doors.

"It's not my usual, young lady. I'm watching my weight." Bromley was indignant.

"Something's changed since that dog was here. It's not the same anymore. I think it's all due to that dog." Claire's voice was a sad whisper.

"Now, Claire, don't get started on this again," implored Bromley.

"Here's your eggs and bacon, Bromley," Cynthia set them down with a big flourish and then leaned forward, elbows on the counter, her chin resting on her overlapping fingers. "Claire, you know that collie wasn't my dog." Cynthia wasn't paying much attention to Claire. Instead she was looking out the windows and across the town square. Chip Frozen Bear was walking out of the hardware store. Red Trueheart had stopped him on the street and the two were talking.

"That collie did something to my little men. Ever since the dog was here, my little men haven't been visiting me."

"I wonder what my Daddy and Chip are talking about," mused Cynthia.

Thelma, taking a short break, turned around in her stool and also watched the two men across the street. She swirled back to look more carefully at Cynthia. Cynthia's attention was across the square, and her face was alive with energy.

"Wally, what do you think of that Chip Frozen Bear?" Thelma asked. "Do you think he's handsome. Or just good looking?"

Mr. Packer broke in. "No need to ask that question. Everyone knows he's a very handsome man. There's none that would deny that. More to the point, he's quite an intelligent and ambitious man. Look at what he has done for the Lattigo. There's progress in that town."

"Why would the dog tell my men to stop visiting me? Does Arthur want them to stop? Is Arthur trying to tell me something?"

Bromley turned to Claire and snapped. "Would you shut up!" All the diners turned to stare, and Bromely gave them a stare back as though to dare anyone of them say one word.

"I think he's just plain cute," said Cynthia.

Thelma got up and walked around the side of the counter and motioned Cynthia back against the cabinets of liquor bottles. She bent close to her ear and whispered. My hearing was better than Thelma gave me credit for. "Can I tell you a secret," Thelma asked.

"Sure! You know I love secrets," bubbled Cynthia.

"Gilbert and I are planning to get married this spring. He asked me on Sunday night, I slept on it and Monday morning I told him yes. Isn't it wonderful?"

Cynthia squealed with delight. Now everyone looked at her. "Oh, mind your own business," she said in a mock voice of crossness. She grabbed Thelma's hearty arms and did a series of baby jumps. Thelma tried to hush her.

Claire pulled her muffin plate back toward her. "Tonight," she muttered, "I'm going to wait in the field until they visit me."

Cynthia stopped jumping. She moved in close to Thelma's ear. "I have a secret too," she said. "Can I tell you?"

"Go ahead," a look of victory flashed across Thelma's face.

At that moment, Officer Campbell walked into the restaurant. His big black and unbuckled galoshes, fully prepared for tromping through the spring melt, made a squishing sound and his usually timid face was strangely morose. He didn't even try to catch Thelma's attention, which proved to be a more effective tactic that his usual behavior.

Finally Thelma couldn't take it any more. "What's with you, Campbell?" she asked brusquely. By now, all of our attention was focused on the town cop. His shoes made one last squish and he was up on a stool.

"A cup of coffee, please?" he asked.

Wanting to cheer him up, Claire tried to push her basket of strawberry jams toward him. "How about a muffin and some jam?" she asked.

He shuddered. "I don't want to see anything red the rest of the day. Neither would you if you had seen what I just saw."

That was like throwing a lit match on a pile of oily rags. Suddenly he had the full attention of Bromley, Mr. Packer, Claire, Thelma and even me. Even Cynthia came back out from the kitchen. Thelma took down a cup and a saucer, poured the man a cup of coffee, and set it in front of him. Campbell was beginning to perk up a bit, realizing that Thelma was paying attention to him.

Finally, Bromley would have no more of the suspense. "Well, god darn it man, tell us what's got you moping. Did you see some of Claire's little men?"

He had my attention as well, though I was loath to admit it. Something lingered in the air of Thread and sooner or later you were infected. Perhaps the agent was in the water. Or maybe it floated through the air like a virus in a cough. It was as though a weird tale engagingly told made you move in too close and then you breathed in the germs of narration from the storyteller. Whatever the process, you couldn't be quarantined and remain in Thread. Sooner or later, you caught the story bug. Once you had it, it was incurable. You felt compelled to pass along to whomever whatever you had already uncovered. Sooner or later, everyone in town caught Loon Town Fever.

Like all the others, I needed to know what Campbell was about to say. I knew there was no way his tale could possibly live up the expectations we had set for it. But then these little coffee klatches were much like a parasite that always took more than it gave back.

I finally had to give in. I was powerless in the face of the fever. "Tell us Officer Campbell. You know we all want to know."

He straightened and puffed up a bit. The galoshes made another squish as moved about for the best storytelling position, and he began his tale of the doomed rabbits at the Siilinen farm. The Siilinen boy's 4-H project had long ago grown out of control. According to Cynthia, who loved visitng the rabbits, the kid had nearly two hundred rabbits running loose in the ground floor of his father's otherwise unused barn. Needless to say, rabbits being rabbits were only ensuring continued growth. It was unfortunate that I couldn't get anyone in town to order a nice braised rabbit dish. I certainly could get the ingredient on the cheap from the Sillinen farm.

Campbell was explaining how Mr. Siilinen had "called me out because he thought aliens had been in his rabbit barn. He didn't know how else to explain what had happened."

"I knew they were up to something," Claire said with disapproval.

"Explain what?" I asked, not really wanting to know.

"Every rabbit was dead," Officer Campbell said. Cynthia gave a little cry. "Every rabbit had its little throat torn out. Must have been two hundred of them." Cynthia gave several little cries. Thelma now had her arm around the girl. "There was blood everywhere." Cynthia now was in furious tears.

"Dogs," said Mr. Packer simply.

"That's what I figure." Campbell and the others all nodded in agreement.

Everyone knew about the emergence of those packs of wild dogs every spring and how they could go into a killing frenzy, killing for the sake of killing. I've seen when they've run down a deer and killed it that way. Then just left it behind, not a bit eaten. They're not hungry. It was just bloodsport. I recalled from my buying visits how the Siilinen barn was quite a way from the house. The parents probably didn't hear a thing.

"Anyway, I figure I got to round up a posse of men to go hunt down that pack of dogs," said Office Campbell. "Now that they've tasted the blood, they won't stop with the rabbits. They might go after a hog. Or worse. Could be far worse."

Bromley had been quiet throughout Campbell's story. Now he spoke but still very quietly. "Maybe it wasn't dogs. Maybe it was the Lattigo."

Cynthia tears quickly transformed into anger. "Why would you say such a thing? How could you even think it?!"

"I don't know what they might do these days," Bromley was calm. "I'm told that when the walleye start running for the spawn between the lakes this spring, they plan to go spear fishing. It'll be like a pack of dogs in a barn of helpless rabbits if they do that. Maybe you should be planning to set up a posse to keep the Lattigo in place, Campbell. If they kill all those fish, there won't be a decent fishing season around these parts for years."

"Then why would the Lattigo do it?" I demanded to know.

"To prove a point. They say the laws allow them to do what they want. So they're going to do it. I guess they want to show us who's the real boss in these northwoods.

"If they want a war, maybe they'll just get one." Bromley stood up, threw some bills to the counter and left. None of us remaining had a thing to say. Our tale telling was momentarily cured.

Four state patrol cars were parked in the town square. Thelma, Cynthia, Danny and I watched them out the window. They seemed to glow in the afternoon light of the spring day. Since arriving earlier that morning, occasionally one or two of the cars would be dispatched to drive around the town, eventually returning to the square. Everyone wonder why we needed so many police. Yet at the same time everyone knew why the cars had been dispatched to Thread. It was just that no one wanted to acknowledge the reason.

"Daddy made Bromley and Officer Campbell call in the state police because he's afraid of what might happen tonight," Cynthia said as though she were telling us a secret.

The tensions in town had been building, ever more rapidly over the past week and a half, with Bromley serving as a bellows forcing oxygen onto little flickers until they burst into flames.

For example, everyone knew that Rueben had been killed by his girlfriend over his cheating behavior and that she snipped off his pony tail only because he had been prouder of that hair than anything else. When she was captured by the police in Green Bay she proudly said she would have cut off his penis as well if it hadn't been too small to find. So everyone knew the missing pony tail had nothing to do with scalping or the Lattigo. Yet now everyone was whispering that because Rueben refused to sell some land to the Lattigo, they contracted his killing. Some even claimed a few landowners were sent a lock of hair in the mail as a warning.

Of course, I knew this was all nonsense. The Lattigo weren't even the people behind the land purchases. But between the rumors of planned strip mining and the Lattigo revenge, a panic was building. While some wanted to unload their land and get out of the county, others were more afraid of being cheated. Despite the trust Van Elkind had placed in me, no one in town would actually listen to any calming insight I might give.

Rumors and anger ratcheted up one more notch when Olli-Pekka Siilinen told Reverend Mall that he had been offered a good price for his farm, but that he refused to sell. Immediately, it became common knowledge throughout Thread that his son's rabbits had really been killed by a band of wild Indians. No one wanted to work with Officer Campbell to hunt down the pack of dogs because no one believed the dogs existed, even though the Siilinen farm had been surrounded by muddy dog prints. Officer Campbell told me one of set of prints looked like the puppy paws of a Norwegian Elkhound, but I hadn't the heart to tell Danny that.

Bromley was always quick to nod sagely from his stool at the counter as though he had a secret reservoir of knowledge about such matters. When I would attempt a logical explanation, Bromley would interrupt with some non sequitur like, "Who's to say that the Indians weren't telling the pack of wild dogs what to do."

To make matters worse, the Lattigo electronics plant was beginning operations and not one person from Thread had been hired. Since it had clearly been the Lattigos' intent to provide employment first to the residents of the reservation, this shouldn't have been a surprise to anyone. Yet this too had been transformed into another hostile act against Thread.

So when the State Supreme Court in Madison ruled that Lattigo tribe members were not covered by state fishing and hunting laws on or off the reservation, the fuse was lit. Bromley immediately issued a statement that he would instruct his officers, namely Officer Campbell, to arrest anyone found breaking state fishing and hunting laws in the jurisdiction of Thread, and that the township would fight this ruling all the way to the national Supreme Court.

Hearing of Bromley's bravado, Chip Frozen Bear tracked him down while Bromley was having coffee in my cafe. Frozen Bear threw a copy of the court judgment at Bromley's plate and laughed at Bromley. "We can fish where we want. Tomorrow night, we're going after the walleye in the Sapphire Run. Just try and stop us."

The Sapphire Run flows from Big Sapphire Lake to Little Sapphire Lake, skirting the southern edge of Thread. This mile-long, slow-moving creek, while shallow, has a steady current in its center where the water remains clear and aerated. The stream is just deep enough in its center that a wooden fishing boat can float along it and move from one lake to the other. But as you drift beneath Highway 17, you must duck low or you will bump your head against the concrete culverts that were used instead of a bridge. The old railroad trestles further up the run are higher and more forgiving.

Each spring thousands of fish swarm into this run to mate. The walleye pike and its smaller cousin the northern pike are normally solitary fish. And then there's the big brother—the muskie. They prefer to cruise the lake waters hunting for food. Voracious eaters with thin bodies and long jaws lined with rows of fierce looking teeth, they are ready to eat whatever meat falls within their reach: other fish, frogs, snakes, even the occasional young duck or muskrat. Muskie occasionally grow as long as six feet, the height of an adult man. Even when that long, they are seldom more than twenty pounds, but twenty pounds of fight. The muskie is the supreme trophy for any fisherman in northern Wisconsin. It is for this reason that Thread treasures the abundance of muskie, walleye and and northern in the Sapphire Lakes. These fish and no other are what lure the ardent fishermen up from the big cities to the south.

But during the spring, in the Sapphire Run, the pike are exposed. Their urge to mate overcomes its solitary nature and caution. The shallow run takes on the appearance of a koi pond in which someone dropped a bag of corn one week after the last feeding, erupting into a frenzy of motion with giant fish seeking to reproduce.

Everyone from the smallest child to the oldest adult knows how easy it would be to simply sit over the stream with a flashlight and spear a fish while its attention is caught by the light. One could probably pick the fish out of the water with one's hand.

Black bear, newly awakened from a winter hibernation may do this with walleye along secluded streams in other parts of the northwoods. But here in the heart of a town that thrives on fishermen, neither Thread nor the the state has ever allowed fishing during spawning. Until today.

The four of us stood still at the window, watching the police cars that had responded to Bromely's request. But the cards were turned on him when the governor ordered the state police to uphold the state court's ruling. The Lattigo would be allowed to fish if they wanted. Bromley, Red and others were stewing at the Northern Nights, meeting with a lawyer from Timberton. But an injunction was only a remote possibility. Another four police cars drove in the square to make a total of eight.

"My Dad says there will be trouble tonight," Danny confided. "He says the people in this town are too pigheaded to admit they've lost. He thinks if they just ignored the whole thing, the Lattigo would spear a few fish and go home. But I don't think that will happen."

"Are you going?" asked Cynthia.

"Josh thinks it could make for a movie of the week, and maybe he could sell the idea if he sees it first hand, so I'm going with him. He's thinking of going back to Los Angeles." Danny gave a disappointed half smile.

"You two listen to me," Thelma said. "Stay away from the run tonight. Nothing good can come of it. I don't know why Bromley has this bee in his bonnet, but it would be better if he just let sleeping dogs lie."

We didn't listen to Thelma's advice.

The night was cold, nearly moonless. We closed the restaurant early since no one had shown up for dinner. We walked toward Homestead Park and caught the path that ran parallel to the run. As we crossed over the square, we soon escaped the streetlights. The stars began to pop out of the sky. I pointed out Orion and Pisces to Danny and Cynthia.

Ahead we could see torchlights burning brightly along the water. There were two encampments, one on each side of the river. Between them but on the firmer side of the Run's shore stood a line of Wisconsin state police in full uniform. On the same side milled the Lattigo. They were carrying high-powered flashlights that they shined into the river. Each was dressed in ceremonial garb. Each carried a spear. Even from the distance we could see some brief ceremony took place and then first one person, then another jabbed a spear into the river, and frequently they would pull it back up with both hands. They would push the spear up into the sky hoisting aloft an enormous fish, flopping to and fro as it died, its spawning incomplete.

As each fish was raised, from the other shore, the townsmen would break into boos and jeers. It seemed as though half the town was present. There were many that I did not recognize. Where had they come from? Timberton? Emerson? They weren't locals. As we got closer, I spied Officer Campbell in the crowd. He saw me and averted his eyes. It was the first time I had ever seen him out of his uniform.

Cynthia shivered, "Maybe, it's not a good idea to be here."

The state police forced the townspeople to stay on the marshier side with its thicket of cattails. People moved about from bullock to bullock trying to keep their feet dry. Some had thought ahead and were outfitted in hip waders. They were ready to rush at any moment across the shallow creek, but the police were there with guns clearly visible in their holsters.

The Indians had built a huge bonfire. Its flames leaped in the sky like a madman's war dance. The crackling of the dry wood as it popped and spurted kept up an irregular rhythm that set us all on edge.

Danny, Cynthia and I stood on the Lattigo side. Across the narrow water, Chip, looking slim and strong in his beaded loincloth, saw Cynthia and smiled at her. She did not smile back. On that same side of the stream, we saw Josh stumbling through from the rear of the crowd. He was dressed in a flamboyant red windbreaker. He caught the eye of Danny and smiled. Danny smiled back.

Some townspeople were holding crudely written signs:

Spear Indians, not fish.
It's our land now. Get out.

Then someone started chanting:

Fuck the timber niggers

As the obscene words were loudly pounded into the heads of the Lattigo, they began to spear into the water with incredible abandon. What at first seemed ritualistic now became a frenzy. The fish came flopping out of the water and were tossed in a pile with such careless disregard that it was clear no one cared what happened to the fish.

Someone on the town side cried out, "They're going to kill them all."

Another shouted, "Stop 'em!"

Madness broke out. The townspeople surged across the Run and broke through the thin line of troopers. The Lattigo stepped back from their their fishing, then repositioned their spears to use as prods to push their attackers back into the cold spring water. Screams and curses filled the air.

One Lattigo looked around and saw us. Thinking we were an attack from the rear, he released an enormous cry and came running at us. His spear was pointed directly at Danny.

Frozen Bear lurched from the melee to stop the spearsman. At the same time Josh jumped up from the creek bank to lunge at the feet of the rushing man. Josh was the more successful. But in tackling the Lattigo man, he sent the spear flinging through the air. Its length caught both Danny and me across our stomachs, knocking the breath out of me and sending us both to the ground.

Groggily, after a few moments, I sat back up. Near me, Josh was tenderly kneeling over Danny, wiping a trickle of blood away from Danny's nose. Frozen Bear had his arm around a crying Cynthia and was shouting at the others in his group to stop.

A policeman shot his gun into the air.

"Holy shit, look at that!" I heard Sam, the bartender from the Northern Nights bar, say reverentially. "What the fuck is it?"

He was pointing several yards away. A long shadow was moving beneath the water's surface, traveling from the direction of Big Sapphire Lake, heading northeast toward Little Sapphire Lake. It stopped and its body shook as though it were spreading milt. Then it continued moving.

By now, all of us were quiet and watching this shape move toward the melee. It was the largest muskie any of us had ever seen. As it neared the crowd, it moved beneath one of the Lattigo spears that was floating in the water. The fish seemed at least an impossible nine feet in length.

"They can't grow that long," Red said in awe.

One of the Lattigo said quietly, "It's a fish of the Great Spirit."

The muskie stopped directly below us. From the light of the bonfire and the torches, we could clearly see the enormity of it. It floated just below the surface nearly grazing the bottom of the sandy floor of the creek.

It stayed there for a moment or two. Its bulging fish eyes seemed to look into each of us. Then it flickered its dorsal fins and with a wave of its tail, it was back in motion. Moments later, it had swum into the safety of Little Sapphire Lake, hidden in the darkness of deeper water.

It was the giant muskie. I felt elated. I did not imagine that enormous shadow in the water glimpsed so many months before. The children had not been making up a story. It knew us, and it had saved us from ourselves.

One of the Lattigo spoke. "Gather up the fish we've already caught. We're going home."

I looked at the townsmen standing in the marsh and in the water. They seemed somehow chastened. Red and Bromley both stood there, soaking wet, having fallen in the stream during the melee. They clambered up onto shore.

In the distance, along the shore, I saw Chip Frozen Bear walking with Cynthia, his arm protectively across her shoulders. They were walking in the direction of her home. They did not seem concerned if Red should happen to see them.

And back on the grass where Danny still lay against the dry reeds of last summer, I saw Josh lean over and give Danny a quick kiss on the lips. They too seemed unconcerned if anyone should glance their way.

The smell of spring was in the air.

Behind the bonfire, I saw someone I had not noticed before. It was Kip Van Elkind. He did not see me. His eyes were totally focused on the disappearing Cynthia and Frozen Bear. The glare of the fire danced across Kip's sullen face. He was too lost in his thoughts to notice if anyone watched him hunger after Cynthia.

I felt some winter still linger in this spring.

Thelma was indignant. "What fool notion moved you to go and buy all of this damn fish?"

"It was an opportunity too good to miss," I said in my defense. The walleye pike has delicious white flesh. Because they are relatively difficult to catch and thus rare, you can't buy them commercially. Yet I knew out-of-towners would pay top dollar for a good piece of fried pike. When Chip Frozen Bear approached me on the night of the Lattigo riot about purchasing the fish they had speared, what could I do but say "yes?"

"Sometimes I swear you just want to plunge yourself into trouble," continued Thelma. "Don't you think Bromley and Red are going to scream to high heaven when they find out you have a freezer full of protected fish?"

"They were caught legally. Lattigo have the right to spear fish."

"In your eyes maybe. But not in the eyes of this town. There ain't a person in town who would order that fish. They ain't going to be traitors to Thread." Thelma was thumping the bread dough across the floured table.

I was alone in the kitchen with Thelma. Danny and Cynthia were in the dining room serving a few members of an early lunch crowd. Over the past two days, any time spent alone with Thelma had quickly evolved into an argument over fish.

"If I hadn't bought the fish, they would have spoiled. The Lattigo had no way to transport them anywhere for processing. And the Lattigo didn't want the fish. They had just planned to spear a few to make their point."

"Well they shouldn't have been spearing any." Thelma was not about to concede.

I shrugged my shoulders which only infuriated Thelma more. "And another thing. I didn't appreciate getting called up ten o'clock at night to bustle down here and help you gut a tub of slimy fish."

"I couldn't fillet them all by myself," I said in defense.

"Then why did you buy them? You knew I was waiting for Gilbert that night. And because of you I missed him, having to be here, scaling fish that no one's going to eat."

I was having none of her pessimism. "Just wait. Memorial Day, I'm going to put fried walleye on the menu. Tourists will be lined up around the block. No one's going to care or remember where I bought the fish."

"Another thing," Thelma was flinging the dough into separate bread pans for its final rising before baking. "I think the whole town was taking drugs that night. What were you all fighting for anyway? And seeing a giant muskie. Next thing you know, you'll be inviting Claire's little men to dinner."

As far as I was concerned, Thelma was talking to herself. I had others things to concern me. I had two dozen fish in my freezer. Thelma would really scalp me if she found out how much I had paid for them. On the other hand, maybe she was right–I must have been on drugs that night. On yet another hand, there was no need to wait until the end of May to use the fish. "I'm going to place some of that fish on the menu tonight. Disguise it a little. You know what I'll do. I'll make quenelles of pike served with kasha dumplings."

"Quenelles? Ain't you learned your lesson the last time you tried that?" Thelma had put the bread pans in the top shelf of the oven to get out of way and to rise in a protected place. "No one's going to order something they can't pronounce."

"They make quenelles all the time in France from pike. They're nothing more than fish mousse shaped like little dumplings. It's perfect. I won't have to worry about anyone choking on the little bones in the fish. People will love them . . . if we can just get them to give the things a try."

"I told you before, I ain't monkeying with it. If you want to offer this French nonsense, you can make it. Just don't let anyone know where it came from."

I strolled back into the walk-in freezer and surveyed my kingdom of fish. They were all neatly cut into fillets and stacked like piles of frozen lumber. I picked up a few of the pieces and calculated the combined weight at about six pounds. That should be enough to make ten servings. There was no sense in making more than that, even though business had picked up a bit after the fracas down at Sapphire Run.

The town was filled with unease. Rumors of strip mining continued to flourish. I knew at least four people who anxiously sold large plots of land at bargain prices. Fortunately, there hadn't been any follow-on confrontations to add to the uncertainty. The Lattigo felt they had established their rights, backed by the state police, a governor's order and a court decree. Bromley still puffed his way around town recounting the heroic stance he took to repulse the madmen from Lattigo.

Occasionally, I saw Hank Van Elkind in town. Once we met on the street while he was walking with Priscilla Jouer and they jointly teased me with details of a new twist they proposed adding to the Winter theme area.

"We're thinking of having an adults-only section that plays off the wicked past of Timberton. Sort of a wild, wild north with an end-of-the-century motif," Priscilla laughed. "I thought of the idea after Hank told me about the eighty houses of prostitution that once lined Silver Street. Such a naughty town." She and Hank moved on down the street toward Amanda Manny's studio. Priscilla maintained her elegance and grace even as her weight bore her stiletto heels into piercing the remaining hard icy patches on the square.

"Wally, are you in there?" Danny poked his head into the freezer, and then walked all the way in. "Where did you get all this fish. This isn't that fish, is it?" He wouldn't even acknowledge the source by naming it aloud.

In the last few weeks, Danny had seemed to flourish. Even Cynthia could see it. Instead of mooning over the boy, she had now taken to finding ways to ensure Josh and Danny spent time together. But they no longer needed the machinations of Cynthia for that. On nights Josh wasn't working, the young man invariably showed up as the Loon Town Cafe closed to offer Danny a ride home.

I didn't know if Toivo had noticed what was going on with his son. Toivo now came to the cafe occasionally to order a light meal. I suspected that he appeared only after spending an hour or two at the cemetery. He would sit quietly in the cafe, normally ordering the least expensive item–the fish fry which I had added to the menu as a standard item. He ate slowly, never interacting with other customers, always preferring a small table to the counter. Sometimes, Danny would talk to him between bussing tables. But more often, Josh would have already arrived to wait out until closing, and Danny would be entranced by the jokes of Josh's. Toivo never sought to join them.

I suspected Cynthia was also receiving nightly rides. But Chip Frozen Bear was more discreet. He never sat in the restaurant waiting for Cynthia. Although I never saw an idling car, somehow, I still knew he was a waiting presence

"Is this the fish that the Lattigo caught?" Danny finally asked.

I just looked at him and shrugged my shoulders. Let it remain a mystery. I stepped back into the restaurant and Danny followed.

Outside, for a moment I caught glimpse of a robin. The first of the season. It was hopping in a bed of purple crocus that were blooming in the town square. There were still a few piles of hardened snow in the square, the last melting remnants of the piles left behind from from the winter plowings. But beneath the hot sun of days like this one, that snow too would be gone within a few days

In the woods, I knew the first wild flowers of the season were already breaking through the ground. In a matter of days or weeks, the white bloodroot would be everywhere. Yellow cowslips would crowd the small streams with their bright blooms. The wild plum and apple trees would break into blossoms. Bees that had stayed within their hives all winter, surviving on the honey they had made last summer, would venture out, busily flying from flowering branch to branch.

I thought about Danny and spring. There was no doubt that he was infatuated with Josh. All he could do was talk about the things that Josh and he did together—the movies they saw in Timberton, the walks they took in Thread, the heart-to-heart talks that kept them awake to two or three in the morning. His eyes grew animated every time Josh walked into the cafe.

Everyone in town knew that Josh was gay. Yet none of us teased Danny about his crush on Josh, as we would have if he had loved a girl in his senior class. No one ever asked him, "Are you gay?" I suspected that not even Josh dared ask Danny the question that would force a changed set of rules.

It was as though each of us wanted to leave the options open for Danny, allowing him to make his own decisions, letting him breathe the spark of life into his choice when he felt ready to say whatever words were his right words. But if Danny was given the space to discover his own route, there was a different aura around Cynthia. No one seemed to want to acknowledge that she might be seeing Chip. It wasn't because he was eight years older. In this town, nineteen-year-olds like Cynthia were often quickly married. Nor was it a skepticism that a worldly person like Chip would truly be interested in a high school senior. And it wasn't because they were afraid to somehow tip off Red. It was as though they just couldn't see it as a possibility.

Henry Van Elkind slumped back in his chair, staring morosely at his half-eaten apple brown betty. The scoop of vanilla ice cream, completely melted, had congealed into a turgid sea surrounding brown-bedecked apple glaciers. He listlessly moved his spoon through the mess.

Ever since Kip's public attempt at suicide by burning, Van Elkind had become more of a loner when he appeared in the restaurant. Today, he ordered a steak and a bottle of a good merlot. Although he didn't eat much of the steak, he drank most of the wine. I had already called Stephen at the camp because Van Elkind wasn't in any shape for a ten-mile drive on a narrow road through the dark woods.

"Wally, get over here," Van Elkind commanded. "You know what I want? Not this old pie. I'm sick of it. I'd like a good dessert wine. Keep me from facing reality."

"It might be better if you have some coffee," I suggested.

He waved off my suggestion. "Don't patronize me. You still got some bottles of that late harvest wine from Chateau St. Jean? Open one of those for me. I need something sweet, but with a kick."

"I don't think you need any kick, Henry," I felt compelled to say.

"Aw, fuck, just get me one of those god damn bottles. Bring over two of those tiny little glasses. What do you call them? Cordial glasses, yeah. You can help me drink the bottle."

Stephen was already on his way into town to drive the man home, I reasoned, and the Chateau St. Jean Select Late Harvest Johannesberg Riesling tasted great and it did have a nice markup. I brought over the small bottle and small glasses. I removed the cork and passed it over to let Van Elkind sniff the incredibly rich, thick, sweet raisiny smell of this American version of an *eiswein*. "Smells damn good," he said, "sit down and have a glass with me.

"Hell of a world, isn't it." He raised his glass to clink it against mine. He then gulped the highly alcoholic wine in a single swallow. I sipped mine to enjoy it more fully. He had already refilled his small glass.

"I had to put my time in at the Emerson Hospital again today. If this continues, they'll consider me a patron so they can put the screws to me for donations."

"What do you mean?"

"Mother Rabinowicz had a stroke last night. Stephen found her on the floor early this morning. She had tried to reach the bell to call him, but she only made it to the floor. The ambulance took her to Emerson because they say it's a better hospital than the one in Timberton. It has that big endowment left from a friend of some old president. The place still looks third-rate to me. But she's there now in intensive care. Doesn't look good.

The doctors say she could live a day, or she could live a month. But she'll never be the same.

"I always thought seeing the end of that old woman would make me happy. And I don't know why it doesn't. Maybe it's because Kip took the news so hard. I guess he loves that old woman more than any of us knew.

"And that old woman loves him. I wish I could say that I do. So now he's back in the same hospital where he was mended after the incident, only this time he's watching over her, instead of her over him.

"It's kind of ironic when you think about it. If Mother Rabinowicz's condition had the least bit of hope, we'd have her transported to the best hospital in Chicago. If your busboy and Frozen Bear hadn't been so quick at rolling my son, he'd still be in that place, or shipped back to a Chicago hospital burn center.

"So Regina and Kip are together in the Emerson hospital, where they can both stay as far as I'm concerned. And I feel like shit because I wish it were Rita's mother surviving, instead of my own son. What kind of father could feel that way?" He downed another glass of the riesling. "You sure you don't want more?" he asked.

"Sure, why not," I said. He poured one for me and then he poured himself another glass. The bottle was nearly empty.

"Rita chartered a plane to get up here. Couldn't wait for the morning flights. It's probably already landed in Timberton. She would have flown into Emerson, but their little airport isn't equipped for landing private jets at night. I should have gone to meet Rita at the airport, but I figured, 'Let her rent a car.' We're going to face the music soon enough.

"If Rita's mother dies, it'll change everything. It puts all that money into spin. Will Rita get it? Will Kip get it? Or did that nasty old woman leave it to some charity back in the old country? We just don't know. She's a secretive bitch, but in the long run, I don't think it much matters. Whatever way it turns out, I'm pretty sure that Rita's going to realize she doesn't need me. She cheats on me, you know. I cheat on her too. That's just what we do. We just don't talk about it." Van Elkind had finished the bottle and was eying the last remnants of a swallow in my glass. Then he looked at me and asked, "What don't you talk about?"

What *did* I talk about? Food and the restaurant and the town stories. But not what I really wanted, to recapture a moment of happiness, to find again what I once had. But was that to be found by returning even further in my past, to a time that had seemed more innocent?

"It's not a secret, you know." Van Elkind was twirling his empty glass.

"What's not a secret?"

"That your friend Patrice was murdered during that mugging, defending you. I did my research on you before I ever involved you in American Seasons. Maybe the rest of this town doesn't know or care why you fled back home, but we all know. And we don't care."

Patrice. Strong, smart Patrice. The happy Sunday mornings as we read the New York Times in our sunlit studio, the hunts through Strand Books searching out some treasured tome, the plans for a future that included both of us. Yes, I understood Toivo Lahti and his urge to visit that tombstone, trying to grasp on to one's dreams and visions and hopes. I could understand, but I could not be that person. I had to flee to a place where no one knew Patrice and where no one ever knew what I could be with Patrice. And now this greedy man with his warped son and dying mother-in-law wanted to destroy that illusion. I couldn't even look him in the eye.

"You got another bottle of this stuff? It's good shit," he said. I shook my head no, unwilling to risk speaking. Van Elkind decided to shift subjects. "All of this is bad timing, you know. We're ready to do the public announcement of American Seasons. Once we do that, then it's out to the market to raise more capital. We're doing okay. We've finished acquiring all of the important parcels of land. There are still a few pieces here and there we would like. But if we don't get them, it's no big deal. We can live without them.

"Of course, that bastard Chip Frozen Bear shot an arrow in our backs when we weren't looking. His tribe bought up some of the most important pieces. Parcels that we really wanted. He says it doesn't make any difference because the consortium has the land it needs.

"But he's fucking wrong. It does make a difference. Now my company doesn't have the land under our full control and we'll have to lease some key pieces from the Lattigo. Sure we got the agreements in place, but they still own the land.

"Chip says it's like the royal family of Hawaii and most of Honolulu. Do you know what the fuck he means by that?"

279

I shook my head to show that I didn't. I still couldn't speak. Cynthia came over quietly to clear away the dessert dishes. Had she heard? "Would you like some coffee?" she asked tentatively.

"No," said Van Elkind. "We got to get you more involved, Wally. It's time for some good press. We plan a big announcement set for Madison. We lined up the governor and the senator. Tes has all the investment money nailed down. Oxford will be there. But we have to figure out how to break the news to Thread."

Stephen walked into the restaurant. I waved him over to our table. I was barely able to say, "I called Stephen to drive you home."

"Ready to go, sir?' Stephen asked as he helped the unsteady man to his feet. But Stephen looked at me more closely, as though he felt I might be in more need of his help that his employer.

"We're on our way now," Van Elkind said drunkenly. "We got a future to build. I'm counting on you. You're my man. Don't let me down."

CHAPTER EIGHTEEN

Reining in the bucking rototiller borrowed from Emil Urho, I thoroughly worked the damp and fragrant dirt behind the cafe until it became almost fluffy. I worked up quite a sweat in the hot spring sun. With my tattered plaid shirt laying on the steps to the kitchen door and with a lunchtime beer in my hand, I surveyed my handiwork. The garden plot was ready. And hard labor felt good. Moving to Thread was good. It was time to be over Patrice.

Last summer, I started too late with planting and because my garden ailed, I was forced into buying produce from locals. This summer I wanted control. I needed to have my own herbs–parsley, basil, tarragon, dill–growing in my own garden. I wanted rows of baby lettuce, little radishes, green onions. I wanted the best tomatos, the best green beans. I wanted it all.

"Here you are," said Thelma. She came out the kitchen door and down the back steps. "Had you forgotten we were going to Agnelli's Funeral Home to pay our respects to Mrs. Rabinowicz."

"Shit," I said. I had forgotten.

Stephen called two days ago to let us know that Regina Rabinowicz had passed away and that the Van Elkind family would hold her funeral service in Timberton instead of Chicago. After her cremation, they planned to cast her ashes across the camp's broad lawns. According to Stephen, Rita claimed this was to be a memorial to her mother's love of the camp's many roses. No one suggested it was simply the most expeditious way for Henry and Rita to get the old woman out of their lives.

"You haven't gone and started planting anything, have you," warned Thelma. She stood over the garden poking at the dirt as though it were one of her bread doughs. "Needs to be worked a few more times," she said, "so there's more air in there."

Thelma was outfitted in a simple black dress, low heels, and a small hat with a veil. My observing made her self-conscious. "It's left over from when Fred died. Bought it just for his funeral. I thought it made me look sexy, and I hoped that if there was anything left of the real him in that box, that he could see me looking good before he went on."

I nodded pretending understanding about the remains of love, but I was forcing myself to think about Thelma's garden warning. The soil looked ready for planting to me. It was loose and free of weeds. I reached down and grabbed a handful of the dirt. It clumped together, but not in a hard ball. As I opened up my fist, the ball fell apart in small chunks to land at my feet. Right texture. Right moisture. What was Thelma talking about? This soil was perfect for planting.

"Besides," she said, "It's way too early to start planting. Everything will come up and then die in a freeze. You know there's bound to be a few hard freezes still. Wait at least ten days before planting anything."

"But then the growing season will be too short for some of the vegetables I want to raise."

"This ain't California," she replied. End of discussion.

We stood there quietly for a moment in the warmth of the daylight. Occasional sounds of cars from the square were muffled by the buildings between us and the street. In the distance, I could hear the muted roar of a fishing boat's small motor racing across Big Sapphire Lake. Fishing season had opened.

"You ain't going to the parlor like that, are you?" Thelma said. "I know it's not like those snooty kids of hers care one bit about Regina dying, but you liked her. You should put on a dark suit. The old woman deserves at least that."

There had a been a small obituary about Regina Rabinowicz's death in my post-office-delivered copy of the New York Times. Most of the story dealt with the fortune that had been amassed by her husband. It mentioned that she and her husband had emigrated to the United States in 1919 at the end of World War One and the beginning of the short-lived independence of her native country, Latvia. For some reason, I wondered about that. Those brief years after World War One must have seemed a time of great promise. Yet this couple had packed all their worldly belongings and moved halfway around the world. Why had they exiled themselves? And for that matter why had Rita Van Elkind exiled her mother to the solitude of our quiet Wisconsin woods?

"Gilbert's stopping by before he leaves town," Thelma said. "He's about ready to set a date for the wedding. We've sort of talked about it being in June. I know he wants to do it soon, and so do I. I'm tired of living alone. The Sundays and Mondays he spends with me are the happiest times of my weeks. When he's around, I feel important and young."

"I'm happy for you."

"Are you?" she asked worriedly. "Are you really? Sometimes I think you don't approve of Gilbert."

"Whatever makes you happy," I said. And I truly did approve. I had grown to love Thelma with as much depth of feeling as I held for my own mother. Thelma was more than a cook in my restaurant. She was my mentor and guardian angel. How could I not wish her every happiness?

There was whistling in the alley. Gilbert, sporting his always well-knotted bow tie, was strolling toward us. "Beautiful morning, isn't it?" he said. "And behold the center of beauty. How is my always lovely Thelma?"

She smiled indulgently. Thelma and Fred had had no children. But today there was something in her look that made me think of a grandmother watching over a brood of grandkids. Gilbert evoked a softness from Thelma that no other person could.

Gilbert pulled from his side pocket the shiny gold watch that he always wore. He made a great show of opening the lid and checking the time. Then he snapped the lid shut and flipped the watch in a practiced move that was meant to have it land once more in his hand so he could dramatically return it to his pocket. But the fob chain snapped and the watch went sailing through the air. It landed in a soft plop on the tilled soil. I jumped over to pick it up.

"Back to the garden, huh?" I smiled, "The watch is trying to return to its original roots from those days when Luigi owned it."

Gilbert smiled at me halfheartedly. I turned the watch around in my hands to admire this historical artifact. The watch seemed remarkably light-weight. I had anticipated the old timepiece to have more heft. I weighed it in my hand for a moment.

"Could I have my watch back?" asked Gilbert. "I really need to be on my way. Have to get to Duluth by tonight. You know a traveling salesman's life is travel, travel, travel. Always on the road."

"You should ask for a smaller territory," said Thelma.

"But if I wanted a smaller territory, then I couldn't have Northern Wisconsin, and I would miss seeing you," he said with a smile. He put the watch back into his pocket. "I just wanted to stop by and say goodbye once more. See you next week." Whistling a song from Snow White, he stepped back in the alley, walking toward the highway, where he had probably parked his car.

"Wally, get dressed, so we can go," Thelma said. "Even the dead won't wait forever."

We drove north on highway 17 in Thelma's convertible toward Timberton. With the top down, it felt more like we were going on a vacation than toward a funeral home. As we crossed the continental divide between the Mississippi River and the Great Lakes basins, we caught the expansive view of the woods marching downhill toward Lake Superior. In this soft spring light, the treetops shimmered in the wind as the lightest green of lace. On every deciduous tree, the tiny buds had broken into little leaves. Just the smallest of green shapes. But within days, they would grow larger and assume the distinctive shapes of maples and elms, of poplars and beech. But at this moment the northern highlands were a single web of the first sprouts. And even the stands of evergreen seemed somehow fresher than at any other time during the year.

An exhilaration was in the air. Not a bit of snow remained in even the darkest corners of the woods. The thick carpet of leaves in the forest was drying. Tiny wild flowers were springing forth. Tadpoles were hatching in all the small puddles and streams. Birds had returned from their wintry retreats. The air itself smelled cleaner, fresher, bigger than it had all winter long. Even in the rush of driving, the sun made us hot. As we drove into the streets of Timberton, I found the tall dilapidated houses lining the streets charming and inviting.

"Agnelli's is two blocks off Silver Street, in one of the mansions built by an old lumber baron," I said.

"Ain't I lived here all my life?" said Thelma. "I know where Agnelli's is."

The Agnelli family had bought the house after the crash of the lumber market in the early part of the century. Originally built in 1885, the house was a fantasia of carved stone and wooden bric a brac. Three stories high, with a circular tower at one corner, it combined Romanesque and Queen Anne Victorian features in a peculiar hodge-podge of stylistic details. The Agnelli family had converted the ground floor into a funeral parlor, with multiple viewing rooms. The necessary workspace was in the basement. The upper two floors had been transformed into their home, but after sixty years, the family had abandoned it for a new tri-level on the outskirts of town. The only exterior change had been extending the wraparound veranda into a tacked-on porte cochere to shelter mourners in bad weather.

The family had taken good care of the mansion over the decades. Other than the Penokee House, it was probably the only building in town that fully exhibited the exuberance and extravagance of the town's rich history. Along the side of the large porches were elaborately cut topiary. A few still had their winter wooden crating around them that protected them in the winter from the crushing weight of the never ending snow.

Thelma and I walked into the foyer. The young Mr. Agnelli, a few years older than Thelma, quickly appeared. "Are you here to see Mrs. Rabinowicz?" he asked with the slightest air of astonishment.

"Yes," I replied

"Please follow me," he said motioning us to the front parlor, a large room that may have been planned as a reception room and dining room in the blueprints of the original house. It had ten-foot ceilings and elaborate woodwork surrounding the windows and doors. The floor were beautifully maintained hardwood maple strips. Each of the windows had a frieze of stained glass along the top. In the bright sunlight, the colored panes seemed almost alive.

"If you wouldn't mind," Mr. Agnelli motioned to the guest book that was set on an intricately carved stand. I noticed that the only signatures in the book were those of Kip Van Elkind, Stephen from the camp, and a most surprising one: Thomas Packer. Could that be the signature of my Mr. Packer? I realized I had no idea if the old man's first name was Thomas.

Thelma and I walked into the room. The casket was on the far side of the room against a pair of double pocket doors that perhaps had originally led to another parlor or the butler's pantry. Today these doors were nearly hidden by the banks of floral arrangements that filled the room.

"The flowers have been wired from all over the country," Mr. Agnelli said in sibilant whisper. "Regina and her husband had so many business interests and acquaintances. She was much beloved. I have never seen so many beautiful blooms. Sylvia at the flower shop had to get a special rush order of roses and of gladiola flown in today just so she could fill all the orders. Aren't they lovely?" He stepped backwards and out the door.

Despite there being several rows of chairs lined up for mourners, only one person was on hand to pay his last respects. Thelma and I walked past the seated Mr. Packer to look at Mrs. Rabinowicz. The Agnellis had done a nice job. Even in death, she looked lively and frisky. I said a silent prayer and then went to sit down next to Mr. Packer.

"I didn't expect to see you here," I said.

"Nor I, you," he replied. We were both silent. I didn't know how to respond. He didn't seem to want to talk. Thelma sat on the other side of the old man.

"I heard once," Thelma began, "that Regina worked for the Oxford family when they lived in Chicago. That's the family that built the Van Elkind camp. In fact, I think she worked at the camp when the Oxfords would summer here. Odd that she would end up rich and owning it."

Mr. Packer smiled sadly. "I first met Regina in those golden days. She was such a lively and playful young woman, but only a maid at the camp. Mrs. Oxford couldn't abide her. For Mrs. Oxford, everything had to be the most modern and the most cosmopolitan. She only vacationed at the camp because it had been in the family so long. And then later when she needed the money, the camp was impossible to sell. No one wanted or could afford such extravagant summer homes during the Depression."

"You knew the Oxfords?" Thelma bored in.

"I've known many people in my life." He stood up and walked next to the coffin. He looked down at the woman. "I always wondered why Casimir Rabinowicz bought the monstrous old camp. It had to have been Regina's doing. She hated working for Lotta Oxford, yet I think she made

Casimir buy this place because she knew Lotta needed the money. Regina was a very kind woman."

"But how do you know her?" I pressed on. Some day I needed to really talk to this old man. He had broad knowledge and obvious intelligence. Over the course of the past year, I learned that he had traveled throughout Europe, had fought in World War I, had once taught college and apparently mingled with the mighty. Yet I usually dismissed him as a crazy old packrat.

"After the second war, there was a period in my life that was very bad and very rough. I had wanted to believe more in the possibilities of man. Somehow Regina found out about my troubles. I don't know why she would have remembered me from the old days or even why she would have cared. But she did. She rescued me. She helped me move to Thread and begin my life again. She saved me, but she never wanted anything in return. She deserved far more out of life than she ever received. Regina was a genuine woman. She was no Van Elkind."

Mr. Packer stood up. "I better get going, or I'll miss the bus back to Thread."

"But you could ride with us," I said. He just shook his head and exited. Moments later, Henry and Rita Van Elkind walked into the parlor. I wondered if they had been outside and overheard Mr. Packer's condemnation of their family.

"Was that the old coot who hangs out at your cafe?" Van Elkind asked.

""His name is Mr. Packer," I said. "And he knew your mother. Apparently from when she was a young woman and a maid for the Oxfords."

"Really," Rita said with disapproval. "How like Mother to have such unpleasant friends. I certainly hope he doesn't plan to come to the memorial service."

"We could still change our minds," Van Elkind said, "and fly your mother's body to Chicago. We could hold the service there and then all of Mother's old friends would be able to attend."

"Dear, we've been over this before. There's really no reason to bother with all that. We agreed Mother would be happiest to have her ashes among her roses. Having a service in Chicago would just mean we would have to fly back here after the service, so let's keep it simple. The service will be here. Most of her friends have long since died anyway. We're the only ones left who care."

Thelma sat quietly on her chair. But her back was rigid. She was primed to light into Rita Van Elkind, and I suggested that we leave. Although Thelma was more than willing, Van Elkind had his own ideas. He dragged me across the hall to the tower corner room. There were windows surrounding us on three sides. Looking across the hall, I could see Rita Van Elkind sitting in the front row near her mother's coffin, simply staring into space. Thelma had stood up and was beginning to pace. The black purse she was carrying seemed to swing more and more with each step.

"I think I better get Thelma out of here," I said.

"Just a minute, Wally, I want to talk about American Seasons. We are going ahead with the public announcement next week. This damn inconvenience of my mother-in-law dying has made it difficult to plan a local briefing, but the more I've thought about it, the more I'm convinced there is no need for anything local."

"But you always said you wanted the town on your side," I pointed out. I wanted to get away before he mentioned Patrice again. But he had other things on his mind.

"And they will be. Look at the facts. Everyone is going to breathe a sigh of relief when they realize that our resort plans will stop dead in the tracks all plans for strip mining."

I protested, "There never were any plans for strip mining."

"Technicality," he waved it off. "And when we start talking about the jobs that we are going to create, everyone will be happy—especially after the way Frozen Bear screwed the townsmen out of jobs at his electronics plant. There is not a person in town who won't benefit from this development. It will mean more tourists and that will mean more money for everyone. Why waste time priming a pump that is already flowing with water?"

"I'm not sure it's that simple," I said.

Henry Van Elkind was smug as we walked back toward Thelma. "Trust me, it is exactly that simple."

We left the car parked where it was on the street outside the funeral home. Van Elkind's BMW was parked nearby and next to a fire hydrant. I was pleased to see that there was already a pink parking ticket stuck beneath his windshield wiper.

"Let's walk over to the Penokee House for a late lunch," I suggested to Thelma. "We can check out the competition."

No matter how many times I saw the Penokee House, I was always entranced by its glamour and scale. It had been constructed at a time when many expected Timberton to reach a population of thirty or fifty thousand, and by a man who believed the city would be a major center of commerce. Who imagined then that a city of nearly twenty thousand could so quickly slink back to a few thousand people, that the streetcar tracks could be so easily pulled up, that the cheaply built housing on the narrow lots would be simply moved away or torn down and that the mines and forests that fueled the economic growth could play out so quickly?

But the one hundred rooms of the Penokee House were not so easily dispensed with. Built to last for centuries, insulated with asbestos for fire proofing, the four-story Penokee House was a masterpiece of frontier optimism. Through the years, it had played host to such national luminaries as President Grover Cleveland, orator William Jennings Bryan, and novelist Edna Ferber. Who knew what other famous people may have walked up the broad steps from Silver Street and promenaded along its two-hundred-foot veranda, watching the comings and goings of a once bustling town?

Today, there was little activity on the street. The hotel catered mostly to couples on a weekend getaway, who imagined in the grand old hotel a romance that may never have existed. Travel writers praised its ambience, although seldom its food. Nevertheless, and despite it being nearly three in the afternoon, Thelma and I were told we would have a fifteen-minute wait for a table.

When we were finally seated, I took a look at the menu. Boring. Only the usual items that you would expect at an overpriced tourist spot. Nothing to show imagination or a connection to the history of this town. Just steaks, deep-fried chicken and the like.

Thelma saw my look of dismay. "You're paying for the ambience so you might as well order a martini and drink it in."

I followed Thelma's advice and ordered a martini, extra dry, up and with a double olive. I would indeed enjoy myself, I thought, especially since Thelma was driving. I ordered a New York strip steak, rare, to go with my cocktail. "And bring me a glass of cabernet when you serve the main course," I told the waitress.

"Our only wine by the glass is Gallo. Will that be okay?" she asked.

I grimaced. Thelma was giving me her most severe look of disapproval, although I wasn't sure whether it was for my reaction to the wine or the fact that I had ordered it. "Don't give me that look," I shot back. "This will be my lunch and dinner. Besides I have worries."

Thelma would have none of that, and it turned out her disapproval wasn't over the alcohol. "Months ago, I told you to watch out for people like Van Elkind. Have you figured out yet what he wants of you?"

"No," I replied, "besides who said anything about Van Elkind. Okay, okay, it is about Van Elkind." It was the most honest thing I had uttered in months. I had no idea why Van Elkind had ushered me into his inner circle. There was nothing I could offer. I had no land, money or political connections. Even the public relations acumen he claimed to see in me had never been to put to use. I was just a useless appendix. And I was ready to burst with anger over the whole resort plan. In a way, I was afraid that Van Elkind was right. Everyone in Thread would agree that the development was a wonderful thing. It wouldn't be clear to them what they were tossing aside until it was too late to retrieve. The forests would be destroyed one more time, and the land would be mined in a new way leaving scars of highways, airports and condominium complexes, the pulsating sores of strip malls, cheap motels and get-rich-quick schemes.

Thelma set down the beer she had ordered. "When you were in school, did you ever notice how often really pretty girls had a very plain gal as their best friend?"

I smiled, "Rhonda Jackson and Sylvia Makinen were like that. Rhonda was gorgeous. Let's just say Sylvia wasn't. Yet they were always together. I always thought it was odd."

"Why do you suppose that is?" Thelma pressed, "Sure, the ugly girl probably hopes some of the beauty rubs off? But what's in it for the gorgeous one? Don't you see how the pretty ones look even better in comparison? People think, 'Isn't she nice to hang around with such a dog.' And the dog is always there wagging its tail in appreciation. The beauty can always look at the beast and think, 'I'm so much better looking than her.'"

"So are you saying Hank likes to hang around me because I'm so beautiful?" I was feeling the effects of the martini. I needed another. I signaled the waitress for a new round.

"That's not what I mean Wally. You're more like the ugly girl. Don't you see how Hank wants you around so he has an admiring audience? He knows you're a big city boy who's smart and clever. But he also knows you have no talent for the kind of business shenanigans he plays. He's the one behind all this land-buying, isn't he? What's he planning?

"Don't blush on me. Who am I going to tell? Anyway, your face just gave it away. You're like an adoring puppy. He's got you wowed. You'd admire him even if he beat you black and blue. He wants an audience, and you're it. You were his chosen one. Ain't you lucky!"

"Maybe I should write a book," I muttered.

Thelma didn't answer. I stared down at my salad, a poor mixture of iceberg lettuce with a few strips of spinach for contrast. It was drenched in blue cheese dressing. I tasted a pinch of truth in what Thelma had just said. But would a rich and successful businessman risk so much just so he could have an intimate admirer? I thought of Amanda Manny and how she was also included in Van Elkind's inner circle. There was no way that she was providing anything of use to the American Seasons project despite her fancy title. Everyone assumed that Van Elkind was screwing her. Was I just a variant of his whores?

I looked over to Thelma who seemed lost in thought, gazing across the room. Maybe she was just making me stew in the pot she created. I looked around the room for something to anchor my thoughts. The dining room had been carefully restored to a Victorian sensibility. The walls were covered with a large and intricate turn-of-the-century pattern. The chandeliers had the appearance of brass gas lamps converted to electricity. The room looked much like it did the 1890s photos they had hanging in the lobby. Only the long tables once set for mass seatings had been exchanged for contemporary small tables designed for individual parties.

Thelma was still staring across the room. She ignored her fried shrimp. I wondered if I had offended her somehow. I was reminded of the time we had picked raspberries in the woods, and I decided to play it safe, so I ate my steak without saying a word.

But minutes later, she was still staring across the room. I turned my head to see what so entranced her. I realized then she wasn't upset with me . . . perhaps with herself, but not with me. Across the room in a small alcove, nearly shielded from us, sat two people engrossed with one another even as they ate. One was a woman similar in age and appearance to Thelma. The other was Gilbert Ford. He leaned over and kissed this other woman on the cheek. Even across the crowded room, we could hear her flirtatious giggle. Gilbert. Here, and with another woman.

"Maybe we should go," I suggested.

"Yes, let's go," Thelma responded. As we stepped out onto the veranda and the brightness of the late afternoon, she handed me her car keys. "You're going to have to drive," she said.

"But I've been drinking," I said.

"And I can't see," she replied. "Something happened to my eye." I looked over at the wonderfully weathered face of this warm woman. Her left eye was as bloodshot as a man on a two-week bender. A blood vessel had burst in her eye.

"I think I was staring too hard," she said. She said nothing more. No mention of Gilbert or his dinner date. It was a long and quiet ride back to Thread.

Days later and the restaurant was abuzz with the biggest news to ever hit Thread. Television crews, with massive satellite dishes on their vans, were packed in the square. All the state's television stations were present, as well as national correspondents from the major networks. Even Charles Kuralt had flown in. He was going to do an update on his decade-old Eye on The Road Loon Town piece.

In Madison, the governor and senator were basking in the glow of a major coup. An overnight poll by *The Milwaukee Journal* and the Roper organization showed that seventy-six percent of Wisconsin residents approved of the American Seasons resort plans. On Wall Street, the stock of Haligent Holdings trading on the American Exchange was up five points. In the cafe, my breakfast business was booming. I had even met an old friend from Manhattan who had been sent out to do background research for *Business Week*. No one could have predicted the enthusiasm the media had for the unveiling of plans for a new mega-resort and casino in the northwoods.

"It'll never get built," Bromley fumed. "They don't have any of the right clearances. There's zoning laws in this county. And there aren't any god darn liquor licenses left to be granted. How do they expect to get any of it done if they didn't even ask for my help? You know the Lattigo have to be behind all of this. Never would have happened without them. Chip Frozen Bear is out to get me, I tell you. Red is my friend, and he's known me for years. He would never have gone along with this cockamamie plan if it hadn't been for that Indian. What does Frozen Bear have over Red?"

Josh was in a slump. "I should have known something was up when people started a bidding war over my useless swampland. I never would have sold it so cheap if Chip Frozen Bear hadn't shown up in person to make the offer. He's so damn cute. I'm always a sucker for a cute guy. But I could have been rich. I sure hope Dad at least can look down from up there and see how that his old swamp is going to turn into a casino. That would make his day."

"They came back. My men came back last night for the first time in weeks. I had been having all these horrible dreams about Arthur. At least I think it was Arthur. In my dreams, I was a young girl and Arthur would come crawling into my bedroom late at night trying to get into my bed. And I would scream. Then I would wake up. I'm going to ask my little men tonight what it all means." Claire was having a double muffin. She was very happy to be in touch with the cosmos once more. Local doings were of no concern.

Cynthia waltzed from table to table, pouring coffee for all of the news reporters who were buying breakfast. She had seldom been happier. "Just imagine. Daddy and Chip are in business together. That explains why they have been meeting so often and talking. Chip is already almost like family."

"Someone took my new police light," Officer Campbell was in an uproar. "I placed it inside the car, so I could use it if I needed to pull over any of these out-of-towners for speeding. This town is busier than during Loon Fest. Bound to be some speeders. But some prankster took my light away. When I find out who took it then there's going to be hell to pay. I'm the law in this town, and no big city newsman can get one over on me."

Amanda Manny pranced into the cafe bedecked with clothes and make up, all perfectly geared for a television camera. "Has anyone seen my partner Henry Van Elkind?" she announced in a regal tone loud enough for all in the restaurant to hear. "I need to show him my latest plans for the interiors of American Seasons. Oh, are you with NBC? How nice to meet you. You're interested in talking to me? Really? How delightful!"

Danny was bewildered by the hubbub in the establishment. Only the presence of Josh at the counter kept him calm. He confided to me, "Dad got really upset when he heard the news last night. He's afraid that this development will destroy what's special about this area."

"You knew this was coming didn't you?" Thelma had been depressed ever since we had spied Gilbert and the other woman in Timberton. She was dreading the arrival of Sunday when Gilbert would once more appear for their weekly rendezvous. "Wally, you knew it was coming and you helped it along. Is this what you came back for? Do you want Manhattan rebuilt in your own back yard?"

Mr. Packer held his coffee cup close to his nose. He allowed the steam to rise up to his nostrils before each sip. His beard seemly recently trimmed, and I thought he had taken a bath. I had never seen him look so presentable. He moved around the restaurant, pausing at tables, never saying a word, just letting the reactions of everyone float up like the steam of his coffee.

"I'm the mayor. I should have been told . . ."

"I wonder if I could rescind the sale to try to get more money . . ."

"If you turn your camera on, I'll tell you about the little men who visit this town. . ."

"Everything will turn out okay now . . ."

"That van just did an illegal u-turn in the square. I gotta go . . ."

"Hank is my dearest friend. I met him when we redecorated his camp . . ."

"Dad says the woods should be sacred . . . "

"What did you get out of all this . . ."

The cash register never stopped ringing. The coffee never stopped flowing. The voices and opinions swirled about me.

The door from the street flung open. Pastor Paul Mall stood there with his arms outstretched. He was an imposing figure, dressed all in black, his close-cropped silver hair brushed to perfect attention. All of the reporters stopped talking, stopped eating, stopped drinking. He had the attention of them all.

"This town is filled with sin. You need to know about . . ."

Mr. Packer calmly strolled over to the pastor, gently pushed him out the door and closed it. "Sometimes you have to step in and put a stop to things," he said to no one and to everyone. "I think that time is now."

And he was out the door.

CHAPTER NINETEEN

When I stepped out of the kitchen door into the back yard, I was quickly surrounded by little clouds of midges, newly hatched in the remaining puddles of spring. I looked around my garden and soaked in the temperatures high in the '60s. I didn't care what Thelma said. My plot was ready for seeds.

I liked to imagine my future flower beds that would let me decorate my cafe each evening with home-grown flowers. All winter, I pored over the seed catalogues, trying to guess whether dahlias would be better than gladioli, concerned that zinnias might have too strong a smell, and wondering if bachelor buttons were too frail for a vase. In the end, throwing caution to the winds, I bought everything I fancied.

Behind me Thelma walked into the kitchen, her arms laden with branches covered with delicate white buds. "The pussy willows are in bloom again," she said.

I laughed.

"What's so funny?" she wanted to know. I shrugged, unable to explain. She grabbed a mason jar from the shelf, filled it with water, and arranged the branches. "I hope you're not still thinking about getting into that dirt. You're like a little boy with a sandbox. Don't complain to me when you end up losing everything in a freeze."

"I called my mother last night," I replied, "she didn't think it was too early to get started."

"What does your mother know? She moved to Arizona. I bet it

don't even freeze there. Say, did you hear about Reverend Willy?" she asked.

I hadn't heard, and no matter what it was, I didn't care to hear. But Thelma had to tell me about how Pastor Mall had heard about Willy's nighttime film showings and was convinced the poor man was breaking some law or another. There had been talk of him sometimes watching the movies naked. The pastor had even called in the county prosecutor.

"All that Pastor Paul Mall's doing," groused Thelma. "He just can't let sleeping dog lies. Why, I bet Willy's one of the best people in his church, and he does their janitoring for free. Wouldn't hurt a fly."

I tried to imagine the potential investigation. A handful of cars purring in the field outside Willy's house, their lights turned off, their wheels gently coasting them forward; their motors extinguished—and on the exterior of the tiny house, the flickering lights of a Charlie Chaplin or a Clara Bow. Then out of nowhere, like a posse in the dark, the gravel is spit into the trees as the heavy police cruisers crash over the bumps of the lake road, their blazing headlights streaking across the nights, sirens echoing in the black woods.

Cynthia flounced in with exuberance. She was carrying a tray filled to capacity with dirty dishes. "Wally, you should get back in the restaurant. I had to help Danny with the bussing, 'cause he can't keep up."

"Wally's moping about his garden," Thelma said in a dismissive way. In the dining room, Bromley, Claire and Mr. Packer were at their usual spots. By now, Bromley and Claire's morning breakfast rituals had spilled over into lunch and afternoon coffee. It seemed as though they never left. Mr. Packer came and went on his own schedule. They too were talking about Revered Willy and his supposed crimes of exposing Thread's youth to the flickers.

Claire was worried. "But what if they put him in jail. I'd feel terrible."

"They should institutionalize you," muttered Bromley.

"Don't you talk that way to me," snapped Claire. "I know who crawled into my room, and it wasn't Arthur. So don't you talk that way to me."

"I don't know what you're gabbing about," Bromley grabbed the last of his strudel and strode out the door.

"Touchy, isn't he?" I said.

"I don't know why," Claire replied, "He's been that way ever since my men stopped coming, you know, after Arthur's dog visited Cynthia. Something's on his mind. I don't know what. I never seen him this way before, not in fifty years. But he shouldn't be so touchy no more because my little men are back."

Outside, Officer Campbell and Henry Van Elkind were shouting at one another. Dressed in a double-breasted, vested suit, Van Elkind appeared decked out to brief his board of directors. But his hair was falling out of place on a windless morning. Officer Campbell was in his usual disarray, with his leather jacket unzipped and his hat with its plush ear flaps at an odd angle. Van Elkind kept trying to walk into the restaurant, while Officer Campbell tugged at his opponent's arm trying to pull him back. Finally, in an act of disgust, Van Elkind flung Campbell's grasping arm to the side and stomped into the cafe.

"Fucking little pissant," snarled Van Elkind. "Get me some coffee." Despite his recent triumphs, our Chicago financier had grown increasingly surly. At first, he gamboled delightfully in the initial shower of glowing reviews; now, he had to face rising opposition to American Seasons. It was as though a thousand noxious weeds had only been waiting for a sprinkling of publicity to sprout into opposition. New groups blossomed daily. There were the environmental concerns. There was the anti-gambling contingent. There were those who were against anything Native Americans wanted to do. Then there were those entrenched interests who opposed anything counter to their personal vision of the best interests of a reservation they had never visited. The anti-development crowd quaked about the need for new highways. The taxpayers union hoisted the threat of new taxes to pay for infrastructure. The lumbering interests and paper mills fretted about their source of cheap pulp. The mining lobbyists had a sudden thunderbolt that there was still ore to mine in the area despite decades of geologists' reports to the contrary. Everyone across the state and the region found reasons to claim interest in the project.

For every life-or-death concern, as each seemed to be, someone was on hand to deliver its truths for the television cameras. The old hotel on the square had overflowed its sullen rooms with crowds of do-gooders. Even the Timberton hoteliers was basking in the financial radiation emitting from the much-publicized and controversial American Seasons.

Through it all, Henry Van Elkind was the man on the spot.

"Don't you go running away from me, Mr. Van Elkind," Officer Campbell stormed into the restaurant.

"Do your job. Find Mother Regina." Hank shouted back.

"And I told you I need the state police. I got no resources to conduct a kidnapping investigation by myself. Your mother could have been taken across the state border to the U.P. That makes it a national matter for the FBI." Officer Campbell was quaking ever so slightly, but he stood his ground. Two days ago, Bromley had authorized him to deputize two men to help control the jamming traffic of television trucks. His new authority seemed to have given him added backbone.

"And I told you. Keep them the fuck out of it!"

Bromley waddled over. "Boys, boys," he intoned, "there's no need to argue. Not in front of a restaurant full of people. Come into the back room with me and we'll work this out. I'm the mayor here. I can help." Bromley's face glowed like a highwayman discovering an unexpected opportunity to fleece an innocent traveler. The two fighters sullenly agreed to Bromley's suggestion. I followed all three into my back room.

Here we were in the room where I first learned of American Seasons. Of course, Van Elkind had romanced most of the needed players before my first meeting them at that dinner. Now the whole world knew of the pregnant possibilities. Nearly a year ago, flush with the thousand-dollar payment made by Van Elkind for the dinner, I had felt unique and had overlooked any apprehensions. Now as I looked at the livid Van Elkind, I wondered what havoc we had let loose.

Bromley leaned against a shelf laden with boxes of canned goods ordered by Thelma. "Hank, do you think it's wise to yell in a crowded restaurant about matters you want private?" he lectured. "You know I can keep a secret, because I've known about your park for quite some time. And did I ever hint at it? Not once. Now did I? So just tell me what's got you so riled up here? And I'll help. I run this god darn town, after all."

"Regina's been kidnapped."

"But she's dead," I blurted out.

"Precisely," Van Elkind replied.

Bromley leaned back even more, and tapped his chin slowly with an air of perspicacity. "I see," he intoned. Officer Campbell shifted uneasily from foot to foot. His usual flush was creeping up his neck, spreading into the lobes of his ears. His hat, now in his hands, was being twisted like a spent dishrag.

Van Elkind was incensed. "You do not see, you old man. You don't know what the hell I am talking about, any more than you knew one god damn thing about my resort. Don't posture with me. I have more important things on my mind. Like getting Regina's body returned. I can't let the press find out."

"Unlike Bromley," I said, casting the mayor a look of apology even as I began, "I don't have the slightest idea what you're talking about. Your mother-in-law was scheduled to be buried today. People don't kidnap a dead person. What would they do? Threaten to kill her?"

"No, but they're threatening to throw her body off the highway 2 overpass onto highway 17," Van Elkind said as he slumped into a chair. The fight had suddenly gone out of him.

Casting a human corpse into that particular intersection would be a bit messy I had to admit. Highway 2 connected Bangor, Maine with Seattle, Washington and was the only moderately busy highway in all of Northern Wisconsin. Its intersection with 17 just north of Timberton's downtown actually sported a highway cloverleaf. A dead grandmother thrown in front of a Mack truck wouldn't make for a pretty picture, but even I could see how it would make for a great news story.

"Rita and I went to the funeral home this morning, after we decided to have Regina buried instead of cremated. We were going to airship her body back to Chicago and have her be buried next to Casimir. We walked into the funeral home to give Mother Regina our final goodbye, and then have the funeral home handle the air freight and the internment in Chicago. There was going to be no reason for us to be involved further.

"So we walk into the viewing room, and the casket is empty. Fucking empty. 'What have you done with my mother?' screamed Rita. Agnelli was frantic. The stupid jerk hadn't been in the room until he walked in with us. He fucking didn't know someone had broken in and stolen my mother-in-law.

"All that's left in the casket is a poorly-typed ransom note. The scum demand half a million dollars or they'll drop Regina off the highway 2 overpass. They threatened that if we bring in the state police or the FBI, they would alert the press. They're clever enought to know I can't have this kind of publicity and make American Seasons seem like some fucking joke.

I'm sure one of these fucked-up demonstrators is behind it. They'll do anything to stop me.

"Rita says 'Don't pay.' If they keep the body, what's the difference? Regina is already fucking dead. But imagine the headline: *Amusement Park Tycoon Tells Crooks: Keep Grandma's Body*. It would destroy me."

I gave Van Elkind the truth. "You have to call the police. They'll know what to do. They're not going to tell the press."

Van Elkind nodded glumly in agreement. Officer Campbell finally stood still. Bromley beamed brightly as though he had negotiated the solution.

"I told Daddy last night. I told him everything," Cynthia said. She had come into the cafe, following her last class at school, radiating a curious aura of joy and dismay. My only customer was Danny's father, Toivo. He had starting coming in for a cup of coffee and a piece of pie after finishing his shift. I suspected that after he drank the last drop from his cup, he went to the cemetery to spend an hour with his memories of Lempi.

"Told him what?" Ever since the showdown at the Sapphire Run over the spawning muskie, Red Trueheart had become an unpredictable, even irrational, man. He and Barbara had been in for dinner a couple of times. Each instance, he was glum and unresponsive to anyone's attempts to start a conversation. Even when Bromley tried to insinuate himself into Red's notice, Red couldn't find the energy to snap at the old man.

With the announcement of American Seasons, Red's spirits should have lifted like a joyous hosanna. The connivery of two generations of Truehearts was about to pay off and transform rugged second-growth scrub woods into a playland for the nation. Much of this "Las Vegas of the North" would be built on land controlled by Red. Vast riches surely awaited him. Yet as the only kid in the schoolyard who owned a ball, he didn't seem to want to play.

Cynthia reported that Red hadn't gone fishing since the fishing season opened. He was usually the first to be in the trout streams, walking the river banks in his waders, casting his hand-tied flies. After the spring thaw hit Big Sapphire Lake, Red always kept a fishing boat tied to the dock in the front of his house. It might be just a little wooden model, with a tiny Evinrude motor under ten horsepower, something totally different than the monster speedboat he zipped about in when he was trying to show off, but he called this little boat, True Heart, and Red always seemed the calmest and most relaxed when he pulled up to his dock in True Heart, his basket full of freshly caught fish, the sun setting in the west, and his sunburnt nose gleaming brightly.

But something about that spring evening spent in the tense light of the torches had unnerved him. Whether it was the raw violence that hung over the water current, or whether it was the promise of a protecting earth that coursed through the stream, who could say. Cynthia didn't know. I didn't know. And it was clear that Red didn't know.

Red didn't like revelations, and I feared that Cynthia's bubbling good news had been about her feelings for Chip. To anyone else in town, this would have been no news. But as with so many of us on so many topics, the only people in Thread from whom a secret could be kept were precisely the very people closest and dearest to those individuals who hid the truth.

"You didn't tell him about Chip, did you?" I asked tentatively.

"Of course, I did," Cynthia exclaimed. "What else could I be talking about?"

"And he gave you his congratulations, I bet ya," said Toivo. For the first time in the months that he had been having coffee in my cafe, Danny's father entered voluntarily into a conversation.

"Yes, he did. And so did Mommy," she said as though any other outcome would have been totally impossible to imagine. Yet I knew that she herself had been trying to keep her parents from encountering the least hint that there were sparks flying between Frozen Bear and her. Moreover, she didn't sound convincing.

"Cynthia, I know your father is involved in business with Frozen Bear. But money and families are two very different things. Your father, I am sad to say, has never shown great tolerance for the Lattigo. After all, he kept them from getting the liquor license to this place for decades."

She was dismissive. "That was business."

I was astounded. "What was different between them giving Red money for an unused license and my buying it? The license wasn't being used. The Lattigo would have paid as much to the penny as I did."

"Well, Daddy was pretty happy when you bought this place. He had been trying to sell it for years. And you paid him way more than he ever expected to get."

"Oh."

"Anyway, it wasn't the money from the license that Daddy was thinking about. He wanted to get rid of this building, and you bought it. And he didn't want anyone to use the liquor license who would compete with his store. He knew the Lattigo would use the license to open a liquor outlet closer to the reservation. Then the tribe members wouldn't drive into Thread anymore, and they wouldn't shop at our store. But you . . . well, he knew that you wouldn't be able to run a business that took away any of his liquor sales."

"Thanks a lot."

"Why get offended? I'm just telling the truth. I should be upset that you think Daddy wouldn't be happy I'm in love."

"But Red hates the Lattigo," I protested.

"Wally, you don't understand love," Toivo jumped back into the mix. "Someday you're going to find that right woman. Somewhere there's that person who makes you feel complete. And if you're lucky enough to have a baby with that woman, and you see that baby grow into a beautiful young lady like Cynthia, then when you hear her come to you and say that she's in love, then that day, that day for sure, you are going to be the happiest man in the world.

"Let me tell you, there's nothing richer than love. Once you have it, nothing else takes its place. You could catch the biggest fish there was. You could lumberjack the oldest tree in these woods. You could even have more cash than any of these tycoons coming to town. But if you know you're missing real love, then none of those things can be all that important.

"And when you see your baby has a chance to get it, every inch of your body will want it for them, and you'll cry to the heavens, 'Thank God my baby has found love.'"

He handed over two dollar bills for the coffee and pie. "I gotta go now." He walked quietly to the door. He moved with such dignity. We could see him walking slowly in the direction of the cemetery. Even in his gait, we could somehow sense just how much he was aching to hold onto the hand of his dead wife, how much he wanted to reach out and complete a union that could never be held again.

"Was he talking about me?" whispered Cynthia.

"Maybe he was talking about all of us," I said back almost as quietly. I watched him walk steadily, unhurriedly, until he turned a corner and disappeared from my sight. And then I felt immensely sad remembering Patrice.

It was very early in the morning. Officer Campbell was standing in the kitchen with Thelma and me. He was nervously twirling his hat. "I have to ask, you see? It's my job."

"And I told you," Thelma replied calmly, "that I don't know what you're talking about. There's no way I could be a witness for the state."

Officer Campbell had a problem. Up in Timberton, the ambitious district attorney for Penokee County had run into a small snag in his case against Pete Sullivan. Not surprisingly, there didn't actually appear to be any laws against showing silent movies on the siding of one's own house. But the district attorney sniffed that there was something untoward about the Reverend Willy and wasn't willing to drop this bone. But people liked the Reverend Willy, even if they thought him odd for showing old movies to no one. Besides he cleaned all the churches for free. Moreover, even his own parishoners considered Pastor Paul Mall overly sanctamonious. No one was going to admit that he had ever done anything other than show movies.

Stress was building up in Officer Campbell's face. For a man whose chief worry had been replacing a broken police light and catching the occasional speeder, he had become a very busy soul. He was caught up in two investigations involving the state police: the kidnapping of Mrs. Rabinowicz's body and the somewhat undefined case against Willy. Added to that was his new role with multiple deputies trying to deal with the crazy rush of news traffic. Ever since someone had leaked the tale of the bodynapping to the press, the news media had truly descended on town to delightedly lap up the oddities. Between the press and the investors visiting American Seasons offices, which had taken over much of the bank as the information center for the planned resort complex, the town square was always packed.

But the Reverend Willy case was particularly challenging. Both the county district attorney and the state police were persistent in attacking Officer Campbell for ignoring the so-called Willy problem.

"Help me out here," he said, "I know both of you were out to

Reverend Willy's place. I heard you guys talking about it last summer. I was here in the cafe the day you planned it. I know you went there. What was he really up to? Was he naked?"

"I don't recall going there, Thelma, do you?" I wasn't about to feed this frenzy. Reverend Willy may be a weirdo, but he was the town weirdo. The way the town was swinging verbal clubs against American Seasons, I didn't need to offend the locals.

"I don't recall that either, Wally." Thelma was smiling.

"No one in town seems to recall that," Officer Campbell said glumly. "I could subpoena you, you know."

"Would that change my memories?" I asked.

"You're telling me you would perjure yourself on the stand?"

"The thing is I just don't recall ever going out to the Sullivan place. Maybe I did, but I just don't have any memory of it," Thelma said. "I don't think that would be perjury. I'm getting old. My memory just isn't that good."

"You're going to force me into talking to the Lahti boy," Officer Campbell sighed. "Danny's bedroom faces that house. He had to have seen what was going on. He probably knows if there was anything wrong going on."

"No," Thelma and I said in unison.

Officer Campbell looked at both of us. A slight grimace pursed his lips. Across his face flitted the pros and cons of fighting the town over this, while stacking it up against his need to meet the demands of outsiders. He sighed and a weight seemed lifted from his shoulders. A little smile began to creep into the corner of his mouth. "I guess there's nothing here to worry about, since no one else in town can collaborate it. It's just a nasty rumor. Now why would anyone want to start such a rumor about a good God-fearing man like Willy who goes to church so many times a week?" The man was trying on the story for size and liked the fit.

I jumped in. "Yup, Willy's a god-fearing man. That's why we all call him Reverend Willy."

"How about a cup of coffee before you go?" Thelma asked. The room now seemed bright with early morning sunshine.

"Don't mind if I do," he replied. "And how about one of your sticky buns? I haven't had breakfast yet today, and I should be getting our of your hair anyway. Aren't you supposed to be opening up for breakfast."

"Don't worry about that. I'd be delighted to serve you. And it'll be on us, won't it Wally?"

I nodded in agreement. Thelma quickly hustled up a mug filled with fresh coffee, and then set down a plate with the largest of her sticky buns. She eagerly waited for Officer Campbell to take the first sip and the first bite. Only after he did both did she really relax, as though Campbell had made a commitment that could not be broken.

"Any news on finding Regina's body?" I asked.

"We have our suspect, and it has nothing to do with the resort plans. I can't really say more," Officer Campbell said with pompous authority. He was back in charge. "By the way, some seem to think I have another missing person. Either of you seen Mr. Packer in the last couple of days?"

I pondered the question. "Now that you mention it, he hasn't been in for a couple of days. But that's not unusual. He isn't like Bromley and Claire who are here absolutely every day. But he has been gone a while." Because my cafe had become the in spot for out-of-town reporters who liked my food and used me as their lodestone back to the big city realities, I hadn't paid much attention to my regulars.

Officer Campbell looked pleased that he knew something we didn't. "Don't worry about it. His neighbor called me yesterday because she hadn't seen him for a day, and you know how he's always walking about. Hard not to see him. She was afraid he might have died in that maze he calls home. I looked around his house. Bookcases full of books, and the guy hasn't thrown anything away in decades. The rooms inside are nothing but paths between piles of junk. But it looked like he had been searching for something. Things were all thrown about. It made me worry that someone had robbed him.

"So I checked around, found out that Harvey had sold him a bus ticket to Madison. He left day before yesterday. Why do you suppose old man Packer would be going to Madison?"

We never had a chance to answer. An enormous woman rushed into the kitchen without warning. I wondered how she got in since the cafe wasn't even opened. Then I remembered I had left the front door unlocked for Officer Campbell. This woman had enormous red hair, piled high in a bee-hive hairdo. She skidded to a stop next to Officer Campbell and teetered on her high heels.

"We're not open yet," I said.

"You . . . You . ." she said, pointing a long finger, bedecked with two-colors of nail polish, at Thelma. "Where is he?"

"Who?" Thelma asked dismissively. I could tell Thema had cast her eyes over this apparition and dismissed her as a floozy.

"My Gilbert, of course. What have you done with him?"

"Why would he be here? Beside he's not your Gilbert, he's my Gilbert," Thelma's voice was strong, but her tone had changed, mixing an undercurrent of fear with preparation for a truth already suspected.

"Is that so?" she snipped. "I know you know that Gilbert spends every Tuesday night and Wednesday with me. We were going to get married, but you kept trying to lure him away, so when he didn't show up this week, I called his landlady. Gone off and gotten married, she told me. I knew it had to be you. How could you? After I've done his laundry for ten years." She started to sob.

"I haven't seen Gilbert since Monday. I don't know where he is." Thelma was faltering. Officer Campbell and I moved closer. I was afraid she might faint. I thought of the woman Thelma and I had seen with Gilbert at the Penokee House. I knew that Thelma was thinking of that same thing. Her eye was still slightly bloodshot from that dinner sighting.

The other woman was crying and hesitant. "If it's not you, and it's not Tillie, then who is it? What't happened to him?"

"Who's Tillie?" asked Thelma in a very quiet voice.

"I know you know about Tillie!" Thelma shook her head to the contrary, and the woman seemed taken aback. "How about me?" Another shake from Thelma. "Oh, dear, I was sure you knew about both Tillie and me. I'm Tina. I guess Gilbert liked his T's. You really don't know?"

Thelma shook her head again. The other woman was clearly astonished, and now a little bit embarrassed.

"Well, it was a deal how we shared Gilbert. Gilbert spent Fridays and Saturdays with Tillie, 'cause she's an accountant, and she always helped him balance his weekly books. She's been dating him almost as long as I have, nearly ten years now. He told both of us he would marry one of us one day. But then he met you. Before you, he used to alternate Sunday evenings with us. You changed that."

"I've never heard one word of this." said Thelma defiantly.

Tina was now shy, almost demure. "I just assumed he was honest with you, like he was with us. Sure, Tillie and I know he's a playboy, but we always thought he was our playboy. Then when he left a phone message for Tillie that said he was going to Florida to get married with someone new . . . well, Tillie and me figured it was you. You were the newest, so who else could it be. We just knew it had to be you, and Tillie said I had to come and find out for sure."

The four of us floated in the early morning sunlight. Officer Campbell's coffee and half-eaten roll sat forgotten on the counter. Tina seemed eager to leave. Thelma was adrift. I felt moored to the spot, anchored by my concern for Thelma. Time ticked on, and I thought of Gilbert's watch and his many stories.

A transformation came over Thelma. It was as though the very broken blood vein in her eye instantly scarred up, and she took on an attitude more frightening than her behavior when we had seen Gilbert at the Penokee House. Sensing the change and the desperation behind it, Officer Campbell tried to give Thelma a hug, but she shifted away.

"Wally, we're supposed to be open. We better get going. So Gilbert is gone. Good riddance, I say. Never liked his bow tie anyway. He just better not come around here again trying to sell me canned goods.

"Why isn't Cynthia here already. We got work to do How are we supposed to run this restaurant if we don't have dependable help?"

Tina slinked back out the door, her tiny heels making a tip-tapping sound in retreat. Poor Officer Campbell's hat was nearly destroyed by his wringing hands. His face was fully flushed. He wanted to say something, but couldn't imagine what would be worth saying. I knew exactly how he felt.

"Thelma," I said softly, "You once warned me that people are more complex than I thought and to watch out. That was good advice, and maybe I should have given you the same warning."

Immediately, I realized it was a stupid thing to say. She glared at me with astonishment and anger. "Get out of my kitchen."

Officer Campbell and I hurried out. The moment we were in the main room, Thelma's sobs burst forth, rising as a keening wail into the spring.

The square was filled with angry people. Hundreds, maybe thousands. More than had ever attended Loon Fest. They focused their fervor on the old bank building on the east end of the square. The bank–now owned by Haligent Holdings, an investor in American Seasons–was currently in a swirl of sandblasting, sawdust and new paint, all endeavoring to restore the building to its turn-of-the-century promise of northwoods glory. Haligent had opened the bank's long-empty third floor to house the local offices for American Seasons. In order to direct operations on site, Henry Van Elkind had temporarily moved from Chicago to live at his camp. Now he looked out from the bank's third floor onto a square of seething protesters. At least a thousand tumultuous souls.

Jacqueline Grant was currently urging the group in its chants and waving of placards. The mob was a strange conglomeration of Native Americans dissatisfied with the role of the tribe, environmentalists from the big cities, locals fearing the loss of their world, and disgruntled landowners who felt swindled out of their worthless swampland. Josh was among them, lazily waving a sign that read: You Cheated Us. Danny claimed that Josh was now worth over a half a million dollars thanks to his parents' inheritance and the sale of the land. His outrage lacked conviction.

The more I watched the milling mass, the more it seemed a mess. Danny and Cynthia were at my side. No one dared to cross the sea of seething humanity to come into the cafe.

In the town's eyes, I was still an innocent in this maelstrom. Thelma suspected my involvement with the resort's planning. Maybe she even knew, but she was too caught up in her anger and hurt over Gilbert to focus on my perfidies. I was glad no one knew. After all, the town should embrace the development. Its enormous investment would bring new tax revenues to the community allowing up-to-date schools, a full-time librarian, better services. There would be thousands of new jobs: hotel managers, restaurant hostesses, shop owners, amusement ride operators, croupiers, bartenders, managers, computer programmers. The list was endless. And all of those people would require new shops, banks, offices. Doctors, lawyers and accountants. Teachers for the children. New roads. New airports. More people to build the roads and airport. This was a town that catered to tourists. Why wouldn't they welcome more of them?

But that was the problem. More people. Somewhere, somehow, a whole new city would have to emerge. Most who lived in Thread didn't like a lot of people. They tolerated the summer folk, because they were essential to eking out any kind of living. But who needed a bowling alley or a movie theater or a newsstand? A fishing boat, a snowmobile, a friendly bar, and a church were more than enough. Many of them didn't even need the church.

They lived in Thread because they hated the big city. Now, the big city was coming to them: Congestion. Pollution. Inflation. Crime. Anonymity and indifference.

Van Elkind was trying every trick I ever suggested to change their minds. He engaged the country's largest public relations firm, Hill and Knowlton, and with the firm came sensible advice. Stress the positives. More money. More jobs. Nature preserves. Revived economies. Grants to protect endangered species. New investments. Keeps out the nasty mining companies and saves the earth. More money. Opens nature to the enjoyment of millions. More money. More money. More money.

Nationally, such tactics worked. Serious publications estimated the costs of development, computed the net worth and connections of the principals, noted the risky legal aspect of tribal gambling, and duly reported the positive conclusion. Haligent Holdings went up twenty points. Capital venture firms started swarming to Thread to discuss potential investments. Brokerage firms paraded by.

The regional press was even more enthusiastic. They were in a party mood, taking full advantage of new color press capabilities to run complex artist's depictions of the new Thread. And why not? They catered to the millions who lived in Milwaukee, Chicago, and Minneapolis who wanted a playground closer to home than Orlando, Las Vegas or Anaheim.

The checkout stand press never bothered to discuss the development. They were too interested in the story of the kidnapped corpse. The body of Regina Rabinowicz remained missing. Any chance of Van Elkind quietly paying the ransom had long since vanished.

The FBI, having taken an interest in the case, visited Cynthia one day. When they left, she said she thought they suspected Kip Van Elkind, who had disappeared at about the same time as Regina's death. So far the tabloids hadn't picked up on that minor detail.

Back in the square, the people joined voices in a rendition of "We Shall Overcome." I was tired of seeing them. The demonstration had been going on for over an hour. None of the reporters were going to eat in my cafe as long as they might find a good camera shot.

The bell on the door tinkled and Jacqueline Grant walked in. She was truly a woman of style. She smiled at the three of us, "My part is over, so I wanted to come by and say hello to Cynthia. I don't get to see as much of her as I would like now that Chip and I are on opposite sides."

"I must say I'm quite surprised you're leading this demonstration," I said.

"Did you see Josh?" Danny asked of no one in particular. "I wish he would get out of there."

"Wally, are you surprised that I would get involved or are you surprised that I would take this position?" Jacqueline asked.

"To be honest: Both."

"I'm just a romantic at heart. I believe in the land and all the old legends. Chip seems so willing to destroy it all."

Cynthia protested, "Chip doesn't want to destroy anything."

"You believe that because you love him. But I've loved him a very long time as a sister, and yet I have no idea of his true intents. I'd like to think of him as the original Frozen Bear in our legends, ready to restore us all. But I know that he isn't."

A hint of an old story and Cynthia was immediately hooked. "What old legend?" she asked eagerly.

"Just a story my grandmother used to tell me. A story handed down in our tribe. I can tell it if you like."

Cynthia eagerly encouraged Jacqueline, who began:

"This story takes place before time was defined, when the Great Spirit Father still moved among us. Days and nights had no specific starts. More things were possible then because there were no clocks to pace off the passing of our lives. We lived simply, in touch with our mother, the earth, in touch with all of the creatures the Great Spirit had made.

"A Trickster lived in the great forest then. The Trickster had powers not found among normal people. He plotted things for the pleasure resulting from the confusion caused by his actions. He didn't care if anyone was hurt by his japes, because he paid no attention to such things.

"The first people of our family lived then, and they were much happier than they are now. They lived on a beautiful island surrounded by a vast lake. And on all sides of the lake spread a neverending forest.

"One of these people was Snow Flower, the most beautiful of all women in our tribe. Another was Frozen Bear, a man so handsome and so strong that all other men in the tribe wanted to be like him. Snow Flower secretly loved Frozen Bear, and he her. But they had been afraid to tell one another.

"But the Trickster saw their love and was annoyed by it. He didn't like any hint of true happiness, and so he thought he would have some fun. One spring day when Frozen Bear was hunting in the vast woods, the Trickster transformed himself into an enormous buck and lured the hunting Frozen Bear deep into the forest, far, far from home.

"The darkness of the night descended. In the night, the Trickster simply vanished from sight, leaving Frozen Bear in the woods. But the Trickster returned to the island in the middle of the vast lake. Once there, he froze time across all of the island and all of the lake. Nothing could move, nothing could change.

"On the lake, the other men had been spearing for muskie. They had been floating in shallow water in small boats. One man in each boat held aloft a blazing torch to light the waters for signs of the fish. There were many boats, because we were many then. Their fishing created the sight of a lake of flames, and in the freezing of time, the flames never flickered, never burned. The light just reflected from the dark water.

"But deep within the forest, Frozen Bear still moved. The Trickster had not enchanted him. But he had deceived the handsome hunter. During the earlier chase, the Trickster had given Frozen Bear the fleetness of a mighty stag, and so unknowingly, Frozen Bear had raced deep into the dark recesses of the forests. Now his fleetness was gone, and he was far from home.

"Yet as far as he was from where time had stopped for Snow Flower, Frozen Bear could sense that something had happened. He knew that he had to return, and to return quickly. Snow Flower needed him.

"The Trickster knew that Frozen Bear would know. The power of love is mighty and soars far. But the Trickster was set to have fun with Frozen Bear. And so as Frozen Bear started to retrace his tracks, to return to Snow Flower, the Trickster caused the moon and all of the stars to retreat, and he forbade the sun to arrive. The enormous darkness that had once existed when there was only the Great Spirit had returned.

"The Great Spirit could see what the Trickster was doing. He did not like it. And so he decided to help Frozen Bear discover the strengths within himself. He whispered through the wind, 'Look inside yourself for the powers you need.'

"And Frozen Bear thought of all the animals he knew throughout the land and into the seas. He thought of the bat, and how it could fly through the darkest of night. In thinking of the bat, he became the bat and began to fly through the darkness, listening to the noises that bounced in front of him.

"But the Trickster was not to be so easily stopped. Allowing the stars and moon back, he instead grew a wall of briars that reached to the moon, that touched the stars and kept on growing. There was no way for anyone to fly over its great height, or through its enormous thickness.

"Frozen Bear stopped and descended to the ground, faced with this daunting wall of thorns. The wind rose up once more, and the Great Spirit whispered, "Look inside yourself."

"Frozen Bear thought of his friend, the badger, and he began to claw at the ground with a ferocity and strength not imaginable. He dug beneath the briars, far down below their roots, then back up, and soon he was on the other side. He had to reach Snow Flower and help her.

"The Trickster smiled to himself. Frozen Bear was a more formidable human than he had ever encountered. He conjured up a battalion of wicked and deformed spirits from within the earth. They came up and out of the ground and surrounded Frozen Bear.

"In Frozen Bear's ears, he could still hear the wind and in his heart he could still hear the cry of Snow Flower. He thought of himself as the courageous bear with fierce claws and a mighty jaw. He clawed and fought through the Trickster's minions.

"Finally, he was at the lake's edge. He was at the watery edge of movement, caught outside of time. He touched one foot to the water, and sensed that it would become frozen there, encased in time. His mind and body, still on the mainland, could move and think. But once he entered into the timeless zone, it would be caught fully in the Trickster's snare.

"He looked at the lake, lit by the flaming torches of his many friends, now fishing in eternity. He could think of no one who could cross through this, except for the wind itself, the wind of the Great Spirit.

"The Great Spirit was much impressed with the power and intelligence of Frozen Bear. Not even the Trickster's might could affect the Great Spirit, and so he entered into the water as a powerful muskie. He swam outside of time to the edge of the shore, and the wind whispered to

Frozen Bear, 'Stand on the back of the Muskie. It will carry you to the island.'

"Frozen Bear listened to the wind. He trusted it and it became his heart. And on the back of the Great Spirit he was conveyed through the Trickster's snare, until he was face to face with Snow Flower, who was caught herself in unmoving time at the water's edge, standing on shore, watching the fishermen, waiting for the return of Frozen Bear.

"The Great Muskie could bring Frozen Bear to the edge of the lake, but there still remained that gulf between Frozen Bear and Snow Flower. If he stepped off the muskie and into the water to cross to shore, he would be ensnared by time.

"'How do I save her?' wondered Frozen Bear, and he looked into his heart, and he saw his love, and he saw the love of everyone around him. Their love of life. Their love of the earth. Their love for one another. He saw the love of every animal for life itself. He saw the love that was everywhere but in the Trickster's soul. He knew that love could trick the Trickster. Still standing on the muskie-back of the Great Spirit, Frozen Bear stretched his body across the gulf of water until his face was close enough to kiss the lips of Snow Flower.

"As their lips met, the flow of time returned. Snow Flower returned the kiss of Frozen Bear. The flames of the torches across the lake flickered and jumped in the breeze. The Great Spirit, leaving the giant muskie, allowed it to break into a thousand smaller fish. As the fish dissolved into many, Frozen Bear's feet landed in the water. Snow Flower caught him with her arms and they kissed once more.

"The many fish sped throughout the lake. Soon all the fisherman were holding aloft muskie on their spears. And in the sky and the wind, the Great Spirit had returned to his home and he laughed. And he called forth the Trickster and said, 'Leave my people alone' and cast the Trickster into the form of a skunk.

"That night, all of my people held a great feast, enjoying the muskie given to them by the Great Spirit, and celebrating the love of Frozen Bear and Snow Flower.

"And this story was told by Snow Flower and Frozen Bear to their children, who told it to their children, who in turn told it to theirs, and so on and so on, and now I tell it to you, so someday you may tell it to yours."

We were all entranced. I thought of our own Chip Frozen Bear.

Would he fight so hard for Cynthia? Would he battle so hard for his tribe?

"What a beautiful story," Cynthia said. "But what does it mean?"

"Listen to the wind. Listen to your heart. Love is what will always save us. I'm glad you love my brother," Jacqueline held her hand across the table to touch Cynthia and smiled at us all.

In that moment, I felt hope that things would turn out all right.

SPRING FORWARD AGAIN

CHAPTER TWENTY

Around the town square, vibrant swatches of purple pansies alternated with yellow beds to create an interweaving border of color. From our third-story perch in the bank building, it was a floral tapestry of bright color caught within the light breeze and bright sunshine of a June afternoon. Taking a cue from landscapes at Disneyland, all of the planted pansies were a specially cultured breed that had no faces. The result was uniform and intense.

The management of American Seasons was moving quickly to demonstrate to the world their user-friendly, all-American and antiseptic vision of a northwoods retreat. Bromley Bastique rolled over for any requests made by the corporation. First to change was the town square. A battalion of landscapers and gardeners descended one weekend with flatbeds filled with roses and hedges. This was followed by a semi-truck transporting a wooden jigsaw puzzle that was quickly assembled into an octagonal turn-of-the century pavilion, open on all sides. This ornate Victorian addition to the Square was covered with curlicues and intricately carved balustrades. One day, it was assembled. The next it was painted white. And on the third, hanging baskets of red begonias were suspended in the center of each of the eight archways.

Next came the refurbishment of the buildings surrounding the Square. First the sandblasters roared through, restoring the red brick by blasting away decades of peeling paint. Then the scaffolding went up, and the teams of painters, an army in white pants and shirts, marched out each morning carrying paint brushes and an ochre-cast rainbow of Victorian paints. The tints and tones were carefully applied to highlight each detail of forgotten filigree. Had the town ever looked so smashing, even when the buildings were new?

Sadly, nothing transformed the shops within. So the same old washed-up souvenirs graced the Little Papoose. The same bizarre fashions were showcased in Lil's. The same local crowd guzzled beers and boiler makers at the Northern Nights.

All that remained problematic was the Piggly Wiggly. The optimistic, futuristic bare-bones steel and glass front of Red's grocery store stood as rebuke to the rest of Thread. The American Seasons team had already devised a new false facade, making a liberal use of logs and moss to transform the final side of the square into a simulacrum of an old trading post for the original French trappers. But Red balked. He had become testy about destroying things he had discovered that he truly loved–the quiet and serenity of his favorite fishing lakes, the small town simplicity of Thread. Cynthia reported that Red often awoke early in the morning, sweaty and gasping, murmuring of nightmares involving a giant muskie.

Bromley had no such miasmas. He walked the streets of Thread with a pomposity that more than matched his significant bulk. He was the spokesperson for all local views. He voraciously sought out every reporter. He had been quoted internationally. He preened on each request that came from the American Seasons folk. But even he balked when they asked to take down the giant wooden loon at the town's edge. It seemed too silly, the town's redesigners said, and besides the sculpture was riddled with carpenter ants and beyond repair. Bromley declared the bird could never be removed. They argued. The designers even asked Red to apply pressure, who ignored their prods.

The loon belonged to the township, which meant it was under Bromley's control. And he refused to budge. Finally, the lead American Seasons designer made a last valiant try while Bromley drank morning coffee and ate sweet rolls in my cafe. Once more, Bromley refused, this time threatening to revoke all building permits if he were asked about the giant loon one more time. The fellow made a hasty retreat. Claire leaned over and planted a giant wet and sloppy kiss on Bromley's cheek. "Thank you," she said.

He smiled at her indulgently, but said nothing.

So the new Thread had begun. It was a town filled with the smell of fresh paint and of profits to be made. Real estates prices were jumping each day, as speculators circled in to scavenge the best parcels that were still to be had. And those of us who had made this renaissance possible gathered in the large conference room on the third floor of the newly named American Seasons Building in downtown Thread. The heavy glass and chrome conference table glimmered. The black swivel chairs smelled of new leather. The walls, hand painted to look old and weathered, were covered with optimistic watercolors depicting the lands of Winter, Spring, Summer and Fall at American Seasons. And the uncurtained windows were sparkling clean, providing an unencumbered view, the highest in town, flinging our senses across the lakes and woods that were ours. The place bore no resemblance to the old bank building, except in the optimism that had spawned its original construction a century ago.

Tesla Haligent sat stolidly at the head of the conference table. At the opposite end Henry Van Elkind tried to convey the impression that he held the head spot, but the pull-down screen for the slide presentation said otherwise. Between these two tycoons were the others: Red Trueheart, the Oxford heir, Priscilla Jouer and a dozen other new directors of the corporation. At some point in the past few months, Hank had been forced to kick Amanda Manny from the inner circle. Her lack of talent had become too obvious. Today, only Chip Frozen Bear was missing. The rest were waiting, impatiently, for this remaining key person to arrive.

As for me, I too had been kicked from this inner circle, serving today only as a caterer for the luncheon meeting of the Board of Directors of American Seasons, Inc. The Hill and Knowlton people had seen no need for a small town cafe owner to be part of any marketing campaign. Regis McKenna, fresh from his marketing success in introducing Macintosh for Apple Computer, had been brought in at several thousand dollars a day to offer his advice. He too had been quick to boot the chef.

"I was so sorry to hear about your son," said one of the Hill and Knowlton flacks to Van Elkind. Overhearing it, Haligent glared in disapproval. Van Elkind simply suffered.

The body of Regina Rabinowicz had finally been found last week secreted in the cavernous attics of the Van Elkind camp, where she had been hidden by Kip Van Elkind. He had been the body snatcher, the blackmailer, the crazed villain. No one knew his motives. They only knew that he had placed his embalmed grandmother leaning against a wall in the top floor of the camp, her face turned toward a small window that displayed her favorite view of the sparkling waters of the lake.

"Thank you for your concern," replied Van Elkind. "Unfortunately, Kip has serious mental disorders, and we have placed him under the best of psychiatric care. I do not think the state will charge him with anything. Obviously, neither Rita nor I would press charges. And no one was hurt." He made that final statement with quite a grimace. Tesla, who had been eavesdropping, smiled indulgently. Even I knew that Van Elkind had been enormously damaged by his son's bizarre plot. The tabloid press enjoyed the story tremendously, and the resulting headlines were even worse than anything Henry had envisioned.

Investors in a billion-dollar project were not interested in having their projects led by a person with a crazy son and burdened by a ghoulish story gone national. After a quiet reorchestration, Tesla Haligent was firmly in control of American Seasons. Based on the news, Haligent Holdings had risen another 20 percent in value over the past week.

Still, Van Elkind's soul must have held at least a bit of happiness. He had seen an opportunity, unimaginable to most, and had created a new reality. He had combined bits of land, acquired under somewhat questionable tactics, with re-emerging Native American rights and integrated it with a vision that could attract investment dollars on a magnitude that would never have been imaginable to me.

It was his concept. Now it was becoming our reality. The town that he once considered a hellhole would make him far wealthier than his wife's father had ever been. The Van Elkind legacy would reign supreme over the Rabinowicz.

The group was getting restless. Frozen Bear was still missing. The directors had already finished their coffee and apple turnovers, which I had made with Macintosh apples in honor of Regis McKenna. Danny and I were in the process of making a second round of pouring coffee, when the large double doors opened.

Chip Frozen Bear walked in, dressed casually and carrying a small leather satchel. With him was an elderly gentleman, who walked quite erect. Then I noticed this man had only one arm. It was Mr. Packer.

A transformed Mr. Packer. Gone was the long scraggly beard and unkempt hair. He was sporting a closely cut goatee and a traditional, neatly combed haircut. His usual tattered and smelling clothes had been exchanged for a nicely tailored three-piece, pin-striped suit. It hung on his body perfectly, accentuating the healthy trim lines of his quite elderly body. One empty sleeve was neatly pinned back. His silk tie was in a perfect Windsor knot. His good arm held onto a very large lawyer's briefcase. His eyes were bright and he was smiling.

Van Elkind stood up. He just now realized that this elegant, lawyerly looking fellow was the usual compatriot of Bromley and Claire. "What is Mr. Packer doing here?"

Frozen Bear Smiled toward Red, but his eyes were focused on Tesla Haligent. He took no notice of Van Elkind. "Actually, I invited him, and we should begin by saying that the real name of Tom Packer is Tom Ferber."

Jonathan Oxford jumped to his feet. His heavy jowls jiggled, and his annoyingly squeaky voice seemed stretched to the edge. "No! It can't be. Tom Ferber died years ago. My father and aunt both adored their radical college professor named Ferber, but he hasn't been heard of in years. What kind of sham is this!"

"On the contrary young man," said Mr. Packer, or should it be Mr. Ferber? "Your family simply lost track of me. The years after the Depression and then yet another war took so much from me. I suffered and simply disappeared. It was only through the help of Regina Rabinowicz that I survived, not only physically, but emotionally. She helped me get settled here in Thread, so we could stay in touch when she and Casimir vacationed at the camp."

"Now you knew Mother Regina? This is preposterous!" Henry Van Elkind was seething with indignation. Not only had he lost control of this meeting and of American Seasons, but now the town eccentric was claiming ties to his family. He looked over at Jonathan Oxford with embittered curiosity. They seemed tied together in a forgotten scandal.

Tesla Haligent stood up and lightly gaveled the table with his Mont Blanc pen. "This is all very touching, I am sure. Old families reunited. And all of that. But it has nothing to do with the purpose of this meeting. I am very disappointed in you, Mr. Frozen Bear, that you should think it acceptable not only to be late for this session, but to then disrupt it with this curious sideshow."

Frozen's Bear expression had been non-committal, almost stoic, until this point. But now a grin escaped, and his eyes glinted with a self-satisfied amusement. "Actually, Mr. Ferber's presence has quite a lot to do with this meeting. You see the Lattigo nation–through the agent of Lattigo Electronics–plans to tender a takeover bid for American Seasons, Inc. And I'm hoping that by the end of this meeting, all of us can be in agreement that such an acquisition is mutually acceptable and in the best of interests of each and every investor."

Danny caught my eye and looked at me as though to ask, "What is going on?" I had no answer. Instead, I wished I had a video camera to immortalize the expressions of everyone else in the room. Cups remained suspended in air, only halfway to the lips. Jaws were dropped. Eyebrows were arched. People were sputtering. Priscilla Jouer was nervously scanning the room, ending her review focused on Haligent's face seeking clues on what to do. Only Chip Frozen Bear and Tom Packer, or Ferber, seemed calm. No one seemed to remember that the caterers were still in the room.

The tiniest of twitches at the joint of Haligent's jaw suggested that he was anything but a calm meeting leader. He casually dismissed Frozen Bear's comments. "That should be simple. Quite simple. I have no doubt that we can settle this matter by the end of the meeting. In fact, we can settle it right now. Your proposition is out of the question. Lattigo Electronics couldn't be worth more than a few millions, if that. Your firm has been in existence for less than a year, while the people in this room represent decades of business experience and billions in investment resources. Why would we suborn our interests in a major opportunity to some new-on-the scene entity like Lattigo Electronics? We might as well give it away to the caterers."

There was general laughter in the room. I guess we weren't forgotten.

Frozen Bear's smile grew larger. "Because if you don't agree, American Seasons will never be built. Your significant investments already made will be worthless. Because the Lattigo are the true owners of the majority of the land you plan to use. You have bought worthless titles."

Red was outraged. "You're full of shit. I own every piece of land I've sold to this corporation. Any title search will prove that."

Oxford was quick to agree. "And I'm equally confident that will be the case with my properties. All of this land originally belonged to my great-grandfather as part of his huge lumber holdings." All the while Oxford spoke, he kept his eyes on Tom Packer, as though he recognized some power this man might have. Oxford's pupils nervously flitted to and fro.

"Don't bet on it," said Mr. Packer. "The land belongs to the Lattigo tribe as part of their treaty of 1854 with the Federal Government. The Oxford company never obtained clear title to any of the land, and Barney Oxford knew it."

"My great-grandfather may have cut corners. But that treaty was nearly one hundred and fifty years ago. Land sales have been made since then without dispute. The land titles are legitimate." Even as he spoke, Jonathan Oxford seemed to lose conviction in his own argument.

Haligent was having none of it. "It's ridiculous discussing this. There's no proof the Oxfords obtained this land illegitimately a century ago and even if they did, too much time has passed to reopen the issue. No court would agree to return the land to the Lattigo. Let's just drop this childish dream of yours Mr. Frozen Bear, and return to the purpose of the meeting."

Mr. Packer walked over slowly to the large glass table and set his heavy case on it. The weight reverberated through the glass, jiggling coffee cups on saucers around the rectangle. He opened the case's lid and began removing old, yellowed papers. Many, many old and yellowed papers.

Frozen Bear spoke, "I must admit that I had no idea myself about the true situation. It is thanks to Mr. Ferber, or Mr. Packer if you prefer, that we Lattigo became aware of our own heritage. The original treaty was signed with President Franklin Pierce, when our reservation was formed. And a second, signed with President U.S. Grant when he visited our lands and acknowledged the great bald eagle we had provided to the Civil War battalion. We only had a copy of the first treaty. The latter was apparently forgotten or deemed ceremonial at some point in our past. But it was the second that granted broad ownership of additional lands, which we all knew we once had. What we didn't know is that that particular treaty prohibited the sale of those lands. We could only grant mineral, timber, and other specific rights of usage. The land itself had to remain with the tribe in a perpetual trust.

"Therefore, Mr. Oxford only bought lumbering rights from us in the 1880s. We did not sell him the mineral rights, and under these Federal agreements, we could not have sold him the land. But over time, and because of the loss of certain papers and memories, Mr. Oxford was able to present his sale documents as proof of land purchase, not simply as timber leases. He never had a right to resell the land. He never even had the mineral rights that were so effectively used to frighten some towns folk into the recent resale of lands.

"Mr. Ferber knew some of this because as a younger man he had reviewed Mr. Oxford's papers. Oxford's daughter, Jonathan's grandmother, had at one time considered authorizing the writing of a biography. As some of you may know, Mr. Ferber is not prone to throwing things away. He kept some of those key papers."

"This is a lie. My grandmother never knew this man."

Frozen Bear cut him off. "Please, Mr. Oxford. There is no doubt that Mr. Ferber is the person he claimes to be. These past two weeks, he has been in Madison and then in Washington researching both the state's archives and the Federal archives at the Bureau of Indian Affairs. The documents his briefcase contains are quite convincing. The land belongs to us, the Lattigo. You know, I've been told that our tribal name means 'small whip' in Spanish. You are about to feel the sting of the lattigo."

"I'm sorry, Red," Mr. Packer said to his fellow townsman, "but I couldn't let this area be destroyed after all the ways it has helped me. Seeing Regina Rabinowicz in her coffin is what convinced me. I had to do something."

"Maybe it's for the best," said Red quietly.

"Stop chattering this nonsense," Haligent was livid. "Old documents mean nothing. We will fight it through the courts. There's no way you'll reclaim this land after a century of ownership by others."

"Maybe. Maybe not," said Frozen Bear. His expression was once again his poker face. "But does it matter? During the court battles, the Lattigo would feel compelled to withdraw our support for the project. We wouldn't want to build casinos as part of your plan. And we would quite naturally seek a court injunction preventing you from beginning construction until questions of ownership are settled."

Haligent didn't reply. No one said anything. Outside, a small sparrow was hopping on the window still, jumping up every other moment to hit the window pane, as though it could fly through the clear glass. It created a strangely unnerving tapping sound. I wanted to throw my coffee pot at it. I also wanted to get out of the room. Perhaps sensing my unease, Mr. Packer caught my eye and winked.

Except for Red and Van Elkind, all of the directors were watching Haligent for signs on what to do. Fight or give in. Red sunk in the leather of his chair, looking defeated already, sensing the loss of all that his father had built up during the Depression. At the same time, it seemed as though a tension and roughness was lifting from him. Van Elkind, on the other hand, had the air of a condemned man awaiting his last meal. He had lost all interest in the proceedings. Haligent studied the face of Chip Frozen Bear, who stood impassively, watching Haligent in return. Neither said a word. No one drank a sip of coffee. No one stirred their coffee cup. No one smoked a cigarette. Two wills were in battle.

Haligent spoke first. "Let's say, purely hypothetically, that we were interested in the Lattigo Electronics offer. How could you fund the acquisition? Speaking for the group, I am certain we consider our current holdings to have quite a significant value."

Frozen Bear did not hesitate a moment. "I have a friend waiting in the lobby who specializes in mergers and acquisitions, particularly in the use of specialized financing. The press likes to call it junk bonds, but I think this approach would be quite easy to use to fund the acquisition to the satisfaction of everyone in this room. Perhaps you even know my friend. His name is Caleb Wheeler, and he has long ties to the area. Shall I invite the gentleman in?"

There was only a moment's hesitation. "Yes," said Haligent, "I'd be delighted to talk to Mr. Wheeler again." Van Elkind groaned, but no one cared any longer how Van Elkind felt.

Loon Fest had begun. One full year had passed since the opening of my Loon Town Cafe. Four seasons had come and gone. Once more as before, the town Square was bedecked with finery for the celebration. As tradition required, a large dance floor was being set up in the Square. This year, thanks to the largesse of Lattigo Enterprises, a high-quality, steel-braced dance floor was erected over the beds of pansies. But to stay in tune with tradition, the eccentric musical stylings of Jerzy Jerzyinski and his Jelly Jesters would again be the headline event.

The streets surrounding the square were strung with thousands of twinkling lights, another bonus from the Lattigo. And the town was filled with more tourists than anyone could ever recall hosting. Business was good. Every table in the cafe was reserved this evening for my special Loon Fest Feast.

"Doesn't our town look beautiful?" Cynthia said to me in a quiet interlude between serving. Indeed it did. The refurbished main street, the magical lighting, the redecorated square . . . it truly was a wonderland.

A few minutes later, as I was going to the kitchen to place an order and she was heading out with a platter of fried muskie, she said, "I'm meeting Chip after work to go dancing. We're going to celebrate how everything has turned out. Isn't it wonderful?"

Maybe it was. Maybe it wasn't. Chip Frozen Bear, upon his successful grab for control of the American Seasons company, quickly redefined the resort plans. His new approach was more scaled down, focusing on a true interface with nature. He brought the Nature Conservancy and the World Wildlife Fund on board. Taking the approach of certain eco-minded countries like Costa Rica, he proposed a resort community in keeping with natural balances. In the process, he was defining a more expensive and more exclusive resort. Furthermore, the plans still involved a smaller amusement park and more casinos. I doubted that the new plans were any more in keeping with the Great Spirit than the original, but the debate had vanished. The press had already reported the victory of the Native Americans over the white men, and had moved on to new battles.

But the coverage encouraged a new wave of tourism to the town. People were discovering the pleasures of our lakes and woods.

"Cynthia sure looks happy tonight," said Danny, his arms up to his elbows in soap suds. The other busboy I had hired, Brent, agreed quickly. "She told me Kip Van Elkind is locked up in some nut house, which makes her pretty happy. Plus Red completely supports her dating Chip Frozen Bear. She also said Red plans to sell everything and retire. Just go fishing. Isn't that weird? Red's not even fifty, but she says that's what he wants to do, and she thinks it's wonderful."

I agreed with it all.

"Wally," Danny said with authority, "I'm going to be quitting too." I looked at him with surprise. "Well, now that I'm out of high school, I have to think about what I'm going to do next. And Josh asked me to go to California with him. He said I could live in his place and go to college there, and use the time to figure out what I want to do with my life. And I've decided that's the way I want to start it.

"You're not mad at me, are you?" The old tentative Danny returned for an instant.

"How could he be mad?" Thelma said, then she quickly turned back to her broiler and flipped over five fillets of muskie. "Wally wants you to be happy, just like I do, isn't that so Wally?"

"Yes," I had to agree. With Danny gone, it would be a new life for Thelma and me. Who knows? Cynthia had been accepted to the University of Wisconsin in Madison and would be starting this fall. When she did come back to Thread, it would probably be to spend time with Chip Frozen Bear, who had seen in Cynthia a seriousness that most of us had missed. "I guess we'll be starting over, huh, Thelma?" She nodded in agreement.

We swirled through the night, eager to finish with the last of the diners, eager to close the restaurant and spend the last hour or two of the Loon Fest dancing in the Square. We seemed to occupy a new world already: a restaurant full of people, a new busboy in the kitchen, a Loon Fest Parade that earlier in the day had been transformed by vigor and vitality.

The parade, of course, still included the Thread Screaming Loons Marching Band, but again thanks to the patronage of the Lattigo, the band members paraded in new uniforms which seemed to give a never-before-achieved precision in both their marching and playing. And they had not been alone. The new-found national recognition of Thread had resulted in acceptances from every area band that had been asked to participate. Emerson. Timberton. Grosselier. Ashland. Every neighboring town was there.

And the floats were amazing. Instead of being the best of the lot, Red's annual tractor-driven, tissue-paper-covered float, seemed the drabbest this year. Perhaps it was because there no longer was a pony-tailed Rueben Cord to drive it. But in reality, it was because of the unexpected arrival of floats sponsored by the multinational corporations hoping to be invited to participate in the Lattigo investments. The parade had become a mini-proving ground for their intents. Floats from Hilton, Hyatt, American Airlines, Carlson Travel. The list went on and on.

But at the front of the parade, as proud as ever, was our one and only Claire de Loon, marching in her purloined Nanoonkoo loon costume, highstepping to the brightened beats of the Thread band. Claire basked in the adulation of thousands, adored by more than ever before in her life. And she floated through the day.

Now as my cafe closed for the evening, I slipped out into the crowded square. The dance floor was jammed with people stepping lively to the polkas of Jerzy. As the evening went on, Jerzy had completely abandoned top forty songs to play what were in fact his true love—the polkas, waltzes, and foxtrots of his youth. And in the crowded space of the wooden floor perched above the pansies, it seemed as though everyone knew how to dance.

"This must have been how it was when Thread was young," Cynthia whispered to me as she was whisked to the floor by Chip Frozen Bear. In one corner of the floor, I saw Josh leading Danny in a rambunctious foot-jumping polka that would have done Warsaw proud. No, I thought, this is not how Thread was when it was young. But this is how Thread can be as it ages. And it made me happy.

From the corner of my eye, I caught a glimpse of Officer Campbell, in his newly provided uniform, courtesy once more of the Lattigo, approaching Thelma, a Thelma who had been adrift in depression since Gilbert's betrayal. Campbell was so diffident in asking her to dance. But Thelma accepted, and he led her buxom form up to the floor. Soon she too was smiling and hopping and laughing her famous laugh to the four-four beat of the polka.

Seated at the side of the park on newly-purchased cast-iron benches, sat Claire, Bromley, and Mr. Packer, laughing above the music as they talked and drank coffee.

The Reverend Willy walked by the trio and gave them a friendly wave. They returned the salute. Pastor Paul Mall, so outraged by the release of Willy, had stomped out of town, refusing to preach in such a Sodom and Gomorrah.

Someone stood near to me. Feeling his presence, though he said nothing, I turned. It was Stephen from the Van Elkind camp, and I realized I was happy to see him.

"I heard you might be needing a new waiter," he said.

"Yes," I replied, "Cynthia is leaving this fall and Danny even sooner."

"Perhaps you could hire me," Stephen said smiling. "The Van

Elkinds have had enough of Thread and they're closing up their camp. They're going to try to sell it, though God knows who has need for such extravagance these days. But for some reason I don't want to go back to Chicago. And I thought a job with you might keep me busy while I plan what comes next. What do you say?"

It was a great idea, though I couldn't imagine Stephen working as a waiter for long. But what did that matter? Things change. Things evolve. Take advantage of them while they're at hand. "Let's walk away from the Square, and we can talk about it where it's quieter," I said.

We strolled to 17 and turned to walk south along the highway, away from the crowd, quickly reaching an agreement. Then we stopped and gazed on what lay ahead on this moonlit road that stretched before us. In the background, the music and the laughter of thousands filled the night. Above us, a million stars shone. In the distance of the night, above the glimmering blue waters of the Sapphire lakes, there rose the call of the sounding loons, merging with the wind.

And ahead of us one hundred yards, walking slowly into the night was Toivo Lahti. And he held his hand out to the side, stretching slowly across time and eternity. And stretching back were the lightly shimmering fingers of Lempi. And their fingertips touched. Their hands enclosed. Their eyes met. And they walked once more. Like before.

In the moonlight. Along the highway. Amidst the sounds of life. With the wind, they walked in love again.

ABOUT THE AUTHOR

Dennis Frahmann is a journalist, writer and award-winning marketer who grew up in small towns in Wisconsin and now lives in Cambria, California. *Tales from the Loon Town Cafe* is his first novel. You can learn more about the novel by visiting *www.loontowncafe.com*.

Made in the USA
Charleston, SC
10 July 2013